A LETTER FROM MY FATHER
Volume Two (1931-1947)

We drank a lot and after dinner we undressed and the three of us went to bed together. Jarmila loved Melba, sucking hell out of her – while I took her from the rear. Then to top it off, Melba sucked me while I ravaged Jarmila with my hot tongue until she came with a spasmodic burst. Those two girls – the one blonde and slender, the other jet black and buxom, both with beautiful bodies – were red hot with passion. When I had had enough I left them to their own devices for the balance of the night. Jarmila was really hot about us both – she always contended that she was torn between Melba and myself – she could never make up her mind which of us she loved the most . . .

A LETTER FROM MY FATHER

Volume Two (1931-1947)

Edited by Page Smith

A STAR BOOK
published by
the Paperback Division of
W. H. ALLEN & Co. PLC

A Star Book
Published in 1985
by the Paperback Division of
W. H. Allen & Co. PLC
44 Hill Street, London W1X 8LB

First published in Great Britain
by W. H. Allen & Co. PLC, 1984

A Letter From My Father was first published in one volume in the United States of America by William Morrow and Co. Inc., 1976

Printed and bound in Great Britain by
Anchor Brendon Ltd, Tiptree, Essex

ISBN 0 352 31564 4

Contents

1931–1932

On the morning of May 13th, 1931 with the May issue not yet on the stand, altho it had been due there the 25th of April, I informed the Nomad Publications that unless they came to terms by 3:00 p.m. that Travel Publications would file [bankruptcy] that afternoon. The stupid people thought that I was bluffing. Trying to high-pressure them into giving me better terms.

I was desperate—my publishing castle was crumbling about me. They didn't offer any relief, and that afternoon Travel Publications just before 4:00 o'clock "filed"—and that was the end of our thrilling experiment in the publishing world. *Nomad* had been going for five years—I had been with it for 13 months. . . .

At 5:00 o'clock the afternoon of the 13th we closed the doors, pasted a sign on the doors stating that the corporation was under the jurisdiction of the United States Federal Courts of the Southern District of New York and to apply to them. We never went back there again except to confer with the receiver's agents once.

We took a complete file of the magazines during our reign with us—a few pencils, erasers, notebooks and rubber bands—the rest was left just as it was in action, but quite still—for *Nomad* was dead. . . .

We didn't have much cash left out of the wreck—but we were able to stay on at the Beaux Arts because they owed us a good deal for ads that had been already run. . . .

[Soon after the failure of *Nomad* Melba got a job as editor of *This Week on Long Island*.]

Melba's name went to the Mast-head with the second issue, Vol. I, No. II. [She put an ad in the *Times* for a stenographer.]

One girl who replied to her ad . . . with an excellent letter, but whose test did not compare with the work of some of the others, called Melba up a half dozen times pleading with her for another test. Melba finally weakened and told her to come around—she made an appointment for 3:00 p.m. of the afternoon of the 2nd of June, 1931.

I thought I would never forget that date—but I had to hunt it up to record it here. About a quarter to three, Mr. Garrett called Melba up to come over to the office forthwith—it was a new job so she felt she shouldn't offer excuses. She asked me to give the girl the test (in those days we would dictate from some *Nomad* copy, keep a record of the time it took the girl to take it down and then to transcribe the notes).

Our studio apartment was a large one-room affair on the ground floor—the windows were right on the street, a side door opened on a little setback garden upon which other apartments opened, but all on the street. There was also a rear door to the hotel proper—we had a kitchenette and a bathroom. The apartment adjoining ours was occupied by the bookkeeping department—their door opened right at right angles to ours—they could see into our apartment, we into theirs. An iron grille work covered the windows to protect us from forceful entry from the street—principally kids.

It was a sunshiny June day—our doors were open, our windows open—the bookkeeper had her windows and the door next to ours open. The painter was at the window painting the grillwork. There were doormen or carriagemen dressed as gendarmes on both sides of the street, in fact right outside our door and windows—also taxi drivers on the line awaiting fares.

The girl arrived a few minutes after three. Her real name was Hannah R., but she had given us an assumed name, which slips me at the moment. Her husband's name was Martin. I gave her a notebook and pencil, and dictated.

Then when I finished I gave her the paper and set her down to the machine right by the window. The painter almost fell through the grill looking in at her trying to transcribe, which she wasn't doing very successfully. Finally it became so painful that I told her not to bother further, that I would show her work to Mrs. Smith. She hung around the door—said she wanted to talk to me about getting a book of hers published. I said I couldn't talk to her as I was in a hurry to join Mrs. Smith. (We had a tea date with some friends of my mother's at 4:00 on Riverside Drive & 86th St.—some friend who wanted to meet Melba.)

The R. woman then said she would wait and walk out with me. She continued to stand by the door.

The kids were beginning to hang around as they came from school to watch the painter and pass remarks. I was in my shirt sleeves but I slipped into my coat and putting on my hat and picking up my cane set forth. I was quite lame then and walked with a perceptible limp. The bookkeeper greeted me—the doormen, carriage men, painters, taxi drivers all hailed me as I passed. I am a friendly soul—even the cop at the crossing (2nd Ave. & 44th St.) who was there to help the school children across, called to me. R. continued to jabber away about "the best way to get a book published"—how should she go about it, would I give her letters to publishers, did I think she would get the job with Melba. I said I didn't think she would. Would I pay her for coming over from Brooklyn to take the test—she had lost the entire afternoon. I answered all in the negative. It was a slow process because I walked slowly in those days on account of my hip. When we reached Lexington Ave. & 44th Street, to be sure I would get rid of her I asked which way she was going. When she told me, I said I was going in the opposite direction. And that ended that—I took the shuttle and at 3:45 I met Melba at the Times Building. In fact I was there ahead of her.

We took the trolley up to meet Mother—visited with her friends and then we three went to dinner.

We returned home and went to work getting copy ready for Melba's next issue.

I had two phones—a private wire and the house phone. All my friends used the private number and came in the front way. The hotel was supposed to say we were out to anyone trying to reach us on the hotel phone—all the creditors of Travel Publications Inc. were after me.

It was 4:00 in the morning—we had been collaborating on a review of Konrad Bercovici's new book. The phone rang violently; for awhile we didn't answer— when it kept up I finally picked up the receiver. The night manager said there was a man in the lobby who wanted to see me—very important. I asked who it was—he pretended not to know. I suggested that he come around to the apartment, but he asked if I would come out, said the man wanted to talk to me there. I replied they would have to come to the door—I went to the door and there were two men. I asked them their business. They said they wanted to talk to me alone—didn't want to disturb my wife.

When I persisted in knowing who they were they showed their badges. Then I insisted that they come in—they were reluctant, said they wanted to discuss a matter I might not want brought up before my wife. I replied I had nothing to hide from my wife or anyone. Then they asked me if I knew a Hannah R. The name was a new one to me—I replied that I did not. They said she had been there that afternoon. I said not while I was there, that the only person there other than myself had been—and I gave the name I had for the lousy bitch. They announced that was the same girl.

Then in a whisper they wanted to know if I had had or had tried to have intercourse with her. If the building had suddenly been swept away to sea, leaving me standing naked atop Turtle Bay Hill, the shock could not have been greater. That question to me spelled ruin—it was a shock I never fully recovered from. From then on for weeks and months I lived a virtual hell.

I told the detectives frankly just what had occurred—just as I have related it here. They walked over to my Mexican holster and I think were disappointed that they were unable to find a revolver in it—they looked the entire place over pretty keenly. I phoned Bob Marsh and Christie Bohnsack

(Secretary to the Police Commissioner at the time of Grover Whalen).

Detectives are sly fellows—after their preliminary conversations they announced—especially after I had called the police commissioner's secretary—that they wanted to be helpful, that they knew I was in a tough spot—it would be better if I told them the entire truth, that I could trust them, then they could help me, could tell me what to do. I could only answer that I had told them all there was to tell, that it was a frameup for a shakedown, and that the girl had asked me for money that afternoon and I had refused.

Judge Marsh talked to them—told them that if they arrested me without a warrant they would be liable to a charge for false arrest and possible imprisonment themselves. They had no complaint in writing, not even a warrant. They hinted that the matter might be all fixed up for a little dough to them and to the girl.

Christie Bohnsack told them not to take me down for lineup—not to photograph me and to keep me "out" until just before court.

I tried to get Joe Galletti for some money but he had closed for the night—I had only a few dollars in my pocket. I called Harry Greenberger, Vincent Astor's right-hand man—he said he would bring his brother, a small court lawyer to court for me. Bob Marsh agreed to be present and to represent me. He loaned character to my picture, but he was a Republican and not familiar with the rough-and-tumble Magistrates Court. All agreed the case should go over to enable us to get our witnesses.

While we were waiting around during the early hours of the morning, one of the "dicks" went over to Brooklyn and came back with word that the girl might withdraw her complaint for Five Hundred Cash. Judge Marsh felt that wouldn't do.

After going over to see Joe Galletti at the Italian Cellar Restaurant where they played Bulla (like bowling) we went uptown to a restaurant at 51st Street & Lexington Avenue where the "dicks" had something to eat on me. Then we strolled leisurely to the East 51st Street Station House where I was booked, finger-printed—you have to be finger-printed to get bail—then for more coffee, then up to the Magistrates Court on 57th Street between Lexington & Third, the Fourth District Borough of Manhattan.

The charge was attempted rape. The R. woman claimed I laid her on the couch, took my cock out, pulled her clothes up and asked her to screw me (all in plain view of the painter and the passersby on the street)—that I rubbed my cock against the outer edges of her cunt but did not enter or try to force my way in when she asked me not to (what a gentleman!)—then she said I took my cock and put it in her mouth (THAT IS SODOMY according to the statutes of the State of New York)—that I came in her mouth, that she swallowed it, that I went into the bathroom, got a towel, wiped my cock off, followed her back into the bathroom when she went in to pee.

The case was put over and I was held under five thousand dollar bail—Judge Marsh and Greenberger's Brother were prepared for that.

Before my case was called for a period of half an hour while they were drawing up the complaint and getting the crazy cunt to sign it, they put me in a cell with all the bums and drunks. That was even worse than the shock of the charge, and arrest and the fingerprinting, and the knowledge that the tabloids would have a front page field day—which they did—at my expense.

The premium for the bail was $500. I called Nathan Hugg and Eddie Hurd on the phone and asked them to get me $1,000 without delay, but not to tell Mother about it. Nevertheless they told her and got the money from her. Teneralli brought it to me (he was Miss Hugg's husband)—I turned it over to Judge Marsh.

Joe Gransky—proprietor of the Ball & Chain, a protege of Charlie Hilles, a secretary (probably steno) at the White House under Bill Taft—suggested that Freddie Pecora, famous Tammany District Attorney would be an excellent man to defend me in court. Freddie was then a member of the firm of Banton Sheridan, Hartman & Pecora or something like that.

Melba never left me for a minute all night except for the half hour I was in the "jug" with the scum from the middle East Side (New York).

While awaiting trial we left the Beaux Arts and went to live at the Piccadilly. The torture of the publicity—the humiliation and the fear that I might not beat the rap, that I might have to do a stretch—were ghastly. It was a period of continuous day and night nightmares of the most hideous and terrifying type that could possibly be conjured up. . . .

[Ferdinand Pecora, a famous prosecuting district attorney, was hired to defend my father along with Judge Marsh.]

[A newspaper account of the episode appeared in the New York Daily News, *June 4, 1931, under the headline]:*

MAD ATTACK BY RICH MAN, WORKING WIFE'S CHARGE

It isn't always so pleasant to work for a wealthy society man as the movies so often suggest. Mrs. Hannah Rentzer, an attractive blonde wife and mother, of 1259 56th St. Brooklyn, found that out Tuesday, when she answered an ad for a secretary, inserted by W. Ward Smith, 37, No. 310 East 44th St.

Smith, former executive secretary to Governor Nathan Miller was held in $5,000 bail in Yorkville Court, Wednesday, as the result of the story that Mrs. Rentzer told police.

"I answered the ad I saw in the paper by writing to the box number. Monday, while I was out, there was a phone call, but I got the message too late. That night I got another call from Mr. Smith and made an appointment to go to his apartment, where he lives with his wife, Mrs. Melba Smith.

"When I got to see him, I was impressed by his good looks and aristocratic manner, and thought that he would be a fine boss, if I could get the job. He dictated several articles to me from travel magazines," Mrs. Rentzer said, "and then told me to transcribe my notes.

"I sat at my desk and started. Suddenly I felt a hand on my shoulder. I looked up into the eyes of a wildman.

"'You're going to work for me, aren't you,' he muttered, tearing and ripping at my dress and arms," Mrs. Rentzer's voice broke.

"His wife was out. I was at his mercy, the beast! As soon as I could, I fought him off, and rushed into the street. As I neared Lexington Avenue (and you can imagine the condition I was in) Smith overtook me.

"I shuddered as he took my arm again. 'Please don't say anything about this', he pleaded, 'I will do everything I can for you, but promise to say nothing. We want to part friends.'

"I shook him off and staggered to the train. When I got home I told my husband. We decided that for the sake of other girls who might fall into similar traps, we must make a complaint."

Former Supreme Court Justice Marsh represented Smith in Yorkville Court. Marsh said that the charges brought by Mrs. Rentzer were unsupported.

Smith is a member of a wealthy family. He has been a Member of the Republican County Council for years, deserting it in 1928 to support Governor Smith in the presidential campaign. For a time he acted as general manager of the American-Canadian Lumber & Pulp Co. here, was an associate director of the Savings Division of the United States Treasury, and chairman of the board of directors of the Valley Stream National Bank.

A private detective [was] put on the case by Judge Marsh to find out what he could about the family. Rentzer had a baby, a husband, and a father who worked intermittently. Her sister was in an insane asylum.

Rentzer had framed several small shop owners in Brooklyn. One of them put up a fight and the matter was in court and disposed of while my case was pending. Her racket was to go to some store where she had bought stockings or lingerie and try to return items she had bought and washed and worn. When the salesgirls objected she would then demand to see the owner or manager and blandly announce that unless they exchanged the raiment for new articles, she would run from the store screaming that she had been attacked and call a policeman. In some cases she had gotten away with it—the proprietors or managers giving her the new garments to avoid a scene that might adversely affect their business.

One little Jew wouldn't fall for her line or threats, so she had him arrested—he fought it and beat her.

She had a slimy Jew uncle who was a lawyer and advised her badly.

The painters, the taxi-cab drivers, the policeman on the beat, the doormen at the Beaux-Arts, and the bookkeepers, telephone operators, etc. were all in court to testify for me. When the hearing got under way the Judge told Melba that she could leave and it would not be held against me, that she wasn't by my side—but she elected to remain.

The detective first told of the arrest, and when asked by the D.A., a fellow by the name of Kantor, what I had said, he replied quoting me, "She asked me for money and I refused to give it to her." Then he went on to say that I had denied every bit of her filthy story.

Then the bum herself was put on the stand, with her Yiddish Papa and greasy husband nearby, her Jewish uncle to rave and rant about her chastity.

She burst into a violent tirade when they asked her about her sister in the nut house—at times dribbled like a half-wit herself.

When they got around to her underclothing—what did she have on underneath, did her drawers have a slit in them—she objected with vehemence to that question as being indecent but admitted they didn't have a slit. On direct testimony as led out by the D.A. she had virtually confirmed the contents of the complaint she had signed, written up for her by the cops.

The charge of attempted rape holds good even if you don't partially enter the cunt—rubbing the cock around the outside is all that is necessary to put you in the "jug," provided the dame says she said with violence "no."

They all say "no," even when they most want it. Bobbie R., a cunt from Savannah, Georgia, once said after she had said "no" right up to the last, "It's so wonderful to resist—and so marvelous when you insist."

When they brought up the Brooklyn case, Rentzer tried to squirm out of that—but when faced with the record she nearly collapsed.

Judge Gotlieb, getting tired of Pecora's indifferent cross examination took a hand with the questioning himself. He asked her to open her mouth, to show her teeth, to turn her head, then he wanted to know if what she said was true—if I had put my cock in her mouth and she had sucked and she had not wanted to—why hadn't she turned her head to avoid my penis or closed her mouth tight or bitten my cock when it was in her mouth. She said she was too cowed to resist with the turn of her head or the closing of her teeth and mouth.

They then asked her if she had noticed the painters at the window—she said she had—she had also taken notice of the bookkeeper and admitted that the doors and windows were open, but claimed I had pulled a screen around to the foot of the couch. She admitted the cop was on the corner, that we passed Railway Express guards and other policemen as well as the doormen, that Lexington Avenue was crowded, that she had walked from Second to Lexington with me as I limped along, that her clothes were not disarranged or torn or her hair mussed and that she had made no outcry and had at no time called for help, that she had done some shopping afterwards, had gone home in the subway and made no effort to make a report to the police.

She calmly admitted that it was not until after dinner with the family gathered about that she had discussed the matter with her husband, father and her (lawyer) uncle and that her uncle had advised her to go to the station house (he went with her) and have me arrested. Even then apparently the uncle and the father and husband hadn't been quite sure that was the way. . . .

When the State rested, Judge Marsh made a motion to dismiss and the Court asked for briefs on the subject of corroborating evidence in cases of attempted rape and Sodomy. . . .

[The judge granted a motion to dismiss on June 20, 1931.]

The year 1931 had started out on thin ice and it had ended very close to the poor house—it was tough going.

Nomad had failed, father had died, the rape case had laid me low—what money I could get leaped away from me. . . .

It was my tough year—the end of my 37th and the beginning of my 38th. . . .

We took an apartment at $50 per month at 42 West 52nd Street south side—two rooms, one small one for the children—they slept together—and a large room which served as a livingroom and bedroom for us, a good bathroom, a tiny kitchen—but it had a Parapet for the children to play on.

We organized a group of our friends who were short of cash—we called it The Parapet Club. Each one chipped in a dollar and we bought an awning to cover the Parapet—very colorful—linoleum for the roof floor to resemble brick, flower boxes, a lattice screen to shut out the neighbors and grow vines on. We charged 60¢ for meals prepared by Melba—the girls helped her cook, the men helped me wash the dishes—liquor bootleg was extra. Walter Piel brought real beer from his brewery in payment for his meals—he was that short of cash. Harry Millar kept us supplied with a motion picture projector and we showed pictures of our travels and filthy pictures as well. I got out a typewritten sheet nearly every day called *The Parapet News* with dope about what the neighbors were doing as well as our friends and what we thought of them as well as of the nation and state of the world. We always had at least half a dozen every evening—it was hard work, but it meant meat for the children. 52nd Street was a busy street even then with the best speakeasies in town on it and a number of good eating places. We had a lot of fun—we put on a campaign against the telephone company for its high rates and charges and generally enjoyed ourselves. On Sunday, Mother would drop in and take the children for a walk in the park and during the week, Kaye Lyons would take them out too. The toughest part of the deal was keeping the place clean, scrubbing down the roof on the Parapet—I would get up early every morning with broom and mop and give the place a thorough going over while the sun was on the rise. That helped to dry it off quickly. We grew sweetpeas and sunflowers in the flower boxes and other things in season so that there were always flowers blooming. The children adored morning glories. After dark we hung out Jap lanterns (made of tissue—colored— lighted by candles).

The tables were lit by candlelight.

We had drop curtains in the event of rain arranged so that we could enclose the entire porch. . . .

The best way to tell the story of Parapet View is first to set forth "The Whys and Wherefores."

Parapet View was first, last and all the time our home, Melba's and mine and the children's and we never failed to make that clear to all.

It was also the home of our friends, as my home has always been and will always be, whether it is a palace or a broken down porch—or without porch at all.

The Parapet Forum was developed spontaneously and voluntarily by a little group of understanding friends who in those times, that tried men's souls and women's chastity, realizing that Melba and I were not in a position to carry all the expense of entertaining our friends alone, felt that they could do no less than to pay for the actual cost of their food, iced tea, and incidentals.

We did not run Parapet as a public restaurant—it was a convivial gathering place for our friends and acquaintances who came as paying guests. . . .

A la the Provincial Forties, we gave our guests for 60¢ per head—

Tomato Juice or Fruit Cocktail or Soup, hot or cold

* * *

Lamb or Pork Chops with Peas and Potatoes or
Hamburger Steak Sandwich
or
Chopped Beef and Fried Potatoes or Cold Ham and Potato Salad
or
Spanish Rice and Salad or Spaghetti and Salami
or
Cold Cuts and Potato Salad or Eggs, any style
or
Waffles and Bacon or Griddle Cakes

* * *

Jello or Peaches, or pears or shortcake,
or any fruit in season, or layer cake, or prunes, or applesauce,
or puddings when we had them.

* * *

Tea or coffee—hot or cold.

We charged the guests who brought their own gin—for the mixing ginger ale, etc. 50¢ per mix.

The dues were $1.00 payable in advance.

By that plan we were able to maintain open house all that summer. . . .

We were glad to carry any of our friends on the cuff for a week, but we tried to get settlement on Fridays in order to pay the butcher, the baker and the candlestick maker—Melba put all her enthusiasm, energy and strength into the game and we felt that we should get the money in, so the housekeeping bills could be paid weekly.

We had a lot of trouble getting the guests to put their ashes in the ashtrays and not on the plates.

We charged a 50¢ deposit on any of our ordinary books that were borrowed and a rental of 10¢ a week.

On a special—or obscene book—a deposit of $5.00 was required and a rental charge of 50¢ a night or a dollar a week was made.

We did not serve dinners unless we were notified in advance not later than noon of the day of the reservation.

No cancellations after 12 noon were accepted.

Two helpings were allowed to all 75¢ meals and one helping to the 50¢ and 60¢ meals—additional helpings after the regular allowance one-half the cost of the meal extra.

Van Loon's philosophical leaflets were on sale at 25¢ a copy.

The big excitements of that summer were the B.E.F. [Bonus Expeditionary Force] in Washington, being driven or burned out by MacArthur and Hoover, and the Presidential election.

We felt it was a great political blunder to call out the troops to disperse the recalcitrant members of the B.E.F.

It never helps to call the police to oust an obstreperous or unwelcome guest—it leads to disastrous results.

We agreed that soup is better than tear bombs and that bread is cheaper than bullets.

We were opposed to bonus raids, but we believe it the right of every citizen to petition Congress and in the obligation of the state or nation to care for the needy in their hours of distress.

If the Reconstruction Finance Corporation could dole out eighty million dollars to save Charlie Dawes from abject poverty, why wasn't it possible for the Hoover administration to barrack the unemployed that came to Washington, whether they were war veterans or not, and ration them on McFadden meals or prison fare?

All that were physically able to labor could have been employed in improving the waste areas in and about Washington at a nominal fee, namely, sufficient to cover the bare cost of the food and a cover for their heads and medical attention.

If a centralized national employment exchange had been set up, as Mr. Hoover advocated before becoming President, it would have been possible to shift those men to places where there would have been work for them.

As it was they were thrown out of Washington and thrust upon other communities. . . .

It did seem as if it were more or less appropriate when cities like Toledo and States like Ohio ran out of funds and ways and means to care for their unemployed, that those men and women should trek their way to the seat of government.

Undoubtedly there are grave abuses in our bonus and pension systems, but some provision should have been made for the poor as well as the rich in those troublesome times.

We wondered then if Jesus of Nazareth would have answered the starving pleas for bread with machine gun bullets, tear gas bombs, drawn sabres and tanks.

It certainly was a great blotch on the fair name of these United States that martial law had to be declared at the seat of our government, particularly when the chief of the district police had the entire situation so well in hand. . . .

The parties were very gay—many times that summer strangers tried to get into Parapet, thought it was a speak or public restaurant. It looked bright and gay from the street.

Bad as Herbert Hoover was, he didn't try to pry into your

private life—and we were unmolested by local, federal or state authorities. In fact we were left alone except for gay couples on pleasure bent—there were no questionnaires to fill out, there wasn't any rationing, and we weren't worried about income tax returns. We were poor, but still free men and women. The Jews hadn't taken over to wreck our way of life—women were safe on the sidewalks of New York any hour of the day or night if they went about their business and didn't flirt with pickups. The negroes knew their places and kept them—Eleanor and the New York Jews had not turned the darkies' heads. A man could screw as and when he wanted to without permission of a bureaucrat in Washington.

We were only trying to feed ourselves—we were not bothering too much with feeding or running the rest of the world and they weren't trying to force their political or economic standards on us.

Morris V. always said he didn't have the longest but he had the prettiest tool in the world—he was everlastingly screwing [his wife] Lyle after dinner on our couch for the guests to see or participate in (he only thus indulged when drunk). He invited John M. to watch one time—it was too much for John, he wet his pants.

On one occasion when we all had been drinking and looking at filthy movies, I screwed Lyle in front of Morris on the bed. She sucked my prick first and Melba sucked Morris'—then we both fucked hell out of each other's wives—it was hot, as those doubles always are, and the guests enjoyed the picture. Lyle was a "hot" natural—she would rather fuck and suck than eat. She and Melba would have quite a time of it when they would get together. Morris' tool was not long and neither was it thick, but it tickled the girls—he was insane about having it sucked off. I can think of no better method of giving a lucid picture of Parapet than to quote from some of the copies of *The Parapet News* as they appeared at that time. These choice morsels that were pounded out by the old maestro on those hot summer days of 1932, when freedom still rang throughout the land—show you what we were thinking and doing then.

It would be false to say that Lyle didn't get you sexually, no matter how many other women were around—I was always hot about her, but she was a double-crosser with men—and as swell a bitch as ever double-crossed a horny bastard.

During the summer, Lyle decided to take up professional dancing so she could be on her own. . . .

Lyle wanted to buy a dancing costume so I went along—I don't know why except that Melba was taking the children to the Park and thought that I would be of help to Lyle in deciding on her costume, which consisted of black velvet (shorts), trunks and a white silk waist. She made the purchases at Nat Lewis' original place on Broadway between 47th and 48th St. (east side of street). The fitting rooms were in the basement—they didn't have doors, just curtains.

I have always had a weakness for buying women's clothes and watching them dress and undress. Well—that performance made me plenty "hot" as she tried on the different outfits—in fact, the memory of it as I write stirs my blood and makes the old pecker stand up and look me right in the eye.

When Lyle was about to take off the outfit she decided on, she sent the salesman away for a bow. Unable to withstand the pressure, I laid her on the floor of the dressingroom, tiny as it was—she was tiny too, and the mirror on the three sides helped. Fortunately we were through before the salesman returned—screwing women in dressing rooms or bathrooms has always been a passion of mine—maybe that's my perversion.

When Lyle lays you she lays you—that was all there was to it. You never forgot her—there was something very insidious about that child. . . .

Stanley H. was staying at the famous 42nd Street Whore house that summer, the St. Margaret Hotel, fucking his head off. Lyle fell for his prick and the poetry of his soul—Stanley would read his manuscripts to her by the yard, work her up with his poems and a touch of liquor and then take her over to the St. Margaret for an incision of his long episcopal tool. . . .

We opened the Parapet on the 4th of June—we closed it on the 9th of October. Our last week was our biggest—we took in $79.40. Our poorest was our first—$10.25—no sales taxes then. After the third week we kept above $20.00 weekly. The last nine weeks we averaged around $30.00 per week.

The last night was Melba's birthday. The children dressed up for the occasion in paper caps, etc. Diane in her best "bib and tucker" came out on the porch carrying the cake with its candles lighted and singing "Happy Birthday"—a gust of wind caused the candles to ignite her costume. It would have been a horrible mess had not Walter Piel grabbed the cake from the child and John McNeil grabbed her in his arms thereby smothering and extinguishing the flames in a flash.

Melba and Diane and all were pretty well shaken—but the party went on—we had a wonderful evening.

Near the end of the season (the taxi drivers had always been friendly) we noticed a taxi driver waving to us from across the street. He beckoned us to come down—at the door he said the Federal men were in the street to raid the speakeasies. They were on the roofs, and he had seen some of them in the empty apartment in the house next to ours. He said he didn't know whether I had any liquor or not, but he thought he had better warn me.

Under the children's bed we had champagne, real beer, gin, and bootleg rye. I thought I better act fast (to prevent any nonsense in our place) so I called police headquarters (they answered the phone quicker then—LaGuardia wasn't Mayor) and reported thieves on the roofs and in the apartment next to ours. They sent out a riot call, closed 52nd Street at both ends—trained searchlights on the buildings and turned dozens of cops and plainclothesmen loose in the street, through the buildings and on the roofs. To the chagrin of all the cops, they only uncovered the undercover prohibition agents—but we saved ourselves and the other speakeasies on the block. . . .

One night when Harry and Frenchie were at Parapet,

Walter P. was also around. The discussion turned, rather extraordinarily to sexual intercourse. Melba got on the subject of married virgins and Frenchie agreed with her premise—Walter came up for air. When Frenchie complained that so few American men understood the fine art of preliminary stimulation, how necessary it was for the female and how "cunt-lapping" helped, Walter was horrified. Frenchie reiterated that unless a man kissed a woman's cunt and caressed the lips of her "pussy," as well as the lips of her mouth, he couldn't expect the female to experience real joy.

The more versatile the tongue the greater the joy. We trapped Walter on the discussion by asking him if a cunt tasted salty—he fumbled that one (I hope you know it does—if it is ripe).

Walter said he had never "gone down" on a woman and wouldn't—little Wally contended that a woman's cunt was filthy and that it was revolting to him even to think about it. I commented that for years I have been under the impression that he was a finished swordsman—and that he had his "Union Card" for sexual intercourse, and I asked with surprise, "Why Walter, haven't you even caressed a female asshole with your tongue?"

We accused him of being selfish, thinking only of himself and not of his girl's pleasure—we told him that he could never hold a woman that way, that they would try him once and then let him go if they could get anything better.

When he reiterated that cuzzies were filthy, I asked him if his mother's had been dirty, too (the one he had come out of)—that got him.

We all agreed that the female slit was the holy of holies, sacred to most men—and to be loved, admired, caressed and worshiped.

Walter thought it was all right to have a girl "suck him off" and to come in a girl's mouth—but he didn't want to go down on the girls.

He and a friend, while in their cups, had taken two girls to Sophia's for a night—they started playing around and the dames agreed to go down on the boys and suck them off if the boys in turn would go down on them.

The deal was made and they took their girls into the bedrooms. After Walter's girl had sucked him off, Walter refused to go down on her thereby breaking the bargain—that infuriated Walter's girl so that in her drunken rage, she raised merry hell, throwing the furniture around and smashing the bric-a-brac.

It took all Walter and his boy friend could do to hold her down and get her out—she didn't want money, she wanted to be sucked off. When it looked as if the police would have to be called, the other fellow, to quiet the jane, went down on her—which made Walter very sick.

After that we all started riding Wally—telling everyone that he had not won his "Union Card" as a fornicator. This upset him a great deal.

During that period they often had parties—beefsteak parties at the P. Brewery. We went to one such—the entire P. family and their close friends were there—there was much beer drinking and the steaks were "rare"—it was a great feast with much singing.

It was at one such party that Walter met a girl he especially liked. He invited her to take a trip to Bermuda with him—she agreed, then a few days before the trip she spent the night with him at Sophia's and the next day called the trip off. He decided then and there that he hadn't been able to satisfy her because he hadn't gone down on her. Personally I thought it was a combination of an inadequate prick and tongue—he didn't love her properly to begin with, did nothing to stir her—even animals sniff around their girl friends with their snoots—and then when she wanted more rope, he didn't have any to give. . . .

In October 1932 we rented an apartment at 2 Horatio Street. It was new and very attractive—high up—overlooked the entire City—a big fireplace graced one side of a dropped living room. Modern bath, kitchen etc. completed the picture. . . .

Our credit situation was so tough that we rented the Horatio place under my pen name of "Dudley Brooks."

Chelsea moved us and we left 42 West 52nd in a battle

over abuses we felt we suffered from the landlord—and owing a month's rent. We sold the awning to the woman next door and that was the end of Parapet View.

We fixed the Horatio place up attractively with our Mexican things, but much to our dismay discovered that the couch which we slept on had bed bugs—it was a box spring on legs and difficult to clean.

During this period I had a mail address with a Miss Holzer at 11 East 42nd Street—telephone messages etc.—cost $1.50 per month.

One morning shortly after our arrival at Horatio Street I went out to phone the office (our phone had not been installed yet). I only had a nickel with me (you could get a loaf of bread at that time for a nickel)—if I was to phone and get the loaf of bread without sacrificing one for the other, I would have to beat the phone company. I felt that they could stand it so I dropped my lonely only coin in the slot, called the operator and explained I had received the wrong number—she returned my coin, I got my number and my loaf of bread.

Miss Holzer informed me that she had a red star telegram for me. She was excited—said that that meant it was very important, like a death or accident or something special. I had her open it and it was a wire from Charles M. in Dallas stating that Melba's mother was dead. She had been run down while crossing Hollywood Blvd. en route home from the movies alone. The driver of the car had been window shopping and had not seen her at the crossing where she had the right of way—for the green light was with her.

Charles' brother had seen a small notice of the accident in the newspaper and had wired Charles and me and Judge Marsh.

I returned immediately to Melba who was still in bed trying to sleep in the day time when bed bugs don't come out and bite—if you keep a bright light on at night it has a tendency to distract them. I gave her the glad sad tidings.

Melba was greatly excited. I went to Paul Alaimo's stationery store at 11th and Greenwich and phoned from there on the cuff to mother and Bob Marsh. We went down to see Marsh and to map a campaign. Melba knew that her mother kept large sums of cash around the house hidden all over the place, and she was afraid her Aunt Dora would swoop down and grab all. It was decided that Melba would have to get a California lawyer right away to protect her interests. I called George Barr Baker for suggestions and he recommended Joseph Scott (Scott had put Hoover in nomination at Chicago in 1932) who was an outstanding lawyer and the leading lay Catholic of the West. Melba remembered that she had gone to school with a daughter of Scott's so we went to "Honey's," mother's, and Melba called Scott on the phone. I did the preliminary talking and then she chatted with him. He agreed to take the case, learn the details about the accident, get in touch with Edwards, Mrs. M.'s lawyer, and see to it that nothing was touched.

As Melba was talking to Scott, Dora was racing down to San Francisco with her daughter Alfreda, having sent Melba a delayed wire in care of Judge Marsh as she departed. She got into the apartment ahead of Scott, but he made her put up elsewhere. We wired everyone we would leave for the coast at once.

In order to give Marsh and Scott time to prepare their side of the picture we decided to fly instead of going by train. Scott made all funeral arrangements etc.—in fact attended to everything—undertaker, services and cremation.

Melba had to get mourning clothes—anyway her wardrobe was badly depleted—I needed a presentable suit. Mother advanced us a thousand dollars.

We engaged air transportation to the coast—in those days they were flying part air and then going by part rail—you flew during the day (clear weather) and rode on the train at night (or bad weather).

Melba's mother died on the 29th of October. We set forth from Newark for Glendale the night of the 5th of November. It was the first scheduled flight—all air 28 hour service—from coast to coast.

Walter Winchell's daughter broke a bottle of champagne over the nose of the ship. Slim Lindbergh was there. It was quite an occasion. Mother and her sister, my aunt Lucy, rode out in a hired limousine to see us off—the news photographers and reporters were all present. We had not been aware that it was to be an inaugural trip.

Scott, Judge Marsh and mother knew how we were going out but no one else did. They all thought we were coming out by train. We had excess baggage and had to pay extra for that ($45.00).

Camden was our first stop—we arrived there to the blare of a band and the greeting of the Mayor and the inevitable press. After the ceremonies we were told to disembark, that the ceiling over the Alleghenies was too low and we would be taken to Pittsburgh by train. Cabs were waiting and we were bundled off to the Broad Street Station of the P.R.R. They gave us a drawing room and we slept quietly into Pittsburgh.

When we reached Port Columbus, Ohio (after having traveled all but 90 miles of the coast-to-coast-all-air-route so far by train) we were advised that we would be laid over in Kansas City all night. That meant that we would be not the fourteen hours we were then behind at Port Columbus, but 24 hours late coming into Los Angeles.

[The passengers protested and TWA flew them to Glendale, California, by substituting air mail pilots and division superintendents for the commercial passenger pilots.]

What a trip that was, especially from Albuquerque into Glendale—bump, bump, bump over air pockets as we crossed the desert and hedgehopping—there was hardly a second when the plane wasn't bouncing and banging all over the air. I thought my guts would come right up through my mouth—I hadn't been so sick since the *Siberia Maru*.

The so-called meals aboard were a snare and a delusion—the picnic boxes served in flight were appetizing but hardly would constitute a meal. We had none served us on the ground—we had to buy those ourselves and it would have helped to have met up with just a hamburger cart or a hot dog stand or a soft drink cooler or a newspaper or candy stand at any of the airline stations. . . .

The fiasco of that first trip had but one redeeming

feature—it avoided publicity on our arrival in Los Angeles. If we had flown straight through our arrival would have been spread all over the papers as the first "coast-to-coast-all-air" passengers.

We went straight to the Hotel Biltmore as soon as we arrived—we were so shaken from the trip that we had to go to bed for several hours after bathing, in order to settle our stomachs, rest and hear normally.

Then we met Scott [the lawyer]. After that we met Dora and her daughter and the other members of the family, then we went out to Mrs. M.'s apartment. Before Scott had gotten there, someone had looted the place of all the cash and some of the clothes.

Mrs. M. was cremated and her ashes put in the urn with her father and her husband. At the services in the Memorial Chapel in Hollywood's great showplace, Joe Scott sat with Melba and myself in the first pew—Dora, in the next pew, the culprit, the scavenger, the abused one, the boot licker, became hysterical—and her only interest in "Teetie" had been to get what she could out of her. . . .

Mrs. M. had left a will leaving all the property in the original trust set up for the children which she had attacked and broken—in trust, by will, for them just as she had had it in the trust that she spent so much money breaking. Such are the ways of women—emotional not logical.

The lawyer disclosed that it would be necessary to get Charles M., the father of Diane and Melsing, out of the picture in order to expedite the settlement of the affairs. He wanted Melba appointed sole guardian of the children.

Scott felt that that should be done at once. We discovered that it would take longer to go by train than to motor to Dallas, so we bought a second-hand Packard phaeton for $1,000. . . .

We set forth for Dallas driving night and day. We took Mrs. M.'s chauffeur with us. He rode on the back seat during the day and at night up front with me—while Melba dozed in the rear. The nigger worked the radio—going through mountain passes you keep losing your station unless you change your dialing or volume. That may not be true today but it was then. The radio tended to keep me awake.

We made that trip in forty hours.

We registered at the Adolphus. The papers had arrived by Air Mail for Charles to execute.

We had a nice time with the children and Charles signed all the papers consenting to Melba being guardian in California. And the papers Mark sent on making her guardian for them in the State of New York. We had sent Bob certificates of death etc.

In Dallas I bought the chauffeur Lee a heavy coat for motoring in the North.

Our job completed in Dallas we started back to Los Angeles—driving leisurely taking it easy now that we had Charles signed up and the guardianship matter safely tucked behind us.

Melba bought the children new clothes and gave Charles spending money for them. . . .

[On the way back from Dallas, Lee, the black chauffeur, complained that my father had done all the driving. In response, my father turned the driving over to Lee. Lee went to sleep at the wheel, the car turned over and my father's shoulder and collar bone were crushed. No one else was hurt but he spent several weeks in the hospital at Globe, Arizona. The following article appeared in the Globe newspaper.]

VISITOR HERE ENJOYS WESTERN HOSPITALITY ON FORCED STAY.

"Though I had visited most countries of the world, seeing all kinds and conditions of people, I have never been treated with more consideration, thoughtfulness for my comfort and with the true hospitality than I have right here in Globe during the past 10 days."

That was the statement made last evening by W. Ward Smith, wealthy publisher of New York City as he lay in his room of the Dominion Hotel swathed in bandages as a result of an automobile accident south east of Globe November 25th when he suffered a broken right arm, a broken shoulder and various other injuries.

CAR OVERTURNS.

Mr. Smith accompanied by Mrs. Smith and their chauffeur was enroute to Los Angeles when the accident occurred. The chauffeur was driving. The car, a big Packard, turned over one and a half times. Mrs. Smith suffered bruises to her head and body. The chauffeur escaped with but minor hurts. . . .

"My friends brought me bass from San Carlos Lake, turkey, chicken, duck and other fancy foods which I enjoyed to the utmost. I shall long retain a memory of my enforced visit in Globe. Usually we drive right through these mountain towns and never knew just what they are like. It has certainly been a revelation to me and Mrs. Smith."

During the past couple of days Mr. Smith had been in a wheel chair and was noticed by many residents of Globe while being pushed up and down Broad Street. He talked to New York by telephone from one to seven times a day to keep in close touch with his business affairs there. He kept the telegraph wires hot between here and the eastern metropolis.

Mr. and Mrs. Smith had left New York on November 5th in the inaugural of the 28-hour schedule of the Trans-continental Western Airways, arriving in Los Angeles Nov. 6th. After a week there they motored to Dallas, Texas, to visit with their children and were on the return trip to the coast from where they had intended taking a boat through the canal to New York when the accident happened.

LEAVE FOR NEW YORK

They left this morning over the Southern Pacific for New York.

Mr. Smith was executive secretary to Nathan Miller, governor of New York, in 1921 and 1922. He came west in that year to organize Hoover-for-president clubs, being a great admirer of the president at that time.

While in California in 1928 he met and married Mrs. Smith.

Besides publishing a high class travel Magazine, "Nomad" Mr. Smith engages in banking and lumber business in New York City. While he was here James A. McNary, head of the Cady Lumber Co. of McNary was a visitor.

In a radio broadcast from New York shortly after Mr. Smith was hurt, Hendrick Willem Van Loon, noted author, and Heywood Broun famed columnist gave Globe some advertising by mentioning that their friend Mr. Smith was a temporary resident of the City.

The chauffeur was sent to Los Angeles to buy a new car and take personal effects of the couple on to their home in New York.

While still in Globe, I wired the Gotham and the St. Regis for rates and then made a reservation in both hotels from Chicago. There was little to choose between the room rates—the St. Regis had the advantage for me, of having the barber there (Frank Fisher) who had cut my hair and shaved me on and off since my days of Berkeley School. Fisher was the manager, in fact, he owned the barber shop at the St. Regis, and the accommodations there were nicer as were the manicurists.

The New York Central people were as thoughtful and considerate of my comfort as the Southern Pacific people were, and I went thru the performances of being looked after by station masters, division superintendents and pullman representatives from Chicago to New York.

We sent Charles M. the money to bring himself and his fourth wife to New York for Christmas.

In order to cut down expenses we took a large suite at the Gotham with a big, high-ceiling living room, a room to be fixed up as an office for me, and a double bedroom, also a room for the children, a room for their Governess and a room at our expense for Charles and his wife all on the same floor, connecting with our suite.

We had bought the Christmas tree and were at the Gotham arranging to have it set up—all the furniture removed from the living room—when the management of the St. Regis got hold of me and breathlessly offered me the same accommodations in their hotel, at the same rate that the Gotham was charging me, which was as I recall it $150.00 a week.

I paid the Gotham for one day's occupancy—they had gone to a great deal of trouble to fix up the suite for us—and remained at the St. Regis.

The tree that was set up in our St. Regis living room was a large one that reached from the floor to the ceiling. My breaks were still tender and I was not able to personally set up the Christmas display for the children.

The Lionel people sent two men up to the St. Regis after I had the tree brought back from the Gotham.

It took the two Lionel men nearly all afternoon and

evening to get the tracks laid and trains working after the tree had been set up—they had a great deal of difficulty with short circuits. There was an outer track of standard gauge (large size) that circumvented the extreme outside borders of the room—went through tunnels and across bridges, criss-crossed with crossovers, in the center of the room and then came back to have two inner circles, all of which was connected up with a roundhouse and additional side tracks.

There were three standard passenger trains and one long freight train; signal towers flashed the all-clear and danger signals as the trains raced by switching from one track to the other and passing one another in their headlong electrical rush.

There were signal lights and crossing gates and signal bells that indicated the approach of the various trains. One train of cars could not enter a block until the other train had cleared it.

From a central switchhouse, it was possible to throw the switches by remote control—the switches were marked by conventional red and green lights (in miniature). In addition to the roundhouse and freight stations, there was a passenger station with miniature passengers, porters and baggagemen—around the base of the tree was still another setup, that was a narrow gauge track—and a small passenger train just circled around the tree in and out of tunnels constantly. Melsing also had a sleigh and some other toys such as soldiers, a fort, etc.

For Diane we bought a large doll's house completely outfitted from cellar to garret with miniature furniture and dolls. She also was given a complete set of *The Children's Encyclopedia*, a small writing desk, and a complete and workable electric stove and oven. For her dolls, she had a three-tiered baby basket with all the little accessories that one would have for a real baby, only they were for her dolls.

A Santa Claus was placed near the tree and the management of the hotel hung a very beautiful silver-tinseled drape on the wall as a backdrop which set the tree off in stunning fashion.

Melsing was thrilled with his Christmas—Diane seemed

disappointed and morose. She sulked and was quite unpleasant—she has never been able to explain her Christmas attitude as a child. She always appeared disappointed with her Christmas (altho she now says she wasn't) no matter how much she was given. She contended that it was a mixture of shyness and jealousy of Melsing and his Christmas gifts, altho we always struggled to make sure that she received more than he got, because she was older.

Due to Diane's manner on this annual festive occasion, Melba usually flew into a rage at what she considered Diane's ingratitude and then there would be tears and the little girl would go to her room in great distress. I don't suppose that she ever really had a spontaneously happy Christmas the whole time I knew them—her reactions were always the same, whether we were in a railroad flat in Montreal, a tenant in New York, a house on the grounds of the Santa Barbara Biltmore, or a lavish suite at the St. Regis. . . .

Hendrik van Loon sketched an Xmas card for us that year to send out in addition to the books we distributed. It was about seven by ten and showed what purported to be a catastrophic world with the deluge about to encompass all, to which we added in Melba's scrawl "The world is a bit shaky, but nevertheless, Merry Christmas, Ward & Melba." . . .

1933

The ushering in of 1933 was more auspicious than the ushering in of 1932—it promised much but hardly held its own—1932 had actually been a year which had started with rags and ended in, for us, riches.

1933 was to see the closing of the banks, the beginning of the reign of Franklin the First, a hilarious visit to the Mardi Gras at New Orleans, Palm Beach in season at the Breakers for the first time, the World's Fair in Chicago, Jarmila M.'s visit to the United States, an affair with her and Claire T., a trip through the Canadian Rockies, a visit to Victoria, a trip to Europe with the children, and the purchase of Melvale, a tax fight in the State of California and a Federal Suit with United States Government Department of Internal Revenue over the Melsing estate, as life went marching on—and not the least, September 24th, 1933 was to see my 40th birthday when life is reputed to begin. . . .

At the St. Regis suite, we occupied at Xmas while Charles and Margaret were with us, including room 809, 808, 807, 806, all with baths—living room 805, dining room 804, bedroom 803, 802, 801, 835 and 834—all with baths and better than half a floor of the old building 55th Street & Fifth Avenue side all for $150 per week.

That December 1932—while lavishing presents upon Diane and Melsing—I had not neglected you or your brother, as your "thank you" notes and your beloved mother's acrimonious communications attest.

I sent you sleighs, toboggans, skates, skis, boats, soldiers and other things—perhaps not many in quantity but high in quality—Alex Taylor's best. Clothes would also have been forthcoming had it not been for your Mother's constant wrangling—the record speaks for itself. On the exchange of letters between your Mother and myself you can judge the motives involved. It was a sort of tug of war—you were the prize—and she had possession and possession is nine-tenths of the law. . . .

Following my letter to my Mother you will find a letter I wrote you from the Hospital in Globe, Arizona—it was the philosophical outburst of a man in great physical pain marooned in a desert town.

My letter to you is followed by a note to your Mother which I wrote her on the Twentieth Century Ltd. enroute to New York, December 9th, 1932, asking her to let you and your brother stop over in New York for a few days with your Grandmother Smith or anyone else your Mother might choose—also inquiring as to what clothes you might need for Christmas along with your toys, etc.

Then comes the correspondence about the things I sent you for Christmas—your Mother seemed to feel they were too lavish and was constrained to question my good faith and taste—but that was her wont, whether intentional or not. Attorneys who read them professionally felt they were shallow and condescending.

With this correspondence, you will find the letter about the tuition for the McDonough School—as you will note, I felt your Mother had her figures a bit confused. The school's statements are here for you to judge for yourself.

I have steadfastly refused to permit myself to gauge your Mother by the rigid standards I apply to most—either in my discussions with you or with others—primarily because Ellen West Page Smith was the Mother of my sons, for better or worse, and because I was aware of the provincial environment of the old conservative South that had produced her.

That correspondence ushered out the old year 1932 and in the New Year, 1933. . . .

Melba and I bought a specially built Lincoln convertible—

the body was designed and built by Broun of Buffalo. There were only three others like it and they weren't finished in the same way. Ours was black and silver and the leather was of an almost white color, probably beige. Tommy Manville, Edsel Ford and the Shah of Persia had similar cars with different color combinations. The job cost between $5,000 and $6,000 delivered New York—I turned in the Packard limousine as a down payment arranging to turn over the wrecked Packard Phaeton at the time of the Lincoln delivery, along with the balance in cash. They allowed me $2,000 for the two cars.

The Lincoln was not to be ready for delivery until May. In the meantime I used a rented Rolls-Royce with chauffeur.

In February we cut down the number of rooms that we were using to four (809-810-811-812). They charged us $90.00 a week for them. However, our rooms, meals, telephone calls, laundry, valet, newsstand, theatre tickets, motor hire, beauty parlor and barber shop charges, postage, telegrams, florist, drugs, totalled approximately $1,000 a week. . . .

All during our stay at the St. Regis we maintained the apartment on Horatio Street for midnight parties—we kept a Jap there on full time so that we could drop in whenever we liked for food, alcoholic stimulations or love. . . .

[My father and Melba decided to go to New Orleans for Mardi Gras. The letter includes a lengthy description of the social events surrounding the Mardi Gras and the pageant itself.]

On our way home [from the Mardi Gras] the morning of March 2nd, we bought one of the Extras from the newsboy announcing that Huey Long, as he boarded the Crescent Limited en route to Washington to attend the Inaugural of Franklin Delano Roosevelt, had announced his proclamation closing all the banks in Louisiana.

New Orleans is on Central time, an hour later than New York. We did not go to bed—we took baths, ordered breakfast, and at 7:00 o'clock New Orleans time, 8 o'clock New York time, I telephoned my mother and urged her to draw enough cash out of the bank to take care of her incidental expenses for a month or two. She was then living at the La Salle Hotel and didn't need much cash—I told her what had happened in Louisiana, and warned her that more than likely the New York banks would be next, and in fact the entire nation would have to follow suit.

A few minutes before 8, which was just before 9 New York time, I got Arthur Bowen of the Corn Exchange Bank, Grand Central Branch, New York, on the phone and instructed him to wire me fifteen hundred dollars by postal telegraph and fifteen hundred dollars by Western Union, and to do it immediately, before the telegraph services shut off funds in New Orleans. I also told him to send me $2000 in cash by Air Mail registered to the Breakers Hotel in Palm Beach and to send it in $20.00 bills.

At 8:30 the Postal informed me that they had the wire and a few minutes later similar words came from Western Union. It caused great consternation in both offices but I didn't give them time to catch their breath. I was at the Postal almost as soon as the wire got there and before they opened their safe—they paid me out in cash. The Western Union gave me half cash and the balance in their own $50.00 checks—which I proceeded to cash whenever I could at Western Union offices all the way from New Orleans to Palm Beach. . . .

On with the Melba trip—we rode bicycles, we rode in chair cycles, had our favorite pushmobile boy and the bicycle man who always produced the bike that he said was Grover Whalen's favorite. We enjoyed the swimming, the massages, and the night life at Miami. Clark Davis was in business then in Miami and we went the rounds with him to the hot spots and the track.

The one and most emotional experience that lingers with me is the recollection that I'm not particularly proud of. One evening—it was moonlight—the night of Franklin Delano Roosevelt's first fireside chat. He had closed all the banks throughout the country—the nation was jumpy, starvation seemed just around the corner, even in Palm Beach. We went out for a spin in the car. It was a heavenly night out there under the stars. The radio was on and we had just been listening to a program—the Consolidated Gas, a plain steal of Stanley Howe's "Musical Epic of American History." It was coming to us way down there clear as a bell from a New York station—right out of the dashboard, as if we were sitting in a New York studio witnessing the show.

At the conclusion we were taken to the White House to hear the president. We left the damn thing on—why? Curious I guess. That address will always go down in my mind as the best and most inspiring F.D.R. ever made—or has made to this writing. All his others have been an anticlimax. It stirred me to my very depths—it brought the tears, the thrills and ripples—it moved Melba too. We were for Roosevelt that night if we never had been before—whole heartedly—and never were again. He stood before us that night out there under the blanket of stars, as a true savior—a knight errant—a real leader of his people, guiding them out of the wilderness into the light.

There were quite a few of the top-flight Jews—the big money gents—at the Breakers. That month the late Adolph Ochs then owner of *The New York Times*, with Mama Ochs, tottering along behind him, and Adolph Lewishon, were among the shylocks present.

The Breakers that season perhaps more than at any other time because of the depression and the stock market debacle that had cleaned out so much of the youth of the nation, had a preponderance of distorted, dried up, wizened beauties—parading about in beautiful feathers and startling bathing suits in a useless attempt to appear thirty or forty—when they were in fact between sixty and seventy.

At times the old dames would even spoil the natural beauty of that charming citadel—which was the personification of resort luxury.

The housemaids, waitresses and masseurs were the sole attraction—sexually speaking—in 1933. . . .

I never forgot the gypsy at West Palm Beach—like most wenches of her tribe she sat by her tent letting her tits show. In passing she called to me—my cock got hard and I went in. She professed to read my palm—it was during the hell that reigned following the bursting of the Florida bubble. Altho I took my prick out and covered her with semen as I came, she continued to read my palm, as her baby crawled around beneath the table we sat at—nothing perturbed her. She told me that I was not a lawyer, but that for many years I would have much to do with the law. She explained it would be litigation over civil actions in equity—I thought then, and I still think (when I am rational) that that was a natural conclusion to reach regarding anyone who was in Florida at the time doing business in that panic. Yet, every time anyone has threatened to sue me, or sued me, or I have been in a tight place financially, I have thought of her predictions and like a dope wondered. I know that nothing in my hand has had anything to do with my life—it was just an obvious conclusion to come to at that time, and sufficient—with the sex by-play—for me to cross her palms with silver.

In Baltimore there was a friend of your mother's—in fact of the entire Page family—some old crackpot who reading my palm before we were married, predicted that we would live in a small unpretentious Harlem flat (only niggers there now). That prediction like the one of the old roadside gypsy haunted me from time to time, especially during reverses—I never thought of them when I was on the top of the wave.

Ethel Barrymore once told me that an old witch had predicted she would die in poverty—an inmate of the old "Actors Home"—and she freely admitted that she was fearful that she might spend her last days there. John died broke—their recent years particularly hers have been tough—and would have been tougher if it had not been for her brother Lionel.

I don't take any stock in the palm reading. I have known many who have told me of their tricks—how they get people to tell them things and then turn around and tell it back as part of their wisdom—they go by appearances also. Astrology is just as bad. The trouble with all those things is the fact that (if your mind isn't strong enough to throw them off) the power of suggestion is so great that by thinking the thoughts that the witch has imparted, you bring about the actuality of the prediction—and it is seldom the actuality of the pleasanter things or the things you think you would like to have happen—but usually the things you don't want to have come about—the things that you wish to avoid.

Nothing upsets me more than shortage of funds, threatened lawsuits or lawsuits, yet I have been everlastingly involved in all my life in litigation—principally from over-extending myself in moments of affluence. . . .

I suppose I would have enjoyed greater substantial and permanent success in life if I had not been such a rolling stone—primarily interested in women—suffering acutely from an inferiority complex. Shyness and the fear of being rebuffed held me back in my youth—but in maturity, lack of fervent partisanship, the ability to see both sides to every argument, did much to deter me. Then, too, I always relied on memory rather than an accurate record to keep track of important contacts—and I failed to keep up with friends. I could do for others and push others, but found it hard to push myself. My mind was never nimble enough in emergencies—I could think clearly before or after but never during. Pop a question to me in any gathering or on a witness stand and I would draw a blank—pop it at someone else and I could always give the other fellow the answer. It was a form of what some people call "stage fright." Telling friends off that displeased me or who tried to cheat me, either face to face, violently, or through the medium of the pungent pen, never helped me—in the long run it hurt, especially at crucial times when those friendships would have been helpful. . . .

I took a very nice office on Liberty Street for the Airecooling Corporation which I organized, and which I owned. It was fitted up as a work shop for Mr. Anderson to continue his developing and improving on both the Airecooler and the Electric Ice Box. . . .

[In March] I drove down to Baltimore, and by arrangement with your mother, took you and your brother to Annapolis for the afternoon . . . In the gymnasium we all had a try at the Circular Track. We did the old Navy yard from one end to the other. It was a very delightful afternoon and we took a lot of pictures both still and movie. As we drove down past Carvel Hall a very gorgeous young vision appeared on the stoop. As I remember she had on a white Leghorn hat. You couldn't take your eyes off the vision, and when I chided you with "what are you looking at son" your rejoiner was "The same thing you are Dad."

We were a little late getting back to Ruxton, and I gave your mother $50.00 for a Junior Membership for you in the Ruxton Country Club.

[A flurry of letters and gifts followed the Annapolis trip.]

It has always been my wont to write letters. If the art of letter writing had only not been lost it might have been profitable for me. When I say lost, I mean not only the art of writing but of appreciation as well—letters.

The letters will all have to speak for themselves.

7 East 42nd Street
New York, N.Y.
March 20, 1933.

Mr. Charles Page Smith,
Ruxton, Md.
Dear Page—

I cannot begin to tell you how much I enjoyed seeing you and your brother and your mother the other day.

I was especially glad of an opportunity to see you in your uniform and then to see my very much grown-up son starting off in his dinner coat.

Of course, what interested me most were the very excellent drawings that you gave me to show Mr. Van Loon and I also liked your poetry and was much impressed by the modeling you had done. I think it all most excellent and I think you should continue to keep up your interest.

I notice that many of the sketches were done in 1929 and 1930 and that apparently you have not been drawing much lately and I wonder why?—I would hate to see you give up when you have displayed such real talent for depicting life in a satirical mood as well as being able to do the more serious things.

I hope now that we have succeeded in breaking the ice that it will be possible for us to see one another more often and that our visits will be more frequent than they have been in the past. I feel that perhaps your mother and I are approaching a more agreeable understanding than has been possible in years past. . . .

I appreciate having been to your school—now—I realize the great distance that you have to travel each day, I am amazed that you are able to find time to write at all. . . .

As I told you, I gave the women at the candy store a dollar for you and a dollar for your brother for you to buy ice cream and candy with. I will write you more in a day or two, but I am very busy catching up with a lot of work that accumulated during my absence. . . .

Your devoted father

7 East 42nd Street
New York, N.Y.
April 6, 1933

Dear Ellen:

I have been so busy since I returned to New York that I have not had time to write and thank you for your consideration the other day when we passed though Baltimore and dropped in to see the boys.

I hope from now on that you and the boys and our side of the house can meet together from time to time in the same amicable manner.

The financial situation is such that it isn't possible for me to be of any assistance at the moment, but I feel that within the course of the next two or three months that we should be able to sit down and work out some way of alleviating part of the burden that you have been carrying so bravely.

It was nice to be able to talk to you without acrimony and I am sure you must appreciate how much it meant to me to see the boys and to talk to them, and learn about their work. I think Page's drawings, many of which he apparently executed between 11 and 12, are excellent and certainly his modelling shows great promise. He looked very well in his military uniform and exceptionally attractive in his dinner coat.

They must indeed be a great comfort and joy to you. . . .

I have already set to work to find something for Page on one of the trans-Atlantic liners, but before discussing it further with him I should like to talk to you more about it, and also to have a frank talk with you about a lot of problems with which Page is bound to be confronted.

I am rather glad that you and Melba met the other day. Melba for her part found you very attractive and a surprisingly nice person—which of course does not speak well for me—but then I have always been aware of your attributes while unable at times to reconcile myself to some of your ideas and theories. . . .

This communication is a sort of preliminary word to let you know I have not forgotten the boys and that they figure very much in my plans for the future. I sincerely hope that we can work together agreeably for their best interests. It was nice to see you and the boys, and Melba joins in sending best wishes and the hope that we may be able to repeat the pleasant meeting in the not too distant future.

Sincerely,
Ward

Wednesday April 15th 1933

Dear Father;—

Thank you a lot for the pralines they were very good and we all enjoyed them very much. I hope you are having a good time in Miami. Poor brother has had the chicken-pox and on top of that Dr. Dabney had to operate on him for two awful abscesses on his arm. He is very brave about it. I have taken up clay modeling a little and have done two statues. Mr. Van Loon has been so nice to autograph all those books that I thought I would write him a short letter. I do not know his address. I am enclosing it and I hope you will either mail it for me or give it to him. I am on the debating society at school and just finished the hockey season on the second line (varsity ice hockey I played right wing). We have started a paper in Ruxton and I am the Editor (just we boys) I write the stuff and they typeright it out. We are running a serial in it called "Red Vengence" by me. Hoping you enjoy yourself.

I remain
very Sincerely your Son.
Page Smith

[My father, armed with his new wealth, gave every indication that he intended to decide where and how my brother and I were to be educated. My mother, of course, was equally determined to rebuff his erratic interpositions. She explained to him that my whole academic career had been precarious in the extreme and that only the interest and help of the Gilman teachers and Mr. Pickett, at whose tutoring school my academic deficiencies were repaired each

summer, had enabled me to avoid expulsion for bad grades. As she wrote my father, "Mr. Pickett has agreed . . . to tutor Page in two subjects at no extra cost. He and Mrs. Pickett are devoted to Page and anxious to get him back to Gilman. He says that the teachers (at the camp) who are all Gilman masters, can decide after working with Page, whether he can make the grade or not."

My father, after having promised my brother and me that he would put up the money to send us to camp had then stipulated that if he were to pay he must name the camp. My mother was furious. My brother, as she wrote, asked every day when he returned from school "Has my father sent the money for me to go to camp? I don't mind Page's being disappointed nearly as much for he is never as keen about anything as poor John is, and being older has more philosophy or resignation or whatever you care to call it . . . John has come in at the small end of things always. Everything that I have had to spend has gone on Page. Not only because he was older but he seemed to be more of a problem and need things more. Johnny is so fine and manly and I have been able to do so little for him. I have never seen anyone with a nobler or finer character . . . You made a promise to the child and I will have one more big score against you if you disappoint him and keep the matter dragging on any longer."

My father replied: "This will acknowledge your dictatorial communication of recent date. It both amused and interested me—I had hoped that you had outgrown these tirades of rhetoric—they are so futile—however your imperious letter would have done the Gazi Mustafa Kemal Pasa proud." My father then went on to reiterate that if he was to pay for camp and school he must have the last word on where we were to go. Culver Military Academy in Indiana was his choice, for summer as well as winter. I should take Naval Studies at the Culver Summer Camp in preparation for Annapolis—which I hadn't the slightest interest in attending—and my brother should take woodcraft. We could both attend the Chicago World's Fair on the way.

My mother, knowing a lost cause when she saw one, left it to me to reply to my father's letter. I wrote: "Dear Father, . . . Neither Johnny nor I have ever wished to go to the World's Fair and Mr. Pickett's camp was the choice of both of us. If you are interested in sending us to any camp you could not find a better one than Mr.

Pickett's. We have always been very happy there . . . The things you wrote about Mother hurt my feelings terribly. When I am older I will express my opinion. I only know that mother has worked hard for years to help grandfather take care of us, and we have had no help from you since you left us all in Morristown. Thanks for the fireworks, we all enjoyed them very much. Yours truly, Page."

To which my father replied:]

If your last letter had been read to me aloud, I would have been sure that it was your Mother's composition and phraseology. At that, even your hand-writing is quite unlike your normal script as I know it, and I can appreciate that you were forced into taking the position and writing such a letter which you couldn't help but be contrary to the true feeling of you and your brother.

I am glad the responsibility is not mine of having robbed you both of a most interesting experience of a lifetime, to-wit, a visit to the Century of Progress Exposition at Chicago and a summer in the finest Boys' Camp in the United States, particularly adapted to you, if you . . . plan to go to Annapolis.

The letter was not a bit your style or like your real, true self.

If your mother prefers to play the role of the harassed, the abused and the martyr there is little I can do, but regret her stand for ultimately you both will be the real sufferers.

Of course getting around as little as you all do, you do not have the opportunity to see and understand and appreciate what is going on in the rest of the world and how other people live and do things. . . .

You are quite right, when you are older you will see and understand all in its true light, for I hope as you grow older that in spite of the circumstances in which you now find yourself and the narrow confines of your present environment, that you will be able to see things in their true perspective.

If your Mother steadfastly refuses to accept the assistance which I can arrange for you both, or to accept tuition for you in good schools simply because of a desire to wreak an inverted passion upon me, I can do little at the present moment to stop her.

As far as the so-called sacrifices she feels she has made in order to look after you both I doubt if she would ever have had to make them if she had been civil to me and my family, but her arrogant manner was not conducive to eliciting sympathy, particularly when she has so consistently refused to cooperate or to compromise in regard to you and your brother, your education and making it possible for me to see you from time to time, or have you see your grandparents, or your cousins. . . .

At times I wonder if she and her family are not suffering from a violent inferiority complex and if that is not the real cause of most of the difficulty. . . .

When the time comes, when you are old enough, if you are interested, I shall tell you or I shall have some unprejudiced, disinterested party tell you the truth of the whole situation. It's a long story, and I shan't set it forth now, or for some time to come. For the present, let me say, the impartial persons have been amazed at your Mother's letters and have all felt that in view of her attitude, my communications have been considerably moderate.

I am sorry to have to write you this way and I am sorry that your mother will not let you go to Culver or to the World's Fair or to the type of school that would best fit you for Annapolis or that she won't let you see your grandmother who has been ill for so long and so anxious to see you. I am sorry that she won't make it possible for you to meet and know men and the wisdom of them, of the type of Hendrik van Loon, Carveth Wells and others. . . .

I am glad that you and Marshall enjoyed the firecrackers. There would be a good deal in the world for you to enjoy, if your Mother didn't so consistently and deliberately stand in the way.

As ever, your devoted father

[This letter marked the virtual end of any exchange between the Northern and Southern divisions of the family. I did not see, or so far as I can recall, correspond with him until I went to college, four years later.]

And so, we slothfully wended our way through April—a bit dull, but busy with plans for the new office, Airecooling, *Nomad,* Ampro Distribution, Harry Millar's new corporation, and a multitude of other schemes were brewing all around as we approached the Merry, Merry month of May.

I rented a beautifully panelled office (old Colonial Style) high up on the 39th floor of One Wall Street—the entire floor. It had a magnificient view of the Bay, the East River and the Hudson. As far as the eye could see, North, South, East and West, the Metropolitan area was spread out below me. It was truly Manhattan's inspirational point.

Watterson Lowe did the entire decorating—a friend of Hamilton P.'s by the name of Howley sold me the furniture—both charged me well. I had a big open fireplace in my private office with a colonial mantle. On one side of my desk was a stock ticker and a news ticker—on another side a small board, upon which the stocks I traded in were listed with the purchase price and the high and low changes as the market fluctuated.

My brokers were Baar Cohen & Co., and Satchkin & Pell (this latter firm I always suspected of being a bucket shop and my only reason for doing business with them was because of my friendship for Hamilton P.). I had two private secretaries, a Miss McClean and a Miss Murray—I dropped Miss Hendricks after my return from Florida.

My luncheons were brought in every day from the Savarin Restaurant—I seldom went out but often had business appointments for luncheon in my own office. Melba had a desk but she rarely occupied it. A ship's clock that she had purchased from Abercrombie & Fitch for $150.00 graced the mantle, and my most precious autographed photographs hung on the walls, and my Governor's chair was in place behind my desk. The office was air-cooled, the rent $250.00 a month.

When I say the office was air-cooled and conditioned I mean by my own apparatus in the single cabinet, which Anderson had made for me and which you will see in the pictures—the first of its kind patented in the world. . . .

After Diane and Melsing had finished their schooling at Peekskill—St. Mary's Episcopal School for Girls, and the Peekskill Military Academy for Boys—Melba took the children out to Chicago to see the World's Fair.

We had had word from Kauder that Claire T. was coming on to see her mother-in-law and to settle up her husband's estate. We telephoned her step-father's parish house at Islip and learned that the Reverend Mr. Garth and Mrs. Garth were at Keene Valley. We phoned there and Claire got to New York just before Melba left for Chicago, with the children. I had developed quite an urge for Claire in Berlin in 1929, and was thrilled with the prospect of seeing her again.

She arrived in the morning and came straight to the St. Regis—we got her a suite adjoining ours, connecting rooms. We all had lunch together, mother coming over to bid the children good-bye had lunch with us on the roof, and then mother, Claire and I went to the station to put them all on the train.

Mother didn't think well of my having to remain behind on business—she thought Claire attractive and suspected the worst of me—and Melba was sure. As we parted at the station mother warned me to watch my step, which I had no intention of doing, in the direction I intended to go.

That evening I took Claire to dinner—(she had arranged to take over the representation of *Variety* in Berlin, one of the jobs her husband had had before he died, while here she was writing for some German papers of a similar type). She was very eager to see our burlesque shows which had had a revival and were then in full bloom and assiduously patronized by me—I bought through the broker in the hotel, tickets for the leading one on 42nd Street, and also a Box for the one on Irving Place. We dressed for the evening and after dinner we went to the 42nd Street show for the first half. Still high we took in the Irving Place show for the second half. That night we used the Rolls-Royce, so we were really cutting quite a figure. When we got to the Irving Place theatre we found some people in our box and had to have them put out. As was my custom I offered a prize of $10.00 for what I considered the best strip-tease—that is the most complete, and a second prize of $5.00. . . .

From Minsky's Irving Place Theatre we drove down to my office at 1 Wall Street where, from the 39th floor we scanned the city in its fairylike glory of dazzling lights—before the days of blackouts, New York always reminded me of an over-lighted Christmas tree prone on the ground.

Claire was intrigued by the office and the view. From Wall Street we went up to my studio on Horatio Street. The purpose of that visit was to show her the film negative taken of herself and Melba in the nude when we all visited the Nudist Club in Berlin in 1929. By the time I located the roll, we were both pretty tired and so we returned to the St. Regis—all had been most circumspect. We sat up for a while, in the living room of my suite—purpose a night cap. She told me then that her husband always contended that if anything ever happened to him, she would within a fortnight have an affair with some other man, probably one of his best friends—and under the emotional stress and strain of the accident, she had done just that—"Bundy" M., Jarmila's husband, had been the lucky man.

The next morning, James [Taylor], finding the door unlocked between our suites, felt certain, I am sure, that we had had an affair but such was not the case.

After breakfast we set out for Sadie Weiss'—Claire wanted to outfit herself with a new wardrobe before returning home. Dressing the female carcass has always been a weakness of mine and, as usual, was my downfall then—the whole performance was too much for me to stand.

I had subconsciously coveted Claire for years. Alone with her in the dressing room as she fitted one costume after the other my excitement grew to uncontrollable proportions. My cock was hard—I showed it to her—she felt it—I caressed her, got my hand down on her box—she had a lovely garden. I nearly came I was so hot.

The wardrobe complete, we returned to the hotel for luncheon.

I was taking the Century for Chicago to rejoin Melba and the children there at the Fair—the time was short. We sent James off to the kitchen for a sumptuous repast. I could hold back no longer and she seemed eager too so there and then I laid her—for the first time.

Claire was something to conjure with, she knew every trick in the trade and what a "Dutch" girl does not know about sexual intercourse or the ways of a maid with a man are not worth knowing. By luncheon we had completely satiated ourselves and had agreed that she would return to town from Keene Valley on receipt of a wire from me.

The plan—I would return a day ahead of Melba and the children and that 24 hours we would spend together at the studio—the surroundings there were more conducive to unlimited sexual consummation.

After lunch I caught the train for Chicago and Claire took the train north to rejoin her in-laws in the Adirondacks.

When I reached the Blackstone Hotel, Melba lit into me. It was the first time I had seen a flash of jealousy from that quarter since we had been married—but she was hell bent for election then. She accused me of having stayed over for the sole purpose of fornication—I frankly admitted the allegation but only as it developed the second day. There was no sense of making any bones about it because she knew I had an unquenchable urge for Claire.

As a matter of fact she really was sore because she was not in on the show too. After the first excitement blew over, we took the children and visited the General Motors Exhibit which was the most complete of all. There they not only assembled the motor but they built bodies on the endless chain production plan and turned out cars for immediate delivery as they came off the line.

The Transportation Exhibit showed aeroplanes, the latest in Pullman cars, special frieght cars for carrying shells for the Navy, the famous London, Midland and Scottish train "The Royal Scot." They had been big advertisers with us in our *Nomad* days. The Chrysler Exhibit was in a modernistic building but did not approach the General Motors Show. There were wild west shows for the children, Pony Expresses, American Indian villages, a midway with all types of side shows and an enchanted island for children with a mechanical dinosaur and other prehistoric animals, a replica of Fort Dearborn and of Abraham Lincoln's Birthplace attracted the elders more than the kids.

The Hall of Science and the electrical exhibits fascinated the children—a transparent man, a model of the human body which when illuminated by trick lighting, clearly showed skeletal, vascular, respiratory, digestive and muscular systems which excited the kids no end.

Hundreds of young college boys dressed like the State Troopers pushed the customers around in wheel chairs for 50¢ or 75¢ an hour. College athletes, many from good families, were the rickshaw boys. They had a radio and communication building containing a complete international telephone system in active operation. They had home planning exhibits, agricultural exhibits, dairy exhibits.

The Firestone people made tires while you waited and watched.

The Sky Ride was an attraction difficult to get the children away from.

In the lagoon was Admiral Byrd's polar ship, the one he used on his trip to the South Pole.

Innumerable restaurants dotted every part of the Fair.

Mammoth Greyhound buses, built like railroad observation cars at the New London and Hudson River boat races—Harvard and Yale or Poughkeepsie—went from one end of the Fair to the other passing thru the midway at a maximum charge of 10¢ per entire ride.

After several days of this exhausting performance, I returned to New York 24 hours ahead of Melba after wiring Claire.

My train arrived ahead of hers the next morning and I met her at the station. We went immediately to the studio where we freshened up as the Jap prepared a delicious luncheon. Luncheon over, having consumed a moderate proportion of alcoholic stimulant so as not to adversely affect our sexual desires, we sent the Jap on his way.

Claire had a passion for playing with assholes. She would put her finger up mine and I'd put mine up hers. I even tried to get my cock up her rear end. We sucked one another off at first—and then we played with our tails until we both came again. Eventually we both shit the bed—it was too much and my first active encounter with that performance—manipulating assholes—an old German custom.

Claire liked to ride on top—in fact she had great joy no

matter what the position. We never got out of bed until the next morning—we both came at least once every hour—we didn't sleep all night. Sometimes in the early stage we came more often—we drank just enough to keep us going. She was a seductress of no mean proportions.

The next morning Melba arrived in town with the children. Claire and I met her at the train and we all returned to the St. Regis together—we had luncheon on the roof with mother and Mrs. Van Loon. That night Claire returned to Keene Valley—we had hoped to meet her that summer in Germany but her boat did not arrive until the day ours was leaving so we missed her by 24 hours. I did not see Claire again although we corresponded frequently until after Melba and I were divorced and I had remarried for the third time "legally.". . .

At one time we contemplated chartering Roy Howard's houseboat but it wasn't in particularly good repair and so we passed that by. There were also some other hitches which I do not recall at this time.

We looked at boats from $1,000 a season to $1,500 a week and we finally fell for the S.S. *Sydney*, owned by Sydney E. Hutchinson a brother-in-law of Mr. Stotesbury in Philadelphia. The latter part of June I chartered her for $1,000 a week. It cost me another $1,000 per week for fuel and food. The charter ran from the 23rd of June, 1933 to the 7th of September, 1933.

At Melba's special request we put our own little upright studio piano on board. The *Sydney* was a twin screw motor houseboat 100′ overall in length. The crew consisted of 11 men and from time to time as we gave parties, I increased the number of cooks and stewards. In order to fly the Seawanhaka-Corinthian flag, it was necessary for me to charter this boat with Rayford Alley, who was a member of the Club (and my attorney for the aircooling corporation).

My personal insignia or private flag was the *Nomad* "trademark"—a Nomad riding across the desert on his horse, gun held aloft in black and white.

One of our most successful parties was considerably

photographed, both stills and movies. Among the guests were Mr. and Mrs. William O'Donnell Iselin, the Sterling Ivisons, Major Stanley Howe, the Howard Chandler Christys, the Seton Lindsays, the Ongs, Freddie Davenport, the Hamilton Pells, the Mulhollands, the Clay Morgans, Lyle Volck, Eddie Ballou, the George Genungs and a hundred or so others whose names for the moment slip me.

Our bedroom was attractively decorated—it contained two single beds and two comfortably upholstered chairs, a writing desk, a vanity table and a dresser. Our bathroom contained a full size tub, dresser, shower, etc.

The dining room was beautifully appointed, large enough to seat 12 or 14 comfortably.

The living room, as you will see from the photographs was also quite sumptuous. There were 4 guest staterooms on board, each with a private bath.

In addition to the well-furnished quarters for the children and their French governess there was an aft deck below the main decks for them where they could disport themselves undisturbed by the rompings of their elders.

A charming sun parlor completed the main deck before coming out on to the main aft deck.

The galley crew quarters and engineer's were forward.

In addition to the three lifeboats, we had a fast motor boat which was used primarily between the *Sydney* and shore. The top deck amply accommodated a good many guests.

The bridge was my favorite spot especially when we were under way. . . .

We did most of our cruising on the Long Island Sound, around Oyster Bay, Shelter Island and Lloyds Neck. . . .

Coming out of Greenport or Shelter Island, we ran into quite a storm (thru Plum Gut). We had to lash down the piano and the furniture. The old *Sydney* rolled and tossed but we came through without any great difficulty. That trip was reminiscent of the days when I used to sail through Plum Gut with father on his racing sloop, the *Syce*—we had no motors then—the wind was all we had to propel us against tides and seas.

We set off several hundred dollars worth of firecrackers for the children along the shore of Port Washington Harbor the morning of July 4th; we arrived there the night before during a beautiful sunset and anchored.

At noon of the 4th, we weighed anchor and proceeded to Oyster Bay where at night fall on the signal of a flare from the *Sydney*, over a $1,000 worth of firecrackers which I had donated for the occasion, were set off on the lawn of the Seawanhaka Club. At one time it looked as if that display would not take place because rainy weather temporarily settled in. After the firework display we went to Piping Rock Club for supper and dancing. . . .

Wherever we went by water the Lincoln followed by land and was always awaiting our arrival. . . .

At the Piping Rock Club I met a luscious young thing. I got hot and so did she—we left the dance floor and took to the private hedge. Although in evening dress she first sucked me and then laid me there in the bushes to the beat of the dance orchestra. . . .

I had one of the aircooling apparatuses in my stateroom for demonstration purposes and Anderson, the inventor was frequently aboard. James (Taylor) was always along as valet. . . .

As I had said I had chartered the *Sydney* from the 23rd of June, until the 7th of Sept., and when I tried to extend the Charter to cover the week of the boat races at New London, the owner tripled the charter rate for that occasion. This made me so mad that I *cancelled* the charter and returned the *Sydney* to her owner on the 7th of July. . . .

On our return to New York we went to the St. Regis for a day or so and then down to the Essex and Sussex from where I commuted by motor daily between New York and Spring Lake.

As an item of interest, I am including herewith our hotel bill from the second of July to the eighth of July, 1933. This was in addition, of course, to our expenses aboard the yacht *Sydney*. It shows a total of approximately $1,900 for the week and that, of course, does not include cash gratuities although many of my tips were included on my checks.

We found mother and the children enjoying themselves immensely at Spring Lake. Mother said they had behaved very well during our absence, that Charles M., their father, had been down to see them with his new wife Margaret and that they had both spent the night as our guests. The children had been given swimming lessons in the Club pool to the tune of $50 apiece and had progressed very well.

[In the fall of 1933 my father, Melba, Diane and Melsing took a European tour. The trip started in England. From there they went to France, Germany, Spain, Switzerland, Austria and Italy. The descriptions of Germany where Hitler had recently come to power are the most interesting of my father's characteristically voluminous travel accounts.]

[From France the party went on to Germany.] The Germans were marching and counter-marching all day long and well into the night. Hitler had wiped out homosexuality and scattered the lesbians far and wide closing all of the notorious joints or assembly centers—even the street walkers were few and far between and the Jews had lost their arrogance and become servile again. . . .

Our last night in Berlin, we went out with Knickerbocker, Carl Dickey and John Gunther. Knickerbocker's mistress, whom he afterwards married, also came along. In the party was a very beautiful lesbian who in the days prior to Hitler had been the proprietor of the most notorious lesbian restaurant in Berlin. A Black Shirt was very much in love with her which gave us the entree to several night clubs that presumably were being run very much on the Q.T. and underground. That evening we had quite a night of it: along with us on the party was a German College Professor who also was smitten with the lesbian. It was a gay night, Hitler or no Hitler.

I had letters of introduction from the head of the German tourist Bureau in New York to Propaganda Minister, Dr. Goebbels.

I didn't meet Goebbels, he was in Nürnberg at the time in charge of the festivities that were taking place there, but he had left word that Melba and I were to be provided with transportation and accommodations if we wished to attend that all important celebration, when hundreds of thousands of Germans descended upon that famous historical city.

We wanted to go very much and we always regretted that we didn't, but we had the children with us and we couldn't take them to any such shindig, and we feared to leave them behind.

Instead of going to Nürnberg, we hired a limousine and drove to Vienna by the way of Dresden and Prague. We stopped for lunch in Dresden—it was a most attractive City and the German Troopers, Brown Shirts, Black Shirts, war veterans, local Guard and village burgers were marching and counter-marching all over the City to the beat of drums and the blare of trumpets. The Germans were again holding their heads high—they were no longer a beaten or oppressed people hanging their heads in shame. Even passing through you got the thrill of it, a thrill that Americans have not yet experienced in this present war—it was a martial thrill, an inspirational thrill—although you were no part of it, it made you tingle all over as you witnessed the preparation for the onslaught to come. It was the spirit of their enthusiasm that was infectious—the spirit of a people who had found themselves again, who had thrown off the yoke of semitism. . . .

On the way back [to the United States], as on the way over, I talked constantly with my brokers in New York, and traded over the ship-to-shore long distance telephone—I talked to New York at least once or twice a day every day while I was in Europe, carrying on my business and giving my purchase and sale orders.

Mother was at the pier to greet us—James Taylor, my valet at the St. Regis, the St. Regis porter, with his truck—Henry the chauffeur was there with the car. Madamoiselle was also on hand to take over the care of the children. . . .

* * *

The fornicating manicurists at the St. Regis were ready to take up or off where they had left off—they were beautiful girls who loved to screw (for money) and they knew their business. I always had two come up at a time to manicure me—Melba's masseuse had an electric vibrator that they used to stir me up with. Then when she had me hot they would fuck the guts out of me while Melba watched and played with herself.

Immediately on my return, I continued negotiations with Anderson and concluded an arrangement with him in September, between the Airecooling Corporation, Anderson and his partner, whereby they granted the corporation an option to acquire from them all their rights and interests in certain Airecooling patents and Ice making patents for a period of two years for a consideration of $8,000.00. . . .

As soon as we returned to the United States we set to work looking for a farm. Somehow or other I had the feeling that a place in the country would be an anchor to windward, come a war or any other national or international devastating catastrophe.

In October I paid the St. Regis $500.00 a month for rooms 805-806. . . .

I was keenly interested in Fiorello's campaign for Mayor—I had always been one of his staunch supporters. I had hardly returned to New York when I started handing out free advice to the Little Flower and his campaign manager—Stanley Howe and George Bell were both active in that fight. . . .

When the Mayor considered having a big rally at Madison Square Garden, I suggested to the Campaign managers that they have a series of torchlight parades converging on the Garden that night from all parts of the City. The suggestion met with approval and the parade end of the rally was worked out in my apartment at the St. Regis, and although I did not publicly take the lead I planned it and directed it. They marched up from the lower East Side—they marched up from the lower West Side—they marched down from the upper West Side—they marched down from the upper East Side, and they marched across 59th Street from Queens, carrying their "transparencies." Most of these units were composed largely of the active members of the various political clubs. It did not begin to reach the proportions of the Torchlight Parade that Karl Behr and I had put on for the candidacy of John Purroy Mitchel when he was running for Mayor. Nevertheless, it was a good turn out. . . .

During the campaign I gave a cocktail party for the Mayor, Stanley Howe, Heywood Broun and Theodore Dreiser. When they first arrived none of them would take a drink—La Guardia was very much on the defensive. He had a terrific inferiority complex when it came to men of letters. As time went on they all broke down and proceeded to do a bit of light drinking, which was a great relief to James, who having prepared for a sumptuous alcoholic repast was fearful at first that his efforts had all been in vain.

Dreiser contended that no man was ever completely honest even with himself—to say nothing of being honest in dealings with his fellow man.

He accused La Guardia of harboring, perhaps subconsciously, an ambition to be Governor of the State of New York and then President of the United States. La Guardia replied, without a moment's hesitation, that he had no such ambition in the first place and in the second place there were too many vowels in his name.

Following that up, Dreiser then said, "Mayor, have you ever spent a night in a hotel with a woman other than your wife?" This question was prompted by the fact that a short while previous (when investigating the so-called ruthlessness of coal operators in a Pennsylvania mining town, where Dreiser had really gone to lend a hand to the striking miners under the guise of a writer) he had been arrested on the ground of moral turpitude by the local authorities. The charge—he had had a woman in his bedroom all night. The evidence—when he entered the room with a woman, the hotel management and local authorities at the instigation of the operators and their private police, had placed toothpicks outside Mr. Dreiser's door. In the morning when they entered the toothpicks had not been moved, which proved conclusively to the authorities' satisfaction that the young lady had not left the room during the night. To Mr.

Dreiser's query of the Mayor regarding his personal morals, the Little Flower snapped, "Mr. Dreiser, if I have ever spent the night with a young lady in a hotel room, other than my wife, or if I ever do, I have always made sure, and shall always make doubly sure, that all the toothpicks have been removed from the premises before I retire." The Mayor was tickled to death with his quick rejoinder and promptly repeated the episode to his wife and the intimate members of his campaign management.

As our guests became alcoholically stimulated the conversation became more and more scintillating with the little Mayor on the defensive most of the time.

Theodore Dreiser engaged Melba in a discussion of the virtues of black flesh. He having had a negro mistress was a great advocate of the cross-breeding of the races—Melba did not agree with him.

It was Dreiser's contention at that gathering that anyone could start a revolution in the United States at that time because of the dire poverty of the unemployed, by simply crossing the country, holding aloft a red banner. To the contrary, Heywood Broun contended—and I agreed with Broun—that such a movement would get nowhere outside the industrial centers, where the foreign-born predominate. Broun was emphatic in stating that the American farmer, the American landowner, the American suburbanite would not participate but would in fact oppose any such revolutionary uprising. Fiorello didn't get into this discussion too deeply, but he inclined to the Broun theory. Broun had a great respect at that time for the rural backbone of the nation.

During the arguments, Dreiser sat on the livingroom floor—he seemed to find that more to his liking than the chairs or the couches. Like many of his statements, it was but a pose to get him attention.

After the party was over, I took La Guardia into the bedroom and there I gave him $250.00 in cash for campaign expenses. In doing so, I told him that I knew that there were many expenses in an election campaign that could not be included in the returns to the Secretary of State, and that I did not wish any favors in return.

All fall, I was busy visiting various parts of the country looking for a farm—a farm that could be a subsistence farm in the case of dire need—and a commercially operated proposition under fairly normal conditions. I felt strongly that war in the Pacific was in the offing. In those days it seemed to me that we would do battle in the Far East before we went to war again in Europe. From World War I, I had learned the importance of agriculture. We scoured the Virginia countryside; the Maryland countryside; the Delaware countryside; going down the Peninsula of the Eastern Shore of Maryland to Cape Charles, Va. and back. We looked at property in Pennsylvania, in Connecticut, in Massachusetts and all over New York State. . . .

Election Day I went down to La Guardia's headquarters at the Astor Hotel and in the presence of Rosalie Love Whitney, I gave La Guardia my final contribution. . . .

One day, while driving thru Columbia County, New York, we came upon an old house, 150 years old—about half a mile in from the highway at North Chatham, New York. We were taken with the place and the rolling country around it; it afforded a great deal of privacy and was just what we were looking for. The real estate agent took us to the village, and I made the owner and his wife—the place had been in her family ever since it had been built—an offer of $4500.00. There were 112 acres in the place. They went into a huddle and decided to accept the offer, so I made a deposit of $50 or $100, subject to the search of the title and the closing. The deal was also contingent on their ability to persuade a neighbor owning 12 unproductive acres of knoll overlooking the house, to sell same to us for a couple hundred dollars. We then returned to New York and I engaged John Crandall, the Republican County Chairman of Columbia County, a former County Judge, to look after my interests in connection with the transaction.

The place was devoid of electric lights; there were no telephone or electric lines from the highway to the house, the only toilet facilities was a two-holer in the backyard—the water was from a well not too far from the two-holer. The fireplaces were in great need of repair, and the only thing about it that really intrigued us was the lay of the land, and the age of the hand-hewn timbers that were the frame of the house. But we will return to that later. . . .

We were enthusiastic about the place at North Chatham—I had a corporation set up to buy the property—we called it "Melvale Inc." after Melba. We decided to call the place Melvale Farm. While the title was being searched and the purchase negotiations completed we made many trips to North Chatham, meeting with carpenters, plumbers, electricians, plasterers, painters, and the like, getting bids on the work we wanted done, and done in a hurry. . . .

We took deed to the property in the name of the Corporation on the 8th December and on the 23rd of December, we moved in. . . .

Ninety acres were tillable and the rest of the farm was in woodland, meadow and marsh—the soil was rich black loam on flat limestone top mixture and the place entirely fenced by wire, much of it erected by me.

It was a truly lovely location, nestled away in the foothills of the Berkshires.

Hank Van Loon, Hendrik's son, who had been an architect of considerable ability, came over from Dorset and gave us pointers, particularly on the importance of timing the work so that it would run along properly synchronized, in other words, the plumbers and the electricians would get their work done before the plasterers, the carpenters preceding most of the gang, and then would come the painters, etc.

We started our construction work on the 9th of December and we literally tore out the entire inside. We removed the back stairs—we built on an extension with two rooms and a bath for the servants—we turned three rooms on the ground floor into one living room, and then we made closets out of a single room and a bedroom and dining room out of four other small rooms. To boot we added a bathroom—Crane's most modernistic—the tub, the longest they had, black of course, a black toilet bowl and wash basin, and the whole thing finished off in black and white tile with curtains to match, and a black Medicine Chest. We built a new main staircase.

We sank two great big highway tiles down over the spring, which was about 100 feet from the house—this gave us an unlimited supply of drinking water which never dried up. On the upper floor we also constructed two guest rooms with connecting baths and fixed up two adorable rooms for the children with a balcony overlooking the living room so that we could keep an eye on them. The Balcony served as a play room.

There was an ice house on the place, carriage house, tool house, a farm office, a sheep barn with 70 ton storage capacity, a cow barn with 20 stanchions, concrete floor, newly shingled, a manure runway and a spring and milk cooling shed. The horse barn was of 4-horse capacity—the poultry houses took care of 100 hens—there was a silo.

I had the stables, the barns, the garage (which was big enough for two cars), the farm office and milk house electrically wired.

I installed an electric pump to pump the spring water to the house and I cleaned up the well back of the house—the water for the barns was supplied from springs that never dried. When I bought the house there was a hot-air furnace in the cellar which heated the center of the house downstairs—but I changed that, altho I kept the hot air, I installed steam heat.

Being fearful of fire, I had all the chimneys torn out, three in number, and had new ones built from field stone which we gathered on the place. It was quite a proposition. We papered the bedrooms and the dining room—the living room we left bare with rough plaster between the hand-hewn timbers. We bought old wrought iron fixtures. The living room fireplace was large enough for a man to sleep in.

During the construction work we had over 60 men employed on the place at one time—to add to our troubles we had to go thru a snowstorm right in the middle of the work.

Not only did we have to sink the caissons around the

spring but we had to pipe the water to the house, and in addition we had to run drain pipes to take the water out of the kitchen and away from the bathrooms, and not only was it necessary to lay the drain pipes, but we had to construct a cesspool and in addition I put in a septic tank—I directed the entire work myself, letting the contract for the plastering, the plumbing and electrical work, as well as the papering. I coordinated the entire job as well as planning and designing the work.

During this time I rented a room from the Village Parson, but spent a good deal of time commuting between New York and the farm by motor—I was invariably too tired to drive myself so would have Henry drive me.

Van Loon agreed as usual to make up our Christmas cards for us and also design a letterhead for the farm.

But that promise was never fulfilled—the correspondence relating to it follows and tells a more eloquent story than any I could set forth as to just what occurred.

As so often happens in such matters, Hendrik's failure irked me to no end—and on the last day of the year I wrote him a letter which terminated our intimate friendship, and altho years later there was a reapproachment, we were never really close again.

He showed my letter to many, and I distributed copies far and wide—many people who knew him delighted in my vitriolic tirade—it was probably a mistake to have ended a friendship with such an illustrious one, but I doubt if it was ever much of a loss to either of us.

I am including that famous letter of December 31st here, altho you yourself may have seen a copy of it before this—I thought then that Van Loon had it coming to him, and I still think he had it coming to him. A re-reading of that letter today, almost ten years later, convinces me that everything I said was substantially correct.

Dear Hendrik:

. . . Apparently you have found the post of glorified Lecturer, Barker, Ticket Seller, and Professional Host for the Cunard Line preferable to carrying out agreements to speak before distinguished audiences. Despite all the ballyhoo, on a reservation basis, the excursion is not such a howling success. There have been bigger and better trips without you as the drawing card—it disgusts me every time I think of you having sunk to the level of the moronic creatures directing—as Host or Hostesses, according to their perversions—the lectures and the tourists on various excursion steamships cruises. . . .

Although a great literary genius, you are still but a human being who has prostituted his Art to Commercialism and therefore no longer entitled to abuse the rights of others, in a world where a lot of people have to live together.

I am sorry that I have been forced to write you as frankly as I have, but then I had to do it, because of your lack of appreciation of true friendship and common ordinary decent conduct. The real fault perhaps lies with your friends who, because of their admiration and devotion to you, have gone on overlooking your bad manners and insolent ways. . . .

I hope you had a miserable Christmas, for that might in some small way have atoned for the shabby treatment you have accorded others for years. . . .

Sincerely,
[Signed]

While the construction work was going forth furiously at Melvale, Jarmila M. took the train to Poughkeepsie one morning and I met her at the station. Henry drove me down from the farm and I dropped him off at a gas station with his transportation back to New York, while I took the car over—met Jarmila and went to the Nelson House for lunch. It was a beautiful day and we were able to drive with the top down—altho winter was about to descend upon us it was more like Fall. From the Nelson House we crossed the River and drove down the West side to West Point, where we stopped at the Thayer Hotel. Returning to New York, I left her off at her hotel where she proceeded to freshen up a bit and then she joined Melba and myself at the St. Regis for a late dinner.

We drank a lot and after dinner we undressed and the three of us went to bed together. She loved Melba, sucking hell out of her cunt—while I fucked Jarmila from the rear. Then to top if off, Melba sucked my cock off while I ravaged Jarmila's lovely cuzzy with my hot tongue, until she came with spasmodic burst of love flow. Those two girls—the one blonde and slender, the other jet black and buxom, both with beautiful bodies—were red hot with passion—when I had had enough I left them to their own devices for the balance of the night, while I retired to the guest room to recuperate. Jarmila was really hot about us both—she always contended that she was torn between Melba and myself—she never could quite make up her mind which of us she loved the most. She was an ethereal creature heavenly to look at and wonderful to screw. . . .

We were having a dinner party the night she sailed, but I left the party long enough to give her a farewell suck in my study, and then screwed her on the way to the pier in Brooklyn.

On the 23rd December, the vans from the Chelsea Storage arrived with all our belongings. The chimneys had been built, the plumbing installed, the bathrooms were in working order, the lights on, the house was heated, the spring water was running, the telephone was connected, and the painters were putting on the finishing touches.

We were in for Christmas—a white Christmas on our own farm. Melsing and I set forth with the chief handy man (Hoagle) the afternoon of Christmas Eve for our own woods, where we found the ideal pine tree, which we cut down, brought back to the house and set up in the living room—it reached from the floor to the topmost rafter—it had been a struggle, but we made it.

Melvale was 128 miles from New York, and with the roads a good deal narrower in those days than they are today, and traffic much heavier, and parkways but for a short 30 miles of the trip, it took us on the average of 2½ to 2¾ hours from the St. Regis to the farm or vice versa. . . .

1933 had certainly been a full and vigorous year—it started out with the trip to New Orleans—it wound up with the farm at Melvale. In between had been the House Boat *Sydney*, the World's Fair at Chicago, the trip to Europe, the affairs with Claire and Jarmila, the La Guardia campaign, the falling out with Van Loon, stock market manipulations and trading, the passing away of our dough with easy living and sex orgies.

1934

The transition from 1933 to 1934 was rapid and marked a definite turn in my life—a life full of twists and turns that had now turned rural with a vengeance—and a frantic almost panicky effort on our part to save a little of the thousands that we had scattered to the four winds. . . .

We had spent Christmas at the farm but the bright lights of the big city were irresistible for the New Year's celebration.

We still kept a suite at the St. Regis—we owed them so much. Hamilton Pell threw a party atop the Hotel Delmonico—Freddie Davenport and Jarmila were there—it was festive but not rural—Melba especially was finding the change over from fast-moving urban life to slow-tempoed country, irksome.

When Hendrik failed to do our letterhead which we were going to use as a Christmas card, we decided to get out a mimeographed sheet to send to our friends in lieu of a Christmas card, telling them all about the pleasures and hardships of life in Columbia County—or the "Trials and Tribulations of Country Life in America—". . .

Everyone thought we were "lousy" with dough—we were such free spenders—Mother thought so too—when as a matter of fact we were but two jumps ahead of the sheriff most of the time. I was trading heavily in my Wall Street Office, but my gains were small.

The wallop I received the previous summer when Ham Pell bought instead of selling liquor stocks in violation of orders given him on long distance from the West Coast and then got the money out of my account from Bowen of the Corn Exchange without authority from Miss Murray or myself to the tune of $10,000, had been a blow hard to recoup on a sluggish market.

The office eventually grew to be a place to go to receive summonses, in suits from creditors to collect large sums. In fact at the end that was its principal activity.

We paid $1.40 for two lamb chops at the St. Regis in those days, but up in the country we could buy two whole live lambs for that amount.

It was bitterly cold that winter (1934) at Melvale—we kept the Lincoln at Nassau, 8 miles away, or in Albany—using the station wagon or the cutter (sleigh) to get in and out. The drifts of snow would be ten to twenty feet deep in the cuts along our drive-way into the place and the highway ploughs couldn't get in for days—we only kept the road partially open by the utmost diligence, and that took the constant effort of six men daily. Even then it was closed completely on many days. . . .

Chickens and cows were scarce—the State discouraged breeding in single lots—they wanted you to do it wholesale or not at all—and the Federal Government was out to make it as hard as possible to raise anything. The State said the local people shouldn't keep single milk cows—they wanted the ruralites to buy their milk, cream and butter from the big distributors—more sanitary said they, more dough to the milk barons we said—and so it was.

When we first arrived at Melvale, the local telephone company wasn't able to put in a private wire—didn't have the copper and the entire community would listen to our long distance calls.

I suspected a Mrs. Magill of being the worst offender—so with the aid of Hank Van Loon I framed her.

One night after the usual conversation with Hank I asked him if he had heard that Mrs. Magill (the treasurer of the Sewing Guild of the local church) had stolen the church money in her care. Our last words were hardly out when a shrill excited voice (Mrs. Magill's) shrieked over the wire, disclosing her tuning-in presence, "No such a thing—it's a lie, it's a lie—" and then bang went the receiver.

Altho the local telephone company was very independent and we had lots of trouble with them, they finally strung the private line out to the house—that helped some but the operators in the country exchange always listened to our choicest bits—they got much more fun out of tuning in on our wire than tuning in to their radios.

The great question that January was whether life was really beginning for the Squire at age forty.

I had always lived the usual high pressure life of New York, nothing but rush and bustle—accomplishing little or nothing—on the island my ancestors had settled—now I was to see what farm tempo would do for me.

I felt we were living too fast in the machine age—in olden times men built for permanency, homes were handed down from generation to generation. Today nothing is permanent—new buildings have a life in peace time of but 15 or 20 years—men lose their homes, their savings of a lifetime overnight. In the twinkling of an eye all is swept away by the shifting quicksands of our ever-rapidly changing economic modern way of life in America. Just when men feel they have achieved the success they have always desired, when they believe themselves on the firmest ground obtainable, all about them crumbles and is laid waste. That was true in 1933–1934 when we bought Melvale and it is truer today than ever—only today, thanks to the global war, it is worldwide. The monuments that men have erected over the ages are destroyed in the flash of a second by steel hurtling downward from the skies—such are the ravages of the machine age. It's all so in vain—it always has been so and it always will be so, peace movements to the contrary not withstanding. . . .

We found that the farmer was more regulated and dictated to by the State than the city dweller. The Farmer is told how to farm his farm, how to raise his cattle, what he can raise and what he mustn't breed or grow, what to sell his milk for, and is taxed for this, that and the other thing—he cannot even have a gun or a dog to protect his home without permission from the state—and his cider must not get hard, for that is a crime too.

In February one very stormy night, we returned from New York—it was fifteen below—the wind howled and the snow had drifted high.

We drove out from Albany in a cab—the driver left us at the entrance gate on the main highway. It didn't look so bad at first but the cut was impassable—so we started across the fields. We had wired the farm superintendent to have the cutter at the gate but we were late—we had dillied in the Falcon Room at the Ten Eyck for a nip. It being bitterly cold, he had returned to the house when his fire died out—our men were always so considerate of our horses. It was tough going—time after time we were in the snow drifts up to our middle with hardly the strength to drag ourselves up and out and on—poor Melba dropped exhausted twice.

That quarter of a mile was the longest quarter of a mile I have ever traveled—it took us nearly an hour and a half to make the house. Calling was useless—no one could hear—more than once it looked like the end was going to be right there in Columbia County. . . .

The servant problem became quite a problem at Melvale—urban maids didn't go for the hardships of the country and the country people were not cut out for waiting on city folk. . . .

Mother hung on thru February—sinking faster and faster. On the 9th of March she passed away at Elise's. The day before she died I went into personal Bankruptcy—she never knew, she and father were spared that humiliation. I did it quietly, using my first name William and my middle initial. My schedule was something to behold—I failed for over a quarter of a million.

At Melvale it was always a great relief to learn that our innumerable callers were frigidaire salesmen, horse and cattle dealers, automobile salesmen, fertilizer salesmen, feed salesmen, tree salesmen, furniture salesmen, etc. and not process servers. We had a hard time getting accustomed to country solicitation. From our city experiences, we always suspected the worst of strangers—and awaited the inevitable presentation of that slip of white paper (known as a summons and complaint) with palpitating suspense.

We were happier in Columbia County than we could have been in New York—Columbia County was opposed to reform and progress, and while we inwardly admit that both are essential, if the animal is to survive, we, in our old age, are satisfied to let things be as "they be" and watch governors come and governors go while the State goes on forever, as the younger generation sweats and fumes and chafes at the bit.

By the last of February, the financial pressure had become quite unbearable—there wasn't any light. I engaged Sam Falk to take me thru bankruptcy—not a pleasant performance at best—it's a job that requires some one with skilled training, with a particular aptitude for such work in order to assure a safe journey without complications, avoiding the pitfalls that might cause difficulties with the Federal Government. . . .

In February 1934 I predicted that the New Deal Administration would eventually fail and in the long run we would all return to that time-honored game of dog eat dog and the survival of the fittest, to solve our problems in the trenches, in the air and on the high seas. And that's exactly what happened. I also said in that issue of the Booklet—*Moo*—the question was simple—either the machine would have to be destroyed and the race returned to manpower or man would destroy himself, and destroying himself is what he has been doing these last three years.

It is interesting to note our political dogma or private views on public matters in that year 1934, and I think I shall set them down now before continuing with the retelling of the bankruptcy proceedings. . . .

> We are rapidly racing into a governmental paternalism that may eventually so weaken us as to destroy the nation. The day of strong men and hearty individualism has gone. But all the king's horses and all the king's men, all the Hoover Committee, and all the Roosevelt alphabets with their artificial panaceas cannot defy

the time-old economic law of supply and demand. Water will not run up hill, and until man can harness and control the elements, political jugglers cannot reestablish the national or international equilibrium by artificial stimulation.

The virtues of the modern machine age have proven a boomerang and are destroying western civilization. The saturation point of production can be reached so much faster than man can consume, the world over. In other words, the machine in the home, on the farm, in industry and in business has brought about a vast over-population in this age of mediocrity. . . .

Foreseeing the bankruptcy—and knowing that bankruptcy only clears you of the indebtedness already incurred, especially under a rental lease, and does not relieve you of the contractual obligation extending on and passed beyond the filing of the petition—in bankruptcy, I decided that it was important to get myself clear of my Wall Street office liability. . . .

As to the St. Regis, I had quite a bill there running into $6,000.00 or $7,000.00. It had been my home for some time and while I lived there I had paid from $50,000 to $60,000 for rents and extras.

I didn't want any difficulty under the Innkeepers' Statutes with the St. Regis and while they couldn't have gotten anywhere, they might have made it unpleasant and caused disagreeable publicity. I went to them and gave them a series of notes to cover my obligations. I paid the first two that came due in order to confirm the transaction. That left their attorney without a case. It wasn't pleasant, but there was no other way out. One has to think of one's own skin in such an emergency—and they had made plenty out of me.

Maybe I am dead-beat—I can't judge myself—but whenever I have the money I pay in full. In fact, I get a thrill out of drawing cheques to pay off the bills, if I have the money in the bank. The hell commences when you haven't got the dough and can't pay. . . .

The services for my mother were held in Elise's home in Red Bank. Mother was buried next to Father in the Ward plot in Trinity Cemetery, New York City.

She hadn't changed the will that she had written in the Roosevelt Hospital the year previous, so Elise fell heir to all the stock in father's lumber companies. At that time, I could have inherited it direct without danger of creditor attacks, but she couldn't have known of that. Elise received the cash and securities in her safe deposit boxes and the cash in her different savings banks accounts. She had around $10,000 or $12,000 in her savings accounts and about $6,000 or $7,000 in cash in her safe deposit box, and there were approximately $7,000 or $8,000 worth of other securities besides the company's stock. All of this went to Elise. She and I were executors without bonds. . . .

I am sorry to have to admit it but I fought with both my Mother and Father constantly and violently.

The rows with Mother were especially bitter during the first year or so after father's death, when Melba and I were very short of cash. I never got over mother's avowed partiality to your Aunt Elise, altho she always denied it. Mother was warped on the social angle—Elise had made an effort to maintain the position into which she had been born.

After your mother and I were divorced, I failed to keep up with my family or strictly social connections—my friendships took on a distinctly democratic hue—cosmopolites appealed to me more than social gad-abouts. My mother, your Aunt Elise and your Mother never could gracefully accept such within their circle—so the strife was bitter. Maybe it was jealousy—Elise and I never liked the same people. She lived an indolent wasteful luxurious existence—I wanted only to know and be with people who were vital and doing things in the world, affecting the daily lives of others for better or for worse. Mother was interested in national and international affairs, well versed in them—but her main concern was Elise's social success and her children. Both the Hurds (Eddie's father and mother) and my father and mother supported them in their extravagant mode of life. . . .

The farm intrigued me more than the business did, and I

was harassed in my efforts to get the land broken, fertilized, planted and cultivated. I had to have it ploughed and harrowed and at the same time it was necessary to keep right behind the Lumber Company business. The shavings and the sawdust!

On the 23rd of April, a little more than a month after mother died, I purchased over $300.00 worth of seed from the Cooperative Kinderhook Pomological Association. . . .

I borrowed a thousand dollars from your Aunt Elise in April—it was quite a job getting it out of her—for the purpose of buying draft horses for the farm. We worked three teams there constantly.

I did a good deal of the ploughing, the harrowing and the planting myself.

I conducted a lot of the business of the Lumber Company over the Long Distance telephone—I had a secretary at the farm.

I fired all the girls in the Lumber Company office as soon as Nathan left and started the New York office off with a new crew—the Lumber Company was a great help to us that spring and summer and kept us going until the crops came in and some of the California money loosened up. . . .

Personal bankruptcy is not a very pleasant thing—the supplementary proceedings—when a bunch of small-minded small-income dopes gape in amazement and try to prove legitimate expenditures were for the illegitimate purpose of concealing assets.

A recap for the bankruptcy showed that we spent on our personal activities in January 1933 $1,118.50; February 1933 $8,619.01; March 1933 $1,809.92; April $3,205.98; May $8,918.59; June $11,621.92; July $9,342.82; August $7,425.37; September $2,125.54; October 1933 $2,505.35; November $1,209.46; December $1,505.31.

Our European trip in 1933 cost $9,421.10, according to the vouchers I retained, but it probably cost two or three thousand more.

We had spent nearly $75,000 in one year for living expenses which was not high for the life we were leading.

From December 1932 to January 1934 we spent $49,000 at

the Hotel St. Regis. . . .

Between my Bankruptcy, which was an aftermath of the collapse of the Florida boom, Mother's death, the Lumber companies to run, the Airecooling Company, Harry Millar's business, the Stock Market, and the planting on the farm, I was as busy and harassed as a one-arm paper hanger—and as disconnected as this tale of those hectic activities.

On the 31st day of May 1934, I was discharged from bankruptcy by Federal Judge Robert P. Patterson, which discharge was attested by my old friend Captain Charles Weiser (a fine cocksman) clerk of the Federal Court, District Court of the United States for the Southern District of New York.

As it always happens, the unimportant creditors—the small ones—howled the loudest but it got them nowhere. It was their nagging that forced me to bail out of my financial difficulties (through the bankruptcy courts). For 8 years I had tried to weather the storm kicked up by the Florida collapse, but it was a losing fight, the handicap was too great—I never recovered from that mess—that was the beginning of my downgrade march financially. I had gotten in so deep that only large sums could get me out—Melba had been no party to that (it all happened before she came into my life), and there was no reason for her being penalized for my past mistakes or transgressions.

The bankruptcy stigma attached was never to be lived down and so when the mechanics of that performance were completed under the adroit guidance of Sam Falk, I returned to Melvale—a new life to lead, I hoped. . . .

In twelve months at the farm, we had fourteen couples in the house. If the men were good farmers the women were terrible cooks and housecleaners. If the women were excellent cooks and efficient in household duties, the men were impossible. . . .

Government paternalism has done more to spoil good honest labor in this country and reduce the produce for feeding the people than any other factor (before the war, labor wanted to be paid for idling—and much labor is still paid for the same purpose).

War or no war until the Franklin Roosevelt labor gangster, labor racketeer and labor murderer coddling policy—

We first planned a subsistence farm. There was much to be done—the place had not been worked in ages—the house was a hundred and fifty years old, and looked it. There was no one to turn to for advice and guidance. The only publications available on agriculture were years old and were designed primarily for the farmer with a lifetime of experience in agricultural pursuits. There were no primers for the beginner. The local people, the farmer neighbors, the Cornell graduates, the agricultural experts were all lacking in practical, authoritative information or ability to guide or explain or suggest as to the proper treatment of the soil, the proper crops to sow, the preparation of crops for market, the best markets, where to purchase seed, fertilizer, bags, baskets, crates, what crops were plentiful, what were short.

They did not know that a lot of Baldwin apple trees and peach trees in the Hudson Valley had been killed by the previous bad winter—so as a guide to all and sundry on our list of friends, acquaintances and enemies, we have set forth in an appendix some facts gleaned from our first year at Melvale as a contribution to a much needed Farm Primer.

When we first took up farming, the lack of knowledge generally as to the breeding cycles of the live stock was so amazing that we decided to gather together the information which we picked up by experience and set forth such breeding, gestation, and sexual maturity data as we had learned at Melvale. . . .

Some of the rural enigmas at Melvale were:

Why it costs more for potato seed than you can get for the potatoes, assuming you can get ten bushels for every bushel planted. Maybe Franklin can answer that one.

Why the N.Y. Department of Agriculture was never able to locate a farmer's almanac, when thousands are published annually? And even Woolworth sells them.

Why no two agricultural authorities agree on any given subject.

In June, 1934, horse feed cost $1.45 a hundred; in August, 1934 it was $2.45 a hundred. That's how the farmer wins. Chicken feed, cow feed, horse feed, pig feed—all going up. The price of farm produce going down. Why?

We spent part of the winter 1933–34—the part when we could get through the snow—pruning our apple trees and then spraying them, only to learn as summer came on, that the trees we took such care of, the trees we had pruned and sprayed and fertilized, would give us fewer apples than the big old trees we neglected. . . .

We planted 100,000 cabbages on our hands and knees—50,000 grew big (300,000 lbs.) but the hell of it was that by the time they were ready for market, there wasn't any market for them.

The following were some of our rural observations that year—

We called on a man about a cow. He wanted to sell the cow to buy cement. It was a grade cow. He had paid $90 for the cow but the market value of the cow was only $35 fall, 1934. Nevertheless, the cement that he had to buy for the farm with the proceeds from the sale of the cow cost him just double what it cost when he bought the cow for $90. That's what the N.R.A. and the A.A.A. and Franklin Roosevelt and the Brain Bust have done for the long-suffering farmer.

An acre—the amount of ground a yoke of oxen can plow in a day.

The farmer gets too little, and the consumer pays too much for produce. . . .

Seasons come and seasons go—farm life goes on forever.

First we were the cherry man, then the strawberry man, the cabbage man, the corn man, the onion man, the celery man, the lettuce man, the broccoli man, the tomato man, the pea man, the bean man, the melon man, the potato man, the apple man, the cauliflower man, the pumpkin man, the cider man, the veal man, the pig man, the turkey man, the goose man, according to the seasonal loads we brought to market. . . .

The farmer has no conception of the urban problems and the urbanite has no conception of the farmer's problems.

Newspaper wrappers never removed, mail never opened on a farm. You're too busy during the day keeping ahead of Dame Nature—and too tired at night.

A farmer cannot be successful unless he has a number of sons to work for him as farm hands in place of hired help. Then he has no cash outlay to make—merely the teeth to feed. . . .

Thirty-five percent of the farms in the United States produce 80 percent of all the farm income—65 percent of the farms produce only 20 percent of the farm income.

The 35 percent have an average income of approximately $2,500 annually, while the 65 percent have an annual income of approximately $250.

The big money in truck gardening is in out of season produce. That's what makes farming profitable in Florida, California and Texas, when the land is purchased right. . . .

The rural routine at Melvale would go something like this most any day—the Daily Dozen—

One of the mares is calling for attention. Attention she craves can be obtained for $15 from excellent stallion.

One thousand strawberry plants have arrived and will have to be set out immediately.

Twenty-five thousand cabbage plants are at the Boston & Albany station. They also crave attention.

Standard Oil man phoned and said he could not furnish drum and pump under N.R.A. code. Buying gas for farms saves from $2.00 to $2.50 on fifty-gallon lots.

Electricity went off during thunderstorm. Oil burners and pails of hot water were immediately put in chicken house as substitute for electric brooders. Quite a few baby chicks lost—seventy-five in all.

Montgomery Ward phoned and said 300 rods barbed wire fencing were not obtainable at Albany, but could be gotten from Baltimore, but this would cost $30 more.

Seed has arrived from Peter Henderson and is at Post Office. Must have attention.

Sows and boar arrived from Bethesda, and craving food and water.

Nursery, in filling order, was compelled to put in fifty first-grade and fifty medium-grade trees on account of bad winter—crave fertilizer.

Plumber held up on account of delay in delivery of his pipe valves, elbows, hydrants, etc.

Peter Henderson shipped plants from Red Bank, N.J. They may arrive Sunday.

The cow came round but we were too busy, so she'll have to wait until next month.

The spring dries up and the cattle cant: "How Dry I Am!" while we fetch and carry water by the gallon to assuage their thirst.

By God, how the cattle eat!—and drink!

Ho hum—nothing to do until tomorrow.

We had 100 hens and raised 400 broilers from little chicks. Our eggs at some seasons cost us nearly fifty cents apiece and the broilers—those not eaten in the house or by the farm hands were sold at a terrific loss.

In the summer of 1934 we planted twenty bushels of Dibble Russet Potatoes certified, at $4.50 per bushel. Total, $90.

We received from the ground, thanks to heavy cultivation, commercial fertilizer and hard labor, 100 bushels, which we sold at "prevailing market price" for approximately 20 cents per bushel. Total return, $20.

From that 20 cents you must deduct the price of the basket or container in which the potatoes are taken to market and sold. Total loss, not counting containers, labor, market expenses, transportation, etc., $70.

We planted about 100,000 cabbages, from which approximately 50,000 survived the woodchucks, the deer, the pheasants, the rabbits, the worms and the drought.

100,000 cabbage plants cost	$200.00
To set them out	150.00
The plowing, the harrowing, fertilizer and lime, preparation, spraying and cultivation of the soil	400.00

Harvesting of the crop, packing in barrels and bags	200.00
Barrels and baskets for shipping	200.00
Expense of marketing, transportation	200.00
	$1,350.00
The cabbages brought us one cent apiece	500.00
Loss on this operation	$850.00

which hasn't taken into consideration the feed for the horses, or any allowance for our time and labor or the grub for the men on the place. But we still have the land, which is probably more than we would have had if we had stayed in the stock market.

Further evidence of what the N.R.A. and the A.A.A. have done for the farmer. All this is on land so rich that the quack grows almost as rapidly as the crop.

"Cider apples" brought 75 cents per hundred. Windfalls $1.25 per bushel, but we only had one-twentieth of a normal crop, and the total income from the apples and cider wasn't enough to cover the cost of spraying, to say nothing of the pruning of the trees.

Cauliflower. We set out 30,000 plants. We ploughed the field, we harrowed the field, we fertilized the field. In addition, we gave each plant a shot of nitrate of soda to speed the growing along. Total cost, without labor, $205; 240 crates cost another $30. Total $235. 2,880 plants matured, were brought to market and sold for $1 a crate of a dozen heads. Total income $240—$5 profit, if you do not charge any labor, transportation, gasoline or packing charges against the crop—the balance of the plants that were doing nicely, thank you, were destroyed by a freeze, a thaw and a freeze.

We sold 4,500 gallons of cider in the Albany area in one month at a profit gross of 2 cents of a gallon, but it did not cover the handling costs, the breakage, and the loss when sweet cider turned hard—it hardly paid for the labels and the cleaning of the bottles required by law—oh, well, we had lots of fun selling it—we guess.

In fall of 1934 general retail prices advanced 2.7 while the price to the farmer went down.

The great trouble with the price of farm produce in this country is the fact, whether Franklin likes it or not, that the buyers simply haven't got the money. In 1933, when potatoes were scarce they didn't bring a good price because the people couldn't afford to buy potatoes as scarce as they were at the prices demanded for them, and the prices fell off, so whereas the farmers with the shorter crop should have had the benefit of higher prices, they were unable to get the proper price for their produce.

Mr. President: The farmers in New York State got much less for their potatoes, sweet corn and cabbages in 1934 than in 1933, before the Supreme Court socked you in the eye. Now answer that. . . .

Agriculture is as precarious an occupation as municipal, state and federal office-holding.

We trust this recital of how truck farming pays will serve to encourage you to follow the President's advice and become another one of our competitors, thereby further depreciating the price of farm produce.

Ah! Hell—anyway, we had a lot of fun delivering produce to the garbage entrance of the Ten Eyck and drinking it up in the Falcon Room.

Life on a farm is one continual round of fighting blights, bugs, frosts, droughts, grubs, wet seasons, groundhogs, pheasants, woodchucks, deer, rabbits and other pestilences that infest the crops. It's either the weeds or the bugs or the weather that are struggling to get ahead of or destroy that which man has planned for the benefit of the race and neither the New Dealers nor Franklin D. have ever been able to do anything about it.

We never understood why the American farmer remains so docile in view of the discriminations against him. All winter long he has to hibernate within his farmhouse shell surviving the rigors of the winter as best he can. When spring comes he must till his soil, cultivate it, and plant it. During the growing season when he is harassed by weather conditions beyond man's control, drought or an overabundance of rain, or blights of various kinds, he must cultivate and weed and keep clean his crops. When the crop matures it must be harvested, made ready for market, packed in bags, in baskets, in crates, or in barrels and then trucked to the nearest market place—sometimes that is 100 to 200 miles from the farm. On the market place the produce, the results of his toil, his labor and the sweat of his brow, will bring him anywhere from 400 to 500 percent less than the ultimate consumer pays for his green groceries.

The Scottsboro decision by the U.S. Supreme Court should tend eventually to stamp out that famous old Southern custom of white men raping colored women with impunity—for too long it has been a heinous crime for a black boy to cohabit with a white woman, while white men from the time of Georgie Washington have gaily enjoyed their dark meat—with negroes on juries in the South perhaps the gallants of Southern aristocracy will no longer go scot free when caught forcing their favors upon the black lassies. Let the whites and blacks keep to their own.

The time has not yet arrived for a racial comingling—until it comes let each race respect the other.

How much of the American foreign policy the world over is dictated by the Standard Oil interests? That's a question we would like to have the State Department answer.

The only people that we have found the world over worth a second thought were the sophisticated bellyrubbers who acknowledged that this was a ballbearing universe, revolving every twenty-four hours on a phallic axis, and once having conceded that, forgot it.

Vice by itself is drab and dull. Nevertheless, we are opposed to reformers of all kinds, sorts and descriptions when it comes to the sex life of the people. We are for snappy shows, snappy movies, snappy burlesques and snappy literature—for adults. . . .

Every time we witness a May Day parade of socialists and communists in New York, we realize how far apart and how fundamentally opposed are the rural and urban radicals. Theoretically, they have much in common, but as individuals and types little if anything. A great many of them in the cities would be happier, we believe, if furnished free transportation to Stalin-land.

Great country America—the aristocrats struggle to be common people—the common people struggle to become aristocrats. Think we'll go back. . . .

Chickens, chinamen and New Yorkers have one thing in common—they love to cross the road directly in front of fast-moving vehicles.

It was gruelling hard work at Melvale—hard in the kitchen, hard out on the farm, it was work, work, work morning, noon and night.

The interludes of getting to Albany were few that summer except to attend to the lumber company's business—and to New York fewer, except to attend to Mother's estate, etc.—we tried to sublet her apartment but without success.

The children when they were home from school loved Melvale. I liked it—it suited me I thought, although most everyone else felt it was incongruous. I liked farm work—I liked going to market—I liked the local people—I liked drinking with the politicos and the newspapermen in the Falcon room of the Ten Eyck.

Bringing your produce into the garbage entrance of the Ten Eyck and going upstairs to drink up the proceeds with judges of the Court of Appeals (the highest court in the state), had its points—if you had my type of mentality. . . .

We left Melvale, I regret to say, before my nature series was complete. To compensate in part for the lack of graphic illustrations, and as a guide to friends who might desire to follow in my footsteps, I prepared a breeding table for all and sundry. There is such a lack of authentic knowledge on the subject in most rural and urban communities.

Speaking of the rural urge to reproduce—while living at Melvale I had the urge to screw one of the sub-normal country maids, the real peasant type, strong in body and muscle but low in mentality, and observe the type of progeny that combination would produce. Somehow or other the consciousness of the complications involved deterred me. I always regretted the opportunity I threw over my shoulder at Melvale for that genetic experiment.

There are so many mental and physical malformations in the country—whether it's the result of the hard life, the incest that is rampant in small places, venereal disease, perversion, over sex-stimulation or what, I wouldn't know.

Farm life is hard—to save fuel and effort, large families, even of long-line Americans, live in squalor all huddled in one large room shut off from the rest of the house, where the cooking, the sleeping, the sitting, the fucking and even the shitting, is done. It's horrible but true—and sometimes they have the stock in with them—that condition is prevalent all over the country U.S.A.. . .

What the New Deal economic dreamers never have understood is that farming is a most senseless pursuit, for you sow that you may reap, and then you reap that you may sow—and let no New Dealer for one instant believe that farming is governed by good judgment and labor, even if you had an abundance of both, but by the most uncertain things—winds and tempests, rains and drought—and above all, as Edward Gibbon once said, let all farmers beware for "all taxes at last fall upon agriculture." And never forget that while the farmer fattens most when famine reigns, he is lean most of the time.

In cultivating any place and producing from the soil you must always remember that constant tillage will exhaust any field.

I liked to plough—I liked to cultivate—I enjoyed cutting the hay—I enjoyed raking the hay—I enjoyed putting the hay in the loft, filling the silos with corn and then as our crops matured, taking them to the City market and to the farmers market at Menands. Some of our produce was so fine that the local hotels displayed it in their windows. The Ten Eyck specialized in Melvale Melons—paid us $8.00 per barrel of eight—but they were all the same size and shape, every day.

The De Witt Clinton and other hotels and restaurants plugged our produce and put it on display. . . .

From July on, we were on our market stand most every day but Sundays—it was a lot of fun, but little money. We had planted many of our crops such as cabbages and cauliflower on our hands and knees—some of the plants we had put in with a horse drawn planting machine borrowed from a neighbor. . . .

I cannot repeat too often the dilemma in which the farmers find themselves—he seldom turns his investment over more than once a year—he must plough his field, harrow it, fertilize it, plant it, and cultivate it—he must fight against insects, groundhogs, moles, rabbits, drought, and in the case of cauliflower he has to take the leaves of each plant and bind them over the tops of the cauliflower with rubber bands in order to prevent the sun from scorching the white heads as they mature.

The animals of the forest will make a good farm their haven unless they are driven away. It's hard going, noon and night and then you have to buy your boxes or your baskets, and after harvesting or picking your crop, get it to market as quickly as you can—if possible, before the market becomes deluged with a seasonable crop. More often than not the poor farmer goes thru all this work only to take his crop to market and find all his neighbors there with tomatoes or corn like his or what have you, with little to choose between his produce and theirs and no buyers.

The tomatoes and the corn are a glut on the market that day—his sales are few—so he is left with most of his load to take back home with no alternative but to feed it to the pigs (if the Roosevelt administration let him have any). It's a disgusting heart-breaking life. Even if the farmer is able to sell his load to advantage, get his crop in ahead of his neighbor, just enough out of season to get the top price, he then returns home with his cash without any prospect of turning it over again until the following year.

A commission broker on the other hand can theoretically turn his capital over every twenty-four hours for approximately 300 days out of the year and a retail produce man can do likewise—but not so the poor farmer.

We tried to protect ourselves against the weak cabbage market by digging ditches in the ground 4 to 5 feet deep and storing the cabbages in the ditches to be brought out in the winter when the price was higher.

It was a good gamble because that year the Texas winter crop was very short—but as luck would have it, the local farmers, feeling that they knew more about it than the city slicker, during our absence while we were on the market, dug the ditches only 2 and 3 feet deep—the result, a hard and heavy freeze completely ruined the tons upon tons that we had buried away, and spoiled our only chance of recovering our cabbage losses. . . .

For a moment this hot June day (1943), I will interlope with a few current observations. . . .

Looking at the war situation objectively I am forced to concede that Herr Hitler is a true German patriot seeking only what he considers to be best for his people—Benito Mussolini likewise is a true Italian patriot, in search of greater territory and riches for his people. The Emperor of Japan is currently engaged in increasing the wealth and territory of his people. Churchill and Stalin are largely and exclusively concerned with the nationalistic interest of their own people—whilst Franklin Delano Roosevelt has devoted his entire time since being elected in a partially successful attempt to destroy the true concepts upon which our Government was founded by the founding fathers—not content with that traitorous behavior, he determined upon a foreign policy of sharing our resources with the rest of the world, lowering our standard of living while raising theirs.

If he can succeed in completely detroying our economic system and reducing the nation to abject poverty with his grandiose globular scheme of sharing everything we have with the rest of the world, he will then have succeeded with his "Franklinstein" cunning to ruin and destroy the land of the free and the home of the once brave—Benedict Arnold was a piker compared to Franklin Roosevelt. . . .

We were at Melvale at the height of the depression, yet with all the unemployment and all of the people out of work and going hungry or selling apples on street corners, it was most difficult to get good every-day farm labor. The New Deal had already inculcated the vicious idea that the laboring class should not have to work—particularly the foreign born or those who had been here for one or two generations. Mr. and Mrs. Roosevelt and the New Deal semites had given these people the impression that they were entitled to something for nothing—they were all looking for government handouts. Government paternalism was their watchword—they wanted the government to buy them farms and to stock the farms for them and to give them the machinery for their farms and guarantee them a livelihood without any effort on their part regardless of the success of their crops.

A nation of non-workers is doomed to destroy itself—only by hard work can a people survive—most morons or mediocrities or mass thinkers never realize that the Government is but a creature of the people, that it gets its support and maintenance solely from the sweat of the people, that when the people do not produce, the Government loses its ability to collect taxes and the entire system collapses. Governments are only as wealthy as the ability of their people to develop their natural resources. When the people stop producing, stop growing, and only take from their government, the whole crashes by its own weight—for without production there is no wealth. . . .

That Fall after Mother's lease ran out, I stayed at the McAlpin whenever in town.

On one of my visits, Ruth R. and I got very tight over luncheon at the McAlpin and we went up to my room. The McAlpin management was very strict so I had George Brelsford stand guard in the hall outside my door—he had had his stenographic agency there since the beginning of the building and knew everyone, housemaids, floor clerks, managers and all.

Ruth was a hot piece of tail, very passionate—a wonderful fuck—contrary to Eddie Ballou, who always contended she preferred sucking to screwing.

Ruth was living at the Saint Moritz at the time in a room on the 17th Floor. Late one fall afternoon we were hot at it, shaking the bed to pieces when a rap came on the door. We ceased firing with paralyzing shock—there was no way out but thru the door or out the window—we both were sure it was Bob (Ripley). The knock was not repeated—so after a long pause of intent listening and waiting, I withdrew my limp cock from her cooling pussy and dismounted. There shoved under the door was a telephone message, put there by a page boy who had knocked (hoping for a tip), announcing that "Believe It Or Not" would be around shortly. That was enough—I dried my penis while she washed out her cunt. Then we both dressed hurriedly and I left by the service elevator—much pleasanter than a fistic encounter with Bob or a 17 story jump to the "terra firma" below.

I was very fond of Ruth—she had a lovely body, a good mind and knew how to love—she was a Jewess—afterwards she took an apartment at the Navarro on Central Park South and I often fucked her there in her seductive surroundings. . . .

The second Christmas at Melvale was a tough one financially—we were in a hole, we had just had a fire, and the fantasy of Santa Claus had flown out the window.

The fire was a determining factor with us—after surveying our situation very carefully we decided to close the farm shortly after the New Year and return to the City. The struggle with nature had been tough—the fire, the blights, the pests, and the lack of market for our produce had all conspired against us.

The cabbages which we had stored for the winter in beds of corn-stalks in scientifically constructed pits (but not deep enough as I have mentioned before) for sale and for our own table were frozen and of no use.

A stupid lug of a farmhand had left the cellar door open one very cold night and our potatoes were frost bitten.

Another farm boy had failed to put leaves in the beet barrels and besides he had dumped the beets in when they were wet, so most of them had rotted.

The only thing that had survived were the turnips—and we didn't like turnips!

The canned goods that we so carefully laid up for the winter with malice aforethought were fermenting in their jars—others had a lovely green mould over the top, and those that looked all right had a peculiar taste, or too much spice or too little seasoning. In other words, the entire canning project had been a dismal failure, and we hadn't laid in any Del Monte canned goods from the local store, and the heavy weather had already set in. We had ripped the rear end out of the station wagon trying to buck one of the early storms—a week before the fire we had spent two or three days with Dandy and the sleigh, and the Packard, with all hands at the shovels and on the ploughs working constantly day and night to get the road open.

All of this contributed to our decision to return to the great metropolis.

1934 had surely been a strenuous year and I learned many a lesson from nature that had not been imbued in me during our summers at Oyster Bay when I was a youngster or on my visits to Purebred Stock Farms thruout the East in the search of orders for our Sanitary Bedding—baled shavings and sawdust. . . .

Farming in the East on the small truck farms is a hard, unremunerative grind—morning, noon and night—it would have been a complete nightmare had it not been for the interlude in the drinking room of the Ten Eyck with the newspapermen and the politicos. We also enjoyed having our friends come out from New York for a weekend or for visits of a longer duration. Like my father I have always preferred to be visited and to entertain than to visit and be entertained. . . .

The end of 1934 found us considerably in debt with prospects pretty dim. I was in a constant state of trying to get in money to deposit in order to cover checks already given or predated; often I had to resort to sheer kiting between New York, Oyster Bay, Kinderhook and Albany—having my usual substantial hotel credit was a help at the Ten Eyck and also of assistance at the McAlpin in New York.

At the Ten Eyck I would cash checks on the Oyster Bay

Bank and deposit the proceeds left over from drinking in the Kinderhook Bank the same or the following day. At the McAlpin I would cash checks on the Kinderhook Bank, or the Oyster Bay Bank and deposit the money in Kinderhook, etc. It was a merry whirl while it lasted. . . .

We had learned a lot about the land, hard labor and laborers—that was our sole asset at the end of the year.

[Before they left Melvale, my father and Melba devised the two "job wanted" ads. That they were ever actually used I doubt.]

JOB WANTED—MALE

Executive, experienced, wholesale lumber, coal, hay, real estate, air-conditioning, banking and brokerage businesses, printing advertising, publishing, editing, commentating. Knowledge farming, politics, photography (16 mm and still cameras); organized and successfully managed national banks, export and import companies, 150 commercial, industrial and professional groups for government loans; established 50,000 sales agencies for government securities, organized state-wide political clubs in forty states of the Union. Executive secretary to Governor Miller of New York State; former Associate Director Loan Division of Treasury; published *Nomad* Magazine; manager of Advertising Campaigns and Solicitations; have raised millions of dollars for charitable purposes; written monographs on economics of railroad freight transportation; and many other subjects, such as banking, travel, politics and agriculture; world-wide travel experience. Advertising or publishing business preferred, but any job from office boy to lobbyist acceptable.

Address W. Ward Smith, Melvale Farms, North Chatham, N.Y.

JOB WANTED—FEMALE

Executive, experienced, editorial, musical. Trained concert and radio singer, widely traveled. Extensive European education with leading masters, unique repertoire international folk songs in Spanish, French, Hungarian, Italian, German and English. Programs on

WOR, KFI, KNX, KHJ, KFWB, CNR, and on the coast-to-coast hook-ups. Former editor world-wide magazine. Complete knowledge magazine make-up, lay-out, caption and copy. Conducted fashion, social, theatrical, motion picture and musical review, columns. Farming, domestic science, editorial or broadcasting work preferred, but will accept anything from musical instructor or copywriter to milkmaid.

Address Melba Smith, Melvale Farms, North Chatham, N.Y.

1935

1935 was to see our return to New York—first to the Mansfield Hotel and then to a sublet apartment at 2 Beekman Place which we subsequently furnished when we took over the lease in October 1935. 1935 was to witness the inception of another burning affair of the heart with complications and ramifications—semitic, but true.

It was the 10th of April 1935 that I first met Ruth G. and succumbed.

In 1935 I headed the Citizens Power Plant Committee—supporting Mayor La Guardia in his campaign for a public Power Plant Authority as a yardstick for determining the proper rates for electrical current in the Greater City.

I had my row with the police over the pushcart peddlers that year which made local history in the inner municipal circle.

I published *Moo*—the second booklet about Melvale our farm—and continued the battle for the reduction of Federal taxes on the Melsing Estate.

On the side I sold printing and managed to keep the O'Connell Press from losing their annual contract for publishing the Fatal Statistical Indices of the City of New York.

In the Spring of 1935 Melba started a regular weekly broadcast on WNYC and an affair with one of the young announcers.

All this I shall tell you about in some detail.

It was not a productive year. It was another struggle—it had its public aspects, but it was not of financial profit. . . .

At the end of January, we packed everything of value to us and sent it back to storage and hied ourselves back to our beloved Metropolis, which we probably never should have left in the first place.

Before our departure we came to New York and canvassed the hotel situation. We first thought of the Iroquois on 44th Street near the Algonquin—but down the street further, near Fifth Avenue, we came across the Mansfield. It was inexpensive, $17.50 a week for a livingroom large enough to park the children when they were in town, and bedroom and bath—the furnishings were not so hot but it was a parking place. . . .

We reached the Mansfield about midnight, unloaded our baggage and boxes and selves, and after tucking the kids in bed, the cars in a nearby garage and ourselves in the bar below, wondered where the next dough would come from. But all hands were glad to be back—for to me, New York has always been home—my roots for too many generations have been too firmly planted here for it to be anywhere else.

We left a couple behind to care for the place, look after the stock and keep the pipes from freezing. They were an indolent pair, but recently married—and consuming one another with screwing—in other words, they were fucking themselves into a decline.

They spent all the money I sent them for the feed, care of the dogs and stock, on alcohol and entertainment in the hot spots in Albany—they busted the station wagon and let everything go to hell.

We stayed at the Mansfield for a month while we searched for a furnished apartment. . . .

We had a lot of fun carousing in the bar at the Mansfield and there, Melba renewed theatrical contacts and got herself a boyfriend.

I busied myself keeping under cover from the farm creditors and trying to get something to do.

We found a furnished apartment at 2 Beekman Place, overlooking the river at an angle east—and the servants quarters of the swanky #1 Beekman Place cooperative.

Directly opposite from our apartment (we had a

bedroom, livingroom, bath and kitchenette) was the bedroom of a lovely little girl—a cook who cooked in her shorts and entertained her boyfriends between courses. She seldom pulled down the shades that warm spring—even when cooking a big dinner, she would leave the kitchen for a caress—on more than one occasion she was "laid" between courses. She seemed to like it that way best—there were four or five servants in that particular retinue, including a butler, but nobody interrupted. I would get as hot as hell watching them—Melba was out a lot singing and I would come as I watched the cook fucking.

One evening in May she caught on to my interest—saw me watching then after dinner she stripped for my benefit. I, too, took everything off and she would watch me jerk off as she fucked.

Often when her boyfriend was not around she would lay on her bed completely nude and play with herself as she watched me jerk off. I never met her, but that performance went on for several months until the apartment at 1 Beekman was closed for the summer.

In the fall when they returned, it started up again. Why we weren't caught, or the police complained to, I never will know—perhaps if anyone saw us they might have liked the show too much to complain. . . .

All through my life I have always had a feeling of unreality—as if I was bluffing my way through. I have always felt that I was inefficient at whatever I was attempting—that even goes for sex. I have always had a notion that I was an inadequate lover—that my prick wasn't big enough or my tongue wasn't long enough—women have raved about my rod and in my youth my caresses, but I had the idea that it was just insincere flattery, for what it was worth—like the barber who always greets you with "I was just thinking about you yesterday and talking to Miss Brown (the manicurist) about you." You like it but you know it's the bunk—so when a dame tells you what a wonderful cock you have, you always feel she wants it harder or bigger or a fur coat.

Much of what I have revealed here to you about my life I have wondered whether it were fiction or fact—or just an old man's flight of fancy, especially when telling stories to others, and I have told many of them to all and sundry within the sphere of my acquaintance. When I have verified my recollections with some of the personalities involved or from documentary evidence still in my possession, I have been amazed to find that my memory has not played tricks.

In my youth my sex interests and behaviour were matters to hide from view—as I grew older I grew bolder.

As a youngster, I thought my varied sex interests, the departures from the straight and basic incision of my sword into the scabbard of the female, was an abnormality peculiar to me, that my sex reaction to lewd pictures, that the thrill of exposing myself to the opposite sex and the reading of obscene literature, was peculiar to me. It never occurred to me that other men and women got hot and came when indulging in such pursuits.

Talking to girls on the phone, getting hot during the off-color or passionate conversation, local or long distance and "coming" while I did so—and my addiction to the practices of the masseuse—I felt set me apart from other men as something strange and peculiar.

While in fact a great lover of my own home and an avid accumulator of personalia I was considered a gay blade with a way with women—a sort of wolf without the "sheep's clothing." How I acquired such a reputation I do not know—perhaps it was largely because I wasn't two-faced about my various affairs, or surreptitious.

Most of the men that I came to know well in all walks of life were doing about as I was doing—and the more successful they were the busier they were at it—but discreetly and under-cover. Most of my friends were busier screwing everything in sight than I was—getting more involved than I was—yet I got the name while they had the game. . . .

[In 1934 my father met Ruth G. and began an affair that lasted some four years. An account of his first meeting follows.]

I didn't take to the idea of dining in Jewish homes on the West Side—I begrudged the taxi fare across town—in fact none of it appealed to me. At the very entrance to the apartment house I balked—Melba protested and urged it would be good liquor and good food without cost, a dividend on the crumbs we had scattered far and wide, so we went in.

That fatal decision was to usher in another burning desire—an unquenchable thirst for an insatiable female.

There were about fifty guests for dinner and we were seated at tables of four or six.

Melba was at a table with Harry Hertz, the wayward husband of the guest of Honor. The guest of Honor and her amour and a Mrs. Benjamin (Ruth) G. were seated at the table I was placed at. Nearly every one there but Harry and Dorothy Hertz were strangers to me. There wasn't a gentile in the place but Melba and your Pa. Some of the others we had met casually from time to time at Dorothy's—such as Mrs. Baron, the Hostess, and Mrs. Goodney (so she claimed) but not impressively enough for me to even remember meeting them.

It was a shock to my staid quakerish background to find that Arthur Kramer, Dorothy's lover, was at her table celebrating her birthday within her husband's very presence—

The cocktails before dinner were potent, and as the meal progressed the liquor flowed freely. Everyone was gay, and the Jews revelled in filthy stories—men would come over to our table to felicitate Dorothy and drink to her health—and use the occasion as an excuse to drop a dirty one or two—some were clever, others just "stank." The women who came to the table would do likewise and would all but open your pants and take your cock out. Their yarns were good and dirty—nothing but sex.

Ruth (Mrs. G.) and I got along fairly well until I caught her switching scotch and rye on me and that annoyed me. I was good and tight—she was lewd to the point of being neurotic—she got me hot as hell and I felt her all over—she fondled my cock under the table as my hand caressed her cunt. I was good and drunk. In my annoyance over her switching the drinks I proceeded to say what I thought of the

Jews, making it very clear to Dorothy, Arthur and Ruth and anyone who might be standing by that the yiddish termites had ruined the beloved, fair City of my aryan ancestors—Holland (dutch) and English who had settled here and done so much to found and build up the town only to have it pass into the hands of the Jews—the miserable lice that they were and are the most hated and contemptible peoples on the face of the globe—a people, truly without a country because no one wants them.

I denounced them for their crooked financial practices. Nothing that I said seemed to faze them in the least—I finally reached the stage where I could hardly stagger to the bathroom to piss—about then the party broke up.

Ruth had given me her private telephone number before I got too drunk. Her husband strangely enough had been at the table with Melba and Harry Hertz as had the Hostess.

On the way out I was still boisterous and "horny" and denouncing the Jews, declaring to all that I hadn't wanted to come anyway.

Ruth G. was living at the Majestic Apartments, on the spot where the famous old Majestic Hotel had stood, the corner of 72nd Street and Central Park West—higher type than West End Avenue but still 100% Jewish. It was an attractive apartment with terrace and plenty of room, furnished conservatively and in good taste. . . .

To get on with this (tail) tale—about ten p.m. that Friday a collect call came in from Cornwall-on-the-Hudson where Melsing was attending New York Military Academy.

I accepted the call altho they had called for Melba—Melsing had been stricken with double mastoid, had been rushed to the local hospital and placed under the care of Dr. Stillman (brother of James Stillman of the National City Bank—Flo Leeds of Indian Guide fame). He was an excellent doctor—his wife and your mother had been good Junior League friends in their youth. The School principal wanted authority to have Melsing operated on at once. There was no way of getting up there at that hour or of getting hold of Melba. I had no idea when she might get home—she had acquired the habit that spring of staying out late upon one excuse or the other—and usually returning home in the wee small hours of the morning with that innocent look in her eyes "having went." The attention that Freddie Davenport showered upon her the previous Thanksgiving and subsequently had gone to her head. She had been having affairs with Davenport, the boy at the WNYC radio station, Oscar Cooper, "Beau of Imogene Snowden," Eddie Ballou, T.R. Smith, Harry Millar, Renato Bellini, Joe Lilly, Charlie Bayer and Henry Clive and maybe others that I hadn't caught on to. So I told them to go ahead and operate—before doing so, however, I talked with the doctor up there and doctors in New York and all agreed that it was the thing to do and do quickly.

Melba did not arrive home until after midnight, full of phony alibis. I told her the story and she phoned the school and arranged to go up on the first morning train—she was hysterical and terribly upset that she had not been home when the call came in.

I had to remain in town in order to raise the dough for the operation.

En route to the train Melba phoned Ruth and told her what had happened. Ruth insisted that I come to dinner anyway—that was a mistake for all hands.

At noon I learned that Melsing had come thru the operation all right and so I went to Ruth's for dinner. It was a large party and I sat on Ruth's right—which marked me as a new something or other.

The dinner went off well enough—much conversation about Melsing, etc. After the meal was over in true semitic fashion the card tables were brought out—not playing cards, I was an odd fellow in more ways than one (I do not play cards—I don't know how—I am not interested). . . .

Ruth and I spent a great deal of time out on her terrace that evening and we took a lot of kidding from everyone whenever we came in.

Her husband, Ben, made a point of commenting after one of our terrace sojourns that Ruth was fickle—that no matter how much she philandered, she always returned to him. In fact he told me that I was just another passing fancy.

That night we agreed that on my return from Cornwall the following day we would meet for tea at the Plaza. God what hot pants I had for Ruth—I could hardly contain myself—but I was devoted to Melsing and I determined to visit him in the hospital the next day. So Ruth would have to wait until evening.

I took the early train up to Cornwall and spent the day there, leaving early enough to get back in time to keep my date with Ruth.

I felt sure that Melba saw thru my subterfuges when I didn't stay the entire afternoon at Cornwall. But Melsing was doing well and I was on the hunt, my blood was tingling and I was almost on my prey.

I arrived on time but didn't stay at the Plaza too long, just long enough to acquire an edge—drinking out in the open was still a novelty in those days.

On some flimsy pretext we went to my apartment at 2 Beekman Place. My real reason was that Melba was to call me there about Melsing and it was a good place to screw. There I fucked little Ruth for the first time less than a week after we had met at the birthday party.

She was a hot primitive number and gave me one hell of a workout. We kept at it all evening until we were both exhausted.

When it was all over she left but forgot to take her gloves which Melba discovered on her return from Cornwall. . . .

Having tasted of the luscious cunt with my cock and tongue, I craved for more. Ruth was brazen, cruel, neurotic, erotic, imbued with certain sadistic tendencies—mental rather than physical.

Ruth had been born in Odessa and brought here as a child. Much of her early life was spent at Sea Gate—almost 100% Jewish—low type. Sea Gate was the once lovely haven at the entrance to New York Bay of well-to-do "micks" (Irish Catholics).

Ruth spoke faily well—dyed her hair blonde (on her head)—and was an inveterate reader. She had drive and a great deal of force and singleness of purpose. She was anything but a beauty—very Jewish in physical construction. With the characteristic hump on her back, well developed tits and small hips.

Ruth had wandered astray from Ben on another occasion—an affair that had lasted for several years and then blown up and she had returned to her husband's bed.

Ruth had a daughter about 9 years old to whom she professed great devotion—she was a nice child, very quiet, a definite Jewish type. Ruth kept her mother hidden from me—she was orthodox. Her brother had been mixed up in some shady business, he could not practice dentistry under his own name, and he and his mother lived in a house Ruth provided for them at Sea Gate. . . .

Her friends always contended that the money was hers—at one time I think Ben had been connected with a shady bucket shop but Ruth always denied it. Her maiden name was very Yiddish—that was the English translation of the Russian—I have forgotten what her first name in Russian was—I liked it better than Ruth but couldn't pronounce it. She always contended that the money was Ben's that he had made it.

Two Jews publishing a couple of men's furnishing trade papers for wholesalers to advertise to the retail trade stores the styles in men's clothes, decided to get out a men's furnishing general magazine to help the retailers educate men to changing clothes and fashion in men's gear.

They (Dave Smart and William "Bill" Weintraub) called the magazine *Esquire*—it didn't go over well at first with anyone but the "fags"—then women bought it but the advertising was for men. The circulation was special and limited and the sources of advertising revenue scarce. The publishers—whoremasters at heart—were in deep water financially. Bill Weintraub knew Ruth and Ben—he was of their smart Jewish social set—first generation immigrants in the United States.

Smart and Weintraub (the publishers) were desperate—they had to get money to keep going. They took their troubles to their affluent friends Ruth and Ben, who by then had moved out of the Coney Island Ghetto (Sea Gate) to New York's smart middle class Jewish apartment, the

Majestic. The Jews migrate from one Jewish neighborhood to the other as their fortunes increase—their financial affluence is all they have in life. They have to climb always upward until they reach the heights of an exclusive Christian community, which they buy into over the misfortunes of some broken down aristocrat—and then they take over, destroying the entire section for anyone but Jews—when the Jews have ruined a place then the niggers move in and that puts on the finishing touch—but I have been over all that in detail before.

Well, Ruth loaned Bill the money to keep *Esquire* going. Weintraub wanted to give them stock but they wouldn't take it—Ben said that if the paper were saved Bill could pay back the loan at six per cent—if it failed he could forget it. Well, that dough was just enough to keep them going until the repeal of prohibition when the big, new (previously unheard of) Jewish liquor companies (which had been speedily organized after the repeal of prohibition) seeking a truly man's organ as an advertising media that was read largely by women—slightly on the risque side—found in *Esquire* their perfect medium—and Weintraub & Smart turned the corner, out of the red into the blue. . . .

I developed the habit at first of dropping in on Ruth of an afternoon for a drink and a bit of wooing. Much of my preliminary courting all my life has been done on the phone—that is usually my approach, lengthy talks—it's cheaper and stalls off complications. You can talk to a girl on the phone for an hour for 60¢ and it appears extravagant, but to take her out will cost from $1.50 minimum to five or ten dollars an hour depending where you go for liquor or food or whether it be peace or war time—and an evening out may run up to a hundred bucks and during the speakeasy era the sky was the limit.

Shortly after Melba returned (from nursing Melsing back to health) she attended a luncheon that Dorothy Hertz gave at the Sherry-Netherland. Ruth was there and trying to be vivacious, blandly announced that she was pregnant, whereupon the scintillating Melba never at loss for words on any occasion, quick as a flash facetiously shot at Ruth,

"You must have found Ward a pretty good lay." Ruth was speechless—she never forgave Melba—but she had brought it on herself, she had given Melba a perfect opening. Ruth was a flop at repartee—she had no fast come back. Melba had scored—a ruthless jab as she invariably did whenever their paths crossed which was seldom after that. This had much to do with Ruth's hate of Melba—she was no match for the firebrand from the Sunset State in a wordy battle—but between the sheets that was different. Ruth had ways of her own and her tormenting preludes to sexual intercourse were irresistible to one of my temperament, who always sought to conquer.

I would rather argue my way to bed than caress my way to the best lay in the world—the more violent the mental abuse the greater the pleasure of the eventual conquest. Ruth knew this by instinct or design and played upon that weakness of mine masterfully.

She would invariably hang up the phone whenever I called her—that is as soon as she knew who it was. After you persisted with frequent calls—during which attempts she would even leave the receiver off the hook for varying periods of time—she would condescend to talk. At first the conversation would be devoted almost entirely to her annoyance at my persistence—then she would be argumentative about some picayune thing and declare that she would never see me again, that there was no need of my calling—she wouldn't, simply wouldn't talk to me that she was fed up with me etc. This would go on for an hour or so and wind up by my coming up there to her apartment, meeting her for lunch or dinner or cocktails and screwing hell out of her—she loved her "nookey."

Her friends and Melba thought she was kidding when she announced she was pregnant but she was with child—I had knocked her up.

Melba became very suspicious the first evening I returned home late for dinner after that with a sun burned face (gotten on Ruth's roof) and I suppose some rouge that wouldn't come off—plus the gloves, plus a tip from Dorothy Hertz that Ruth had been singing my praises far and wide. I passed the sun burn off with the statement that I had been sitting on a park bench writing copy for *Moo* and hadn't noticed the sun beating down upon me.

I was very frank with Ruth about my finances—I told her right off the bat that there wasn't any money to play around with—that's why that April, May and June I saw much of her daytimes (her daughter was at School), in her home, on her roof, and on her liquor—frequently lunching with her in her own apartment.

Ruth spent a great deal of money on clothes—and her lace negligees were numerous and seductive, designed to give her height and take the Jewish hump out of her back.

Her maid was aware of what was going on for I mauled her in her living room, on the terrace, in her dining room, in her bedroom—and fucked her all over the place, usually departing before her daughter arrived home from her school and playtime activities.

Once a week she had her Mother and brother to dinner—once a week she had dinner with them at Sea Gate—once a week she had dinner with Ben's family in her own home or theirs. On Monday nights Ben didn't come home for dinner but was usually home by ten-thirty. Sometimes she didn't go with Ben to his family. Sunday Ben played golf all day. Saturday night they always entertained or were entertained.

When I first saw her ice box and cupboard I was shocked—plenty of liquor supplies but no food to speak of in the ice box or on the shelves or the pantry. She ordered from day to day from an expensive chain grocer, Gristede's, and never had anything over—this horrified me because a full larder has always been the pride and joy of my life. . . .

One evening (a Monday night) in early June I met her down stairs in front of her apartment—we were to go for a ride in her car (a big Cadillac). She thought it safer to go out in her car than in ours—she was afraid of Melba. As she stepped across the doorway she called my attention to a twenty dollar bill on the sidewalk. I told her to pick it up it was good luck. As she did so she announced that since we had found it we should spend it.

So we decided to go to dinner and hit upon a Japanese place between eighth and ninth Avenues on West 58th Street. I had gone there with Henry Clive and Melba and Sonea and had liked it and Ruth loved oriental food—Chinese or Japanese. It was called Miyako—afterwards it was moved to 20 West 56th Street and for a while after Pearl Harbor was closed—but then it was opened again.

The House of Chan when it was on Broadway between 56th and 57th Street was a favorite of the Jewish clique—it was Chinese.

But back to the Miyako. We got very drunk from drinking and very hot from ????—excitement, first fighting then caressing, then she had to pee. The Miyako was in an old fashioned brown stone house—high stoop, the dining room on the first or parlor floor, the privy on the floor above.

It had been the master's bath in days of yore—the tub had never been removed. I stumbled up the stairs after her—my ever present weakness to be in the can with a female getting the best of me—and we went into the toilet together. This seemed to excite the Japanese no end—or on-end for they jabbered excitedly like a lot of monkeys.

We were so drunk and hot that we fucked on the can—being in the "little girls room" with a female has always made me hot as hell. As we stumbled out dishevelled and unkempt, we fell over a Jap who had been at the keyhole—the little yellow bastard had been peeking and jerking off as he watched—in my drunkenness I showed him Ruth's cunt and this excited us all over again and I laid her out on the top of the stairs in the hall outside the can and gave her another shot—as the son of nippon spilt his load all over the carpet. The proprietor and his wife or some Japanese female belonging to the joint came running up the stairs and got us straightened out and back down stairs—fortunately for all concerned we were the last in the place. With another drink we paid the cheque and departed. Ruth drove the car—why or how we got over to Park Avenue I will never know, but there we were going up the Avenue. Twice she drove up on to the Center garden plot right up over the curbing. I had come twice in the restaurant but my cock was still hard—I had it out of my pants—she was drunk and trying to drive and feel my cock as I in my cups played with her pussy—she loved to play with me and be played with in the car.

Ruth liked to fuck in the car—she missed a couple of lamp posts by inches.

We crossed the park at 72nd Street and at the half way loop or parking space overlooking the 72nd Street Lake, we parked and got out. We wandered up a knoll there and I laid her on the grass behind a bench and some bushes.

Everyone was doing something at that late hour—boys were finger-fucking their girls on park benches and fucking and sucking them off in the bushes, or on their ass in the grass—fairies were picking one another up or making new conquests or converts—masturbators were jerking off as they watched boys and girls together, or fairies or lesbians doing their stuff—cock sucking and buggering were rampant—blackmailers and petty thieves were doing their prowling—some just came out to walk their dogs for a pee or crap before turning in for the night.

It was dangerous, exciting and conducive to fornication in its many varieties and perversities. It had always been a favorite haunt of mine since early childhood—for finger-fucking, straight diddling, cunt-lapping or masturbation—and on occasion I have sat on a bench in the park and jerked off as some fellow fucked his girl—and at other times I have pulled my pudding as some other guy on the same bench pulled his and while some fellow across the pad put in his rod, or a dame went down on her boy friend—it was hot stuff—it saved room rent etc. In the warm weather the cops were few and far between and walked with heavy tread on the pavement—the place was poorly lighted in those days and the benches were always in the shadows.

The risk with Ruth was twofold—blackmail if followed home or robbery if her jewels shone too brightly—she always wore row upon row of glistening diamonds—all over her wrists were big wide bracelets, typically Jewish, worth a small fortune.

In addition there were her priceless rings—diamonds, diamonds everywhere.

Ruth liked it on her ass on the grass or anywhere for that matter—those that had autos did their fucking mostly in their parked cars. In the parked cars in Central Park, the favorite practice was for the girls to suck the men off.

That night in the park after we found the twenty dollars (I always thought she planted that dough as a face-saving for me—a way of having a night out on her own money), the night of the Miyako incident, I fucked her three times on that hill and then I went down on her and as I sucked off the load she fainted. It was the first and only time she had ever passed out on me—but we were pretty drunk—too much liquor and too much fucking had been too much for her.

It took her some time to come around—and it scared the piss out of me. I didn't want a dead woman and married at that on my hands in Central Park. I was always in mortal terror that we would be held up and she would be robbed by some bum or thief in the park. If that had ever happened everyone would have said I had a hand in it—instead of my cock.

When Ruth finally came to I got her to the car and got her home. The ground had been damp—it had rained during the evening while we were at Miyako's getting drunk—and we both were pretty messy sights, covered with dirt and mud and grass stains and human semen—our clothes all askew.

On the hilltop between fucks we had quarreled—and slapped and clawed at one another until we were both bleeding from the scratches on our faces made by our respective nails. She was so intense in her love making quarrels that she often clawed and clawed deep and I retaliated.

It must have been something for the doorman to write home about—how she covered up with Ben, I don't know. She instructed the doorman to send the car to the garage and then kissing me goodnight she slapped my face as a parting gesture and went on up to her husband, as I grabbed a taxi and slunk home to Melba. But Melba wasn't home so I removed my clothes, cleaned them as best I could, doctored my face, pissed, washed my cock and then the body and went to bed—a bit more sober than when I had left the Miyako.

The next day we drove out to Jones Beach. She brought along the liquor and the picnic lunch and the balance left over from the "twenty" paid the entrance fee, the parking charge and the bath house fee—she had her own towels.

We spent the day there—she loved the beach—many women do. I got a burn not only on my face, but on my entire body, altho we didn't go near the water. She wasn't much on the swimming end—we read and talked and made love—it was Tuesday and there weren't many there.

When I got home what a time I had trying to hide the body sunburn from Melba. We never wore any night covering or clothing when we slept, summer or winter. I guess she noticed but kept mum because I had so much on her.

At the Hamilton P.s that year Melba got out of hand at their annual cocktail party—so I left around nine and she remained behind. Melba never wanted to leave a party—I went home and after talking to Ruth on the phone went to bed. Melba arrived about 2:30 a.m.

Much to my annoyance she and Eddie Ballou parked in front of the apartment for over an hour and they weren't talking. If they wanted to do that sort of thing it was my contention that they should have parked elsewhere and not in front of the very apartment in which she was living with her husband (still) and children—and I told her so in no uncertain terms.

Most of my friends coveted Melba—many of them made her—all of them thought she would have gone to bed with them had they been willing to betray a friend (me). . . .

A brief interlude—a jump from 1935 to 1943—pardon the interruption.

5:04 p.m. Sunday the 25th of July 1943 at Smiths Folly on the River—East—in our V for Vanity Garden. Eve in her bathing suit sits across from me in a porch chair—your father is in his shorts only—the fountain is playing in the center of the garden. Convoys are passing by up and down the river—operatic recordings are on the air from New York City on Station WNYC—flash-flash-flash—the music has abruptly stopped and Tommy Crown is announcing that Mussolini has been dismissed—King Victor Emanuel has assumed command of the Italian Army. As the music is resumed we hasten to phone *The New York Times* for verification. Eve remarks, "All worldwide dramatic news seems to happen on Sunday—Pearl Harbor, etc.—England goes to war"—I phoned Elise—she was lying in bed at Chestertown resting from her arduous farm labors, worrying about her men in the armed services—Especially Russell [her son] with Montgomery unheard from for three months.

She was incredulous—she said she would stay glued to her radio—while talking, further details came over the radio. I placed the telephone transmitter near our radio so your Aunt Elise could get the story from our own municipal station which had scored a beat.

Hardly had I gotten settled back to normal to go on with my own little inconsequential yarn and sex revelations than Elise phoned back to say nobody down there had heard the great news—the real beginning of the end. I assured her all the New York stations had verified it—the House of Savoy was saving the seat of Christendom from the ravages of the semitic maniacs ruling the destinies of America and attempting to gain control of the world—but more about that in reflection when I come to it. Man will do well if he does not destroy himself completely.

Maybe the wops are just big talkers and little doers when it comes to physical encounter—they just don't fight, no matter what side they are on (and what a false alarm that turned out to be).

I was wondering what you were doing when the dramatic news broke—

Well, back to the letter and the year 1935—and Ruth and the Barbizon Plaza.

I was getting in deep with Ruth—too deep—I had no intention of marrying her, I was ashamed to be seen in public by anyone I knew while with her, except her own friends, Jewish. . . .

I liked Ruth and enjoyed her society but I did not want to be seen in public with her. She wanted to go to all the leading restricted hostelries in the east as Mrs. W. Ward Smith—and that was not for me—I didn't care how much dough she had, or what fabulous jewelry. Later she told me she had taken all her property, stock and bonds and cash over into her own name and to her own physical possession for the purpose of living with me, marrying me, and keeping me while I got on my feet.

That break didn't end our meetings, although I had to make amends by much extra screwing and wooing.

During all this period Melba and I both went in for massages—she for reducing her bodily flesh and some of the personal pleasure from the caressing manipulation of her cuzzy, and I for the reduction of the extended main organ by proper stroking. . . .

During August I spent most of my time, when not out with Ruth, down at the O'Connell press supervising the makeup of *Moo,* reading and correcting proof and I am a hell of a proof reader of my own copy. . . .

Strange but true—I would not cross a "T" or dot an "I" today of my "Topšy Turvy" platform as set forth in *Moo* in 1935—nine long years ago, and years before there was a second World War.

And here it is for re-reading—

OUR TOPSY-TURVY PLATFORM

We advocate a National Central Banking System.

We are for Federal and State ownership of telephone, telegraph, radio and electric utilities. The Federal ownership of all the coal, oil and timber resources of the nation.

We are for the abolition of credit bankers; partial payment loans on household goods, automobiles, real estate, by private corporations. We propose the substitution of a Federal credit corporation in the place of the present money leeches.

We are for Federal maintenance of toll highways and supervision of all forms of transportation, air, rail, water and automotive.

We are for the development of centralized market places, for the exchange of goods and produce rather than credits.

We would keep the church and the state entirely separate and prohibit all prelates from preaching or discussing political or governmental subjects of a controversial nature.

We believe that voluntary segregation of creeds, cults, and races should be respected. We believe our gates should be closed and our births controlled until all but a normal and seasonal ratio of unemployment has been eliminated, then the gates to be opened gradually and the population increased by a rising birth rate until all the virgin lands within our borders are under cultivation and production.

We are for centralized taxation by the Federal Government, with distribution back to the states, and counties and cities and villages under National Government supervision.

We are for Government lotteries, the parimutuels and for Government-owned and controlled gambling.

We are for the destruction of privately operated policy rackets.

We oppose corporations issuing stock representing anything but cash contributions to their capital structure.

We would eliminate all private utility advertising from newspapers and non-fiction publications.

We believe that not more than one-fourth of the legislators in any law-making body should be lawyers.

We would make public hearings on all legislation, municipal, state or national, mandatory before the legislating as well as the executive branches of the government. We would exclude professional lobbyists from such hearings.

We would pay U.S. Senators $15,000 a year, Representatives $10,000 and prohibit their being engaged in any other activity whatsoever. We would pay N.Y. State legislators; Senators $10,000 Assemblymen $7,500.

We are opposed to crop control, destruction and processing taxes.

We are for a quicker, cheaper and more economical distribution between the producer and the consumer.

We would have the Federal Government allot $2,500,000 to each national party polling over a million votes in a presidential year for campaign expenses. No other contributions permitted.

We would have the state and municipal governments

appropriate money for local campaigns to local parties.

We would have the state, local and federal chairmen of the respective parties salaried men paid by their party treasurers.

Political leaders under a statute making it a misdemeanor would be prohibited from discussing legislation with any elected officials.

Moneys should be loaned to farmers with less red tape regardless of their financial condition for periods of thirty-three years or more, at ½ of 1 percent for the purpose of permitting them to discharge their present obligations and to refinance their farms. A tax moratorium of five years should be declared on farm properties.

We are opposed to the squandering of millions to clear up congested areas in metropolitan centers so that modern abodes may be erected for the foreign-born, while not a cent is being spent to rehabilitate and modernize the dilapidated farm homes of millions of Americans.

We are for federal hock shops.

We are for a union of all nations, with legislative, executive and judicial branches, regulating the international affairs of the world, supported by an international air, naval and land police.

The new domestic was Graham De Ryder—photographed one early August afternoon across from the then still-existing Central Park Casino and what a luscious lay she was then and for some years thereafter.

To our Topsy-Turvy Platform as contained in *Moo* we would add a six-year term for President of the United States—nonsucceedable, subject to impeachment, and Congressmen for terms of three years each, but not to exceed two successive terms—Senators not more than two successive terms of six years each. . . .

In the Fall the fellow I sublet the apartment from at 2 Beekman Place moved out and we rented direct from the owner, bringing some of our things in from storage.

Nearly every Monday night Ruth and I went out on a tear on her money—after the stall of finding the first twenty dollars on the street she had no hesitation in offering me the difference between a meal for two at Childs and a meal for two at El Morocco.

She was a peculiar woman—whenever Melba and I

would run across her at a night club, and she was always with her husband, she would immediately depart. I never understood why—she would tell her friends that she was afraid I would do something rash—what, I don't know. On several occasions we took a suite at that "creep" hotel, the Coolidge, across from the St. Margaret. One night we drove up in evening clothes, quite tight, bought a bottle, ordered some chinese food and fucked like fools. About two in the morning, still high, we dressed, checked out, drove around the corner to the Metropole and ate roast beef sandwiches with french fried potatoes at 15¢ a plate plus a nickel beer and pickles—then I took her home and crawled back to Beekman Place myself—Ruth didn't like the St. Margaret for sexual intercourse. . . .

The following was released for the Sunday Morning papers of October 6th, 1935—

CONSUMERS PUBLIC POWER PLANT COMMITTEE
299 Broadway
Tel. Barclay 7-1566
FOR RELEASE IN SUNDAY PAPERS

The Consumers Public Power Plant Committee announced yesterday (Saturday) that it had appointed Mr. W. Ward Smith as manager of the campaign it is conducting in behalf of Mayor La Guardia's proposed "Yardstick" Public Power Plant. The Committee is proceeding with the organization of its campaign pending the decision by the Court of Appeals on the application of the Consolidated Gas Co. to prevent a referendum vote upon the proposal at the elections, November 5th. The Consolidated Gas Co. is trying to prevent the referendum on technical legal grounds, but if the company is successful the Committee will carry the fight to the Legislature.

Mr. Smith, who has been identified with conservative financial interests, accepted the task of managing the campaign and threw himself into the fight despite the fact that his family has been connected with the utility companies and the Consolidated Gas in this city, in high executive capacities, for four generations. The Committee regarded his acceptance as highly gratifying, since Mr. Smith has managed successfully a number of important patriotic, civic, and political campaigns during the last fifteen years. . . .

[My father directed the campaign for a consumer-owned utility with typical energy. La Guardia, having used the threat of a city-owned plant to force down Consolidated Edison's rate and calculating the political pluses and minuses, lost interest in the issue and the plan was abandoned much to my father's disgust.]

1936

1935 hadn't been much of a year—Ruth was a liability, the power plant campaign had fizzled, our money was dwindling as was our interest in one another.

1936 was to offer still less.

The thirst for wealth, filthy lucre, money, or the possession of worldly goods in excess of one's fellow man has so often been the root of much evil in the world—and that goes not only for evil in the dealings between men but between communities, between states and between nations—perhaps it would be better to define it as greed, insatiable greed.

Listening to tales of the vagaries of some mortals—tales that were told almost at first hand—jolted me into realization that before there can be justice and understanding in dealings between nations, there must be a higher standard of ethics in the transactions between men in all walks of life.

We in this country as a whole are much too tolerant of the pettifoggery of men in public and private life. Even grand larceny seems to be condoned by the populace at times—and so being condoned is widely practiced. . . .

The New Year, 1936, didn't begin auspiciously and wound up poorly—that year saw the breakup—permanent—of the Melba interlude. I went West to look after the property in her estate and also to further the candidacy of William E. Borah for the Republican presidential nomination—I visited Mr. Hearst as his guest at San Simeon—I made whoopee in a bungalow in the Hollywood hills—I had a violent affair via the U.S. mails with Mary Dunn of Abilene, Texas. I met Frank Knox, then publisher of the *Chicago News* and a potential candidate for President, which eventually materialized into the vice-presidency under Landon—I met Marion Davies and became enamoured of Mary Pickford.

I returned to New York to live for a while in a hall room in Watterson Lowe's tenement apartment—I then moved to the St. Margaret for several months, and eventually took the apartment at 904 Park Avenue, which you visited at Thanksgiving time when you came down from Dartmouth. . . .

In the summer of 1936, I became associated as an Account Executive with the Lawrence B. Whit organization, a publicity outfit, and prepared a plan for publishing an American edition of the Illustrations published by the Holy See. I prepared a plan to publicize Robert Ripley "Believe It Or Not"—and to steer the Provident Loan Society thru troublesome waters.

I traveled the width and breadth of the country, from New York to California by bus. It was an experience, especially that part of the journey when I tried to sleep in a berth at night between St. Louis and Los Angeles—the bunk wasn't long enough and there wasn't any head room to speak of, so you couldn't double up very well.

In the following pages I will try to make 1936 as brief as possible and hurry on to 1937, 1938 and 1939. . . .

At 2 Beekman Place I evolved the scheme for economy's sake of serving small very thin slices of Hormel Ham out of a can on thin slices of French bread with a thin slice of butter for hors d'oeuvres, and a rum cocktail consisting of cheap light rum, gin, orange juice, lemon juice, grapefruit juice, sugar, and ginger ale. It was inexpensive—and you could give a party for 100 people on that diet and with a "chink" to serve it, it would run around $18.00 for everything.

We became known for our Rum and Ham parties.

We also had potato chips delivered from the wholesale dealers that we had dealt with on 52nd Street, during the Parapet days—we served them in the big cans they came in.

The French bread we purchased from a bakery around the corner on First Avenue, the Betsy Ross, run by a funny skinny Frenchman and his buxom wife—the poor bastard had worn himself out knocking his woman up, and baking his cakes and pies and breads.

In the old days before prohibition was repealed, when I first met Melba, I served tuna fish on crackers for parties.

Before I left for the coast, Alma Phipps—her husband was a partner of Harry Hertz—had a birthday party at the Vanderbilt Hotel—liquor flowed freely and the conquests were many and easy that night. The party was downstairs but the Phipps had a suite upstairs for their guests to repair to or straighten our their hair or their cocks or their cunts—and it was a "friggen" swell party of the Englewood in-betweeners. Twenty-four hours later I was on my way West.

A Mrs. Francis H. of Lydecker Street, Englewood, N.J.—a friend of Alma's—was the best tail there—three times we went upstairs and fucked in the bathroom. She had a great deal of money and a jealous husband—I never saw her again.

Before running off into that story which was a hot one, I want to refer a moment to the stupendous rally that they gave Bill Borah in Brooklyn on the night of January 28th.

The Hall was packed—the press pit was overflowing—klieg lights or flood lights for the movie cameramen were all over the place—hundreds and hundreds of stills were flashed of the colorful old warrior from Idaho, that great individualist in domestic and international politics, undependable, unpredictable, an erratic genius, swordsman extraordinary, that silver-tongued orator, that lovable old potato—did a swell job of it thru nigger heckling and all. It was his opening gun in his campaign for the Republican nomination for president, an honor he was never to attain. Few could have been worthier—I did not always agree with the grand old man, but I did admire his brilliance of mind and tool—intestinal fortitude—it was an inspiring occasion. . . .

William Randolph Hearst, the publisher, with his string

of dailies from coast-to-coast and his magazines, was supporting for President an unheard of, unknown and untried Governor of Kansas by the name of Alf Landon—a good man, but a colorless one—more of that later on.

It was Sunday night, February 2nd, 1936, or rather 2:00 o'clock Monday morning, following a Sunday morning hangover after Alma Phipps' liquid birthday party, Saturday night at the Vanderbilt.

Fortified with the best sirloin steak the Divan Parisien could boast that night at dinner, I was setting forth on my first transcontinental modern motorized stage coach jaunt en route to Los Angeles.

A week before at the same Divan Parisien, Melba and I had awaited Gloria (Mrs. R. Vanderbilt). She was late—she had had a date with her lover, Blumenthal, husband of the Lesbian Peggy F. At that date they had broken off—"Blumey," as she called him was flitting around with the season's debs, forsaking Peggy and Gloria—he found the new crop of fresh young things more to his jaded tastes.

We had a sumptuous repast that can best be purchased at the Divan within reason.

Gloria was full of her former Yiddish lover and how he had let her down. During dinner, among the many anecdotes which she related about herself, Peggy Fears and Blumey and their cunt-lapping, fucking performances, was a story about her sister, Thelma, Lady F. For years, Douglas Fairbanks had fenced around and around, sparring for an opportune opening with Thelma.

Finally, one night while they were still living at the Sherry-Netherland—before they moved to the house on 72nd Street—Fairbanks, Sr. took Thelma to dinner and the theatre and for a nite-cap afterwards to a nightclub. Long after midnight they returned to the Sherry-Netherland and Thelma invited him in for a brandy—and then it happened—the Great Fairbanks laid the former mistress of the King of England.

Fairbanks was all hot and bothered—so hot that he stuck it into Thelma and before he could give her any kind of a workout or preliminary love-making, he shot his load—he just couldn't hold back—and those sisters were accustomed to workouts with finesse.

Fairbanks was chagrined at his own lack of control and flop as a lover—the next day he sent Thelma two dozen American beauty roses with his abject apology.

The trip to the coast was for the purpose of getting an honest lawyer—if such did really exist—one free from the taint of the Barbary Coast days.

Lured by full page bus advertisements in the daily press and in the leading periodicals of the country, claiming that the buses equalled the time of the 20th Century Limited and the Santa Fe Chief at one-half the railroad fare, I set forth on my journey.

There were no sleeping or night coaches out of New York—the tunnels and bridges between the great metropolis of the East and Kansas City did not permit the passage of such super-coaches in those days.

The drivers of those up-to-date chariots on North American highways resembled in looks, youth and physique and vitality and self-assuredness, the pilots of the pioneer airways, the mounted constabulary of the various states, or the North Western Mounted Police—they were God's gift to womenkind.

At that season of the year (mid-winter) sleet, wind, rain and snowstorms blocked the highways and it was sub-zero weather. Few women were being lured forth even by these Adonises for long journeys.

In New York I purchased my ticket thru to the Coast and paid $1.50 to have a reservation made on the night coach out of Kansas City for Los Angeles. The reservation was confirmed and the ticket was bought on the assurance that all connections would be held for this extra express service, which called for a schedule of exactly four days (96 hours) from coast to coast.

On board the bus, I purchased a soft pillow thru to St. Louis for 25¢ and checked my baggage thru to the coast free except for a valuation insurance charge.

I was no sooner comfortably ensconced in my reclining

chair than at the very first stop—all seats out of New York are sold by seat numbers and you are assigned your seat before you leave—a bride and groom entered and lowered their seats in front of mine to a reclining position. That was my first discomfort. Being long-legged it bothered my knees, but I twisted and turned until I had assumed a fairly comfortable position, when at the next stop a perfect replica of negro fighter Jack Johnson seated himself plumb beside me and sprawled his legs in the aisle—for the first time I realized my error in having bought a window seat. By this time it being cold outside—5 above—the heaters were on full blast and the mingled body odors of those who had not bathed recently were becoming unmistakably noticeable—the lights had been dimmed and some snored and some talked.

Every two hours we stopped and a handful of the most venturesome would dismount to partake of a Coke or a hot dog or a hamburger or the pleasures of the unsanitary comfort stations. And so on thru the night, down thru Somerville (for comfort); Allentown (for breakfast); Harrisburg (for comfort); Lewiston (for lunch); Duncansville (for comfort); and points West. With the dawn came the cold white beautiful snow as we climbed thru the rugged Alleghanies on and on—15 minutes here, ten minutes there for comfort—one half hour for breakfast at a nondescript joint, one half hour for lunch.

During the bleak snowy afternoon a couple of show girls in the rear came up for air—they were just recovering from a hangover of the night before—and proceeded to entertain with dances to amuse the driver, or thrill him. How he kept his eyes on the road and not glued to the mirror no one will ever know. One of the dear things sat down directly behind the young and virile pilot of our caboose and proceeded to rest her charming ankles on each shoulder, much to the edification and joy of those on the front seat—oh yes, I had moved forward as the crowd shifted during the day, the better to afford my legs a place to stretch—and never did I relinquish that point of vantage again—seat #3 to the coast and back.

The other dame, not to be outdone, proceeded to kick the rear view mirror on the ceiling of the bus for a pint of rye—this was too much for our driver. He had to stop the bus for a better view of this stunt, or to be frank, the dame's cunt—especially since the charming girls had no panties on at all. Maybe the males on board should have written New York Police Commissioner Valentine and thanked him for the entertainment—it was the night of the big New York raid on apartments of questionable fame—or was it the night they removed the dance studio signs from the Ripping Seventies? And the whores were leaving New York like rats skipping a scuttled ship on every available bus and train.

At Blairsville, the youthful steward was so overcome with the free display of feminine pulchritude that he couldn't help the passengers on and off with their baggage—he was busy fucking one of the bitches prone on the back seat.

Oh well—the party was fun while it lasted, even if the bus never did quite get going again on the even tenor of its usual way—rye was cheap in Pennsylvania, and it was the reward I offered for the best female high kicker. Nearly every guy on the bus, including the driver who screwed one of the girls in the rear of a comfort station, had a "hard" on—one of the lovelies jerked me off on a back seat as I fondled her cunt before we reached Pittsburgh. . . .

All manner and types of people were traveling. There was a soldier returning to his post: he was bound for foreign shores. A boy and girl going back to college—women joining their husbands on business trips—drunks returning from a funeral—a farmer going to town—trained nurses out for a spree. There was a girl making whoopee with everybody on the bus, and trying to date the bus driver up at El Paso for the night before she reached her prospective groom, whom she was to marry within the next day or two—and then there was the salesman who traveled the bus, but charged the railroad fare up in his expense account.

Some folks never entered into the festivities—others kept up the fun-making all the time.

When I reached Los Angeles at the end of the delayed

cross-continental trip, it was with great relief that I registered at the Biltmore for a comfortable bed and bath.

Bus-riding kinda gets you—it's damned uncomfortable at first, pillow or no—but after a while you get the hang of it and sleep well sitting up, provided the driver isn't a city traffic expert out on the open road, for the city drivers are hell on the nerves.

You get interested in their working hours, the personalities of the different division heads, their families, the pension system, the advantages of the Santa Fe Railways over the Greyhound, and vice versa, the salaries, the mileage they make, the experiences they have in fighting the elements, what they do to keep awake, etc.

The fastest run was from Tulsa to Kansas City—310 miles, 40 stops, 20 minutes for comfort, 65 passengers and their baggage on and off, the aisles frequently filled, 7 hours flat for the entire trip. The Eastern drivers say that people in the East have no respect for the buses or drivers, but in the West it's different and I guess they're right.

One of the drivers stopped suddenly, rolling a pair of fucking lovers off the back seat onto the floor—they didn't know he could see them in the mirror—it was dark, but they forgot the small light burning overhead. I thought that one hell of a trick until at the next stop he turned off all the lights and told them they would have a half hour to themselves unmolested, thereby redeeming himself for his earlier prank.

The segregation of the colored folk in the South and the whites who refuse to ride sitting beside them preferring to wait hours for another bus, was difficult, but necessary.

In the big open spaces, the buses are as fast if not faster than the fastest train and just as comfortable as any plane. Many older men of moderate means spend their winters riding thru the warmer climes, calling on relatives and friends, traveling seven or eight hours a day by daylight, sleeping with friends or in inexpensive hotels at night. They say they see the country that way and learn more about the customs than any other way they could travel, except to drive themselves.

Bus-riding is a trifle hard on the system, but then any form of travel is. The big railroads were gradually buying up all the bus lines and with the aid of the Interstate Commerce Commission, will gradually combine them into a few big systems. Then progress in improvements will start to decline after competition is brought under control.

Romance is always sprouting on the bus runs—sometimes it is only a quickie on the back seat, sometimes it is good for an over night stop at some small local hotel away from the home town, sometimes the spell lasts longer, sometimes it endures for life—but that's the way with man and maid most anywhere, that cocks and cunts find themselves together.

[My father, writing of his trip to California, six years earlier, was distracted by wartime convoys passing up and down the East River.]

The flaw—and most distracting day after day, hour after hour, almost minute after minute—passes a convoy bound in from the sea or bound out to the sea—the procession was continuous.

During the writing of this page alone, four ships raced in on the tide—empty—their gay crews cheering and calling to the nursemaids and mothers and juveniles along the river walk—the channel was but a hundred feet off shore at this point. Most of the boats were flying the stars and stripes, a few the British "Jack," an occasional tri-color, and once in a while the Russian Scythe and Sickle. Now and then a neutral ship would glide by—another has just passed (as I write this) going out—she was heavy, moving slow against the tide, like she didn't want to leave—tanks, trucks and all manner of cases lashed on her decks. She was heavy to her water's edge—now a loaded tanker follows.

All fly the gaily colored international code flags for their clearance or their entry. Those flags even give the somber outward bound ships a festive air, which the demeanor of their silent crews belie—no waving to the girls along the walk, they are sailing out to meet the enemy slinking beneath the sea, to send them sprawling to Davy Jones locker. The toll is great—each man knows the danger that lurks without the harbor gate.

A Carrier has just slipped by, graceful and swift. Her commander's orders over the loud-speakers clearly audible ashore. P.T. boats on active duty, Navy, Coast Guard roar up and down on important business bent—landing barges struggle against the fast-racing tide thru Hell Gate in practice runs for the crews and trial runs for the machinery. A Destroyer has just moved past—as I write and glance up, it looks for all the world like a stage set. They all move by so smoothly they look as if they were being pulled across a stage. Smoke pours from the funnels of the busy puffing snorting little tugs—alongside those that don't handle well in fast tides. The whistles blast and blast day and night. Thick heavy soot lays down upon the garden tables, furniture and plants, thick dust hourly pours thru the screened windows and the poor flowers and plants have to be washed like ourselves—to keep their pores from choking up.

A hospital ship, all in white, is moving by—there are recuperating sailors and soldiers on her decks—they call to the girls along the shore as an airplane roars overhead—one of the penalties of war, the maimed and wounded returning from the field of battle. Some will recover whole, others will never be the same—some will always be charges on their families, their state or federal government for the remainder of their helpless lives—worse off than the comrades left so gloriously or solemnly on the field of battle.

This is August 1943.

And before I return to the tale of 1936—I will interlope here a thought often expressed by me in conversation and written word—

There will always be wars as long as man is man—there can never be a permanent peace. Man cannot defy the economic law and succeed—he cannot make water move up hill without artificial aid—man-made aid. Men quarrel amongst themselves—men are always seeking the greener grass on the other side of the fence—man always desires to expand. Just as the Jew thrives on misery and the ill-fortune of his fellowman, the Aryan thrives on success and expansion—the Aryan is the pioneer seeking new fields to conquer regardless of the physical price; the Semite seeks to exploit the established, to chisel in—the Aryan builds for the Semitic to destroy.

New devices—the manual saving machines—over populate the land. Then man must destroy the machines or be destroyed—and when man continues to improve the machine, to perfect the machine, he is in effect perfecting and hastening his own destruction from the face of the earth.

Wars are economic—rudimentally they arise from man's inborn urge to improve his lot in life whether on the Yangtze or the Hudson.

When men are crowded into small areas they crave to expand to break their bounds. The British did it—the Germans have been striving likewise and valiantly—and in fact superbly when resources and manpower are considered—the Japs are having their try at it—the Dutch, the French, the Spanish all took their turns. Just as long as nature implants the basic urge of progeneration—or procreation—in man, so long will there be wars.

Now what are the results of all this fighting and wasting and detroying of men and materials?

Let's look at nature. In plant life—let's take the Tung tree—you plant a tree, you nurse it along, you fertilize and cultivate it. After a number of years the tree begins to bear.

And after it arrives at a normal bearing prolific state, what happens? One year you have ten bushels of fruit, then the next year there may be an unexpected late frost or an early frost and it is just too bad—or it may be heavy rains—but frost is the most damaging. Your orchard may be on the best land for soil and water and air drainage, but the frost gets the tree and you lose most of the crop.

The tree's development has been arrested—the crop will only be a bushel—but the next year it will come back to ten or more or nature may intercede again. The third year the crop will be the biggest yet—then there will be a setback, a recuperation and a surge ahead and then another setback. Nature never permits the trees to race ahead beyond their strength, to give greater and greater bumper crops each year—she always retards, levels off.

Now for war—man races ahead, gets beyond himself, life becomes too easy—there are too many for work and not enough work to do. So come the wars, the normal fatalities around the world from disease, natural causes, normal accidents, disasters—hasn't been fast enough—war steps that up.

In some cases it took the best men, the top cream, and destroyed them—that was nature's way of destroying the ruling class and revitalizing by letting the lower order develop and come to the top—birthrates fall in peace time, but are sharply accentuated in war.

One man said, "In peace time there are more men than women. That is not good—there can be little selectivity of females by the males in such a society, so the race is weakened." After wars there are more women than men—a man can be more selective.

My observation, however, is that man is seldom more selective—a stiff prick arises out of other considerations that have little connection with the male's mature consideration of the type of offspring to be produced by a union.

Seldom does a healthy boy stop to consider the eugenics of a union—hot pants give little thought to the type of brat a fuck will produce if the gal gets caught. . . .

Well, war—in modern warfare, as in days of yore, old cities are destroyed, antiquities are gone forever—that enriches those that are left. New cities will have to be built—out of this conflict as out of the last will come newer and more radical advances in machinery on land, in the air, on the sea and under it. Transportation, communication, television, improvements in the home, in the office, great strides in commercial and personal aviation, household appliances, the automobile, even agriculture and foodstuffs will be improved if the present Secretary of Agriculture doesn't destroy the American farms with his socialism.

Novel and alluring edibles as well as advances in personal adornments, habitats, clothing, etc.—ultra modernistic homes will arise the world over. We will lag behind Britain,

Germany, China, Japan (if we ever get to the mainland of the Rising Sun), because so much of their old has been destroyed. In defeat, Germany will gain.

The air raid blitzes over London were good for London—it has revived that tottering, rotting, decaying capital on the Thames.

Much in New York could have been destroyed to the betterment of the metropolis—as young as she is and prone to tear down and rebuild without the stimulant of destruction by war or fire or quake, it would have been well for us.

New cities rising on the ashes of the old are always better cities—that's progress. It would have been well if Rome and Paris had not been declared open cities—they will have to be destroyed sooner or later to make way for the modern advance of man.

No, we remain alone untouched, except for an upset in our ideologies—our ancestors came here to get away from European methods, old world superstitions, restrictions, jealousies, nationalism, bigotry, corruption and poverty. This war is bringing us closer than the last to a revolution that will return us to the old countries' ways—for the scum of Europe will be in the saddle, in charge of the new order which will be but an embracement of the old countries' discredited ways. Freedom of speech, of worship, the right to work where and when one chooses and to live one's own life is vanishing before our very eyes—in fact, has almost vanished.

No longer do we enjoy or will this generation enjoy or many generations to come enjoy the right to work harder than the neighbor next door, and have a better home because of that harder work.

No longer will one man excel another at his trade.

No longer are we to have the right to enjoy that which we have worked so hard for.

No longer are we to have the right to secure for our children better opportunities than we had.

No longer are we to have the right to enjoy the freedom of initiative and individual enterprise.

No longer are we to have the right to be a Horatio Alger.

No longer are we to have the right to rise from rags to riches.

No longer are we to have the right to rise from newsboy to the White House.

For the future—and even now—we must submit to the dictation of the European minorities—walk alike, eat alike, dress alike, talk alike, worship alike (new Gods—not the old) and fuck alike, as ordered by the state, complete and total regimentation—that is what we are winning out of this war and that is to be our fate until another war or complete economic collapse wipes out the European ruling minorities, and a new regime and form of regulation comes up in their stead.

As we grow older we like to reminisce over the homes we liked to visit, the old plays, the old songs that brought us joy in our jaded youth. We call those the "good old days" that are gone forever—and they were good to us, even better in retrospect than they were at the time. Age tints our glasses—they were nice times—the people we knew then behaved as we were brought up to behave—that was the era of civility in human relations. Altho you were robbing your best friend in business, you were what was called courteous about it. The ruling classes enjoyed innumerable servants to assure them the comforts and ease of life—comforts that the mechanical age strives to afford the ruling classes now on their way into power—none of what the former generations knew as the niceties, the beauties of life are to remain.

Taste in food, eating habits, have all become regimented, have been revolutionized—inevitable with the migrations from the rural to the urban and industrial area.

The family group living together in the home, eating together good well-cooked wholesome food, has given way to mass eating palaces where thousands are fed daily at a fraction of the cost of home cooking—and at much less the wear and tear on the housewife, who now takes her place beside her mate in the commercial and industrial life of the country, reluctantly taking time out for child delivery—and menstruation is a bore—nursing babies is also passé, and so it goes. The last war developed, or at least brought out into the open, large crops of lesbians and homos to further complete the natural scheme of recreation.

To those who knew the old, were reared in it, this all seems a sacrilege, as they moan the passing of the past they knew and loved—their Santa Claus of life has vanished, and so will the generations to come look back upon the glory of their youth and wonder and worry and fret about the changes that have taken place about them and are taking place about them as they mature and ripen into old age.

Just as men and women lose their teeth, their hair, so their eyesight dims, their zest for screwing wanes, and so will they always long for the days when—nature is that way, always changing, never stagnate—life is change, change is life, life is perpetual motion from the womb to the grave, forever tearing down the old, building the new. Wars are great contributors to the process—just as fire, and water and pestilence and volcanic eruptions play their part.

Wars hasten the improvement and progress of life—wars are great levelers, one of nature's compensations for the human race. In present life, war takes up part of the slack created by the machine age, and man will fight until he has exterminated himself, for man is a self-destroying creature at best.

A submarine has just sleeked past, long and narrow and trim—a thing of beauty—her crew on deck, almost awash as she skimmed thru the narrow channel without a sound. She had been preceded by a large tanker, name unknown—PIII was all she had upon her bow. Our flag was at her mast—she was swift too.

But the submarine—the serpentine of the sea—my! that was something to see. It was the first time either Eve or I had seen one under way, down the river or up the bay.

Above me, upstairs in an apartment overhead, a little girl prepares her way—she plays her scales all thru the day—she never stops to see a ship and only ceases when she has to take her pip to pee.

Just above us is a man, crippled—sans furniture sans bed sans light—a candle seems to suffice, and old papers cover the floors for his bed.

His girl friend paid the rent—$1,600.00—in advance. He is a menance to health and a fire hazard of no small proportion. So much for the present.

And so I will slip back into the past again—as Roosevelt blasts drooling words from Ottawa to help Churchill help MacKenzie King, the Canadian Prime Minister, hold his job—and we nominate candidates for Lieut. Gov. that may well or well not seal the early fate of the nation and affect the lives of others outside our borders—because it is on trifles that great issues are made.

And Sidney Hillman decides to implement the newly formed but struggling labor party by taxing all union members for its maintenance. . . .

Yes! Times have changed—an American fast Scout ship roared by a British K and neither dipped their flags in mutual salute, recognition, courtesy, or respect—no greeting. Yes, that is a change too, just like the evolution of the military uniforms. They will get the seamen yet—aboard ship the changes have been slow, too much real tradition still there.

Sometimes I wonder—perhaps it's old age creeping up—if there is not a place for tradition and the lessons of the past. Is there not something in the best of what there was that might not well be preserved as a sacred heritage in the ever-changing scheme of things—might not there be just something a bit worthwhile preserving, something that would be of value and of guidance, something that might be a yardstick for the future generations yet to come. Or should there be no guide posts on the road of life?

On with the yarn. At the Los Angeles Biltmore on the Square, Grimsted the credit manager of the 1931 days was still on hand to welcome me with ample credit and good service—too much credit and too little cash has always been my downfall. . . .

It was a Sunday afternoon. I had been writing to Joe L. and several others—I dictated the letter to my secretary Frieda S. direct to the typewriter as I always prefer to do anyway. In that letter to Lilly as I went along I expounded on Frieda's charms and my attraction to her and my urge for her. Business was dull that afternoon—I had made my interest and eagerness clear in my letter to Lilly—so when I suggested that she close early, she acquiesced, and we went out to dinner and did quite a bit of drinking.

After dinner we strolled over to her apartment. She invited me in for a night cap—we were both pretty high by then. All thru dinner I had been making love to her and dancing with her between courses—I had had a perpetual hard on while dancing and talking to her and she naturally felt my hard prick up against her as we danced—we were both damn hot by the time we reached her apartment.

We had only been in the apartment a few minutes—hardly finished a drink—when while loving her on the sofa, I unleashed the old boy and stuck him in. She took it like a tigress grabs a raw piece of meat—how she loved it. I pulled my pants off—her drawers were already down and off—and we had the next one on the floor—as I came the next time, she pissed all over me and herself—hot pee—that was a real sensation.

Her cunt had been very wet from the first time I put my finger on it, as I fondled it and played with it and as I kissed her, caressed her bubbies and made love to her until I shoved my cock up into her—but the piss when it came was like the rush of the Niagara River over the Horseshoe Falls. It drove me nuts—she must have been holding it back for a long time.

She had to take everything off then and so did I—we were both too drunk to clean up much, so I spent the night there with her.

Somehow or other every time we fucked that night and she came, she peed on me too.

Well, it got me down—the next day and for days after that she would come to my room in the Hotel, ostensibly for dictation—she would strip and we would fuck—God, she was a find. She had me almost out of my mind for a while.

I grew so fond of her—wanted her so much—that I started to think of her seriously, about living with her—but circumstances in my turbulent life prevented, altered that course for me, so to speak.

The necessity for my going out to Ken Johnson's house did much to break it up. She came out there several times, but she couldn't take my fear complex spasms, my hysteria—as she discovered I was in hot water financially, her interest waned and I found new and better tail on the sides of the Hollywood hills that was ever ready and willing and no marital complications. Yes, she was a Jewess, too—in fact that seemed to be my Jewish sex cycle about that time.

I have always remembered Frieda and her piss—if I found myself in her vicinity even today I suppose I would hunt her up to see if she pees as well now as she did eight years ago—and she probably wouldn't.

I have always wanted to write, to express myself with my pen or typewriter, but I have never been able to do it well. In the first place, I cannot spell—of grammar or English composition I know next to nothing—I do not know a split infinitive from an adverb and my writing isn't legible, my vocabulary small, too small for writing and my pronouncing vocabulary much smaller. There are so many words I know but cannot pronounce correctly—because of my deficiencies, the writing of this letter is a slow struggle.

Hotels always make me hot and bothered—the maids, no matter how old or young always stir me up and I am constantly bothered by a stiff prick when in them.

In Los Angeles, they had several get-together agencies or matrimonial agencies or outfits that purported to bring lonely girls and boys together, of all ages and all types. I got in touch with several, paid one of them five dollars down, more to come—fucked the woman who ran the other, and started out on a cheap evening's adventure, selecting gals from the files that were willing to stay at home.

Most of the girls were of moderate means, working, nice girls but not follies beauties. I laid them all. The approach was usually a bit difficult—they were invariably the bashful type, a little stiff at first—but once thru the ice they were damn good lays and hot as hell. They had really joined for scratching—they lacked the personality to attract men and didn't have the chance of meeting them. Some had come to Hollywood for the movies—others were just off balance—most of them wanted to hold on once they got a grip on you. They were great letter writters—one learned of my name and hotel and she became quite a pest writing, phoning and following me around. . . .

The Burlesque Houses on Spring Street were a favorite haunt of mine, where I jerked off during the strip tease acts as they stripped off. Nearly half the customers openly played with themselves in and out of their pants—some fellows were too bashful to take their cocks out and come outside, so they came in their pants—others just shot their loads on the seats in front of them.

At night they had dance halls in the tougher sections. There you danced with a girl for a dime and a drink—if you bought her a round of beers she would fool around with your cock under the table and would give you a look at her cunt—for half a buck you could go in the can with her and she would jerk you off—for a silver dollar she would fuck or suck you off if you preferred.

L.A. also had the shows like they had in Chicago where you paid a quarter each time to see a little more—until at the end you got a look at a cuzy after you had shot a couple of bucks in quarters and a load in your pants. . . .

The urge to take one's life, particularly in periods of adversity, is very great—it doesn't make much difference whether one is drunk or sober. Frequently, the desire is greater during the height of a mental depression as one comes out of a hangover. . . .

Macy and the Borah people in Washington felt that while I was out on the Coast I should contact William Randolph Hearst. The great question came of the best way to reach him. . . .

About the middle of February, the *Los Angeles Examiner* had carried a full page editorial lauding Senator Borah's Washington Birthday speech to the skies and Macy and Thomas and I figured that old man Hearst might be in a receptive mood to consider Borah as his second choice if he couldn't put Landon across. . . .

In one of Melba's letters she suggested "the California situation is simply an episode, a stepping stone to other and better things." And in the same communication—"We need *plenty* in order to live up to our standard, and I propose we shall have it," and then she concluded with "You seem to have drifted very far away from me lately and I can't see why because I certainly have been with you mentally all the time—I have given our matters a great deal of consideration and have even refused several invitations to parties—which you know I love—to stand by and write to you and get your letters and messages and do everything in my power to lend my moral support."

I got involved in two situations—one was that I told the newspapermen in Los Angeles that I was leaving on a tour of the West Coast States in behalf of Senator Borah's candidacy; in addition, several females were a little too eagerly persistent so I had my name taken off the rack, as checked out, but I continued to stay at the hotel until the 1st of March when I moved out. . . .

[Melba, in New York, exhorted my father to greater efforts in settling her financial affairs.]

> For God's sake, don't go hay-wire now—unless of course you want to chuck the whole thing between us and go separate ways.
>
> I know we get just about what we deserve in the scheme of things, and when the big times don't come, it's because we have closed down on our capacity to let in the big thoughts—You and I have come through a period of some pretty small, mean, miserly thoughts, and it's high time for expansion.
>
> When you first went out there, you started out doing things—I don't mean extravagantly—but in a big way—and now you lose your grip—Why?—You certainly have more requisites than anyone I have ever known—brains, looks, ability, intelligence, shrewdness, blood and *guts*—I hope! . . .
>
> As for the future, if it doesn't scare me I don't see why you should be quaking in your boots. All I ask is to have my immediate obligations cleared and the next few months taken

care of, my health and the future to look forward to. I'd like your cooperation but even that I can do without if you want to stop and lie in the gutter. Let's not be noble any more, let's just work and stop thinking about how much you can or can't get until you start getting something, even if you only support yourself that's something and the little the children get will help with them. Who in Hell knows what the future holds for anyone much less just us—certainly the world is never going back to the old standards—a whole new scheme of things and different sense of values is being ushered in and I for one think it's all swell and healthy and I want to keep up with it and if our hard luck is forcing us to keep up with it while we still have our youth & health I say HOORAY for the hard luck. . . .

I certainly DO read your letters very thoroughly but perhaps you do not realize how vague and scattered you have been. Why not take stock of yourself about now—politics, sex, women, drink are only temporary escapes, you still have yourself with you and our relationship, which seems to have some importance to you. Your self-styled hermitage would seem a good place for that but perhaps the desert would be better as an expansive locale. . . .

Lovingly, Melba

Aimee Semple McPherson—the red-headed rip snorting high powered evangelist with "it"—that had the City of the Angels by the ear and the nation all atwitter, was still packing them in when I was on the Coast in 1936. She put on a great show of ranting and raving and threw the sex all over the place.

Judge Carlos Hardy, an old friend of Celeste Ryus, was her attorney—he offered to introduce me to the firebrand of feminine sex unleashed. I chose the hard way—it was safer—I went to one of her Sunday night revival meetings where converts threw themselves at her feet. Out there on the stage in her flowing robes accentuating every line of her body she was something as she exhorted her followers and the shekels poured in.

I waited until after the show was over and stood in line to shake her "mit" and a better close up look-see. Sitting in the balcony as she carried on, I got an urge, slight, but an urge. I thought I might try a piece of it—it looked like a good tail—in fact the idea was taking root until standing almost at the end of a line that must have had a thousand souls on it—mostly eager admirers eager to touch her hand, her gown, and get a thrill—my turn came to shake the hand of the Los Angeles Goddess come to earth. She was older, close to than her picture showed or klieg lights showed—she was worn and a bit haggard, exhausted from the night's effort and her long hand-shaking performance. Her hand clasp was limp like a wet cloth or dishrag—her appearance and handshake knocked all sex urge sky high—killed it there and then. Perhaps it was just as well—but she attracted thousands of men and women the country over.

I think that oftentimes we are attracted—I know I am—to some feminine personage, usually of the stage—not for what they are but for what their buildup or publicity has made you believe them to be. And so it had been for me with Aimee—the reality was a cold awakening. . . .

On the 3rd of March, Kendrick Johnson, who was head of the Borah-for-President Club in Hollywood, drove me out to the Warner's lot to keep an appointment with Mr. Randolph Hearst, that had been made for me by wire and telephone through the Editor of the local *Los Angeles Examiner*.

Cosmopolitan Pictures—a Hearst Organization producing Marion Davies pictures—was sharing part of the Warner lot—there was some tie-in between the two organizations.

Marion's bungalow was in a corner near one of the entrance gates—it was a palatial two-story affair that would have been a most comfortable mansion on any country estate.

I sent my name in at the gate and was ushered to the bungalow where a woman in the garb or dress of a trained nurse greeted me and ushered me into a large and beautifully decorated living room. A few minutes later, Mr. Hearst made his appearance. He escorted me into a large room he uses as a sort of combination office and study. He has a capacity for great cordiality along with his gracious dignity, which puts you immediately at your ease.

Marion's bungalow was very beautifully decorated—it was a two-story affair. After seven years, my vision of it is somewhat dim, but I was impressed.

In Mr. Hearst's study, on the ground floor, we sat informally and discussed the National political situation, as well as many other of his employees. One thing that did impress me was the fact that he seemed to feel much closer to Henry Clive than he did to Howard Chandler Christy. He looked upon Clive as sort of an incorrigible boy.

During the course of our talk the trained nurse came in to tell him that Governor Landon was on the long distance phone—Landon was Hearst's candidate for the Republican presidential nomination. When I heard this I suggested that I should leave the room, as I did not think I should be in on the conversation between Mr. Hearst and his candidate—Hearst protested that that wasn't necessary but nevertheless I went outside until he finished with the call.

The purpose of my visit was very largely to get the famous publisher to commit himself on Borah for a second choice.

Kendrick Johnson, the local Hollywood Borah leader, drove me out to the Warner Bros. lot and waited for me—

The old man was easy to get on with—showed a great fondness for Borah, but unquestionably felt that if he could put Landon across, he would have a more amenable man in the White House than the unpredictable Borah.

Marion's little dachshund was all over the place and Mr. Hearst exhibited a great fondness for the little dog—the glamorous Marion herself did not put in an appearance. . . .

I found Hearst at that meeting in Marion Davies' bungalow on the Warner lot exceedingly charming and delightful. The whole meeting was very cordial and very friendly—you would have thought we had known one another for years. We covered quite a range of subjects—different things we were both interested in. He agreed with me entirely regarding Fiorello—he thought the "Wop" had handled the Building Employees' strike in N.Y. very badly, although he mentioned that it hadn't affected any of his property. It was Mr. Hearst's observation at the time that F.H. was prone to lose his head at critical moments. . . .

I moved out to Kendrick Johnson's bungalow at 6225 Winans Drive, in the Hollywood Hills. It was the type of shack that one finds very largely in the Philippine Islands—there was a living room, fairly large, a good size bedroom and bath, also a large kitchen, and a screened veranda where one could work or meditate and look off over the valley of Los Angeles County for what that was worth, day or night. I gave a cocktail party there—was visited daily by Kendrick Johnson—had several girls working for me part time—and had a lot of fun keeping house. The rent was free, the only thing I had to pay for was the telephone, the electric light, the ice and the food. . . .

One of the great pastimes in California at that time was the interviewing of beautiful damsels that came to Los Angeles in search of movie stardom. They came in droves, yes, in fact by the thousands—they came with parents, they came alone, they came by train, they came by plane, they came by boat, they motored West, they came by bus, and they hitch-hiked.

Grimstead, the Credit Manager of the Biltmore, had told me of the practice some fellows made of coming in and renting a minimum room, and advertising for photographic models or for girls to "cast." Such advertisements in the local Los Angeles paper always brought a deluge of replies from the hopeful. The girls never seemed to be able to differentiate between the legitimate "calls" and the illegitimate snares. The Management objected seriously when the advertising was done by a guest with a minimum who did not patronize the hotel facilities. If a guest had a sitting room, bedroom and bath, and was a good spender, they let him have his fun. While I was out on Winans Drive Ken and I thought it would be a lot of fun to put such an ad in for material, so, we agreed upon a time for interviewing—an afternoon when he could get away from his girl friend, and I put an ad in with the telephone number and without the name in the local Hearst paper. The replies were numerous, appointments were made and Ken came over all ready for the prey. When he discovered the ad had been run in the Hearst paper, he became panicky. It seemed his girl friend had a hobby or made a hobby of reading the Want Ads in the Hearst paper—so, in his confusion he called her up, told her he had changed his plans for the afternoon and took her driving. I kept my local secretary, a skinny gal, Katherine Neuworth of 5946 Sunset Blvd., around for a cover, and what an afternoon and evening I had. Some of them came alone, some of them with their boy friends some with their mothers, etc. They brought numerous pictures of themselves in all degrees of dress and undress.

The parents or friends usually waited outside in their cars, while the young lovelies entered the den of iniquity. The procedure: they would come in, give their names, addresses and telephone numbers, show photographs of themselves, and then walk back and forth across the floor in order to give an idea of their carriage and demeanor. After that they would, without hesitation, display a full view of their limbs and at the first suggestion would disrobe and pose in the nude on a slightly raised platform, which I had provided for the purpose. After passing upon their lovely forms, with a feigned professional eye, I would then take measurements of the various parts of their anatomy, beginning at the ankle or the wrist and working up or down. There was a set professional procedure for this, and you not only took their measurements from their shoulders to their wrists, but from their armpits to their wrists, and from their hips to their ankles and from their crotch to their ankles.

Naturally I would get hot and especially excited when I measured their tits, or from their hairy cunts to their ankles—some of them, in fact many of them had their hair shaved off their "pussies." Howard Christy always deplored that practice—women all over the country are forever sending him pictures of themselves in the nude, with cunts shaved—and he contends it annoys him for they lose all their personality and look for all the world like "navel oranges."

My stiff prick would not be refused, and before more than one measuring job was completed I was laying my rod in up to the "hilt." Variety is the spice of life, and I fucked nine different girls that afternoon—they were young and luscious, beautiful creatures, all eager to please—women were legion in Hollywood then and jobs few. It was ideal for free tail—and I made the most of every piece of lovely ass that came my way. You didn't have to urge—the slightest suggestion was readily understood and they would roll over on their backs before you could get your pants unbuttoned. It was wonderful fucking—a perfect bliss—"Hide," "Hide," "Hide," how heavenly it was.

It is difficult at times, when I reflect, to recall the exact details of all that took place during the periods about which I am writing—especially things that I feel would be of interest to you. So often, in fact most of the time, I am only aware of what others do to me, and not what I do or say to others, and likewise I find that others are able to vividly recall what I have said to them or what they have seen me do, but are not able to remember what they said or did. In retrospect it is difficult without keeping a diary to have even a fairly impartial or unbiased picture of past events.

We always remember things we want to remember, both pleasant and unpleasant—and perhaps not always as they really were or as the other fellow saw them.

I have assiduously tried to hew to the facts as closely as I could, and a perusal here and there of old files and correspondence in order to check my recollection, has more often than not confirmed the correctness of my memory.

Things were getting pretty hot from a financial standpoint—trying to maintain Melba in New York and myself in California was difficult.

Between looking after Melba's property and trying to keep the Borah crowd in Washington from consenting to Campbell's plan for Borah to enter the California Primary, and take care of the lovely ladies at the same time, I was kept pretty damn busy. . . .

[The project to visit San Simeon was revived.]

[Hearst] invited me to come up to San Simeon for a further talk before I returned East. This I agreed to do—he then suggested that I come up the next evening, but I told him that I had just met a very beautiful girl at a cocktail party who was coming to have dinner with me that night—and he said that he understood my feelings and that he didn't blame me in the least for wanting to keep that date. So it was agreed that I come up on the day following.

I had always been eager to visit Mr. Hearst's palace, high up in the California Hills, along the shores of the Pacific, about half way between Los Angeles and San Francisco. Had I been sober I probably would have accepted immediately and cancelled the dinner engagement with the beautiful buyer from Bullocks-Wilshire, who I had met thru Celeste Ryus at a cocktail party given by an old Dowager—a friend of hers—Mrs. Grace G. of North Beverly Drive.

My staying over afforded me one of those rare thrills that only come once in a lifetime, as I shall now relate.

Grace G., an old girl with dough and a big house at North Beverly Drive in Beverly Hills—a friend of Celeste—was giving her annual cocktail shin-dig. She invited me at Celeste's suggestion. So I took Celeste in her Ford.

Altho I took Celeste out to dinner from time to time, it was more to have a male escort than to return my hospitality that she took me about.

It was a large party—the Hamilton P.s were there and many attractive people—but one woman in particular stood out. She was lovely to behold—prematurely gray—she was the belle of the ball. I didn't have any money, but I had a lot of nerve. The Mayor of the town and all the bigwigs and little ones, were laying siege to the lovely creature—she was a vision, and one I never forgot.

Well, your old man plunged in where angels were fearing to tread—and lo and behold, he made it—the grade, I mean. I couldn't take her anywhere and I was going home with Celeste in her car—so I tried it and it worked—I invited her to the Hermitage for a homecooked meal by the maestro, with the stipulation that she cook the dinner. I built it up and sold her a bill of goods—she accepted and I was thrilled.

Thereafter, at the party I had a hell of a time, dividing my time between her and Celeste. She was a widow, Mrs. Harriet Gardnier by name, of South Palma, supporting her two children.

That was the date I had when Hearst asked me to come to San Simeon. That's why I delayed my visit to the publishing Tycoon—I have seldom seen a girl as popular at any party as she was.

Well, I was living on air—I worked myself into a frenzy preparing for the event. She told me what to get and I borrowed the money from Kendrick to get the food and liquor. He was as excited as I was. She was by far the most attractive girl I had seen in California. It was to be my day of days. I was to have her—the loveliest of them all—up there in the Hermitage all alone.

She too seemed eager when I talked with her over the phone.

Slowly the day crept by. She had arranged for her children to visit friends that evening while she philandered.

It was dusk and I was waiting. It was still up there in the hills—the lights were beginning to twinkle in the valley below, the lights of that palpitating, fornicating town. Soon she would be there within the very portals of my shack—my cock was big and hard in eager anticipation.

Then the silence was suddenly broken by the ever-omnipresence of the instrument of mental torture—the tingle of the phone bell. I hesitated to answer—I didn't want intrusion, a conflict of foreign thoughts and ideas forced in upon me. I wanted only to contemplate the heavenly vision that was due to arrive any moment.

The ring was persistent—as if the caller were sure I were there or long distance trying to get thru.

Reluctantly I lifted the phone and there were sobs coming from the other end—it was my gorgeous guest of the evening. Haltingly she cried—a wire had just reached her that her mother had been scalded—she was on her way out the door to me when the boy gave her the message. Rushing back into the house, she phoned her mother's home in Detroit—she had been boiling beets and had pulled the pot off the stove and badly scalded herself. The doctors thought she at her age had scant chance of recovery. She phoned a brother in Texas—she was home alone—she asked me to come right over. She was going to fly to Texas on the first plane to Detroit—now that posed a question.

I said I would come at once—but she was way across the city in the Beverly Hills section—the taxi fare would have been several bucks. I consoled her as best I could—I was brokenhearted—my night of nights was shattered. I phoned Ken Johnson, told him my plight, pointed out the only salvage would be for me to get to her while she was still in a highly emotional state—and before the friends came in to console her. There was a chance, just a chance I might be able to break thru and give her what it takes to calm a female in a highly wrought-up condition. He agreed, conferred on the subject with his lady love, and rushed over in her car, driving me across the city to Harriet's apartment.

She was still very emotional when I arrived—I had gotten there before her children had been reached or friends had come to help her get away.

Ken departed and left me to my own devices. She was more delectable, more tempting than ever—my urge surged within me at the very sight of her. I took her in my arms to comfort her—I started to get a drink to steady her nerves, and we went to the pantry together. It was the first time I had been in her home—she seemed as distressed about the spoiled evening as the contemplated demise of her mother.

Before a drop of liquor was poured, she was again in my arms in another spasm of crying—I didn't wait, I don't think I gave much thought to what I was doing or where I was, but I was hot as hell and she was quivering. Then and there it happened, as I soothed her, stroking every part of her lovely body in passionate embraces—right in the pantry, with couches and beds all over the place, we fucked and fucked and fucked right on the pantry floor in one mad passionate orgasm after the other.

I never had the like before—I have never had quite the same since. When we were completely exhausted we slowly came to our senses. We both wondered why it had been the pantry floor that we had honored.

We hardly had time to adjust ourselves, our clothes etc. when the bell rang and the consolers started coming in to comfort her, and to help her pack. By the time the children arrived home she was quite the perfect mistress of herself. I didn't stay late—I had a long journey of crosstown on buses to get home to Winans Drive.

She was all I had expected and more—but it was all over too soon. As wonderful as it was, maybe she wouldn't have been as exciting or responsive if nothing had happened and she had been able to keep her date at the Hermitage.

She told me on the pantry floor that she had been hoping that I would love her at the Hermitage, that she too had had a great urge for me from the time she met me and had trouble sleeping the nights in the interim.

I heard from her from Detroit and wrote her for a while but left Los Angeles before she returned. We never met East, if she ever came here. Her mother died and I never saw her again—I have never forgotten her or her fornicating ability and capacity under stress and strain—she was wonderful, wonderful, wonderful. It was a passing fuck in the night, but one of those never-to-be-forgotten—the best pieces of tail are that way. A crowning thrill and then each on his and her way—never again to meet and if you were to meet, you would be unable to repeat.

It's the inspirational emotion of the moment that makes for the best in sexual intercourse—and accounts for bastards (born out of wedlock the result of a passing fuck under great emotional stress) being such unusual specimens—frequently superior mentally as well as physically.

Naturally I have often wondered about her, wondered what she is like now—then I was lean and just past forty.

I had had my clothes pressed and dry cleaned and my laundry all done for the occasion. . . . Although we started late—6:55 instead of 6:45 from Glendale—the Sunset

Limited reached its destination San Luis Obispo on time at 1:00 a.m.—and whereas I had left Glendale well fortified with the alcoholic snifters and in fact well heeled, when the journey started, I was cold sober when I got off the train and was met by one of William Randolph Hearst's secretaries who had one of Mr. Hearst's cars at the station to drive me the intervening fifty miles along the Coast to the Hearst Hacienda.

I think perhaps that here is a good place to insert the letter that I wrote Melba on my return from San Simeon—it was fresh then in my memory—and whereas I glossed over certain facts in order not to arouse her suspicions as to my amorous conduct, the letter in the main is largely correct, and so here it is:

Los Angeles, Calif.
March 31st, 1936

Dear Melba:

To San Simeon—took the 6:45 p.m.—the Sunset Ltd. from Glendale. Ken Johnson drove me over to the train—had my clothes pressed and dry-cleaned and my laundry done especially for the occasion—Before leaving fortified myself with a few snifters and was well heeled when the journey started—reached the San Luis Obispo Railroad Station at 1 a.m.—Was met by a Hearst motor car and driven the intervening fifty miles along the coast to the Hearst hacienda—it was a beautiful drive even at night—for miles and miles we could see the castle brilliantly lighted awaiting our arrival—the climb up the mountainside after we left the main highway and passed the Hearst flying field with its twinkling varicolored lights—the house is 1800 feet above sea level—reminded me of the winding roads up the Himalayas on the way to Darjeeling.

The first gate one comes to at the bottom of the hill is guarded by an attendant who takes your pass and then after unlocking the gate releases a secret spring so that the gate moves upward and aside in ghostlike fashion like a modern drawbridge—As we passed thru the attendant telephoned word of our arrival up the hill.

After that, we had to open and shut our own gates—formerly you had to pull a rope to do this, and on rainy days the water would run down your sleeve, but nowadays there are trippers, and when you ride over them, after going through the gate, the gate closes automatically behind you. In the enclosed fields, along the road approaching the castle, are white deer, llamas, ordinary deer, and in fact all manner and description of animals.

When we reached the castle we were met by a guard and a valet and I was escorted to the "Hero Room." I later told Mr. Hearst that I suspected I was assigned to that room with malice aforethought because of my worship of contemporary political heroes.

The room had a huge fireplace of ancient design and above the mantel carved into the granite block was the figure of the Madonna and Child. The ceilings and walls were paneled and beamed, with heroic figures of the ancients painted between the beams with Latin inscriptions in gold lettering below each figure, fully describing same.

The bed was a beautifully carved high posted affair—fit for a king or queen—in spite of my long legs I had to step up on a stool to climb into it. There was a large comfortable couch and several small benches before the fireplace—electric heaters in the wall were the only modern touch—the bureau was outfitted with a toilet set that would have made your eyes bulge.

There were big closets and a private bath finished in marble from ceiling to floor with a sunken tub and up to date glass-enclosed shower—the essentials for either male or female or both—with or without luggage—were at hand—There was a private entrance hall and a private exit—the windows had shutters that were in fact huge panels—they closed you in completely if you so desired—the Pacific ocean lay below and the flying field with its sparkling lights contradicted the medieval character of the room—a beautiful clock ticked the time away noiselessly.

The household had retired by the time I arrived—2:30 a.m., so I took to bed. Thinking of dear Diane and how she would have gloried in it all.

I did not awaken until 10:00 and then I wasn't called—I up and dressed and strolled around the grounds—a beautiful amphitheatre embraces a lovely outdoor pool that the ancient Easterners might well have envied. The indoor pool is even more beautiful—the finest in the world.

As you enter the castle there is a tremendous baronial fireplace and a room that must be nearly 200 feet wide and looks out over the mountains on one side and down over the Pacific ocean on the other—back of this big room is the dining hall, about 150 feet long—it is narrow, and at one end is another huge fireplace protected by glass screens—of course the fires were burning brightly in all the fireplaces—baronial banners hang along each side of the dining hall and the light comes in from small windows near the top—the tapestries are exquisite and the silver service is simply massive—the whole room smacks of a set prepared for the days of King Arthur.

One long table runs the full length of the room and is laden with fruit and every kind of preserve and cheese—there isn't just one centerpiece of fruit but there is fruit from one end of the table to the other—Yesterday was an off day—there were only thirty of us at the table for dinner and the room seemed empty.

There is another livingroom to the rear of the dining hall, not quite as large, but extremely attractive. It too has a fireplace. Off this room are innumerable little dressing rooms for men and women. Then there is a large pool room also on this floor and a sumptuous and beautifully decorated theatre with the most comfortable chairs in the world—one could curl up and go to sleep in them without any trouble.

It was apparent that it was the custom of the house to wander at will into the feast hall uninvited and unannounced—and so I entered and partook of a sumptuous repast (breakfast)—others were doing likewise—strange men and women—people I had never seen before in my life—were constantly drifting in and out, sitting beside me or across from me at the table, indulging in small nothings of conversation—no one being introduced; it seems that Mr. Hearst likes people to get acquainted without knowing the background or anything about one another at first.

After breakfast, I explored again—the Hearst home is a cross between the completed Taj Mahal in India and the uncompleted Cathedral of St. John the Divine on Morningside Heights; the real difference being that the Hearst castle is occupied and a center of great activity and industry.

In every nook and corner of the house and all about the grounds there are telephones galore—little boxes hidden in the trees, at various corners of the swimming pool and along the paths and the highways and the byways—on the tennis court there are two and the damn things are ringing all the time—in fact, there are phones everywhere except on the tennis balls, and when they are not ringing, the valet is bringing memoranda and messages which Mr. Hearst replies to pronto on scribbled memorandum sheets.

There is a large office staff ensconced in a sort of temporary field shack at the west driveway entrance that has every appearance of the headquarters of a military organization in the field, or the engineering shack of a subway construction gang.

There is a menagerie, but before you get to the menagerie you pass dog kennels where there are dozens of every breed of dog, all barking and howling; in the zoo there are bears and lions and tigers, panthers, monkeys, everything imaginable—bigger and better than the biggest circus—it would put Billy Rose's *Jumbo* Menagerie to shame.

When I returned to the castle I read the news bulletin in the large hall. They come in on a teletype machine just as they come into the newspaper offices.

The radio did not work so well despite the fortune that has been spent on it. For quite a time there was a great deal of static and interference from the ships still using the old spark set as they steam up and down the coast.

And so the time crept by till lunch—about 2 o'clock—Marion Davies stepped out of a panel in the wall of the large livingroom—the entrance, altho in the height of simplicity was most effective. She was greeted cordially by several friends nearby and went directly to the dining hall. Shortly thereafter the gong rang and everyone wandered in for a sumptuous buffet luncheon. Miss Davies sat down next to me and after a very respectable period had elasped, turned and introduced herself and was very cordial from then on.

I told Marion about Gloria Vanderbilt's grandfather, General Kilpatrick—How he married a little native girl while he was Ambassador to Chile—and insisted that the trustees of the Smithsonian Institute in Washington allow her tiny shoe to be displayed with his Civil War boots, saber and saddle—or else "no accoutrements" of his preserved for future posterity—And how Mrs. Commodore (Neil's grandmother) Vanderbilt was on the Mayor's reception committee that went down to the battery to receive the Ambassador-General's remains when they were brought back from Chile under naval escort. It seems that those within earshot were enchanted with the tale.

When lunch was about over, just as everyone was ready to leave the table, Mr. Hearst entered—his first appearance of the day—He espied me and greeted me most graciously and then proceeded to walk around the whole length of the table from one end to the other in order to arrive at my chair where he shook hands with me most cordially and was very friendly—the perfect host.

He then returned to the buffet table and helped himself to a heaping plate of lunch—after which he came back and sat across from me; at Marion's suggestion the others all left—except Dr. Barnham, who is a partner of Mr. Hearst in the publishing of the *Herald Express*—who remained for a few minutes—when he noticed the turn the conversation was taking, he left—He has a very nice blonde wife, a woman of about 40 or 42, who felt a little out of it because her square diamond ring was only 10 carats while Marion's was 16—wives are like that when their husbands are in business together.

On the way up to the ranch the driver said Mr. Hearst was famous for inviting people up and keeping them waiting days to talk to him—this was confirmed by one of the RKO executives present and several of Mr. Hearst's secretaries—so I was quite surprised and particularly pleased when Mr. Hearst launched forth immediately into the subject of my visit—we covered all that I had in my mind and from my standpoint it was a highly successful conference.

After lunch we continued the discussion interposed with political gossip and reminiscences—in talking with Mr. Hearst, he bemoaned the fact that there were so few men who could write politics or understood anything about them, in the newspaper field.

After our talk we watched Marion and her friends play Monopoly—tuned in on Bob Ripley's "Believe It Or Not" Hour and then to the tennis courts where Mr. Hearst played doubles with his sons, Jack and George and with Marion—while the others played the other courts. . . .

Mrs. John Hearst—or Jack Hearst—is a very attractive girl. Her first name is Gretchen—and they have the most adorable child I think I have ever seen outside of Melsing, Page and Marshall. At the age of two and a half he is a dead ringer for Charles Augustus Lindbergh, Jr.—makes a great fuss over his grandfather and his grandfather makes a great fuss over him—

Hearst does everything very easily, one never gets the impression that one might be intruding or interfering in any way with his comfort, his pleasure or his business.

Despite all of the conversation about rules for guests I did not see any, nor was I admonished not to mention death in the great publisher's presence. I suspect that this is all hokum.

The safety match covers bore Mr. Hearst's initials and the slogan "Buy American."

Tell Henry Clive that Marion's little dog Gandi was everywhere.

There was a Mr. and Mrs. Harry Joe Brown. Mr. Brown is the production executive at Warner's Bros.—Someone said that he had at one time been Lew Cody's valet—His wife, I do not know her professional name, played with Eddie Cantor in *Strike Me Pink*.

There was a countess who affected the pose of Helen Wills Moody on the tennis court and the screen manners of Greta Garbo in the dining hall of the castle.

Also a seventeen year old girl who expected to marry a man by the name of Eddie Kane, but he died just three days before that and Marion Davies had invited her up to help ease her grief—the death was sudden—too much Scotch I take it. . . .

There were quite a few single girls, ever hopeful of movie careers with their mamas to chaperone them. . . .

We finally got around to dinner and was that something. The place cards indicated it was not to be a help-yourself affair. While no one dressed, the women did change from sport clothes to tea gowns, and Mr. Hearst put on a dark suit. I found myself one seat from the squire's right and next to Mrs. Jack Hearst. Hearst and Marion Davies sat in the centre of a large table opposite one another. Miss Davies seems to be a kind person, a devout Roman Catholic, who does a world of good to people in trouble. She is charming, attractive, and intelligent. Ham Fish, I understand, gave her quite a rush on his visit to Mr. Hearst's other mountain ranch.

The chair between the squire and yours truly at dinner was at first vacant—to my mind most of the women there, in fact all of them, had nothing to offer and were most uninteresting to talk to and not particularly attractive to look at—

At the dinner table there appeared to be a great deal of excitement about some girl who was to sit between Mr. Hearst and myself, whose name it seems was Mary, but it meant nothing in my life, and so I continued to talk about farms and children with Mrs. Jack Hearst—you remember David Cowles told me Jack Hearst was looking for a farm.

Just about then there was a considerable flutter and all the males arose from the table, and Marion Davies got up to greet the late arrival who came over and sat down between Mr. Hearst and myself—while I had no idea who she was, I must admit that for the first time that day I was tremendously attracted, and while I realized that Mr. Hearst was her host, and entitled to all prior rights, I determined to let the very sweet and interesting creature know that I was on her right.

When the dinner was about over, I stole a glance at her place card and much to my amazement the letters on the same spelled Mary Pickford—and was I thrilled. Of course I had nothing in common to talk about as far as her interests and friends were concerned, but I quickly discovered that she knew a great deal about politics and was quite well aware of what was going on in the world outside of her own activities—She had been to Hong Kong and Shanghai and had an excellent suggestion for La Guardia, with the cooperation of John D. Rockefeller Jr., for improving the condition of the dwellers in the New York tenements—To me who was never over enthusiastic for her on the screen, she seemed most lovely. She appeared a bit depressed over the loss of Doug Fairbanks—She was still carrying the torch.

I had only two hours and a half to go before I had to leave for my train, and most of that would have to be spent in a movie, worse luck—nevertheless we chatted together after dinner while Mr. Hearst went off to his office, and when he returned we went to the movies.

On the front row most of the women were seated with Marion, and Marion had saved one place for Mary—but Mary said she preferred to sit in the back—that she did not think it was fair to leave the men alone, and so with a grand fanfare she refused Marion's proffered seat and entered a vacant row. We curled up in the big comfy chairs and I completely ignored the picture, directing my entire attention to the charming young lady beside me. But of course the hands of the clock moved surely around and eventually the major domo arrived to announce that it was time to go and so I had to leave the lovely creature.

Miss Pickford told me that her secretary, a Mrs. Lewis, had some strange phenomena about her. She said she had bought her dozens of watches but that whenever she puts on a watch or winds a clock it stopped and refused to go. It will go for anyone else but not for Mrs. Lewis. It seems this condition has existed all of Mrs. Lewis' life. Mary thought Robert

Ripley might be interested. You might mention it to him, or Ruth Ross when you see them, and if Bob wants to write to Mary or to Mrs. Lewis they will furnish him all the data. I wish he would write her anyway because I told her I would tell him all about it. It sounds like a real "Believe It Or Not."

In my enthusiasm over Mary Pickford, I forgot to mention that we had oodles of champagne for dinner and a perfectly gorgeous meal—more God damn fresh vegetables than I ever saw at this season of the year in my life—farmer that I am. It was novel being in an American household where the servants were American.

Riding in the same motor with me on the way back to the station down the hill, through the wild animal enclosures and thru the gates, were Lloyd Pantages and Mr. and Mrs. Harry Joe Brown and a bottle of Scotch. In the second motor for the train were four or five women.

When we arrived at the station, I discovered that Mr. Hearst had arranged for pullman transportation for all with his compliments. The couples had drawing rooms and the singles had compartments. . . .

That was a week-end visit to write home about—Hearst had crate upon crate of priceless art treasures piled high all around the place—never opened—things he picked up in his travels and for which place had not been found—he told me that the steps approaching the castle were not in proper proportion to the building and altho they were stone blocks imported from abroad at great cost, he planned to rip them up and erect a larger stairway. . . .

Devotedly, Ward

The creditors were crowding in on me—milkmen, stenos, models, icemen, bakers, cleaners, grocerymen, etc.

I hocked my camera and borrowed a few bucks from Johnson. . . .

After a last visit to burlesque houses and clip joints—I boarded a bus for Mecca—heading back East with my tail behind my legs like a licked dog and leaving a trail of bad cheques and unpaid bills behind me. . . .

It was a long hard ride—with the usual merriment of the loose women that boarded between terminals to ride with their bus driver boy friends free, or to see what could be picked up—at a buck a fuck.

One thing that Melba wrote that stuck for a long time—she said if I would only be myself instead of trying to be someone else I would really amount to something—I wonder who I was trying to be then and why I wasn't being myself. Was I just cunt struck—could that have been my trouble I wonder—I often felt it was. When coming to that conclusion I would rationalize that many of our leading citizens (our most successful men in all fields of endeavor) were cunt struck. That they fucked and chased to excess—and that that was true of brilliant and successful gifted women as well. Perhaps I lacked the essential gift of brilliance of mind to offset my preponderant sex urges and uncontrollable cravings—who knows—who will ever know. From Dallas I went by bus to Chicago.

[In Chicago] I was very short of cash—so I had to pull a stroke. I had the Blackstone Hotel porter get me a lower to New York—and a railroad ticket for same.

The charge for the tickets was put on my bill. When checking out, I gave my cheque for my room, restaurant, stenographer, barber, telephone and tickets—to say nothing of room service. Then I drove to the station, cancelled the reservation, turned in the tickets for cash and went down the street and boarded a bus for Washington, D.C.

That ride was boring and uneventful—but I wanted to meet Borah. . . .

I had a very pleasant visit with Senator Borah (the old firebrand of the Senate)—gave him a full report of the West and my talk with Hearst. He was pleased to learn Hearst was so friendly. . . .

I took a bus for New York—the end of my journey—I had been gone almost three months.

When I arrived at the bus terminal I phoned 2 Beekman Place. I had wired the time of my arrival to Melba—but there was no Melba to meet me which was unusual—the phone had been disconnected—I had tried to reach her by phone from Washington, but the phone never answered.

Finally I got hold of the apartment superintendent and he told me that Melba had moved out that very day bag and baggage and furniture—I was disconsolate—I phoned Joe Lilly and told him. He suggested sending her a wire with a request for a delivery report—this he did for me over the phone. Then I called up my old standby when in trouble, Jane H., and went down and spent the night with her—I would have stayed longer but she had a big black cat and I don't like cats—altho I liked screwing Jane. Joe had given her a rush and a bit of screwing while I was away.

All night the telegraph company tried to deliver the message—finally in the early hours of the morning they reported that they had delivered the message to Melba at the Sutton Hotel, a cheap joint on East 56th Street.

That had been one hell of a night—with me in a nervous uproar. I don't know how I ever got in hand enough to screw Jane, but I did.

The next day I got together with Joe and learned all he had to offer and then I phoned Ruth and imparted the glad tidings to her. She was jubilant—at last I was free, for her alone—but I wasn't. It was a great shock, a blow to my vanity—I had Ruth—she was a sex delight but I was devoted to Melba and the children.

I couldn't get Melba on the phone or get her to agree to see me or answer my wires.

I got in touch with Watterson Lowe and rented his hall room for $3.00 a week (in his tenement apartment at the corner of 41st and Second Avenue)—he was away at sea most of the time so I had the apartment with its kitchen, largely to myself. The only annoyance was the few days a month when he was home—then he would have his boy-friends—lovers—in to spend the night—black or white—and I was always nervous about running into them and interrupting their pleasures. . . .

Some days after I wrote Melba on the 24th—she agreed thru Joe Lilly to meet me in Central Park. . . .

Melba said that she was wasting her talents with me—that she had as much as the twins [Gloria Vanderbilt and Thelma Furness] and that she was going to marry a man with lots of money to take care of her and her harassment over finances. Freddie Davenport had been very attentive to her during my absence—it had turned her head a bit. Joe Lilly and Charles Bayer, my newspaper friends, according to Tommy Smith, had also been smelling around.

Well, we decided to do the thing quietly without rancor and without publicity. Freddie Davenport's firm, Chadbourne Stanchfield and Levy, had been advising her thru a stooge named McGrath—a guy who did the dirty work for them.

It was decided that she sue me under the name of William W. Smith and bring the action in Westchester.

I agreed to give her the phoney evidence thru one of my friends. First of all I talked it over with Morris Maltzer, whose office I used for certain mail and phone calls (Watterson Lowe didn't have a phone)—but I decided that Morris was not the man for the job so I took it up with Julius Hallheimer—this was all in the way of stalling—it seemed to throw our friends and the lawyers for as much of a loss as it did me.

Everyone seemed fond of us both and felt badly that we had come to the parting of the ways.

I was torn between two emotions—my devotion to Melba and the children and my relief at being a free agent and clear of the responsibility and burden of supporting the entire family. I have never been a steady provider and the fear of want of tomorrow has always harassed me to death—so it was a relief.

As to Ruth, I had no intention of getting hooked to that Semite—I would have cringed in shame to have been caught out in any Christian Assemblage with her.

Well—I stalled along hoping for some solution that would mean a solution of our marital rift. . . .

Joe Lilly and Gene Early tried to get me the job of Secretary of the Midtown Tunnel Commission—building the tubes to Queens under the East River—but it went elsewhere. . . .

One night after my return from the West I asked Melba to have a steak dinner with me at "Rudy's" Second Avenue Rail—a place famous for its beer and the multitude of free lunch of all kinds of sliced meats, pickles, bread and butter, cheese and crackers, etc. and beer only 5¢—hot dogs were on the house.

While we were dining there, Tommy B. entered with Betty Campbell and a new girl, a nurse he had picked up in a Third Avenue Bar a few days previous when he had first gotten his Army bonus money (from World War I), and started drinking it up as fast as he could.

Her name was Mary—she was a beauty with a very lovely body—as I was afterward to learn.

Mary was a nurse at the Ruptured and Crippled Hospital and a bit fond of drinking herself—in fact I think she preferred drinking to screwing.

Tommy showed me his wallet which for him was bulging with dough—he bought everybody drinks and then we pretended we were going out to piss. We went across the street to another bar where Tommy told me all about Mary and his bonus money and his desire to ditch Betty, while in the gin mill several English beauties leeched on to us to our delight and theirs, at Tommy's expense.

Finally we got away from them—returned to Rudy's and drank until closing time. We insulted Betty and she went home, so we got a bottle from Rudy, and Melba and Tommy and Mary went to Watterson's with me—he being away on a ship.

We were all pretty drunk—the girls stripped and so did we. Melba went after Mary like a house on fire and Mary came right back at her.

Melba certainly loved to love girls—any hot number would do her—it finally got too much for me so I had to give her some of my rod. God, how she fucked me that night—while I was screwing Melba, I was sucking Mary—poor old Tommy was very drunk and confused and tried to get his pecker up for Mary to suck, but he had no luck. Finally in despair, he went down on Melba—after I had left her with my load.

At dawn I took Melba to the Sutton and her children—it had been quite a night. I returned to Watt's.

Later in the morning, Tommy, wanting beer, went out for a few bottles. I was in the tub soaping myself—the bathroom door opened onto Watterson's bedroom—Mary was lying nude on the bed reading Casanova. It was too much for me—I got up out of the bath, soap suds all over my cock (erect) and gave Mary one of the best fucks I ever had out of her—returning to the tub as soon as we had both come.

Tommy came back shortly thereafter. Noticing the wet trail of my footmarks and the wet bed, he accused us—but we denied the allegation with a flimsy alibi.

I don't think Tommy believed us, for the next morning before daybreak, he got Mary up and out of there before I was awake—he couldn't do much for her with his cock, but he was determined that I was not to reap the benefit of his filling her with liquor at his expense.

After that I went to Cleveland for the Republican convention by bus. I stayed at a very cheap hotel with some farmers. I saw a good deal of King Macy—he was busy doing what he could for Borah but it was by then a lost cause. Landon had it in the bag. . . .

The most interesting event of the convention was a press interview—mass interview that Borah gave during the first day of the Convention—It was the greatest intellectual treat of a free-for-all give-and-take I ever saw, Borah matching wits with the ablest political correspondents of the nation. He never appreared to sidetrack or dodge—he stated his position on the platform and what he proposed to have in it. He was fighting to the end but while he got his way as to platform planks he wanted he didn't get the nomination—and he knew he was too old to try again.

I visited Hoover in his hotel room after he had delivered his oration to the convention—a speech which he had hoped would sweep the crowd off their feet, and cause the convention to nominate him by acclaim. It missed the mark—it fizzled out—Hoover was a sad sight that night, dejected, forlorn and neglected. . . .

I was with Borah during the balloting—he too was alone in his room with but his secretary, Cora Rubin standing by. She was depressed and weeping—they both knew that the Senator's last chance to be President of the United States had come and gone. He would be too old to try again—he died before the next one.

American crowds are wonderful—when they think a man may be a winner they crowd around to get on the band wagon—they push and fight and jam to get near him—but when the tide turns and he is thru or licked, they desert him like rats deserting a sinking ship. Then he is left severely alone by all, to commune with himself and contemplate the hollowness of his fellowman. He hasn't changed—he is the same fellow, with the same ability and charm—but the crowd has changed, they have raced off to idealize another hero newly made—and so it goes. . . .

I returned from the Cleveland convention of 1936 to start working for the Lawrence Whit Public Relations Organization on a commission basis. . . .

I got a room and bath at the Hotel St. Margaret for $7.00 per week to be paid for as I could. I moved myself and papers—they were voluminous—things Melba had turned over to me.

It was a creep house where men took rooms and Dave C. the night manager sent them girls to assuage their sexual appetites—and some brought their own women—it was cheap. Stanley H. had lived there in a drunken stupor for several years before La Guardia gave him a job as a Deputy Commissioner of Welfare and then made him "Secretary to the Mayor."

[I remember the St. Margaret and Dave C. very well. My father took me there, introduced me to Mr. C. and told him to get me a woman whenever I wanted one and charge it to him along with the room rent.]

Ruth came there one or twice—on several occasions when we got real tight we stayed at the Coolidge Hotel across the street from the St. Margaret for hours at a time and had chinese food sent in with liquor while we screwed hell out of one another often rowing, beating, scratching and biting in our blind passion.

Melba came to the St. Margaret several times to be fucked. Sometimes I never left the Hotel from one day to the other just laying there fucking my head off.

I picked up a waitress in the Savarin—a hostess. She lived in Brooklyn but came up occasionally for a matinee. She was Alva H. who lived at the Montague Hotel—103 Montague Street, Brooklyn.

One night during the Olympics which were being held in Berlin, Joe L., a Tax Commissioner afterwards president of the Board, and Stanley H. (the Mayor's Secretary) came up to see my dirty movies and get fucked. Dave C. got us three lovely girls—when the pictures started running the boys got hot. Stanley H. wasn't drinking although a bottle was at his elbow—he ignored it, but Joe made up for that—as they got hot they started work on the girls. In no time at all the dames were stripped and the boys had their cocks out—the girls licked them and one another—soon they were in keen competition with the movies. I have trouble getting an erection with professional "whores"—my prick wouldn't rise. They all worked on me but I left the fucking to my illustrious guests—Stanley between long distance calls to the Olympic officials in Berlin tore off two pieces while Joe got in three—Joe had to try each girl. After the girls departed Joe became remorseful—raving about his lovely wife and adorable child and worrying about getting a dose of clap or syphilis. He was so worried he washed his cock in piss, cold water and soap and then took three prophylactics—Sanatubes. After Joe's cleansing outburst we went to dinner at the Brass Rail and Joe swore that never, never, never again would he be untrue to his wife—he was worried to death—he was always that way after every promiscuous fuck. After dinner we went back to the St. Margaret—Joe wanted to take another prophylactic. In the lobby was a pretty prostitute—a blonde. Joe got "het-up" all over again—when we got up to my room he had me phone Dave for the girl—he wanted to talk to her about her life. She came right up and in no time he forgot all about her life's story and was fucking her on my bed—five dollars' worth. When she departed he started to rave and cry about his wife and child as he administered another sanatube—it's guys like Joe who enrich the Sanatube Company.

Across the Street in the Coolidge, on the floor level with my room, were two girls, sisters, with a man who was the husband of one of them. I often saw them having a three cornered workout—it would get me so hot that I would jerk off watching them. One night when I had the light on they noticed me playing with myself—the next day when the husband was out they ran around nude near the window waving to me and playing with their pussies—as I jerked off. After several days of this monkey business I signaled one of them to come over, it was right after supper. The girl had no sooner reached the hotel and gotten up to my room than Melba arrived with some papers for me—but really for a fuck. I hurriedly placed the girl—she spoke only French—in the room next to mine occupied by a Spaniard antique wood worker named Mario and I asked him to look after her until I could get Melba satisfied and out of my way—this he did with Dave standing guard to protect my interests until Melba left. Then I took on Frenchy. She couldn't understand English and I couldn't understand French but we both knew how to screw. All this took place after Melba had sued me for her divorce on the grounds of adultery—and that adultery if there had ever been any real adultery that she knew about and disapproved of she was condoning by her very acts at the St. Margaret. . . .

One time when Melba came to the St. Margaret to be fucked, I tied her hands over her head to the bed posts and her feet to the foot boards or iron, then with my belt I beat or lashed hell out of her until I drew great welts and blood in some places. She loved to have her cunt lashed and slapped, it excited her terrifically and me likewise and then we went to it.

On this last occasion Melba begged me never to use her weakness against her in fighting the divorce. (Whenever a wife has intercourse with her husband regardless of the marital status, in the eyes of the law she has condoned all of the previous acts which she has claimed to disapprove of and object to—many a woman has lost a good divorce case by just such weaknesses.)

During that summer I spent much time on the beaches with Ruth G. going out in the morning for a picnic supplied by her with her liquor, and in her car. . . .

Forty-seventh Street was quite a street—gangsters, murderers, bums, drunks, gamblers, broken down actresses and actors—down and outers of every class or strata of society found their way to 47th Street. Pimps and fairies mingled with the whores, racetrack touts, taxidrivers of very questionable repute, Chinese, Japanese, soldiers, sailors, niggers, Filipinos, Marines, newspapermen—all up against it, hiding out—the drunks were legion.

If you preferred to sleep in the daytime and to stay up all night, Forty-seventh Street before the war was the place. The lights glared there all thru the night—not only was there the reflection from the gay white way always overhead (half a block away) but the hotel lights and signs that were 47th Street's own, announcing the wonders of each tavern's delights or of oriental foods or Chinese laundries, glittered and gleamed from sunset to dawn. I loved it—I was drawing $25 a week for expenses and entertaining—that meagre sum paid for for my rent, for my food, for my liquor and for my women—life was something then.

I bluffed my reports—I had to.

I got up late every day between 3:00 and 4:00 in order to check in.

All night long the street teemed with activity—when the saloons closed the drunks sat on the steps (of the old brownstone rooming houses) and screamed and swore and fought till dawn. Brutal brawls would take place in the wee small hours of the morning—swearing and cursing they would fight and roll in the gutter, women and men, men and men, women and women (the women were the worst).

The police never seemed to bother very much. They brawled and beat one another and fucked as they rolled in the gutter—with or without clothes as the case might be. The daughter of a prominent physician—he wealthy but she a drunkard—would swizzle until the "dumps" put her out screaming—then with an extra bottle of fire-water bribed from some bum she would sit up until dawn night after night—in bedraggled rags, upbraiding the rats who surrounded her, eager for a few extra drams of her alcoholic poison. She would curse them and defame them and feed them liquor in return for their admiring attention.

Life flowed thru that street at its height from midnight to morn—drinking, screwing, brawling—men and women, their pagan emotions bare for all to see unashamed, unabashed—no inhibition on that "drab" (by day) and tawdry glittering by night street.

It might have been an outcast haunt in Shanghai, for food, lodging, liquor and women were cheap there—and sometimes one would be killed.

One night I ran into a very shabby fellow—dejected depressed, listless, and a bit dazed—hardly recognizable—He was loafing in front of one of the creep houses. The last time I had seen him he had been a spry snappy active young assistant Vice-President of the Bank of America in charge of that institution's Southern Correspondent bank.

At the bank he had always been well groomed and attractive—vital and immaculate.

He had been let out when the National City absorbed the Bank of America—then had come the crash of '29. Banks had failed all over the country—there had been a superfluity of banking men and business-getters—there was no place for him. He stood the degradation—the failure—as long as he could—then he committed suicide.

Men having failed in life or on their way up from the depths of humble surroundings somehow seemed to find their way into the 47th street "Maelstrom"—some never got out—some sank further into the oblivion of the bowery slop houses or the Bellevue Alcoholic ward or the City morgue or potters field.

Some merely stopped there on their way down the toboggan. Coming down, they cushioned there and picking themselves up, rose again to a proper place in the sun—others just gave up.

Some went up and then returned as adversity overcame them once again—some never descended so low again. Those that climbed back were mostly men.

Women when they go down down down to the depths of poverty and depravity or become dope fiends or alcoholics, seldom redeem themselves and reclimb the social economic ladder.

The ravages of time—the trials and tribulations—the worries and cares tell on women sooner than on men, leaving a devastating and irradicable scar—women show their misery physically more plainly than men. Their vitality, their virility generally lessens faster with the years than with men.

During the summer months not only were there fights and brawls to keep up the hubbub, but juke boxes, the small string instrument orchestras, the little tavern dance bands, the broken down piano players, the vocalists that huskily rasped out their bawdy tidbits for a glass of grog, a crust of bread or a night's lodging—in order that the visiting firemen and their lady friends of questionable character might be amused.

It all added up to life as she was lived on New York's tawdriest street—47th between 6th and 7th Avenue. That was my home from the middle of June until the middle of August 1936.

There was enough going on at night to make you forget your own troubles and to keep you up until you fell off to sleep near day break.

Watching the men register at the desk and ask for a girl or register with a stray street walker who was always a sight. Men are just as shy in New York about their screwing (the would-be cosmopolite and sophisticated of the big city) as the country yokel, miner or farm boy from the hills of Nevada visiting a crib for a lay. Their entrances are just as nervous and nerve wracking and their exits as embarrassed—and they are hot as hell when they enter, agitation personified—and they all wonder as they depart why they bothered, what the hell had been the necessity—worried for fear they may have gotten a dose—and why hadn't they stuck by their old woman or their steady.

Even the regulars, who were cheating on somebody and came every week on a certain night, were always just a little bit timid—a little ashamed—as they made their arrangements with poker-faced Dave C. for the sexual festivities of the evening. Even the half potted were bashful.

Vice ungarnished is dull and uninspiring and as every whore or madam knows once a male has shot his load remorse sets in and he wonders why he took the trouble. Then the cunt stands cold before him unadorned and shorn of the glitter and glamour of a stiff prick illusion—he might just as well have used the knot hole or a bit of vaseline or putty thinks he, and maybe it would have been just as well or better. . . .

I had gotten behind in my rent at the St. Margaret a matter of six or seven weeks. Dave, (the night man), or Leonard, (the day man), never spoke to me about it, but one day the new owner asked me if he could have a little something on account. I had just had my expense money raised to $35 per week payable every 15 days—and so I announced that I not only would pay him a little something on account, but I would pay up my entire arrears and move out. That meant an immediate search for a new place. Sunday was the day—I read *The New York Times* furnished room and furnished apartment want ads—I checked those I thought would be desirable and sallied forth afoot.

At 904 Park Avenue two flights up in the rear I found a large combination bed room and living room with kitchenette, bath and dressing room—it looked out on an attractively furnished garden—summer tables, colorful umbrellas, swings, flowers, a little pool with fish, etc. and backed up on the Todd Hunter School.

James S., former head of the National City Bank whose wife was Fifi S.—whose girl friend was Flo Leaves of the Indian Guide divorce case fame—owned the house. It adjoined his palatial home on the northwest corner of 79th Street and Park Avenue—the rent was $50 furnished, with linens, until October 1st then $50 unfurnished—Melba had all the furniture so I had no choice about a furnished or unfurnished place.

I was favorably impressed—upon leaving I noticed a very beautiful woman in a dressing gown at the door of the ground floor apartment. She apologized and said she thought I had rung her bell—she was the tenant with the garden apartment. I discussed the apartment house with her and she invited me in, offered me a drink, etc. That decided me—what with a neighbor like that, life should be very pleasant—her apartment was attractively furnished—her living room had a large piano, and her furnishings were all smart and expensive.

From the mailbox or doorbell I found that her name was Harriet S.—before I got back to the St. Margaret I tried to telephone her but her phone was private (non-listed) so I sent her a screwball sentimental wire and some flowers and asked her to phone me which she did about 8:00 o'clock—she invited me back and I came arunnin'—we had a bit to drink—Harriet was quite tight and quite decollete.

She excited me so I spent the night—she had an attractively appointed bedroom and bath, and a full size kitchen and dinette well stocked—she was amusing, full of fun, gay and carefree—and loved to fuck.

The next day I rented the apartment and moved—kissing the St. Margaret goodbye. Tommy B. helped me move and Ruth G. loaned me her car to save cab fare, etc.

All my life I have had a weakness for a home, a place to cook, to entertain—I've always preferred entertaining at home more than going out to night clubs, restaurants, etc. Meals at home mean much more even when I have to cook them, serve them and wash the dishes and clean up afterwards.

Harriet S. was a former Ziegfeld beauty of the bygone days—she was a lot of fun. . . .

That was when Park Avenue was a junk pile—a haven for goats and tramps—it was but an open cut and the New York Central and the New Haven roads burnt coal for steam in their locomotives. . . .

Being free I met many new and attractive women—although I was hampered by a lack of cash. . . .

The incidents were not worth recording in detail. There were others that I have already mentioned and still others that I will discuss as I go on. . . .

I sometimes wonder why I pound this out—I doubt if you will ever read it or if anyone will ever have the fortitude to wade through such a mass of personal junk.

Recently I have been going to funerals of certain friends—something you never do until you have passed the half century mark—and the futility of it all weighs in upon you whether you attend an orthodox Hebrew service, Romanist, Presbyterian or what have you.

Then I listen to people yap who have gone in for science, astrology or mysticism.

Heard the arguments of those who believed in reincarnation.

For myself I do not believe that the set of the planets at the time of our birth has anything to do with our dominant characteristics.

If there were anything to such fancies, it would have to prevail at the time of conception—not after the egg is set and the child has reached the sufficient development to step forth on its own.

Nothing can affect the human's mental processes at that time—it must occur at the time of the blending of the two bloodstreams that produced the fertile egg—so astronomical effects at womb ejection are meaningless.

I seriously doubt if there is any hereafter—except as parents live on in their children and their children's children until the third and fourth generation.

Just as the fruit of the tree fertilizes the tree—unless the fruit is removed and commercial and synthetic fertilizers substituted—so the human goes back into the soil, in the flesh or as ashes—and makes in either case excellent fertilizer for crops to feed his children and his children's children—or being civilized, we waste that fertilizer because of fanatic rituals embraced by man in the various sects that abound the world around. . . .

You cannot deny nature's plan of checking development—we will always have in nature our feasts and then our famines—water will not run up hill unless forced by man using a greater energy than the flow of water—then you can only force it up—it will not run up of its own volition—and after you force it up it will quickly seek its own level.

You cannot waste without wanting—we here have wasted our resources and manpower for eleven long years, and now the nation wants—except for the war plant workers (who are but viciously overpaid draft dodgers) and yet the war workers want, too, because their ill gotten gains will not buy them the things they wish for since they are nonexistent, for Mr. Roosevelt did not permit us to accumulate in times of plenty.

When we had much, our stocks of cattle, pigs and grain and capital were wantonly destroyed by the New Dealers until our National Granary was nearly empty.

It is tragic to see a great nation that developed free enterprise and individual initiative—a nation which was founded to such a great and unlimited degree to escape the embitterments of nationalistic clashes, cramped economy, religious prejudices—surreptitiously embrace all the false and misguided tenets and prejudices of the embittered and warring peoples of the world at the colossal sacrifice of our own blood on the field of battle and the destruction at home of the very institutions that we diligently and painstakingly built to get and keep away from the European mess.

If we are to give the people of the world all our resources every time they go to war they will always go to war and our standards of living will always be lowered by the amount that we raise theirs.

We are suckers for honeyed words—the mental process of the masses the world over is low—the people of China, Russia, Japan, Italy, Germany, England and the United States are fall guys for catch phrases and grinning dictators.

Hitler murders a few thousand jews who had tried to take over the life of the German people, so he is a beast—Stalin exterminates millions of Christians but he is a great hero because after several years of desperate fighting with our Military supplies, our tanks, ammunition, arms, airplanes and food (much of which he cannot use) he is able to drive the enemy (a former ally in rape) out of his own country.

The jews objected to Hitler's extermination program—the Christians were docile about Stalin's massacre of the Russians.

We were propagandized, pushed and shoved into the war by the jews on the side of the murderer of Christians who had by stealth been trying to undermine and destroy our government and our way of life.

Russia, where the standards of living had fallen as low if not lower than in China, was held before us as a great ideal to be obtained.

The jews were at the bottom of it all—they were the real agitators—for war and the overthrow of our constitutional government.

When war finally came—where were the jews? In hiding—using every kind and known type of subterfuge to avoid the draft and getting away with it. . . .

Today we have rabble rousers who are the leading inciters for their own political benefit—in order to perpetuate themselves in office—encouraging the jews to follow their sect line—having the negros front for them on the question of race discrimination.

I can remember when I courted Jewesses—loved them and fucked them—most jewish women are well trained in cock sucking—both the married women and the young girls.

When I had my own office I was scrupulously careful never to show religious prejudice—in fact, I didn't have any—I had as many jewish girls as Christians working for me.

Well I must get on with my story—but every so often I find it necessary to blow off about the jews—they are such mean petty stinkers—and yet there is little to add to the detailed dissertation I indulged in somewhile back when I started that section of my letter, so I will return to the subject matter at hand—my life in 1936 as I recall it.

I gave a party on my birthday that year at 904 and another in December the day Edward the VIII abdicated—I need not go into the details of Wallis Warfield's love affair here as you know them better than I do.

You have read from your Aunt Virginia's diary how those girls, Virginia Page and Wallis Warfield and Emily Merryman got around together—what (as silly young things) they thought of the then Prince of Wales—how they eavesdropped at the head of the stairs in your grandfather's house at 941 North Calvert Street to your father's wooing of your mother, and their comments thereon—and how years later I was unable to recall Wallis Warfield the debutante but always retained a vivid recollection of Emily Merryman, the other one of the trio—who was the first girl to kiss me at the wedding after your mother and I had been joined in holy wedlock. . . .

The sex life at 904 was so rampant that I have a hard time getting around to my other activities.

The bankruptcy had cleared a few debts away and for a time I was in the clear but the farm soon got me down. While it was run as a corporation and worked as such people were always trying to get around the company at me or suing the company—then when I lived at 2 Beekman Place I ran into heavy debt trying to get by with Melba and the children and their schooling on a nickel—and keep going—there were the bills from the West Coast hotel and my travels for Borah etc.—they had a way of sneaking up on me—people were always inadvertently telling my creditors of my whereabouts, and the process servers were forever on the search. It was a useless performance but harrowing to me—I have for the most part lived the life of a hunted man, of a criminal at bay—I knew they couldn't do anything to me—I had not stolen—but I was always getting threatening letters from lawyers and investigators and being hounded constantly by process servers, many who perjured themselves so that judgments would be taken without my knowledge and I would find myself in contempt of court for failure to answer summonses in supplementary proceedings which had never been served—but the process server had falsely sworn to having served me in order to collect his fee with the least amount of trouble.

For years I have been judgment proof—I have had nothing that could be attached—I have earned little yet always they are after me. It hasn't been a happy state of affairs—and has given me what some might call an inferiority complex.

If it had not been for the adoring adorables to bolster my deflated ego I would have expired long ago. To always be expecting such unpleasantness is in itself depressing, disturbing and mentally unhealthy—in fact it affects everything and everyone about you adversely.

Then the trips to court—waiting, waiting, waiting for your case to be called. . . .

[My father rented an apartment on 83rd Street with Tommy B. and then attempted to sublet it at a higher price to create some income.]

Peg H. of 43 West 85th Street and then 307 W. 76th Street was quite a woman—she had two kids and was trying to keep going by renting apartments—she lived with the children in one room in the house at 43 West 85th Street near Central Park West—Peg came to look at the apartment for a client.

Peg spent several nights with me at 83rd Street both when Tommy was there and away—I gave her $25 to get her real estate brokers license with.

I didn't know what it cost then but she got something for

herself out of it. I helped her with small sums for food for the children and we had a lot of fun—she was a wonderful fuck, just built for screwing—enough animation to give her ass to you with lusty thrusts—and she loved it—and so did I.

When she came the whole world could know it for all she cared and she would let out a snort that was something—while she was holding on she had a grip that was nobody's business—and her flood was something. Her first name was Margaret but she liked to be called Peg.

We spent a good deal of time together that month and it helped to get over the bumps—I received three different deposits on that apartment that failed to materialize—they all dropped out—some wanted their money back when they decided they weren't going thru with the deal—but I was relentless, I needed the dough. I never saw a place where so many wanted it on first inspection and then backed out after other members of their family would disapprove.

When renting one or two rooms you have only the individual who is going to live in the place to contend with—but when you rent a seven-room apartment, their mama and papa and the seven little dwarfs all have to be considered—to say nothing of the sisters and the cousins and the aunts. . . .

The stories of those negotiations would fill a volume. That was a tough neighborhood and we were handicapped not having a phone—we didn't turn on the electricity, we had only the gas that came with the rent, we used candles and were out most evenings—there are few sections of New York that are so unpleasant. . . .

Four or five bucks, sometimes three a week, would get a room in that area. There were higher priced ones, and suites or front rooms for the whores—street walkers—the massage artist—the dancing parlors etc. where every variation of intercourse known to man was indulged in. . . .

Christmas rolled around and found us very low in funds—Tommy and your father. I had bought presents for the Ettl children and Joe Lilly's, and for Melba's—she and the children were living at 14 East 60th Street and she was sliding by with work at Sonia's now and then, and help from the girls—Morgan twins. . . .

Tommy was contributing a couple of dollars for his room so he had the room with the brass bed—I slept on the floor.

After selling the plates and brass lamp it occurred to me that the parlour (or living room) furniture might have a value, so I called in a half dozen antique dealers to make offers—two were enraged that they had been called to look at such junk—one offered $75 cash to take it out at once—then I asked $250—another went to $125. Then I was sure I had something—finally one fellow who started at $100 came up to $200 and I let him have it—in a weak moment, I let Melba have half of it for the children—then I bought a folding wire spring bed arrangement on 9th Avenue & 43rd Street for five dollars and took it home in a cab—so that got me off the floor—but Peggy still preferred the floor to the springs, for her fucking—and I think she had something.

During the morning, we got together a meagre breakfast. Peggy came over during the day with a bit of holly and her ass—that left Tommy to the daily paper. For Xmas dinner we went to Stewart's Cafeteria for a couple of bowls of soup and some vegetables, bread and butter—we had a buck between us and we spent 60¢ of it—that was a low point Xmas for me. The only bright spot had been Peggy and her tail—and that had its drawbacks when you took in the surroundings and knew her condition.

After our repast at Stewarts we returned to 83rd Street and slept it off.

The next day a Christmas card from Elise arrived with a $10 bill attached. It was a welcome Xmas present, but it would have been more welcome before than after Xmas—then we could have had a real feed.

It was not a novelty for Tommy—being a bit of a rum hound, he had frequently found himself broke on Xmas day from imbibing too much the night before—but Xmas 1936 was a very sober one, both before, during and after.

I suppose a handout at the Mills Hotel or the Municipal

Lodging might have been worse.

1936 had been quite a year—much activity—income from nothing to $750 per month and down again—visiting with the mighty, living with the derelicts all in the same year, sometimes in the same month or week.

Man is certainly an adjustable creature—to climate, to adversity, to riches—there hadn't been, I can truthfully say, a dull moment in 1936

In the middle of August riding downtown in the subway to have lunch with Joe L. and the other commissioners of the City Government, I caught sight of a lovely thing. I looked and she looked—she left the train at Grand Central. It was the East Side of course, and she headed north by East—I followed—to hell with the Commissioners—they would have done the same. I caught up with the strikingly attractive damsel and she didn't object—seemed she was headed for the Beaux Art Apartments where she had a very nice layout—it developed she was going home for a mid-day repast—she was selling offset printing to some of the large steamship and railroad companies.

I fell like a ton of bricks and instead of eating, we screwed. She was "Bobbie Lee" from Savannah, the daughter of a Georgia cop—she was lovely to look at and wonderful to screw.

She soon became a court favorite, giving G. a close race for number one position in my affections. The only trouble with Bobbie was that she had two or three old guys from Georgia who had made good in New York in a big way, who took her out wining and dining, and to the theatre, dripping with orchids—among her devoted lovers she numbered Bedeaux of International fame—the guy who was going to bring the Prince of Wales to America, but didn't.

Bobbie was a frequent visitor to 904 on her nights and afternoons off. She had a bungalow in the foothills of New Jersey—I was going out there for Thanksgiving with her when I learned you were coming thru—so I took her to the train in Jersey and returned to meet you. I had a habit of introducing her to all and sundry—while I was still tied up to Melba (which was safe)—as my third legal wife to be. . . .

And so I pass from 1936, the year of ups and downs, mostly downs—sex life rampant—I kept my pecker up sexually that year.

Borah — women — California — women — real estate — women—the Republican National Convention—women—Melba's divorce proceedings—women—Mary Pickford—and whores of every degree—William Randolph Hearst—women—public relations—women—an inheritance—women, women, women—and Ruth G.—that was a fast moving year and little change.

And so I turn that page in my life to 1937—and that was an even more turbulent year.

1937

1937 came in with a struggle—alleviated in small part by my real estate deals on the apartment at 904, where I was getting $35.00 a month profit, and the apartment at 83rd Street, which was rent free—I was still in litigation over the Provident Loan account with the Whit Organization, and I was unable to get anything substantial from my inheritance from the Lucy Ward estate.

1937 saw Melba the vocalist with Vincent Lopez's orchestra at the Astor Hotel—saw me move from 83rd Street on the 19th of January to the Ritz Carlton where I remained until the 19th of June, when I moved to the apartment (furnished on 82nd Street East) where I remained until October 1st, when I moved again, this time to the Vanderbilt Hotel and from there I took my apartment at 6 East 37th Street.

That was the year in which Ruth G. was quite a bit on the wane—that is the year that we fell for Jerry Worthing, the actress who had played at Hanover—that was the year I visited Lydia Locke at Yorktown Heights, that was the year that I met Ellen Niehaus, the German refugee, and fell for her—that is the year I gave a party in the kitchen of Joe Pani's Merry-Go-Round on the day when the Hindenberg blew up at Lakehurst, May 6th.

That was the year that Harriet S. and the cat women were having a big time of it—that was the year that Ruth G. and Mabel Baron visited me at the Ritz Carlton, where they had cocktails with Joe L. and myself in my apartment while the movies were being shown—that was the year that the vitriolic Margie K. was in my life.

That was the year that I opened my own business, W. Ward Smith & Associates—that was the year that I discovered the Provident Loan were not seeking publicity when they engaged the Whit Organization and subsequently Ward Smith & Associates, but were in fact, seeking a contact with the Mayor, in order to amicably adjust their differences with him, and when that was accomplished they no longer needed me. . . .

That was the year that the Missing Persons Bureau claimed that Melba had been seen in California, with the missing Judge Crater—when she was singing at the Astor all the time—and which Harold Fowler finally straightened out.

That was the year Melba and Esther S. had an affair at the Ritz—Esther was Lopez's secretary and mistress at the time—that was the year that I had charge of the publicity for the First National Trailer Show.

That was the year that I established agents for my Publicity Bureau all over the world—that was the year I fell for Sylvia Randolph (a Canadian Jewess)—that was the year that I obtained signatures (5,000) petitioning me for a candidate for Councilman under proportional representation (I only needed 2500)—I didn't file because the expense seemed to be prohibitive.

That was the year I met Margaret M. who afterwards played such an important part in the life of Tommy B., that I met and fell for Lorell P.—and that I became enamored of Norah Anderson, the painter, sculptress and dancer—that I made fudge for my Christmas presents—that Ruth G. sent me the turkey from Gristedes. . . .

[My father here lists the names and addresses of thirty-nine women with whom he had affairs that year.]

That was the year that I got high when my teeth were to be extracted and was charged with disorderly conduct (case being dismissed thanks to political influence).

That was the year that I tried to bring Paul and Bob Moses together for the purpose of having Paul tell Bob he didn't know what he was talking about in connection with trailer space at the World's Fair (purpose publicity for the Trailer Show). That was the year that Gypsy Rose Lee was a flop when she appeared at the Trailer Exhibit.

This was the year that I had my famous art [photograph] collection of the feminine beauties that had been in my life, prominently displayed in my apartment at 6 East 37th Street, Apartment 5-D.

This was the year that Lorell P. was going to decorate my bathroom with exotic paintings, but a boyfriend and the Mary Elizabeth candy store blower or air-conditioner prevented.

And it was just at the last of the year, between Xmas and New Year, when you were returning to Dartmouth, that I first met Berenice Holloway—but that little story will have to wait to be told mostly in 1938. . . .

After renting the apartment and settling matters with the Provident Loan, I moved to the Ritz Carlton Hotel—where, because of the poor times, I was able to engage, as you may recall, a fairly large room and bath for the nominal sum of $4.50 a day, payable weekly. . . .

Probably the most important event of that December was unexpected—and at the time I am sure that you never anticipated that my life would be so affected by an event as minor and as innocent as occurred on the evening you phoned me from the station enroute back to Hanover, after spending Christmas at Baltimore.

If you remember, as I remember, you were returning to Dartmouth before the holidays were over in order to undertake some special work, or maybe you were just tired of provincial Baltimore.

Just before you called, Ruth G. had telephoned me—it was after dinner—her husband then had gone to a prize fight or something, and she had an urge to be with me—I too was eager for her. Hardly had I agreed to meet her and hung up the phone, when your call came thru—so I immediately cancelled my date with her. You came over to 37th Street and we visited together between your trains.

We chatted for quite a while about this and that, the

future of the nation and the world—then we ambled off to the station—and that was to eventually change the course of the life I was then living.

In November, December '37, I had seen a great deal of Benjamin Hanft at the 37th Street apartment but I hadn't been able to get anything going from the standpoint of productive activity. I bought a portable typewriter, a copy of *Webster's Unabridged Dictionary*, and a *Columbia University Encyclopedia* and settled down to writing, frugal living and intensive loving—definitely on the promiscuous side—but we're coming to that shortly now—and before we do, I want to finish off the serious side of 1937.

Arriving at Grand Central Terminal, we strolled down to your car, or Pullman, and we put your things away in your berth, and then we returned to the platform for final goodbyes. As we stood there talking, my eye caught and your glance followed a very smartly turned out female of the species (attired in a short Kolinsky fur jacket) coming down the platform. We struck a bargain—if she boarded the train for the North she was to be yours—if she didn't board the train, but was merely there to say goodbye to a departing passenger, she was to be my game.

She passed us, unnoticing our very existence—and headed for the forward cars. Up near the end of the platform she was joined by another girl and several men—we watched them and discussed them—then the cry was "all aboard"—the men boarded the train, the girls remained on the platform. You stepped into the vestibule of your car and as it gained momentum, closed the door—we had said our goodbyes. We had been talking about Charles Meredith and the Little Theatre movement—Charles was in town—you had been eager to meet him—for a moment you had been undecided whether to change your reservation and stay over, or return to College, as you had originally planned—you finally decided to go on. As the train moved out, you tried to call a message to me—it had to do with Meredith, and your plan to write him—in order to get what you were saying, I had to sprint alongside the moving train.

Now the girls had turned—they were walking back. As I

jogged by, keeping up with you, a facetious observation was half mumbled, half spoken in jest—then I waved a fond paternal farewell, and turned in my tracks back to the station. I hadn't gone far, and it did not require many rapid steps for me to overhaul them.

The girl I coveted was on the offside from me and disinclined to enter into conversation—the one nearest me was not in the least reticent.

The girl in the Kolinsky coat—the one you and I had spotted and staked our imaginary claims on—was reserved—she did not enter into the light banter between her girl friend and myself as we strolled back down the platform to the station. In fact, it was not until we were in the center of Grand Central that we got around to introductions—to which I paid, as usual, little heed (mistakenly, unfortunately—a bad slothful habit—always a handicap)—I then suggested that we have a "drinkee."

I had about 40¢ to my name—enough for a taxi to 37th Street and that was all—but there behind the bar I had the grog.

The girls accepted my invitation (thinking, as I was afterwards informed, that I was taking them to a new place. I was—but it was my own, private—not public).

When we alighted from the cab they expressed some surprise, when I escorted them into the self-operated lift they were convinced that all was not well—at the door to the apartment, when I searched for my key, the girl in the Kolinsky balked, but her companion, by that time, consumed with curiosity, and being a bold piece, was determined to go thru with it, and see the inside of the den of iniquity—and she succeeded in breaking down the resistance of the girl in the Kolinsky.

When we got into the apartment, the bold one asked for cigarettes, and I, having no money, it was rather embarrassing. She finally got it thru her dumb head that there were to be no cigarettes at 37th Street that night—so she decided it was time to go, much to the relief of the shy one—so they both departed after a giggling conference in the bathroom—before leaving for their homes, unescorted by men account of my lack of cab fare, cigarette money, etc.

The bold one gave me her name, address and telephone number for the book—the retiring lass (who had a very seductive way of nonchalantly handling her lanky limbs) was disinclined to furnish details about herself—but I had picked up enough from the conversation while the girls were at the apartment to make it possible for me to get the quiet one's phone number from information, but not correctly enough to find it in the book for myself—we will come to that shortly however.

Little I realized that night that the entire course of my future was to be so definitely altered—not without a struggle—and that I was to become another personality molded into the pattern of a "Berenice Holloway design."

June 6th, 1944:—3:45 a.m.—It's D-Day! When I came downstairs I noticed in the darkened Huylers candy store the outline dimly silhouetted of a man and woman—they were loving there in the dark—so I strolled down the street and when I strolled back again it was to see a white girl and a negro boy in fond embrace at the door—they looked up and strolled up the Avenue—he with his arm around her shoulder in fond embrace—they noticed me watching the amorous tableau and waved a greeting—defiant—some might say the degeneracy, the perversity of it caused my prick to rise—well, thought I, this is the new era, the new decade—the crossing of the races black and white, the mingling of men and women of all colors, creeds, nationalities the world over—that's what fighting produces—that's the debris in the wake of war.

At that very minute men were being cut down by withering fire, blown to pieces by the ground and aerial bombings, the bombings beneath the ground or the water's surface, and from the skies above, as they raced ashore to the beachheads of France to destroy an Aryan who had hoped and planned for a superior white race (by the complete extermination of the Semitic scourge from the face of the earth). Hitler may have had the right idea, whereas our monstrous semitic and negro loving dictator may well have been all wrong—only posterity will be able to record that fact long after we have gone.

Those were my observations, my thoughts, my activities on that momentous occasion as the hour struck—H-Hour, D-day.

Now back to the past. . . .

Ruth G. had been away most of that winter in Florida (1937) and I found that I got along much better without her than with her. Despite my promiscuousness—my screwing all over the place—I was able to attend to business better—I always do a better job when fucking the field than when tied up to one dame, legally or otherwise. Discovering this, I decided to ignore Ruth on her return—but that only worked for a short while. . . .

Girls! Girls! Girls! All types, sizes and shapes. All colors and creeds—the Ritz drew them like flies to molasses. After the Ritz, it was the penthouse in the walkup that attracted the wenches—then the Vanderbilt Hotel and finally the conveniently located studio on 37th Street off the Avenue, in the heart of New York's commercial center just down the block from J.P. Morgan's on the Southeast corner of Madison and the National Democratic Club on the N.E. Corner of Madison Avenue. . . .

One evening, as my sojourn at the Ritz was nearing its end, and the pile of bills in the Hotel safe deposit box was getting lower and lower, Tommy B. phoned—an old girl of his, a bit passé—in her late sixties but still with substantial funds—a typical continental cosmopolite who maintained an elaborate salon in Paris. . . .

Julie Batchelder, the old bat—Tommy's gal of the evening had an old battle axe in tow—currently known as Lydia Locke—a former aspirant for Metropolitan Opera honors, so she said.

Tommy not wanting to discourage Julie's desire to provide a festive occasion—food and liquor at no cost to himself—sought to please Julie by getting me to make up the foursome. Altho I was short of cash, I wasn't much interested and didn't care to have old dames buying meals for me.

However, I agreed to assist him in whatever nefarious plot he was up to, and which inevitably was—as it was in this case—an effort to inveigle large quantities of alcoholic stimulant without any expenditure of cash on his part.

Lydia was fat and fifty and must have weighed over 250 pounds—a loud, boisterous, domineering and unattractive whore with a filthy tongue who dwelt entirely on sex and sex perversions—Lydia swore like a trooper, and the uncomfortable part about those old gals was that they always insisted upon going to the smart, quiet places where they were their loudest. Being extravagant guests and tipping lavishly, managements reluctantly put up with them in dull times—now one of the old gals is dead and the other is dying.

During dinner it was decided to go to the Merry-Go-Round to see Melba—it would be noisier there and they would be less conspicuous than at the Old Bijou where we dined, much to my embarrassment.

One of Lydia's greatest claims to fame was the fact that she had either inherited or received large alimony or settlements running into millions from five different husbands—she had been accused of murdering two of her spouses, and had stood trial and had been acquitted in at least one instance.

While I painfully shoved her about the floor at the Merry-Go-Round, she suggested a weekend at her estate in Westchester, and it was an estate—in fact three estates—a stupendous place at Yorkshire Heights—three mansions—one of them her former husband had built for her and lavishly furnished—another built by a previous owner and one she had recently completed for herself in widow-hood.

As part of the new house, she had a very beautiful music room or organ hall more like a private chapel, adjoining the main house—just why one with a career such as hers behind her, should have felt in need of such an inspiring sanctuary, I was never able to fathom, but she had it built herself and she had installed a most valuable organ.

She enticed me—she lured me—with a luscious description of a teen age voluptuous illegitimate niece of hers—so I accepted, protesting all the while that my real interest in going up was Lydia, and that was why I was going.

My tenure at the Ritz being on thin ice, I decided against taking one of my largest suitcases for the weekend in order to avoid any suspicion of a contemplated getaway—instead I purchased for $5.00 a petite overnight case of real leather, it was goodlooking—smart—it is now in storage at the Willard Hotel in Washington. . . .

Lydia met me at the station in a big chauffeur driven limousine and enroute to her main house, pointed out the construction work that was going on—mainly the erection of a dwelling for her sister and a sister's illegitimate child (girl), both of whom she continuously denounced but with the most abusive but artistic vituperation.

Lydia had an adopted son of her own for whom she professed great affection—how anyone ever let her adopt a son, I do not know.

I was given a very charming guest room and private bath which connected with Lydia's sumptuous suite.

At dinner the sister, the niece and a girl friend appeared—there had been much drinking at cocktail time, and the meal was very fullsome and festive.

After a cordial or two, we all retired to our respective quarters—there had been a good deal of suggestive by-play during the evening which indicated that there was no question in the minds of any of those present but what was expected of me for the remainder of the night.

While I was undressing, in fact just as I was about to slip on my pajamas, Lydia opened the adjoining door between our rooms and standing there in a fluffy lace pink georgette crepe negligee—over a flesh colored chiffon nightie—all of which tended to make her appear even larger than she was, but it did give her the somewhat lewd appearance of a madam of a whore house who was not adverse to a diddle herself occasionally with a preferred client.

I was drunk and the picture excited me—as usual my god damn cock stood up and pleaded for a screw—she crossed the room to my bed, threw her arms around me and suggested that I come in her room—the bed was larger there and more comfortable—great resilience.

I got in her bed with her—it was comfort personified—I loved her—fondled her and removed her nightie. She had taken off the negligee when she had climbed in under the sheets, which were quickly thrown back—what a gross but voluptuous sight she was stripped—her nude body was in rolls—in fact rolls upon rolls—like inner tubes piled one above the other, only her rolls were a pinkish white instead of the usual tube gray or red.

She had covered her body with scented powder—the bed sheets and her hair were scented with seductive perfume—I think Lydia was the largest and oldest female I had ever fucked—her flesh was soft and flabby—it sounds revolting yet it was exciting. The wench knew all the tricks of the trade and she used them—her tits were so large that I fucked her between them—she sucked me off—and when I finally shoved my cock into that cow-cunted bitch, I shot one hell of a wad. The novelty, obscenity of it, got me—she loved and wiggled her fat ass all over the place.

I stayed with her all night—we would fuck and suck—oh yes, I went down on her during the night—she loved that. We played with one another and each other—we slept only a little—she always wanted more—by morning she was suggesting matrimony, offering to turn over everything she had to me if I would marry her.

The next day was Sunday. We arose late—after breakfast in bed—then Lydia took me for an inspection trip of her entire property. She wanted to sell some—she thought I might help her to do that—she had grandiose schemes for the balance of her estate and she suggested that I might be interested in managing that for her.

Her proposals were many and frequent and varied. She kept a crew of men, laborers, artisans working Sundays as well as weekdays and she drove them with a firm determined hand, with all the ability, the capability of any road boss or construction gang superintendent—she was a hard task master—she knew what she wanted and she intended to get it, and the most for her money.

She set a very lovely table and we had about completed the Sunday midday meal when her broker, a fellow by the name of Shaskan who had finally married his mistress, the little girl who had come to my father's office many many years before with a Miss Maurer—I had interviewed Miss Maurer and hired her.

Shaskan's wife was with him, as well as another couple whose names escape me at the moment. Shaskan had been a partner of Hamilton P.'s and a notorious bucketshop operator.

We drank mint juleps and again we made a tour of the property, followed by more mint juleps—then it was suggested that we should go swimming in Lydia's lake—as Shaskan's wife and I ambled home from one of the inspection tours, in a slight stage of alcoholic inebriation.

The suggestion was received with gusto—and we all prepared for the bath in nature's best. Lydia, the most playful of the group, was a nauseating sight to behold in her 250 lbs. plus, but S.'s wife was a most delectable morsel in the nude and well worth the effort and discomfort of a dip in the cold still lake, while the early Spring mosquitos did their best to make a meal of the occasion.

After the dip there were more drinks to warm the cuddles—then the uninvited guests departed. Somewhere along the line of the afternoon's drunken conversation, I had expressed a liking for spaghetti with Italian sauce, which caused Lydia to proclaim that she would take herself to her kitchen and prepare my evening's repast for me herself.

This caused great confusion.

When the hors d'oeuvres were served I discovered, much to my delight, that I had some tuna fish on my plate—being tight and with my weakness for Tuna Fish, when it was passed the second time, I rudely took a second helping, then to make matters worse, I asked for more. This incensed Lydia who assumed that I would lose my appetite for the spaghetti she had prepared if I ate so much tuna fish—she remonstrated with me, ordered the butler to remove my plate and I, asserting my independence, and my fearlessness of her domination, became embroiled in a hideous and violent row with the bitch in which she finally ordered the butler to fetch her gun—she was determined to have her way—I was determined to have more tuna fish.

Knowing her propensities for murder and her reputation for a light finger on the gun, I excused myself—ostensibly to go to the can, actually to phone the State Constabulary—which I did over the extension in my bedroom. I requested them to send a cab for me from Ossining and to accompany the cab themselves—this they agreed to do.

Unbeknownst to me, Lydia suspecting that I was up to something had lifted up her extension—and had come in on the conclusion of my arrangements with the State troopers, catching just enough of the conversation to become aware of what I had done.

Whereupon she broke out in hysterical remorsefulness and shedding voluminous crocodile tears and screaming undying devotion implored me to spend the balance of the night, and go down in the morning.

How I packed I'll never know—but I did—and the troopers and the cab arrived in the midst of the peak of her hysteria. With the aid of the State Police I drew myself aloof from her fond embrace and lustful clutches, and departed. As I drove off, her sentimental feelings suddenly turned to vile denunciations.

Arriving at the station with my police escort, I found that I had an hour to wait for my next train. By this time my appetite knew no bounds, but the hour was late and the local eating emporiums were closed—but I bethought me of my friend the Warden of the State Prison, Sing Sing—but a stone's throw from the station—and his full larder—and thence I directed my chariot (taxi).

The Warden—Lawes—was then living in his new mansion outside the prison walls—it had been designed like the new death house, the new cell box, etc. and approved for construction during Governor Miller's administration, and my approving signature had been affixed to most of the plans on account of one of my ex-officio duties.

No one was about on the ground floor when I entered—I called and no one answered. As drunk as I was, I was able to recall the general plan of that ground floor and so I took myself to the kitchen without further ado—but to my great dismay I found the huge refrigerator of that great exponent of Criminal Reformation padlocked and sealed, against the prying hands of the trustees of the much heralded honor system.

During the commotion, the children's maid or nurse appeared on the scene, but she had no key—the "trusty" cook had that—then came the guard. By that time, like the moronic inmates of most of our prison cells, I had given vent to my predicament and pronounced my own opinion of an Honor System so successful that the Warden had to padlock his own icebox.

In my own inimitable scrawl with my little lead pencil on the white enamel icebox door—

Years later Lawes professed never to have seen the pungent epithet I had penned thereon.

The guards had stealthily removed my potent remarks in the wee small hours of the morning. The Warden, I forgot to say, was in the City giving his weekly Sunday broadcast to the nation on the penal problems of the day.

An exhibitionist at heart, eager for the public praise, and the cash commensurate therewith, he was everlastingly during his regime at Sing Sing, writing, lecturing, broadcasting, with the material he constantly obtained in his post of trust, as Warden of Sing Sing Prison—for which he was amply and substantially compensated by the taxpayers of the Empire State.

Disgruntled I returned to the station, caught my train and enroute to our Fair City, regaled all the paying customers of the New York Central Line with my opinion of a Warden who had to padlock his own icebox and then had the audacity to proclaim the virtues of the Honor System far and wide.

[Included here is a portion of a letter from my father to Ruth G. recounting one of my visits to New York.]

Needless to say I told [Page] all about you—he approved—he is for you for his next step-mother—wants to meet you—likes your picture—anxious to go to Russia—Thank God I have a liberal son.

Apparently the latest college slang in this modern age which horrifies most parents, I understand, is SHIT—it even jolts me—and I don't think it very effective, but there it is—

Ever hear of RAT FUCKING—well I hadn't either except to make more rats—but at Hanover that means the raiding of the students rooms on one floor by the students from another floor—the boys go in groups of eight or ten—turn everything upside down in the students rooms—even fire buckets of water are employed to make the wreck complete—that's progress—

At the schools of higher education (our American Colleges)—RAT FUCKING—My, my, what a lot Page will have to tell the boys at Oxford besides the beautiful women of America and the C.I.O. . . .

East 82nd Street loaned itself to fornication.

I had a large livingroom with fireplace, kitchen, and then a sleeping room or porch on a setback, which afforded a nice roof garden, plants, etc.—off the livingroom was a spacious bath—the girls liked that—and I could see into my bathroom from my sleeping porch.

It has always excited me to watch a woman piss on a pot—then when they lift their skirts to wipe their ass or powder their cuzzy, it has stood my cock on end.

A Miss Freeman—who worked in the Museum of Art—rented me the place furnished for the summer from late June, July and August to early September—she only got one month's rent out of me in advance and she made the mistake of leaving her phone connected.

I hired a French maid—to clean and cook three meals a week or whenever I gave a party—French maids are so understanding.

Ruth G. was the first to visit me there—she took sun baths on the roof afternoons and screwed me on the bed on the sleeping porch—the first few weeks she found it handy to run in often—then she got out of hand—she was living around the corner on 83rd & Fifth Ave. . . .

That summer I knocked up Ruth for the fourth or fifth time to add to my troubles—while she always paid the freight on such operations, she raised hell about it—and as I have said before I never knew whether I was the father or her husband—I liked to think I was the fertile one. . . .

Harriet S. was still living around the corner at 904 Park Avenue and frequently dropped in for a drink or a screw. Harriet had found an old girl friend living in the basement of a renovated apartment on 80th Street—next to the famous Todd Hunter School for girls—the old dame had a weakness for cats. Harriet took me to call on her—Harriet was fascinated—the old dame would get a little tight and then flop on a couch in her livingroom, pull up her skirts and the goddamn cats would crawl all over her, lapping at her cunt—until she would go into a spasm and come—much to the delight of the felines.

It was quite a sight to watch—I got so hot watching that I took my cock out and Harriet sucked me off.

Betty C. had taken up with an octoroon that season—Betty always had some good looking younger girls in tow—Betty went in for them and they for her.

Ever since the fall of 1936 when Betty got a peek of my cock while glancing up the stairway at 904—saw the damn thing erect thru the slit in my chinese mandarin robe—she had been clamoring for a ride on my prick—in fact, she had been so impressed that she had sung its praises to all and sundry, far and wide, and she had made up her mind that she would feel it inside her.

I could think of no valid reason for denying her that great pleasure—so I invited her to dine and to bring her current slightly colored female amour along.

After dinner we got down to the purpose of the meeting and all disrobed. Betty nearly swooned as she fondled and caressed my big cock—she couldn't stop loving it—the nigger went to work on Betty first—they had quite a time of it. Betty just couldn't let go of my prick—she kissed it as the nigger kissed her—and I came inadvertently all over Betty's face—then I peed on her and then on the nigger as they lay together—but my cock, to Betty's great delight, wouldn't go down—a bad habit it has always had—deflation being in the case of my prick much slower than inflation.

Much to her annoyance I put on a condom and screwed the mulatto—and kissed Betty as I did so—after that fuck, the old instrument was still standing erect, and Betty was still begging to be laid.

While Betty was washing the piss off her little body, I put on another condom and went after Betty when she got back on the bed. When she discovered that I had on a rubber her annoyance was complete—the first time she objected, mildly—but when I laid her the second time with the rubber still on, her protestations were angry. She wanted me in the raw—she wanted to feel the hot load come within her—she wanted it all. She was such a drunk and rounder that I felt I shouldn't—that it was too great a chance to take. I tried to fool her and sidestep but she would have none of it—in a fit of violent temper she refused to screw again if I wore a condom—and since I wouldn't take it off she dressed and left in a huff—as I gave her girl friend one more—and that was the end of Betty for me. . . .

The 82nd Street apartment had proved a most enjoyable recreational center for me in the metropolis, that summer.

On September 23rd, I moved from 82nd Street to the Vanderbilt Hotel to be near my office and the trailer show.

In engaging girls to do secretarial work for the council campaign, I was careful to select Jewesses, Irish Catholics, etc. A particularly attractive girl that I put on at the time was Sylvia R.—Melba figured I had designs on her from the start and she was right.

Sylvia was a good worker—loyal and attractive—young, luscious, and not averse to being fondled—and to playing with the boss's cock. She began at first by jerking me off—then she would go down on me in the office—she kept me in white heat most of the time. We were very busy and often worked late at night—she was always the last to go home—she had a Jewish boy friend who called for her frequently—and Ben H. (a Jew himself) who was working with me at the time warned her against Jews, said they had no respect for Christian girls—but she went on seeing him—and playing with me.

I was falling for her like a ton of bricks—thought I might like to marry the gal—G. was slipping more and more into the background.

I dined Sylvia every night that fall—in the office or out.

While at the Vanderbilt I ran across Florence M.—she was staying there too—and we managed to be together several times—but it was stale. Outside of Florence, I only had one chambermaid in my Hotel room and a girl on the same floor whose name escapes me—but I still saw Nancy O.—Della and Anita S.—so as not to sluff off in my screwing, political campaigns or no.

After the trailer show was over and I had withdrawn from the councilman's race, I had upon the constant urging of Nancy and Ruth, decided to have my teeth fixed—my bridgework and remaining teeth were in bad shape—the teeth were rotting and the heavy gold bridgework was afloat—nothing to anchor to. Morris Maltzer, the lawyer, gave me the name of a Jew friend of his, a dentist—a younger fellow in the neighborhood named Berke. Berke said I should have all the uppers out, so the deal was made and I gathered together the dough for the job on a down payment.

It was to be done in the evening—I thought I was too busy to have the work done during the day. The evening of the appointment with the dentist Ben H. asked me to sit at the press table—free liquor and food—at some Jewish benefit he was running at the Biltmore. I went there for a few drinks and a plate of soup to fortify me for the extractions, but I lingered too long—when I reached the dentist's office he had gone to attend some lecture where he instructed others.

So I returned to the banquet and the free liquor—the dinner over, I did the rounds of Greenwich Village on my own with special attention to the Lesbian places—about two o'clock in the morning, I headed north, drunk as a lord, woke up Tommy and proceeded to some drinking den of his.

We ordered liquor for ourselves and a couple of

whores—we got their addresses—the drinks were slow in coming and I got into an altercation with the proprietor and departed without paying for the liquor—by that time of night, most places were closed (a few days later Joe L. and I called on the whores and Joe screwed one of them in the kitchen five minutes after he arrived—and then nearly died of remorse and fright) so we went to the Kit Kat Club. The doorman was having a row with a departing guest on the sidewalk over a cheque and didn't see me—the doors were barred and they wouldn't let us in. This annoyed me and when a cop appeared out of nowhere—they always do around those places—Tommy quickly and quietly disappeared as he always did when trouble was afoot and left me alone.

I strolled off by myself after some strong statements about the cop not attending to his job on his beat.

The more I thought about the cop's neglect of duty the madder I got—and so I engaged a taxi to trail the cop when he returned to his post and tour—which was to try the store doors along Third Avenue to see if they were locked.

Now the cop knew that the Kit Kat Club was violating the law—the precinct officers knew it and the divisional inspector of the Police Department must have known it.

I followed the cop for half a dozen blocks up and down Third Avenue hurling critical charges at him—finally the taxi driver sold me the bill of goods that the cop had a family and kids and to let up on him—so we drew up alongside again to call it quits and go home. I am in my cups and use the wrong salutation in calling him over to the cab (there must have been some southern blood in him because his response when I finally hailed him with a friendly "you old son of a bitch—come over here" was to jump on the running board of the car and order the taxi driver to the 51st Street House)—my second trip in seven years.

I was booked on a disorderly conduct charge (but the Kit Kat Club wasn't closed)—after getting in touch with Joe L. and Stanley H., the Mayor's Tax Commissioner and Secretary, I was permitted to go my own way, being booked as William W. Smith, with instructions to be in the 57th

Street Magistrates Court in the morning.

Being highly excited and greatly upset, I took myself at 5 a.m. up to Nancy's—she was enraged at my calling at that hour without phoning first—her profitable lover might have been there, she said—but being Irish and sympathetic by nature toward anyone in trouble (real), she let me crawl into bed—she got me up again at 8:30 and giving me breakfast, sent me to the Vanderbilt to shave and change my clothes and take a bath.

When I arrived in Court I found the Mayor's chief clerk—he visited the judge and when the case was called, the cop said I followed him up and down the Avenue calling him names. I said I had merely been pointing out his duty as I saw it—the Judge admonished me to exercise greater discretion in my choice of language in addressing officers of the law, and to avoid harassing them while doing their work and dismissed the case.

There had been no bail set or finger printing etc. that time. I was released on my own because my friends were in power and they could trust me to show up—in fact I didn't even get a lawyer to represent me. . . .

A week later I went to the dentist again on a Saturday night and had all my teeth—top teeth—removed and a plate inserted at once. As the novocaine wore off the pain increased so I went to a newsreel—I got thru̴ that—but after I got back to the hotel I took the plate out—and even using a mouth wash of salt and water and stuffing swabs in my mouth, I damn near bled to death.

During the night I spat up quantities of blood and when I finally dozed off, after taking many aspirin tablets (4), I awoke to a very bloody pillow and bed—the dentist pooh-poohed my predicament over the phone.

When I phoned Ruth about it, she called her brother and he urged me to insist upon seeing my dentist—I was in pain and the bleeding wouldn't let up—the sight of all the blood made the hotel maid ill—the towels were a sight.

I was weak but managed to get into my things with the aid of a bell boy and get myself around to the dentist. He finally succeeded in clotting up the opening and the bleeding was under control but it took days for me to fully recover and several months before I could wear the plate with any degree of comfort.

As I said before, I moved from the Vanderbilt on October 24th 1937 to the studio apartment at 6 East 37th Street, apartment 5-B.

And there I started to dictate at home—that brought Sylvia over to the apartment—and gave me a freer opportunity to woo her.

When I was closing 904 Park Avenue, after my lease was up and the doctor had moved out, I heard a prospective tenant for one of the other apartments express interest in the decorations of the apartment he had been looking at and asked Wilford (the janitor) about them—he told me and that roused my curiosity so I went up and looked at the artwork for myself. Over the mantel in the living room was a very fine sketch or oil painting of a Chinese mandarin—it was painted on the wall—it was beautifully executed.

I wandered into the bathroom and found the walls and ceilings covered with the most exotic and ethereal nudes—the work was excellent, but again it was permanent. I asked Wilford who had done such fine work and he announced that it had been done by the beautiful wife of a Jew lawyer who had lived there.

That aroused my curiosity further and I got him to give me the lawyer's name and office address—some weeks later I had Sylvia phone the Jew's office—she explained to the lawyer that we had some artwork for his wife, so he gave her address to us. I did nothing about it until I moved into 37th Street—then I bethought me of those nudes for my bathroom—so I had the girl call the wife and explain that I had a commission for her to do some painting for me. Her name was Lorell P.—she had not been married to the Jew—she had only been living with him.

When she arrived at 37th Street, Walter P. was there—I thought it best to have a third party present—she brought a girl friend with her—I don't recall the friend, but Lorell was quite the loveliest thing I had seen in years. I fell for her hook, line and sinker. I told her what I wanted—she said she would submit sketches—and would do the work for $50.00—after a drink or two she departed.

Several weeks later she phoned that the sketches were ready. I invited her to dinner—it was a Sunday evening—she accepted. I had my Chinese boy prepare the meal—I wore my robe—the lights were low—the setting set for seduction. When the hour arrived she phoned to say she had a cold—it was raining—should she send the sketches—I said by all means. Her boyfriend—a jealous kid, the son of Madam Burenilla, a dress designer—arrived, announced himself below, was invited up. The hall door at 37th Street, as you may remember, had a peep hole in it—I could look out and see who was outside, but they could not see in—so I had a good look at the gent. The chink opened the door—I was fully dressed by then, and went out to greet him—took the sketches, thanked him and sent him on his way, without inviting him in—then I slipped back into my robes, as I had called up Ellen N. as a substitute to eat the meal and fuck—and she was due.

Not long after that Lorell came over herself—we talked about the work—she got tight—we fucked and fucked.

While Lorell had a lovely body—she was a bit phlegmatic—she was lovely to look at and wonderful to touch. She was modeling evening dresses for a house firm; that was the beginning of a fine friendship that lasted many years—one you yourself once met up with—and found a bit difficult and complicated.

I offered Lorell my apartment—tried to get her to come in and live with me. But altho low in funds, she had other plans at the time and when she was ready to it was too late, for I had married another by that time—life is like that—but more about the beautiful Lorell later.

I bought this typewriter while there [on 37th Street]—on time (a dollar down, a dollar to come). The trailer account was still dragging on unpaid.

I bought a big dictionary and *The Columbia Encyclopedia* on time too, and prepared to bring this letter up to date.

Before closing out 1937, I shall try to take up 1938 on a

more serious note—altho the wave of fornication that engulfed me at the Ritz carried me thru the days and nights at 82nd Street and at the Vanderbilt and then on to 37th Street and continued on thru to 1938—the forepart, January, February and part of March—and then I married again.

Sexually 1937 had been quite a year for an old buck of 44.

Before leaving 1937 to posterity—for better or worse—I want to add that these fornicating orgies referred to were not the only ones.

Frequently the girls mentioned came to see me time and again and my only reason for not mentioning the encores is that repetition or recounting is as dull and as unexciting as many of the return engagements were—after the first few encounters of the quivering bodies one settles back—in fact, falls back upon a series of variations to keep up the spirit and alive the fire.

There were other girls who failed to make an impression or to leave behind either a pleasant or unpleasant recollection—and there was the usual amount of masturbation always indulged in—just to keep in form. . . .

In this day and age a man's word is no longer his bond—the only thing that counts is his accumulation of material things or temporary fame, regardless of how attained—by hook or crook. Men and women of America, in fact, men and women the world over, have but certain very fundamental urges or desires—they are food for the body, a shelter to sleep in, and sexual relations—and those are the prime forces that activate all mankind.

True, the New Deal, for its own selfish reasons, has tried to substitute an equitable even distribution of goods in equal amounts to all citizens, and not having succeeded in doing so in the United States, desires to do so the world round. As they have not succeeded at home, they will not and cannot succeed abroad.

Nations just as their peoples are economically and politically selfish—and we seem destined for many generations if not for many centuries, to go on living in a world where "grab all" is the principal motivating force in the individual, in the group, in the nation—wherever it be on the sphere.

I could go on at length elaborating on this theme, which is fundamentally the law of the survival of the fittest, but I am anxious to take up 1938, and I must be on with the past, rather than continue to discuss the present and the future, and so, I say Adieu to another hectic year, 1937, in the pursuit of life, love and happiness—and lust.

1938–1939

To begin—1938 was especially eventful because it marked the beginning of my third matrimonial venture, and a revolutionary change in my mode and manner of existence.

The New Year was ushered in—during a period which, for me, was most precarious financially—altho that was not a new, a novel, or unusual situation.

I was in hot water at 6 East 37th Street, Apt. 5-D, over my rent—when I moved in. I had been given a month's concession so that my rent was paid up to December 1st—then when they constructed the air-blowing system right over my head, and used my apartment and my balcony as a runway and scaffold for their construction materials, I raised particular cane.

Aside from my marriage to Eve, which I will go into shortly, I was involved in the tapering off and concluding of my affair with Mrs. G.

In the first months of 1938 I was greatly enamored of a sculptress, dancer and painter by the name of Delores—and of a successful milliner by the name of Anita Andre—and Edwina Powell, Charlotte T., Alice B., Gladys Lafler, Dunn, Graham de Ryder (the Maid of Melvale) and several others.

I circularized all my friends that year in connection with my Public Relations business, emphasizing what I had been able to do with the Trailer Show, and pointing out that I was able to give them publicity anywhere in the world.

I made a bid to get the Publicity Account of the Chinese Government, and also to make a deal to get planes and fliers for them. . . .

I also submitted a plan to obtain publicity in the metropolitan press for the Republican candidate for United States Senator from New Jersey—which was a plan to set up a Publicity Office in the City of New York for the candidate in order to cover the New York papers with large circulations in the Eastern end of New Jersey (the New York commuting area of that State).

I gave a big party at 37th Street in February, and I gave a big party at Sutton Place that year, after I was married—but most of the time was taken up with Eve's illness and the readjustment of our lives, which had been considerably altered by our marriage—it was a trying period from that standpoint, and how we ever succeeded in working out a solution that was feasible, I will never know—but more about that anon.

1938 should not take long in the telling—there was more difficulty with my mother-in-law, with my brother-in-law, with my new sister-in-law, and the period of adjustment was a tough one.

In order to save my financial situation, I resorted to my old trick of sub-letting. . . .

After I moved up to 61st Street, into the furnished room, across the street from the private home of my old friends, the George Washington Cavanaughs, I became a bit morose and at midnight on the 31st of January, I sat down and wrote the following dribble to Ruth G.—I set forth here to show you my irrational state of mind at the time—what a mentality such as mine can sometimes indulge itself in.

RESOLVED BETWEEN JANUARY-FEBRUARY MIDNIGHT 1938

Dearest Darling Ruth:

I have set the date—St. Valentine's day—February 14th, 1938.

I will sell my furniture on the 13th—put my books and papers which are nearly ready now in storage, under Page's name—and set forth never to return alive.

You no longer love me—what brought the change about I do not know—fear of abortions may have done it—I am told that will kill any urge or love.

I have glorified you—worshipped you—loved you dearly—still do—you are all there is of life to me—

If I could have believed that success for me would have in the end meant you—then I could have gone on striving—

Your readiness to hurt me—your eagerness to find any excuse to condemn me and to go out with others—

You denouncing me for things I have never done while you yourself have been unfaithful in thought, has been too ludicrous for words. . . .

By nature I am affectionate—I have wanted you to come to see me—if I couldn't go to you—to talk to me—be near me—if you didn't want to love—well, you could have had your way—but you might have come to 82nd Street and here—

I cannot take it—one doesn't commit suicide on the spur of the moment—

I am going away where it will create no commotion—

I have resolved to relieve you of further annoyance or embarrassment—you will have no more telephone calls—no one waiting at the door. . . .

I don't know what effect my going out will have on Page, I doubt if any—

There is no one that will give a damn—no one that will ever miss me.

How you could have treated me the way you have, after all we were to one another I do not know.

Our lives have been so different—I was born with a silver spoon in my mouth—brought up to believe that I was a superior sort of person because of my parents and their parents and their parents, and the position they had always occupied in the community—only to be bumped and bumped and bumped in the hard school of experience. . . .

No one ever likes you except for what they hope they can get out of you—at least that has been my experience—

No one has ever liked me for myself.

When I was young I was brilliant, or at least people thought I was, and I went ahead rapidly—everything I touched was successful—I was constantly in the public eye—and then time caught up with me. . . .

Now what do you think it does to me—not to have a home—to have to live here alone—in this cold room with little light—so cold it's hard to write—

Have you ever gone for days without food—saving for someone you loved, only to get your face slapped—well, I have and the pangs of hunger are not the most enjoyable in life.

To satisfy your own selfishness your own wilfulness—you have crucified me time and again—broken my spirit, humiliated me beyond words—I have taken it—suffered—because I loved you so—

No, I won't follow you to Florida—I will go elsewhere to my death—

I wanted so for us to have a child—I felt—I always felt you knew so much about all things but me—that you had an uncanny shrewdness about business—that with you beside me I could have recovered the lost ground and gone on to greater heights.

But I was wrong—your passion has really been to set me down—

Well, it won't be for much longer now—

You probably will hold yourself aloof even from a little kiss goodbye.

God, it's cold in here—and so my sweet, my darling girl when I have passed into the great beyond—don't think of me too harshly—try and think of the few happy blissful moments when we were near and close and supremely happy.

As you drive by Trinity—occasionally give a glance to the hill that rises there from the Riverside—and remember—remember—and think what I might have been—what we could have been together as the silver threads slipped in amongst the gold—and blow a kiss—a tiny little kiss from those pretty lips across your lovely hands and fingertips to me—your lover who gave all he had to give—but couldn't take it.

When I go out—you, as I close my eyes, will be with me in my dream world—but no longer will I be around in your real world to worry and harass you—

So Ruth—my Ruth—my only true love—be sweet to me these last few days—I won't mention this again—I am sober—my mind is clear—my life empty without you—the future blank—old man Reaper awaits me and the sod at Trinity is ready for me—goodbye my love—your Wardie—in life so it will be in death.

Sometimes when I write this crap about myself I get restless—my head binds, it doesn't ache. I feel as if I will never get it done—how futile it all is—I feel as if I might go quite mad—the effect is very great—it all must be gone over—but then it probably never will—you may never see it anyway.

Shortly after I moved to the room on 62nd Street I telephoned Berenice Holloway.

She was living at 24 West 59th Street, which was just around the corner from my room. . . .

I had but a nickel left and with that I wished to purchase a can of Campbell's soup—they were a nickel a can then. I also wished to phone B.H. So, I put the nickel in the slot first, dialed the operator, told her I had gotten the wrong number, had the nickel returned, and was duly connected—for the first time she answered the call herself and she invited me to come around and call that evening—I accepted the invitation.

I purchased the can of soup, took it to my room, cooked it, consumed it.

Then I went over to 59th Street—Ann H., the girl who was with "B" when I met her, was spending the evening—in fact, she had been there for dinner, as had Mr. and Mrs. Eric Atterbury. Mrs. Atterbury was the former Marguerite Preece, daughter of Godfrey Preece, the well known polo pony dealer—Eric was an Australian, had been a stable boy, jockey and trainer. . . .

Tiring of my chit-chat, Ann A. and the Atterburys departed—this annoyed B.H., as she did not wish to be left alone with me. After they left, I ambled on in my own dull way, skipping around in general conversation and going into greater details about La Brossie, the fellow who had worked for me in Florida—La Brossie, a waiter for us at the Sands Point Casino, and at the Melton Point Casino at Rye, had married a wealthy widow by the name of Celept. . . .

Berenice Holloway was not inclined to be affectionate, seemed only interested in a conversation. I remained an hour or so, then after having had my timid advances rebuffed, I departed for my garret room.

The apartment on 59th Street was furnished in excellent taste—antiques predominated—it had charm and comfort. After sizing the place up I decided that mother and daughter were probably living on an income of approximately $100 a week—but that's where I was wrong.

My interests had kept me busy the forepart of January—my funds had become limited and I couldn't get about much. I was unable to entertain, so I only called once or twice on the phone after that until!—

On Sunday the 13th of February I had a date with Edwina P.—I was still on 62nd Street—she lived on 55th Street between Lexington and Park, one of New York's loveliest streets.

While I was with her, a former beau broke in on us. He was as attentive as hell—he didn't even sit down. He borrowed ten bucks from Edwina and then invited us both to have cocktails with him at the Waldorf—we refused—Edwina was planning to see her elderly Englishman, and before that we were going to take the dog for a walk—and anyway she saw no reason to go drinking on her own money.

As we strolled along 57th Street I noticed two smartly dressed damsels approaching from Lexington Avenue—they were walking east to west—as they drew nearer, I recognized my "Kolinsky" girl friend of the Grand Central Station episode. It was the first time I had seen her and her compatriot since the evening I had called in January.

One of the most disconcerting things about trying to reach Berenice Holloway (after I met her in December) early in January, 1938, was the fact that in order to talk to her on the phone I always had to run the gauntlet of some uppish female before I could be connected with her—obviously, a ma bent upon discouraging all callers for her daughter was answering the phone.

We all exchanged pleasantries on the street, and after I left Edwina at her boy friend's, I called Berenice from Genay's apartment that evening—the Genays lived on the 58th Street side of the house, and that Sunday night I was showing Ira and Georgette along with Harry M. and his wife V., my "dirty movies"—Ira had gotten hold of a projector for the occasion—I had seen the "dirty pictures" so often myself that I was rather bored with them, so while they were running I went in and called up Berenice and chatted with her at length—she announced that she was leaving for the coast next day—St. Valentine's day—I asked her if I could call—she was busy packing—but she said I could. However the pictures took longer than I anticipated and by the time they were through running it, it was too late for me to drop in, so we postponed the visit tentatively until her return from the coast.

When I went home that night I sat down and scribbled a valentine message on a piece of yellow paper which I took around to her apartment (so that she would receive it before her departure)—she contends that she never took the message contained therein seriously. She thought it fiction not fact—and to this very day says that had she known it was fact and not fiction, she would not have left for the coast.

The valentine read as follows:

WARDIE

I have

Law suits to the right of me
Bills galore to the left of me
Process servers in front of me
Judgments in back of me
No food inside of me
No job in sight of me
Only old clothes to cover me
No place called home to me.

My money has flown from me
My wives have all gone from me
My children are lost to me
My best friends have forgotten me
Only one woman interests me
And she says she is going West from me
So there is no one to care for me.

My debtors don't pay me
My landlord is after me
The hock shops despair of me
My best years are back of me
But a few years are ahead of me
Living is lonely for me
And that's all that is wrong with me.

My mind hasn't left me
So that's why there's hope for me
For that's really
Wardie.

She sent me a picture post card from Palm Springs that raised my hopes.

She was due back on the 14th or 15th of March in order to sign her income tax papers. On that day I called on Bob Ripley ("Believe it or not") at the New York Athletic Club, for the purpose of inducing him to reconsider [a] proposal for his personal publicity.

We did much drinking in his room and as we drank, we denounced the two semitics that had played important and perhaps destructive (although they themselves contended constructive) parts in our lives—the two Ruths, G. and R. . . .

On my way to visit Berenice Holloway I stopped at a corner drugstore to purchase a small can of "Fastteeth" to hold my ("Woolworth's") plate in. It had gone through quite a bit of hard work that afternoon and evening, what with the drinking with Ripley and the heavy chewing at the Genay's dinner table—the plate wasn't much of a fit anyway. . . .

After I . . . crossed over thru the passageway from the 58th to 59th Street side of the house, I poured the powder on the plate to hold it fast. Then I entered the 59th Street hallway and had myself announced.

Mrs. Holloway had not returned with her daughter, so we were alone.

Most of that evening was taken up with the discussion of Miss Holloway's trip to the coast and the heavy rains and washouts in California. After a number of Scotch and waters I left around one o'clock in the morning, after a most discreet evening, for discretion had appeared to be the better part of valor in that instance. I was intrigued—she was different—I was impressed—I liked the girl, strangely I respected her.

I was back at 37th Street by that time and was using my telephone liberally, especially when I found I had someone new to listen to my telephone prattle which went on by the hour—I remember one occasion when I was cooking a rice pudding, we got into a considerable discussion as to the proper procedure to be followed in baking same. She had one idea, I had another (they have never been reconciled).

She had a maid and she ate many of her meals at home—she invited me to come to dinner that Friday and I accepted—in fact, I always easily accepted any invitation to dine in those days.

For the other guests at dinner, she had a Mr. & Mrs. Edward Rutt that she had met in Bermuda—Mrs. Rutt was an employee of the J. Walter Thompson Advertising Agency. . . .

That night I left after dinner when the Rutts left—but I merely walked around the block and came back again. I stayed late and talked much—I thought—I hoped I was making a good impression. My interest was rapidly mounting. That night as I departed I bravely ventured a "peck on the cheek"—and to my amazement didn't get slapped.

On Sunday she called and invited me to drive out on Long Island with her and Ann H. for skeet. I wanted to go—I longed to go—but I didn't have the cash for drinks, for shells or for meals or gas—and I had a tea date with Anita Andre and a girl friend of hers and a dinner date with Walter Piel. But she said I could call after dinner which I did. That night I kissed her and talked marriage—I was bolder.

Then I invited her to have dinner with me several nights later.

It wasn't very successful—I had sent my carving knife to be sharpened—it was late in arriving—the dinner was over done and the meal was anything but appetizing—the roast beef was cooked to a frazzle. She was a slow drinker, taking a considerable time to consume a long drink of Scotch and water, and we lingered long over the alcoholic consumption.

That evening I gathered that she was in some way gainfully engaged in some business in midtown—I hadn't paid much attention. She hadn't discussed it to any degree, in fact she had avoided all discussion of her activities—but she had given me her office phone number. Then the next day she came to lunch as she had been shopping in my neighborhood. I continued to talk of marriage—my desire to remarry, etc.

The following day or on the evening of Friday of March 25th I dined with her alone at her apartment.

Her sense of humor was intriguing me, there was that indefinable something about her that attracted me. She was smartly dressed—I liked her eyes, her good manners, her intelligence, and her integrity—she carried herself well and handled her legs in a most seductive fashion—her good food pleased me, her sexual naiveness captivated me. I knew nothing of her family, except that her father was dead, that she had a mother who was visiting her sister in California, and that her brother, altho a year below you at Dartmouth, was a year older than you.

She was obviously well born, well bred, well brought up—I was reverting to type—in my youth I had see-sawed between sluts and ladies, and in middle age I had hung in the balance with bitches (charming)—Melba and Ruth and Florence. Now I was swinging back to a woman of refinement and culture.

Her maid was not much as a fashion plate, but she was an excellent cook, the food left nothing to be desired, and was beautifully served on a charming service.

We talked about life and the future—I had always leaned a bit to career women—I had been keeping house as a bachelor for nearly two years. I was fed up—she seemed to be the answer to an old man's prayer. We drank a lot—it was Friday night.

As the night wore on, I explained to her that my Valentine message had been sincere, that it genuinely reflected my plight—that my condition had not improved to any measurable extent in the interim—that it still was serious on the financial side.

I truthfully painted the picture as black as I could—but for some unknown reason, all my life, people have discounted my contentions of adversity and poverty—they have always steadfastly refused to admit of my dire straits. That has been one of the crosses I have had to bear, no matter how shabby my appearance, it has been almost impossible to convince anyone of my straitened circumstances, even when they were at their lowest ebb, and she also refused to take my statements seriously.

That night I popped the question—I was amazed when she concurred in the suggestion—in fact it took my breath away. It never for an instant occurred to me that she, or any woman for that matter, would consider for one second entering into such a contract with an old reprobate in my plight—she didn't seem to be the type to do such a thing—but she fooled me. She accepted.

We sat up late discussing what to do—it was agreed that we should be married the next day, Saturday, March 26th, but there were complications, serious complications where I was concerned. It was 3 or 4 o'clock in the morning before we realized the hour and then she panically decided that it wouldn't do to have me depart at such an indecent time, so I remained the night thru, forming plans and preparing for an early start.

My total cash assets consisted of several dollars in pocket—I explained I couldn't buy a ring, engagement or wedding and she produced her grandmother's to meet that contingency. Then she ordered her car for 8—I had an idea for some unknown reason, that it was a dilapidated Model T—instead it turned out to be a Sporting Convertible Buick Coupe, with gaily upholstered seats of red leather.

We had breakfast, hastily gotten together, and then I went to 37th Street for a change of linen.

While she waited below, I phoned Joe L. and told him of our plans; both he and the Public Library explained that Elkton, Md. was out as a quick marriage spot—the Maryland laws had been changed, said they—the Library suggested Alexandria, Va. for a wedding that day. Then there was the question of getting a copy of my divorce papers in the action of Melba vs. me—they were in Rockland County, at New City, the county seat—so we headed there, after I had changed my shirt, shaved and parted my hair.

We crossed the George Washington Bridge—reached the Courthouse and while she waited without, I went in and got a copy of the final papers in the case. We needn't have bothered or taken the time, as they were not needed.

While waiting for the papers to be made out, I phoned Walter Piel and Ben Hanft, collect (my funds were low—I had had to pay the bridge toll and the fee for the papers—and when I had finished and returned to the car, I had but 40¢ left to my name).

I had fumblingly tried to explain my financial difficulties and I was getting panicky for lack of funds—I was all for going South on the Jersey side, but my fiancee feeling that the time was short—it was noon by then—felt we should cross the bridge—thence down the West Side Drive to the Holland Tunnel and back to Jersey again. She was insistent so I had to brutally bare my financial predicament—I had no money left for the license, clergyman, etc.—the car was gassed sufficiently for the trip.

To ease my embarrassment, never at a loss in a spot, she was quick to produce a $50 bill and gaily announced there was plenty more where that came from—so we stepped on the gas for Alexandria.

At Plainsboro, we grabbed a bite at the Walker-Gordon Lunch Room and telephoned her maid—she would not be home for dinner that night. Then on we rushed—thru Camden and Newcastle we sped—at Elkton on the outskirts, as we flew past at 90 to the hour, we spied a sign "Marriage, License, Clergyman." A man was sitting there—he waved solicitously—I jammed on the brakes—we backed up. He offered to arrange the ceremony for a fee—I questioned him at length about the law—he said it was in abeyance—held—pending a referendum that would take place in the Fall.

He wasn't convincing and neither were we—for he finally decided that we had been married some time and were merely pulling his leg. Since time was short we hastened on, and as we reached the town of Elkton, the streets were filled with criers before every house eagerly soliciting matrimonial business for the dilapidated dominies inside—we pulled into the driveway of the most pretentious dwelling in sight, at such an angle as to hide the car's New York license plates from the eagle eyes of the steerers—then I entered and made a deal—$5.00 for the dominie, $2.00 for the license fee, $3.00 for the steerer. We drove around the corner to the Court House or Clerk's Office—there were several couples there in line ahead—a girl sat at a typewriter with a continuous manifold sheet on a roller typing out the necessary license documents—the questions and answers were simple—documentary proof of divorce unnecessary.

With these technicalities dispensed with, we re-entered the car which had been parked in front of the fire house all the time and returned to the clergyman's home—three or four couples waiting were shifting about in the stuffy waiting room, anxiously awaiting their turn.

It was a beautiful spring day, the first touch of Spring was in the air—the bride-to-be could not stand the stuffiness of the waiting room or the people, so we waited on the porch—and as we waited we noticed that the Clergyman in bidding goodbye to each bride and groom shook their hands with his shrivelled "mit"—that was too much for the expectant bride—she announced flatly that she would have none of that handshaking performance.

When our turn came we went inside. It was an ugly uncouth room, the furniture and fixtures were shabby and worn, the place smelled dank. I gave the Clergyman's assistant $5.00, she crammed it in a desk drawer full of bills, then they stood us in the center of the floor, on a worn-out bit of carpet, and proceeded with the Baptist Marriage Ritual.

When he reached the following part in the service: "Then Adam took a bone from his side" and etc. I could hardly contain myself, it struck my fancy so—and when he added "And then he made Eve," I determined to nickname Berenice "Eve" and told her so—Berenice was too long and formal—her friends called her "B" which I thought too short and frivolous, and so Eve it was. We were given a pamphlet commemorating the occasion and set forth on our way—on the porch it was necessary for Eve to turn a complete circle in order to avoid the shrivelled handshaking performance of the Dominie—but he got her anyway.

We went immediately to the local Telegraph office where we wired you that Percy Holloway was your uncle, and wired Percy that you were his nephew—then we set forth for Philadelphia and New York.

We decided not to stop in the City of Brotherly Love but to try and make New York for our wedding repast—by the time we reached Trenton, we were tired and decided to stop for a champagne cocktail—I think Eve really wanted to pee. When she returned from the Little Girl's Room, I sensed that something was wrong—for the second time on my nuptial night my bride was unwell—your mother was the first.

Then we headed North for New York where we went to the Ambassador for our bridal supper and champagne—the bill was $20.00 there and when they gave me change for a $50 bill they shortchanged me $20.00—wedding night or no, I squawked and they made good.

From the Ambassador we went to the El Morocco, the Stork Club, Ceruitti's at 121 E. 54th and several other night spots—by 3 o'clock in the morning I was driving down Broadway thru all the red lights regardless.

I took my new bride home to 37th Street—and in the conventional superstitious manner, well known to many a man and a maid, carried her across the threshold and deposited her within.

That was to begin a new era, or a new episode, or a new reign in my life: the reign of Eve—much of it you know—some of it you've heard—a great deal you are vaguely aware of—and of most of it you are not aware.

It was not until we were homeward bound that I actually learned what Eve's activity was in life—and what her income ($20,000 annually)—and she claimed that it was not until then that I fully disclosed the story of my "Woolworth's" (false teeth).

I was glad to have Ruth G. definitely behind me and nearly out of my life—that had been an unhealthy, unprofitable and impossible affiliation. I was happy in my choice—I was glad to be able to put the Jews out of my life—from a close personal association standpoint.

We were headed and destined for a turbulent beginning, for a hectic and trying period of adjustment—which in the first few months and years nearly wrecked our venture many times.

Eve's father was an Englishman, Charles Holloway—Eve's mother was half Irish and half Anglo-Saxon American—Mrs. Holloway, before her marriage, had been Berenice Evans, the daughter of Katherine Garrett and Thomas Peachey Evans. Thomas Peachey Evans was of old American lineage, stemming from the prominent Peachey family of Williamsburg, Va. (the old Peachey homestead still stands—restored by Rockefeller money—on the village green). The Peacheys were distinguished citizens in the Colonial days of Thomas Jefferson. A sketch of that family which is of considerable historical interest follows. They survived the Revolution and the Civil War:

Two of Eve's uncles, her mother's brothers, were famous Virginia horsemen—Lee Evans having at one time in his early youth been Master of Hounds of the Warrenton pack. Percy Evans another uncle, was the first master of hounds of the Middleburg Hunt—Percy was killed riding Association owned by Temple Gwathmey at the United Hunt Steeple Chase at Belmont Park in 1916.

For many years, Lee Evans owned a stable that he raced on the flat—he also trained many winners. Blockade was once owned by him before he became the famous three-time winner of the Maryland Cup—Lee had raced him on the flat and he wasn't much good at that.

Eve's grandmother owned a large place at Warrenton which was only recently sold by her uncle who was supposed to have kept it intact for his nieces and nephews. The Evans and Holloway families were well known in the horse world—Eve's first cousin, Sidney Holloway, being one of the outstanding trainers in the country, both of gentleman jockeys and of horses.

Having lived in a horse family all her life, Eve was never much interested—but as I look back over our short courtship, I remember being quite thrilled when I learned that she only rode side-saddle—I have never liked women riding astride—in the first place, it requires a much greater degree of horsemanship to ride side-saddle and in the second place, it is much more graceful—too few women have mastered the art in recent years, but then, riding is rapidly becoming one of the lost pleasures of life, except for a few Semitics in the large industrial centers, who were never intended for anything but the back of an ass.

Eve had had part of her schooling at the fashionable country school of Madame Boulliene in Warrenton.

As a little girl she had evidenced great interest in clothes and had made dresses for her own dolls and the dolls of her friends and her sisters—she dressed dolls for little marionette performances, and then as she grew older she made things for her schoolmates, appearing in the amateur theatricals—sewing, design, cut were a passion with her then, and have been a passion with her always. She is always fashion conscious—she loved clothes and her grandmother being a woman of considerable means, from time to time, spent large sums on her wardrobe.

When I met her, she was thirty-five years of age, had never been married, but had crossed the Atlantic Ocean on an average of four times a year, for a period of 8 or 9 years, spending much time in Paris, but also visiting other parts of the Continent—her trans-atlantic crossings were the bright spots in her life.

En route to Elkton, a thought that troubled her most was whether or not we would have anything to talk about after we were married, if, as the years marched by, we might not run out of conversation—well, for the last six and one-half years that fear has proven to have been unfounded.

Part of her life was spent in Virginia, part of it in Washington, part of it at Westbury, Long Island, and Great Neck.

She was no Broadway, or cafe society glamour girl—she had nothing in common with the bizarre—she was and is conservative—a bit aloof, with a degree of shyness, rather becoming in any female. To many she would appear prim and proper—but what many men fail to realize is the fact that the prim and proper female invariably makes the best wife, the best mistress, the best courtesan.

Eve has never forgotten how I arrived home on 37th St. on our wedding night slightly in my cups from too much champagne—I proceeded to take Ruth G.'s picture and smash it to bits on the terrace, frame, glass and all, tearing the photo to pieces.

The next day I wired her, Stanley H. and others, informing one and all of the sudden change in my status—matrimonial—the wire to Ruth never reached her because of an error on the part of the Telegraph Company.

From Miami, Ruth again, against my wishes, had gone to Havana, instead of returning to New York—largely in defiance of me, so I was doubly glad to be able to abruptly and finally strike her off the list.

Sunday afternoon we phoned Melba and I introduced her over the telephone to her successor—she was flabbergasted, she couldn't believe and wouldn't believe that I had ventured forth again and with another. Somehow, she seemed to have believed that altho she had divorced me, she still had me at her beck and call—her emotional tears were audible over the phone—she could not contain herself—Tom B. told me she called on him (hysterically) for confirmation.

None of my friends had ever met Eve—none of them had ever heard of her—I had kept that wooing strictly to myself—I had not bandied her name about.

We also called Ann H. to tell her of the news—she obviously was annoyed, and so great was her annoyance, that from that day forward, a friendship of many years standing between Eve and Ann came to an abrupt end—"piqued" I think they call it—because the other girl got the man.

Eve didn't like the 37th Street apartment, she wanted me to get rid of it—her mother was still away and she felt we would be much more comfortable in her own home. All the furniture she had paid for, she was paying the rent and for the maintenance and upkeep of the place—she had the maid there and the facilities for keeping house—she could see no reason why they shouldn't be made full use of.

In a moment of great weakness, still under the first blush of my bride's charm, I capitulated—and that was my first great mistake. The psychological effect of returning to her apartment was bad—it was bad in the eyes of her friends, more so than in the eyes of mine—but it didn't create the right impression anywhere—it made her master of the house.

Sunday evening, we called you and Percy at Hanover, only to learn that you, with great tact, according to your own statement, when Percy had told you that his sister had always paid for his education, his board and keep was putting him thru college, and then asked you if you thought her marrying of me would make any difference on that score, you glibly replied: "Yes, I think it will—if I know my father, he thinks men should earn their own way thru life and pay for what they get themselves—the hard way." That upset Percy no end and eventually enraged his Ma—it was true, but had been better left unsaid.

After talking to you both, we then called California, to inform the Mater. I had never met her—she had never met me—she had heard nothing about me from anyone save what her own daughter had casually mentioned, but when Eve called her full of joy and overflowing with happiness, her mother received the news coldly—irritated and annoyed that her oldest, the family provider had ventured forth.

When Eve introduced us over the long distance phone, she was cold and distant, almost to the point of rudeness—there was no sound of welcome in her voice, no greeting of heartfelt congratulations—she resented her daughter marrying and marrying in her absence. For years she had interfered with her daughter's life—she had embarrassed her (because of an inherent weakness) on crucial occasions—she had pointedly discouraged courtships of any kind—she was almost a pathological case as far as Eve was concerned. To her, Eve assumed the form, and had for many years, of the provider—of the head of the household—she looked upon her daughter as a woman looks upon her husband, the breadwinner. Her reaction to our marriage was that of a wife who had just learned that her husband and provider had run off with another woman. She was bitter—she never got over the blow—she never forgave.

You could almost feel Mrs. Holloway recoil to the news over the Long Distance phone—it was a hell of a slap in the face. We were both very happy and bubbling over with enthusiasm for the great adventure that lay before us—we were eager to proclaim to all and sundry the union that had taken place, and Mrs. Holloway's reaction placed quite a damper upon our enthusiasm—it was as if someone had dashed a bucket of cold water in our faces. It took us some time to recoil from the shock of that reception.

We had moved back to the apartment Eve and her mother had been sharing on 59th Street, which as I mentioned was a mistake. I had concurred in her suggestion—I hadn't wanted to definitely oppose at that moment, but that's where I was wrong.

There is little doubt that had we set up housekeeping regardless of how cramped the quarters for two on 37th Street, the first three years of our married life would have been smoother, there would have been less opposition on the part of Eve's family to overcome, and it would have placed me in a much better light with everyone. But we couldn't see that then, we weren't concerned with what others thought—we were only concerned with ourselves.

[In 1938, not long after his marriage to Eve, my father discovered he had kidney and bladder stones that necessitated an operation. He decided that the operation would probably be fatal and made arrangements for his death.]

During the heat of our recent campaign, I discovered a certain amount of pus and blood and foreign matter in my urine. I had been rather suspicious for some time that all was not well—for from seldom having to take a leak except in the morning and then at night, I had to piss frequently—and it was not always a satisfactory stream—sometimes a mere dribble or drip drip drip. I mentioned the details to the family doctor who brushed the symptoms aside with a statement that men as they matured got that way.

The condition was so obviously wrong that I went to see another doctor, who after giving me some sulfa drugs for a week or so without correcting or reducing the amount of foreign matter, took pictures of the "innards" only to discover a well developed stone near the kidney and a large stone in the bladder—a condition that obviously had existed for some time—for years in fact.

It will necessitate two operations—front and back—to remove the stones. These operations, cause unknown, are often successful, but there is always the possibility that they may not be and that brings me to a few minor points in connection with what may be my "grand finale."

I face the eventuality of what may come in perfect calmness, for I have gotten much out of life.

I shall not have time to complete this letter insofar as bringing it up to date—it matters little whether I do or not—for nothing in this life individually really matters to anyone but ourselves.

I shall not be able to proof-read the first copy from my first original draft—I have gotten too far behind for that.

I shall endeavor to put Eve's affairs in such state that they can be carried on without too much difficulty—at any rate they are largely matters of tax disputes with the Federal and State Tax Departments.

I shall leave the genealogy part of this letter for the files of the New York Genealogy Society—anyone experienced can review them and then complete them if they wish to.

I shall not apologize for those things that Society would undoubtedly consider I should have done differently than the way I did them.

I shall not apologize for my conventional sins of so-called omission.

If I had my life to live over again it would probably be led the same way.

If you ever take the trouble to read this letter, which you probably won't, you will discover for yourself what my real weaknesses were—you will determine from your lights what you think I should have done, rather than what I did. . . .

People must be accepted for themselves—for what they are as they are—and the best must be made of them as they are, accepting them for better or for worse—they cannot be remade, they were cast at conception and once cast a man cannot be remade. . . .

My great regret in going will be the leaving of Eve alone—I of all those she has ever known have understood her better than anyone—I have admired her rare qualities, her loyalty, honesty, forthrightness, humor and genius—and have revelled in the temperament that has accompanied her extraordinary abilities. She has been a rare and a fine woman among women, she has been a great wife—no man could ever have asked for more—she has given me the love and devotion and understanding that few men are ever privileged to know—and from my experience of women, I know whereof I speak.

She has been generous beyond words in heart and deed—she has sacrificed, she has slaved—but always for others rather than herself. I have loved Eve and literally worshipped her as I never believed I could continuously love and worship any woman. My life with her has been superbly happy. To truly love and be loved, to understand and be understood, and to enjoy a real companionship is the zenith of the happiness and tranquility on earth that I have known with Eve.

Leaving Eve is the only regret I will have—because I have lived my life.

Alice B. upon her return from one of her coast to coast promotional tours for *Vogue*—in January 1938, to be exact—she was with her family in California for Xmas 1937—invited me to dine with her in her apartment at the Beaux-Arts and to see the colored movies she had taken on her trip. Much of the picture showed her tacky parents and their frightful Los Angeles bungalow.

That performance was our after dinner entertainment—home movies of our loved ones are always a bore to others even when well done.

During the showing of the pictures the maid cleaned up the apartment and the kitchenette.

The show over, there was the usual polite chit-chat for a respectable period and then the other guests departed.

The maid followed shortly thereafter.

That left us alone—and my prick got hard.

The moment had come to strike, if Alex Ettl was to have his curiosity appeased—if he were ever to know if Alice were still a virgin or not.

Alice was a willing—yea—even eager subject.

I fondled her on the sofa—kissing and pawing her.

I caressed her cuzzy—and showed her my stiff cock.

Now Alice loved her comfort—she liked to do things nicely.

Many of the apartments at the Beaux-Arts on East 44th—she lived at 310—were fitted with "in-a-door" beds—and hers was one of those.

As I said, Alice liked her comfort—so she, sensing hopefully what appeared destined to occur, upped and opened the doors on the bed closet and pulled the bed out and down—not my cock—that was to come later.

By that time she was in an alarming state of disarray and I knew that Alex was right and Dorothy (his wife) wrong—for Miss B. was no longer acting like a maiden virtuous. In fact she was nearly nude.

She was a tiny delicate thing—flat chested, small tits—my "piece de resistance."

In a jiffy—in fact as she was lowering the bed—I slipped my coat and shirt off, dropped my pants and drawers down all in a heap on the floor—I never was one for wasting time when it came to exhibiting "my manly form" in the nude.

She quivered and shook like a leaf as I stripped her completely and laid her out on her "in-a-door" bed.

She feigned shyness—she wanted to get under the covers.

She professed great ignorance of the sexual ways of a man with a maid or vice versa.

Whether she was "pulling my cock" or not I do not know.

I told her many things she may or may not have known—but I enjoyed the telling—it excited me the more—that may have been her innocent purpose. It pleased me to be a teacher, it helped whip me into a white heat of passion—her cunt was as tight as a virgin's.

But she wasn't a virgin. Alex had won conclusively—for years he had wondered about his wife's college chum.

Alice had had an ardent lover in her life for some years but that had fizzled out.

She was a strange woman. Men often ask women how they compare with other men as lovers—if their cocks are as big or bigger than the other fellow's—they always hope theirs is the biggest, the longest or the thickest, if not the prettiest.

Women seldom ask you how they compare with other courtesans or whores—but Alice wanted to know how she was doing, how she compared with other women as a lay.

I gave her the build-up—and putting a pillow under her tiny ass, fucked the living daylights out of her.

She never protested or opposed when I went down on her and lapped her cunt—she willingly sucked my cock—she let me "frig" her in her ass hole—she was a glutton for it all.

Her only concern seemed to be her fear of getting "knocked up" and she would rush for the "douche" each time I shot my load inside her.

All in all, Alice was a good lay—it was a pleasant evening and when I finally departed I wired Alex in Florida that I had rung the bell five times—and I hadn't been the first. . . .

Norah A., a former model of Harry M. (in his bachelor days Harry really was a commercial artist or illustrator for magazines like *Collier's* or big advertising agencies), was a show girl of some renown—she was a red haired beauty with plenty of fire and "it."

In addition to her modeling and dancing she was a painter and sculptress—from February 28th to March 15th she held an exhibition of her paintings and other work—a one-man show at the Delphic Studio, 44 West 56th St.

Harry M. had taken me to her preview—enroute Harry grew so nervous contemplating the meeting with his former model and love that he literally broke out into a sweat with the perspiration rolling down his face.

The work of hers that I liked best was her "Sphinx Moderne" (in plaster).

Norah had some circulars printed, announcing her showing, and I mailed a lot of them out on my personal mailing list—this was a gesture for the purpose of ingratiating myself—she had a natural bent for publicity and her showing got her a lot of feature articles that attracted the Hollywood scouts.

Remember you saw her dance semi-nude one night in the Greenwich Village Inn under the name of Delores.

After her showing was over, she came to dinner with me at the 37th Street apartment and spent the night—she was an exciting screw—boy how she could lay it on the line.

Just at dawn as I was pounding hell out of her belly I noticed her bust, tits, face and rumpled hair in the early gray light that was creeping in thru the window.

Her poised lips, her disheveled hair, her firm and projecting breasts were a startling replica of her "Sphinx Moderne" in plaster.

Then the truth flashed thru my mind—she had but modeled a self-portrait of herself in plaster—of her exotic disarray following a good working over (sexually)—she looked for all the world like a temptress from Hades.

She was the lay of lays—one of the best fucks that ever crossed my threshold. She put everything she had into each and every thrust of her lovely body and we both came and came and came until we were completely exhausted—we literally screwed the whole night through.

It was a one night stand never to be repeated—I doubt if it ever would have been the same.

In less than two weeks' time I had married again and that was that—I never saw Norah again, except the night with you and then one night when Eve and I went down to the Greenwich Village Inn to see her show. That night she borrowed Eve's silver fox cape to be photographed with Earl Carroll—the picture was printed in some Broadway sheet and she had a part in Carroll's West Coast night club Revue.

Lorell P. has a luscious body—but was a phlegmatic

screw. Her drinking, her oversexed conversation, her filthy, but clever sketches—all roused me greatly.

Whenever I would meet up with Lorell, for luncheon or what have you, she would draw dirty pictures on the menu—frequently of monkeys jerking off or fucking or sucking beautiful nudes.

Lorell was never much of a talker—but she could "draw well," "write well," "drink not too well," and fuck passably—and her body was lovely—she was insidious rather than active.

I would see her from time to time after I married Eve—whenever Eve was lunching with someone else.

One Saturday when Eve had gone off for the day with her mother, brother and girl friend, I had luncheon with Lorell at the Crillon. We got a bit high—Lorell always preferred to drink her meals—during luncheon she told me of her uncle and his wife, how they were both after her—so during the afternoon, we went up there—they had an attractive apartment—the uncle was treasurer of a large and well known woolen firm.

All was well for the first hour or so—then as the drinks took hold, the Aunt and Uncle both became amorous—I, myself, had felt the glow of the liquor and the call of the cunt.

Her aunt-in-law especially resented the obvious affection we were at that moment feeling for one another.

The uncle as he got hotter and tighter became edgier and edgier.

Then as night fell and I went to phone Eve, that I was detained—the sparks began to fly.

I was drunk by that time—showing my cock to Lorell every chance I could get, or whenever the Aunt and Uncle were out of the room snarling at one another.

I was defiant of Eve—because she had left me for the day and made no bones about it—in fact I told her off in no uncertain terms—what Eve said and did is something else again—she packed her things and moved out—women never learn not to leave their men.

Then I went back to Lorell.

While I was on the phone, both the Uncle and Aunt went after her.

When I returned to the room I entered into the spirit of the occasion and between the three of us, we literally stripped Lorell bare—this seemed to appeal to her perverted tastes, but in the fracas, the Uncle became very jealous of his wife and me—insults followed insults, then we starting slugging—that brought Lorell to her senses.

She interceded before anyone was killed—and whispering she wanted to go home and to bed with me, pulled on her bedraggled clothes as I adjusted mine—and we departed as the Uncle slumped to the floor in a drunken stupor.

When I got her home we stripped—and indifferently she let me fuck her whenever I wanted to the rest of the evening.

Lorell had good taste in clothes, dressed smartly and would have made an excellent designer or artist—a keen sense of satire—only liquor and sex always got in her way.

I heard from Lorell some weeks later—she was drunk and called me up to speak her mind. Her drunken tirade was an upbraiding of me for being a pimp—she blandly announced that I had married Eve only for her money or large income—that I didn't love her—that I was a skunk—that I was fucking around with other women. Lorell was so closely allied with the dress business that I didn't want Eve to know who it was—I never told her because she liked Lorell and Lorell grew to like her, as all who know her do—I said it was a friend of Ruth G.'s, because Eve had answered the phone. . . .

Eve was not experienced in the ways of men and women—marital—nor did she know much about "preventatives"—douches, etc.—and the method of self-administration of same.

The night of our wedding, she was embarrassed by nature's monthly call.

Well, that had happened to me the night I married your mother so it was no novelty.

That meant a week of abstinence with a bride as unsophisticated sexually as Eve.

We had been married for almost a week when the coast appeared clear—we had a very passionate affair—in fact, Eve was, without doubt, one of the most responsive, it not the most responsive, affectionate and lovable women I had ever known—her emotions knew no bounds.

Her sexual naiveness captivated me.

Her good food pleased me—but above all her sense of humor and her good mind enthralled me. She was smart, had nice eyes, an excellent mind—a quick, clear, thinker, entirely devoid of bunk or hokum—she was frankness personified. She had had a hard life of bread winning—been kicked around by her family—but she held her head high—she was always to the manor born. . . .

An idea as to how naive Eve was sexually—we were married for over a year before she knew that a "hard on" was not my permanent condition—for my prick was always stiff.

[A few months after his marriage to Eve my father had his final meeting with Ruth G.]

I met Ruth and we drove out on Long Island around Westbury—she was all wrought up—we fought, screwed in the car, out in some field, tore at one another—her clothes were literally in shreds—our faces and bodies clawed and black and blue.

I explained to Eve that my condition was due to a fist encounter with Willie Burns, an old school chum who owed me some money—that we fought over the debt and she should see him. I never saw Ruth again after that except on the street or in restaurants—but not to speak to—I talked with her from time to time, over the phone, for a while, but that was all.

How Eve and I ever survived the rows at 400 East 57th I will never know.

One night I was so drunk and violent that when she locked herself in the bathroom I smashed the panel in to get at her—another night she foiled me by putting on my suit and sitting in the tub—in order to turn the shower on her I had to wet my suit.

I frequently talked of suicide and wanted to make it a double.

All in all it was a tempestuous summer—trying to reconcile our separate ways of life and a conglomeration of weird friends—mine more so than hers.

How she survived—how she lived through it, stuck it out, I will never know.

But we came up to the 1938 finale and the beginning of 1939 much more reconciled than we had been at any other time since our marriage.

It had been a tough row—but we had taken it and were coming through.

The course of true love did not run very smoothly. In addition to several brawls, which we indulged in when drinking heavily, there were many fights about finances, etc.

Eve was forever slipping away to visit with her mother and I resented that—I resented her mother not coming to the house—I resented the way her mother was defiling me and talking about me to all and sundry behind my back. I frankly didn't care much for Eve's brother—I had not met her sister, but I had glowing tales told me about that young lady and her supposed charm. . . .

Into that tense situation, Percy projected himself one morning—I was stretched out on the chaise-longue, promoting my candidacy for Secretary to the State Committee when Percy arrived—I wasn't dressed—Eve was lunching with Ann H. at the Algonquin—I didn't stop talking. . . . I continued to talk, hoping that Percy would leave with Eve when she went to keep her luncheon date—but he didn't.

Some words followed, and I knocked him down on the bed—altho he was taller than I am and younger, he was lighter. When he attempted to rise and continued to struggle, I held him down and choked him—when I finally let him up with the understanding that he would . . . leave the house at once, he proceeded as soon as he was on his feet, to start the argument again—once more I knocked him down and I picked him up by the collar, and literally threw him out of the apartment.

The thing that enraged me the most about the whole proceeding and the reason I threw him on the bed and choked him, was the fact that when we were slugging it out he (with his shoes on—I was barefooted) proceeded to kick my shins and tried to step on my feet—altho I only had my underwear or shorts on, I chased him down the hall and threw his hat after him, as he ran into the freight elevator.

I called Eve at the Algonquin and she was terribly upset, blaming me entirely.

We battled it out all summer at 400 East 57th Street, which was a dirty, dusty place at best—more than once we separated, sometimes for a few hours, and then once Eve went home to her mother for several days, before a reconciliation was effected. . . .

1939 was in many respects all in all a pleasant year for me. There was little to mar the tranquility of our marital status other than the usual mother-in-law difficulties.

We rented a little house at Mill Neck, Long Island, on the Burdicks' property—it was a little too close to their home for complete seclusion, but it was nestled on the edge of a thickly wooded section which kept it very cool in summer and protected if from the worst storms in the Winter.

The rent was only $35.00 a month and from January to June, we used it primarily for weekends; then we sublet the Sutton Place apartment to a little number known as Tony Van A. She sported a car and chauffeur and a little dog—her references were prominent bankers, businessmen and investors. Eventually it became obvious that her profession was one of the oldest in the world—the most widely and universally practiced—her angle I suspect was flagellation—the status with her customers, high—she was versatile in the ways of a maid with a man, professionally. . . .

In January of 1939, we set forth by car for Florida. . . .

[My father describes their visit to the Breakers at Palm Beach.]

We strolled out on the hotel parapet overlooking the ocean after dinner (formal) in the moonlight. We ensconced ourselves on a cushioned settee in a dream world. The setting was perfect—Eve, the moonlight, the glittering ocean, the palm trees, the soft music floating out from the hotel alive with its multitude of lights. Without exception, in addition to her physical attractiveness, Eve was the finest woman I had ever known—able, with an excellent mind, far above the average. She was a woman of sterling character—brilliant, in fact, a potential genius, if not actually one. She was generous beyond measure—a fine sense of humor. It was always a joy to be with her.

Eve truly graced Palm Beach.

It was a perfect setting for her.

We sat there in complete silence for a long time—the silence only comprehended by two souls completely akin—then we talked of life and love and all the sweet nothings that make life "for two" so heavenly—at times we were very very much in love—at least I was and I suspect it was mutual.

Eve was a vision in her evening gown—I was proud of her, proud and thrilled to be seen with her, to have it known that she was my wife.

It was not until we finally arose to stroll along the walk that we became aware that we had been sitting in a puddle left by a gardener when watering the plants—our tails were wet. We had been so absorbed with one another, with the spell of the place, that we hadn't noticed before that the cushion was very wet.

That was tops for me at Palm Beach for all time—heavenly contentment—perfect bliss. . . .

1940–1941

[Shortly after his marriage to Eve my father began negotiating to develop tung oil plantations in Florida. The great bulk of tung oil, a vital ingredient in marine paint, was imported from China and Malaysia and my father tried to persuade the various governmental agencies responsible for military procurement to underwrite a vast program for producing tung oil (made from the nuts of the tung tree).

One of the principal obstacles to this ambitious plan was the fact that it takes at least three years for tung trees to begin to bear and the war might well be over by that time. My father, nonetheless, spent much time and a good deal of Eve's money trying to bring off the tung oil deal. What might be called the Great Tung Oil Delusion was my father's last fling, a demonstration for his new bride of his energy, his initiative, his numerous friends in high places. From the point of view of impressing her it was eminently successful. Eve was charmed by the whole venture, the conferences, letters, phone calls to important officials, the studies, the pages of statistics, the mustering of evidence and arguments on behalf of tung oil, the conviction that tung oil was a vital product, critically needed to keep America strong. To Eve my father appeared a brave and resourceful David battling against the Goliathlike bureaucracy. The tung oil caper enabled my father to overcome the stigma of being a kept man. It was a play in which the leading character was the heroic entrepreneur trying to save his country. To be sure he never prevailed upon the government to make him a millionaire—I suspect he never really expected it to; although it has probably made many no more able or worthy adventurers millionaires—but he did demonstrate his talents, so to speak. These high-level negotiations made the dress business look like small potatoes by comparison. That, at least, is clearly what Eve believed.]

1939 had proven to be for me a year of marking time—I hadn't accomplished much, in fact I hadn't accomplished anything at all—there hadn't even been any outside female or sex interest to occupy any of my time. . . .

1940 was to bring forth a variety of activity, none of which produced from the financial standpoint. . . .

By 1940 Roosevelt, aided and abetted by New York's demagogic little Mayor—the would-be Napoleon, Fiorello H. La Guardia, variously known as "The Little Flower," "Butch," "The Big Hat," etc.—had stirred up religious hatred to a white heat.

The Jews were all yelling for us to go in and beat up Hitler (that is, they wanted the Christians to do the fighting making sure to keep well in the background themselves, far from the actual fighting) altho they had been strangely silent when the Russians were destroying millions of Gentiles.

Lindbergh and his "America Firstists" were cutting quite a figure. "Slim" had put his finger right on the Semitic sore point—their rabid insistence upon our making war upon Germany on account of the way Germans were treating the Jews was revolting.

Our military men who were in World War I were astounded with the capacity the Germans were showing in the early days of World War II as individual fighters—their initiative and resourcefulness in open formation dumbfounded the military experts, who thought the Germans could only operate in mass formations as wholly knit machines.

[1940 saw the acceleration of the war in Europe. One of the consequences of the German invasion of Holland was the problem of Dutch refugees. Through his friendship with Van Loon, which had been to a degree revived, my father undertook to act as Executive Director of the Queen Wilhelmina Fund, a fund collected to aid Dutch refugees. My father was largely responsible for the success of the fund-raising campaign.]

We had sublet our apartment to a Mrs. Barber and her daughter because Eve wanted to be with her mother at Manhasset, where she was recovering in Eve's house (her mother was recovering from the operation on her hip following the fracture from the fall), in the latter part of 1940.

A day or two before we were to turn the apartment over to the sub-tenants, I was taken down with a severe attack of the Flu. I couldn't remain at home, so Dr. Sanford had me removed to the Roosevelt Hospital where I was given a semi-private room without any other patients because I was contagious.

Having hospitalization, I was able to spend a week there without any cost except the doctor's bill. It was inconvenient for Eve, who was living out at Manhasset, and it wasn't a very merry New Year for me—altho the nurses who were very attractive, and the orderly who was bi-sexual (and gloried in the fact that he was married to a prostitute, a street walker who brought him in a tidy sum each night) did everything they could to amuse me and make my stay interesting—and that they did.

The floor orderly came into my room on New Year's Eve (ostensibly on duty) and talked and talked—he told me (he was very young and illiterate) that his wife "hustled"—fucked—for part of their living—he made very little. He told me how he watched her with her customers thru a crack in the wall of their room—how it excited him—how he would come, watching them—then after the customer had departed he would be so hot that he would lap up his wife's wet deck and then "frig" her himself.

His tall tales of his wife and her lovers and his part in the sexual goings-on at home plus his conversational revelations about his alleged fucking of the nurses got me hot—noticing thru the sheet that I had a hard on, he put his hand in under and felt my stiff prick—then taking a great chance (anyone might have come in) he opened his fly and showed me his big tool—it was quite a specimen. I took it in my hand and caressed it as he played with me—then he went down on me—I couldn't resist or hold back—I was too hot. I came in his mouth—then I jerked him off—I thought he would never stop coming.

I gave him a couple of bucks for his pains—it was worth more, but he was only accustomed to small sums.

The next day, New Year's, the nurse who came to bathe me was a lovely lass, short, red-headed, full of vitality, vibrant—she was not one of the regular floor girls—she was up from the "public ward," relieving for the holiday.

The regular nurses when they are giving you your bath in bed (your sponge bath) when they come to your tool are supposed to give you the washrag to wash and wipe your own prick—but that gal didn't—she washed it herself. At her bath manipulations of my cock, the old rod stood up—she toyed with it—her waist or uniform was cut low—I could see her tits when she bent over me and I was in a white heat. In a flash I slipped my hand up under her dress, felt her damp cuzzy—boy, she was hot—then I played with her teats. I could hardly keep from coming—when she bent over me she let her bubbies pop way out and then she rubbed them against my cock—my fingers were working way up her hole—she liked it up the "arse" hole as well as the cunt. She went down on me, and did I come—I gave her everything I had as she came on my fingers—she had a luscious cunt to finger fuck.

I never saw her again—she went back to the Public Ward the next day and I left the hospital shortly thereafter.

My regular day floor nurse lived around the corner in a two-room flat with another nurse. I called on her several times—she was a fair fuck—I never got to her in the hospital, but in her room it was different. Once when I found her roommate also at home with her we had a threesome—nurses are hot numbers.

Driving Eve into town every day left me sort of footloose with nowhere to go but park and sit in the car until I met her for luncheon, for I didn't have an office, so I rented a small apartment on the south side of 27th Street. . . .

When I arrived at the new house, I found the landlord—he showed me a nice clean room on the first floor up, rear, at

$6 per week—a new bath that was shared by three—a fireman who wanted to get away from his nagging wife; a girl who worked in the Metropolitan Life. The front apartment on the same floor had a bathroom and kitchen—that was $35 per month.

I talked it over with Eve and took it. It gave me a place to work on my papers and follow up Tung Oil. I got out all my old pictures of girls, many in the nude—covered the walls with sketches and pictures—I hung the lovely sketches that Lorell P. made for me, the series of the nude beauty having an affair with an ape—one showed the monkey sucking the girl—then fucking her—then jerking off—and then the girl going down on the monkey—she always promised to do one of the monkey fucking the girl between the tits. . . .

The landlord had a French cleaning woman who got quite a kick out of the pictures. Nearly every day she would come into my room while I was there—I would be lying around in the nude—she liked to suck me off—she started in by playing with my cock. The first time she came in my room when I was there I was dressed and she talked about the pictures and looked at them carefully—I got stiff, and felt her ass, then I slipped my penis into her calloused hand—she was coy at first—then I got my balls out—then dropped my pants and got my hand first on her teats, then her cunt—she jerked me off. I don't think she had to do much jerking—I came all over the floor and wall—that delighted her.

The next day I had a robe on when she came in—then I dropped it off—my prick was stiff (it had been just in anticipation). That day she stripped after a little coaxing and sucked me off—after that I never had anything on when she came in to clean—since I seldom slept there, all she had to do when she came in was play with me. I never fucked her—fear of a dose, I guess. Now and then she would bring in a mulatto girl late in the afternoon—a girl who worked in one of the other houses up the street—they would suck one another off as I jerked off all over them.

Whenever Mrs. H. became too difficult I spent the night. Sometimes Eve would stay there with me but it was not comfortable for two—and then I never knew what would turn up.

Eve and I frequently lunched in one of the Armenian or Turkish restaurants.

On the South side between Lex and Third Avenue near the Theatre on 27th Street, there was a private dance parlor—one of those two-room jobs—walkup and dance, belly rub and fuck—also another favorite of mine on Lexington between 30th and 31st and one on 34th St. and Lex.

They always turned the music on as a blind. The fee was $1.00—for that you could come in your pants while you danced—rubbing your cock against their cunts, you could watch yourself in the center of the room before a long mirror. There was always a long mirror—so you could accidentally pull the girl's skirt up from the rear, slowly but surely, until her ass was bare. For $2 they would jerk you off or suck you—for $3 you could fuck them (I preferred to be jerked off or sucked off—thought it safer from disease).

There was always a couch in the next room for the pupils to rest on or fuck on. Eventually most of those small places were closed by the Mayor.

The girls were hot numbers—when you were new to a place they made some pretext of teaching, but not for more than a moment or two—then they would come in close and rub their cunts against your cock. Mine was always hard in expectation—they never wore much, in fact nothing but their light thin dresses which you could look thru and see the outline of their legs all the way up when they got between you and a light—which they always did. Their flimsy dresses were of black silk mostly. Times were not so easy then—women did anything to get by and there were plenty of lovely girls in the business—today they give it away—they make so much at anything.

Usually by the time you got their asses bare in the mirror, you were ready to come in your pants—or take it out and come all over the floor or in their mouths.

I wrote about these places on the upper west side of town when Joe L. and I used to visit many of them along Central Park West and the side streets.

Just writing about those places gets me hot—I wonder if

it's the memory of them or just thinking of the lovely creature who will type this out for me, that makes the damn prick stand up and wave at me—I frequently come just writing about my recollections of those days.

The girl in the room next to mine was a bit on the heavy side—she liked my room too. Ann was good for an occasional workout nights, when I was there alone—and nothing better offered.

The couple that moved into the front apartment were in show business—when the husband was on the road, we would have matinees—she was a swell lay. I picked her up by laying in wait for her to put out her swill.

In a gin mill on 34th Street near Lex I met up with a telephone operator of the Associated Hospital Service of New York. She worked for David McAlpine Pyle who was head of it—she lived in a room in the apartment house above the saloon.

I took her to my room quite often at night—on one occasion I took pictures of her in the costumes that I brought back from Paris—they are in this file—she was also on the plump side—I cut out the background so Eve wouldn't recognize that room if she found them. She liked having me fuck her so much that she was forever calling me at 27th Street.

A few other nondescript lays came and went—I wasn't exactly idle—all told my three months stay on 27th Street was pleasant from many angles.

On July 15th, 1941 Eve and I set forth determined to learn more about Tung Oil. We headed for Louisiana and Florida to inspect existing groves. In New Orleans, after we had washed up, removed the dirt and grime from our persons, I took Eve over to Antoine's for dinner—none better the world around—the gourmet's delight. Nowhere on the face of the globe can such gastronomic delights be found as there—Bouillabaisse, Huites en coquille a la Rockefeller, Pompano en Papillote, Pommes Souffles, Frogs Legs saute demi-Bordelaise and Louisiana River Shrimp.

While introducing Eve to the wondrous edibles of the

place the manager gave us a copy of their centennial souvenir—1840 to 1940.

The Souvenir contained a list of notables that had wined and dined there during the years—with comments by some of them—some such were Irvin S. Cobb, Will Rogers, F.D.R., Cal Coolidge, Alf Landon, Herbert Hoover, O.O. McIntyre, H.L. Mencken, George Sokolsky, Julian Street, Ethel Barrymore, Katherine Cornell, Fiorello La Guardia, Helen Morgan, Hendrik Willem van Loon, Lawrence Tibbett, Eddie Cantor, Justice Felix Frankfurter, Cornelia Otis Skinner, Lucius Beebe, etc.

Eve was scanning the list of distinguished guests who had supped at that "fine board"—men like Theodore Roosevelt, William Howard Taft, Marshal Foch, John J. Pershing, Gen. Smedley Butler, Admiral Byrd, Henry Wallace, Harry Hopkins, J. Edgar Hoover. . . .

Reading thru these long lists of great and near to the great, she came to the list of authors, columnists and artists: Heywood Broun, Sherwood Anderson, Thomas Wolfe, Archibald MacLeish, Stark Young, Will Durant, Rube Goldberg, Drew Pearson, Quentin Reynolds, Francis Parkinson Keyes, Alexander Woollcott, Sinclair Lewis, and lots of others—and to her surprise came upon the name W. Ward Smith in the forefront of that list. At first she couldn't believe her eyes, then light dawned (shadows of the *Nomad* days) when she read my name off, I thought at first that she was trying to be funny—just putting it in herself—but when she showed it to me, I was indeed pleased—it did much for my ego.

That I had not won or deserved the right to be in such company little mattered—there it was for posterity to gaze upon—and that called for another bottle of champagne. My exuberance was complete—I loved Antoine the more, if that could be.

All my life even when in school I had longed to write, to express myself, my thoughts, my opinions thru the written word—to report in writing so that others reading could understand what I had to say, what was on my mind. I wanted so much to be able to express myself in writing on current affairs, domestic, international or what have you—Heywood Broun, F.P.A. Kenneth McGowan, Mark Sullivan, Walter Lippman, Bill McGeehan, F.F.V. (Frank Van de Water) were my early envies—how I wanted to be able to do what they were doing.

In latter years, Westbrook Pegler and Hugh Johnson held my envy—Hendrik Willem van Loon, Konrad Bercovici, John Gunther, William O'Donnel, George Skolsky; I have always wanted to write editorially or a column—I have never wanted money very much, enough to cover the bones, and persuade women to let me make love to them, and for a bit of pub crawling now and then—but that's all.

At the same time I have longed for the society of gentlefolk without doing anything to warrant my getting it or holding it if I got it—for all my life I have defied conventionality and have forever shocked my friends or fought with them when I felt they were not doing or thinking as they should. In theory, I recognize the right of everyone to do as they damn please altho few can (do as they damn please).

Back to New Orleans—dinner over, Roy Louis Alciatore the grandson of Antoine Alciatore (the founder) showed Eve thruout the place and all the treasures therein—principally menus of famous banquets and special occasions—and that too called for another bottle of champagne.

The hour was getting on, so we departed—very pleased with ourselves—at least I was. . . .

Eve has a definite aversion (which I have never been able to break her of or to overcome) to public demonstrations on the lewd or sexual side of life—she is the antithesis of Melba in that respect. In public and before others—even in her own home—Eve is still, after more than 8 years with me, a prude—privately, alone with her hubby, she exudes sex and is curious as hell about it all and will say and do anything almost—her reactions are healthy and when she lets her hair down it is always a surprise and a thrill. . . .

One night in August when I was in Washington on Tung

Oil, Percy (H.) drove me out to Ft. Meade to see you. He was working with Eastern Air Lines (in operations) at the time—he was living with Cecil Moore (Dartmouth '40) in Washington—Cecil was in the ticket selling end. Cecil was engaged to a girl flyer in Eastern reservations named McKenzie—Percy to Ann Loughlin, a girl from Smith living with her family in Montclair.

In addition to Cecil, the Goldberg boy (son of Rube) who had changed his name to George came along. They were all jelly cake when we dropped in on you and saw your setup and found you were a sergeant—the *Baltimore Sun* has just given you quite a writeup in its issue of August 21, 1941. . . .

I couldn't help but recall, as we sat there and chatted and had a drink, that day back in May when I had first called on Oscar at this same home of his in Arlington—and how he had said, as we lolled and chatted on his back lawn as the children romped and played, that the other side would have to start the shooting—and how he had suggested, in answer to a question of mine—that it might be started in the Red Sea by the Germans firing on some American ship carrying war supplies to the British. And I wondered then (Dec. 7th) if Oscar hadn't been dragging a red herring across my vision that May day and if he hadn't known all along that it would be the Japs—and had been really thinking of the Japs in the Pacific instead of the Germans in the Red Sea. Maybe he had said the Red Sea as a blind.

In May I said that to have a munitions ship blown up in the Red Sea wouldn't arouse the Americans enough to go to war—even after the second World War, we sat by and calmly watched the satellites of Red Russia shoot down American air ships and kill American flyers.

There never was any doubt in my mind but that Roosevelt knew that he could eventually jockey the Japs into attacking us—his State Department knew it—every Army and Navy officer who had ever been in the Orient knew it—and Roosevelt's family were very familiar with the Far East.

If I had anticipated it for twelve years prior to Pearl Harbor—certainly the Roosevelt gang were aware of the danger, but they didn't want to stop it, they wanted it to happen—everything I ever heard firsthand or have read or observed, has convinced me that they were yearning for an attack and doing everything possible to bring one about. The Germans wouldn't fall for FDR bait, for they remembered the first World War.

The Japs grabbed the bait and the Roosevelt Brain Trusters had their wish fulfilled.

Roosevelt's place in history is questionable—he will be there, but he will still stink for his infamy and his betrayal of his own country for a few fleeting moments of world glory and power. . . .

The following days were hectic—Washington was a beehive of activity. Inadequate guns were mounted on roof tops—supposed to be anti-air craft—and men were posted at the bridges and guns mounted there—many of the guns were dummies set up to fool the enemy.

Then a rumor came thru about noon that German planes were roaring down the New England coast bound for New York. I tried to reach Eve to tell her to stay indoors—I couldn't get her on the phone, she had gone out to lunch early. The telephone wires were jammed—I was frantic, worried to death about her—sirens screamed about New York and Washington and other cities. I had rented a radio—it was on full blast—people everywhere were paralyzed—but Eve in New York went about having her lunch, doing her chores and ignoring the excitement and confusion. I finally got her but only when she got back to her office after lunch—by that time the all clear had been sounded or announced—nobody knew what it was all about—so confusing—the signals hadn't been properly worked out and anyway it had been a false alarm.

I knew your outfit was returning from manoeuvers and I figured that you would be at the Fort Hill Reservation by Monday night—you being north bound from the Carolina mountains to Fort Meade.

That afternoon, (December 8th) I traveled South to meet you. I picked up a GI on the way down—he was part of the regular garrison at Hill. Every bridge south of the Potomac had a detachment of soldiers guarding it—but I wasn't stopped.

When I reached Hill and let the boy off, they wouldn't let me in the front gate—the boy, however, had told me of a way to get around to the rear of the reservation where you all would probably be—the only reason the kid had given me any hope at all of getting in the front way was to get a ride all the way—but he had tipped me off, so I backtracked and groping around in the dark, found my way thanks to the aid the friendly boys along the way gave me.

To me it all looked like a tangled mess—but that encampment that night with its glowing fires, its mass of equipment and the black outlines of the men as they were silhouetted against the fires, was one of those impressive sights that being seen for the first time and then never again leaves a deep imprint on one's memory. It was a usual sight for you and the others and must have become quite commonplace for you as the years rolled on.

Those hot blazing fires in the pits with the iron rods across them surrounded by company groups keeping warm and chatting until the time to move on came, were a great sight. When you stepped out from the group around your fire in that crisp cold air and we walked over to the car together, it was for me the clicking of something long desired. I married young so that my son—my oldest—and I could be close companions, much closer and nearer of an age than my father and I had been in our camaraderie—but it was never to work out that way for me except on a handful of occasions. The blame?—who is there to judge impartially—perhaps I had been too selfish, too impetuous—whether it was all my fault or not, I do not know.

What I had always wanted most—and that too was no doubt a selfish egotistical parental yearning—I was never really to have consecutively, and that may have been just as well at the time for you. In fact, you would have been better off had you broken away entirely from your mother's influence from college on—you were making headway then as an individual—you continued to be yourself at Camp

James and in the Army and when you married Eloise—but then you slipped back to those provincial surroundings in which you had been submerged so many adolescent years.

I think men and women are the better for developing themselves—free from their parents' ways, customs and influence—children so often not only look like one parent or the other, but favor one or the other parent in speech, mannerisms and the approach to life. It's an insoluble problem.

While it may have been better for you that my plan to have a close pal-ship and understanding with my son did not materialize, it would have been better still if you had gotten away and stayed away from your mother's apron strings. That by virtue of the circumstances and the worldly comforts it affords, and the emotional chords that have always been so adroitly played upon, you will never be able to decide objectively and then do.

I kept the motor running and the heater on that night—in a convertible job, that does not keep you hot as toast, but it takes the chill off. As you will remember, we got in and settled down to a long talk about your future in the reflected glow of all those roaring fires along the hillside and in the flat—as far as we could see in the dark.

The immediate problem was whether you should go to Officers Training School or not—it seemed that there wasn't much difference between the pay of a Top Sergeant with wife and 2nd Lieut.—so why wait for a commission, why not marry Eloise immediately? At the time if you were married, you couldn't train for a commission.

I argued as earnestly as I could (without irritating you, I hope) for officer's training—first and foremost as I told you, your standing in civilian life afterwards would be vastly improved, especially at the war's end if you came out with a rank (later in life, it doesn't matter much, but at the start it does).

Second (a thought I did not give voice to), it would postpone your contemplated marriage to the blonde nugget from the Carolinas. I myself had rushed into so many legal and extra legal affiliations with the female of the species on account of an impatient prick (a stiff tool knows no conscience) that I was fearful for you. When you get hot you lose all perspective and balance, and never weigh the many factors that must of necessity enter into any union if it is to be successful and enduring.

I didn't want you to make a snap decision and be sorry afterwards. I have made snap decisions in such matters and had them successful (Eve, for example)—and then on the other hand, my marriage to your mother was not a hasty decision—ours was a long drawn out engagement that, after marriage, ended on the rocks—all of which disproves my own and the accepted theory in such matters. But nevertheless, as all men know and you yourself have so aptly said, before you get your tail, you think you cannot survive without it, and then after you have had it, you wonder why you bothered.

The professional prostitutes and the demi-mondaines have known all about that feeling thru the ages—that is why they get the five bucks on the mantel beforehand. That's why there has to be something more to marriage than a good screw—all kinds of women can get your cock to stand up and keep you hot for their pussy or their mouth or tongue, but you must have similar likes and dislikes in most cases to last—or else one must dominate the other and the other like to be dominated. Mutual interests are essential if the marriage is to be on an equal basis—with some, the "small fry" are the binding factor, but that is frequently not enough.

Then, too, I felt that if you held off there would always be the chance of your meeting someone that had been reared the same way that you had, that had had the same advantages—someone you would not have to train, that you would not feel superior to. I felt that you should have a taste of marital bliss before going overseas if you were to go—and it was a sure thing almost then that you would go.

Promiscuous tail on the curbstone satisfies for the moment, but the home brew has, as your ma once pointed out to me, many advantages—you don't have to get up and go out or home in the cold of night—some may let you stay till morn—the possibility of venereal disease is considerably decreased.

Finally, but reluctantly, you came to the conclusion that you should try for a commission—it was a wise choice.

Another point which I did not mention to you and never did, was the concern I felt about your going into action—you had had such bad luck as a kid, cutting your face on the scrap basket, your lip on the sleigh, hurting your leg, your colds and many minor things (that I never heard about)—that I feared you would get in action and get hurt—and you did. So I wanted to delay or postpone the inevitable as long as it could be postponed—and going into officers training was one way of delaying you. Another was when you were made an instructor—that was done for two reasons, your ability and my request.

I assume that your mother was also urging you to train for a commission—but you were hot pants to get married.

I knew what you had been up against as far as girls in your own immediate circle were concerned—it is difficult to find them with intelligence, hot pussies and social standing—they seldom have all three. Some have sex unbridled and social position, some are heavily sexed and brilliant, some are stupid and sexy, and many of the better brought up ones are stupid, attractive and cold or have been brought up to keep their cunts in a chastity belt or kotex pad (this latter class are becoming fewer and fewer)—nevertheless, I hoped you might find an intelligent sexy gal in your own sphere.

You sure were lovesick—and the glasses that you used to gaze upon your bride-to-be with were of the rosiest hue—how you sang her charms as you saw them, to all and sundry. Her artistic merit defied the art critics—a great painter not in the making but who had arrived, flawless—a brilliant intellect that had struggled upward and forward against adversity (a la "Honest Abe"). All this you saw with your own eyes and much more—and that was as it should have been and was.

One should never extol their own wares—for what one

man sees in a woman, another never does, and they think you nuts for your raving and vice versa. What one woman sees in a man another woman never does—so both men and women should keep their enthusiasm to themselves.

After midnight the orders came to move out of Camp Hill and we said adieu—you agreeing to apply for officers training, I agreeing to stand by you in your love venture.

I watched the wagons roll away as the embers glowed, faded and then were smothered out—then I too drove away. I passed your motorcars on the highway north of Fredericksburg and I sped back to bed down at the Willard in Washington.

That had been a night of nights for me, my son—one which few fathers ever know, for few are in my boots—and that too is just as well and I hope that you may never be on such terms with your son (if you ever have one and I expect you will) that one night will mean so much—or that in your lifetime there will be other wars and men going.

In frankness I must admit that there is more than an excellent chance for more and bigger and more devastating wars to come within your life—yea, even maybe within my own—however short the balance of that may be.

I have always admired you, Page—admired your work at Dartmouth, your work afterwards and your work in the army especially at Fort Benning—I was always in close touch with your record there. I have not always agreed with your economic thoughts and your philosophy of life—but I have respected your opinions and your right to hold them, and even your right to choose whomever you pleased as your legally wedded wife.

That we couldn't see eye to eye after your wife decided that Baltimore held more for her than New York I always regretted—I never compromise with my beliefs—and I didn't expect and couldn't expect and wouldn't have thought anything of you if you had not taken the stand you did beside the woman you married, for better or for worse.

On the way to the church she told me of her intentions and her ambitions—I hope for your sake and for your daughter's sake, that she attains her objectives—they were large, and time causes shrinkages.

My admiration for you has never waned no matter what our personal relations have been—I yearned in my youth to be and do many of the things you have done and been.

I had been actively interested in the America First movement—most of 1941—attending meetings in Washington (addressed by the La Follettes) with Eve at the National Theatre.

I had been opposed to our involvement in World War I and definitely opposed to the second venture—the futility of it all was always too apparent. Our job was to be an arsenal of defense, armed to the hilt on land, on the sea, and under the sea, and in the air—to keep abreast of any possible combination that might be employed against us if not ahead of the other fellows—leave them alone, sell them for cash, no lend-lease or lease lend—it would have been expensive, but dirt cheap compared to what we have wasted in resources in these last two years.

The America Firsters held a large mass meeting at the Manhattan Opera House on 34th Street—their first big one in New York. Walter Piel had bought a box—we couldn't get near the front entrance, the crowd was so dense. Lindbergh and Senator Walsh (of Mass.) were the speakers—John Flynn presided. When we couldn't get near the front door, we went around to 35th St. to the stage door—the crowd was thick there but we outwitted the "mounties" who were riding human herd and got Mimi and Eve in with us. Inside we bumped into Joe Boldt—you knew his brother at Dartmouth—he was an active official with the committee, sort of an aid to Flynn, and with much pushing and shoving reached our box an hour before the show opened.

What a mob that was—the Irish who hated the English—the communists who were all for keeping us out until Hitler and Stalin tied up—the Germans who didn't want any interference with Hitler—and just plain Americans like Lindbergh and myself who didn't personally and for historical reasons believe in foreign entanglements. I had been opposed all my life to involvement in European conflicts.

Walter Piel (he had been a naval officer in World War I, a flyer for the Navy when they only had box kites, and an aide to Byrd—was a violent America Firster) gave the America First organization large sums of money and was almost pro-German in his excitement. His mother and father were born in Germany and they had large holdings of property there—that naturally raised the question of whether his opposition to war was not really based on his tie with the fatherland thru birth. I think it made him more violent—he was conscious of that interpretation of his position.

I liked Lindbergh and I had always been a great admirer of John Flynn, the chairman of the New York County Committee of the America First Committee. I enjoyed that evening—Walsh, Flynn and Lindbergh were all excellent speakers.

For my part I wanted to do all I could to keep us out. I firmly believed then that involvement in Globular warfare could only mean the eventual destruction of our Republic—the lowering of the standards of our way of life—where every man had a right to worship, speak, think, write or fuck as he pleased and to seek riches or be a bum.

On October 30th, 1941 the America Firsters held their biggest rally of the anti-war movement—this time at Madison Square Garden. . . .

[Edwin] Webster gave a supper party or buffet party after the meeting in his house across the way from 30 Beekman place at #35 Beekman Place for the speakers of the evening and some of the more active workers and the big subscribers. It followed the Garden meeting—Senator Wheeler, Senator Clark, Cudahy, John Flynn, Lindbergh, Michael Strange (former wife of John Barrymore), Walter and his wife, Mrs. Finerty, Dorothy Bayer, Sophia Pinckney, Tommy Brodix came along with Eve and myself.

Eve told Lindbergh that she had seen him in Tiffany's in London some years before and he remembered having been there, said he had been having a watch fixed—he was able to recall the incident because it was the only time he had been in Tiffany's in London.

When I talked with him I recalled the first all air transcontinental flight to California—and the fact that I had been on it and that he had been at the Newark airport when we set off on that inaugural journey—we also chatted about the trips he made thru the West prior to World War I when he piloted his father from town to town in their four wheel jalopy.

Lindbergh was affable and friendly, he mixed easily—Wheeler was a bit grouchy, tired, irritable—Senator Clark was very pleasant, Flynn delightful. . . .

December 7th abruptly ended the anti-War activities of the America Firsters. Theirs had been a glorious but losing fight against the monster, the evil one in the White House who was set upon a venture which eventually brought the entire world to its knees in complete economic and political disaster.

The country was opposed to war—the President knew it—he knew the American people would never enter another world war of their own free will unless they were attacked—that's why he longed and prayed for the attack that came so obligingly for him on that fateful Sunday morning of December 7th when the Pacific Fleet lay huddled together like a lot of duck decoys in Pearl Harbor. The great White Father had gotten his wish—he had baited the potential enemy in—he tempted them as he goaded them and they bit and bit hard, but it was a terrible thing for the people of America—it humbled them before the world and dragged them down to such depths that they may never recover their old standards for generations to come.

Morally they were degraded and economically they were shorn for the fleeting moment of glory of an egomaniac—the vain commander-in-chief who knew so little of military tactics and less of world power politics, yet who was so frequently envisioned as the wise one who knew all and who time and again not only betrayed the blood of the youth of his nation but as a traitor to his sworn oath, again and again bartered away the economic wealth of his people for a few vain moments at international confabs. . . .

1942–1946

Before getting into the serious side of my activities during 1942, I am going to talk about me—thoughts on my thoughts—and then to mention several things that have occurred this year, which I may never get around to report. I did some of that sort of thing in 1943, and again in 1944, when writing out the happenings of many years previous.

To begin with, I am commencing to suffer from a feeling of frustration—I do not know whether that's brought about by the failure of my many undertakings these last few years or whether it's because I have dropped all active interest in the details of political manipulation, plus the fact that the work of restoring the old house at Sagaponack has now reached the point where it takes very little time or effort.

Maybe I have remained actively married too long to one woman—yet I am devoted to Eve.

It may be a combination of all these things and many others that I am not aware of—it may be traceable primarily to the fact that Eve has been producing successfully, while I have been solely on the receiving side. Or again, it may be due to the times—the much greater effort that has to be put forth in order to accomplish only a small part of what it was so simple, so easy to accomplish when I was much younger—perhaps it's just old age.

I'm puzzled at times about myself—my weaknesses—I wish I knew what it was that made me weak. . . .

I wonder why I slip, and when I slipped, and how I slipped—wherein I failed. I would have so much enjoyed the activity of it all—action on a large scale, on a wide front, involving big movements of men, has always appealed to me.

I know I lack staying qualities—stick-to-itiveness—I tire easily, I get fed up, I get bored with most everything I contact—I suffer from great fatigue when I haven't been doing anything to fatigue me, and when I do things that would wear down many men, I feel no fatigue. . . .

It was pleasant to live when we didn't have foreign wars to pay for, or totalitarian governments to support—when we were taking care of ourselves and letting the rest of the world take care of themselves—when we were minding our own business and not permitting outsiders to butt into ours.

When we had no income taxes—when men could buy what they pleased and pay whatever they felt they wished to pay, and could sell what they bought for what they chose to ask without any government interference. The government did not come into your home or your office and tell you what to do or how to do it, and then tax you for doing it—you hired men and fired men, paying them what you thought they were worth, and they worked for a day's pay.

My father worked six days a week, and frequently on Sundays, when he was a younger man, and as he grew older, he always worked six days, sometimes leaving a little earlier on Saturday afternoon—frequently going to his office Sundays for a few hours. To my knowledge, he never took a vacation—I am sure that he was none the worse in health, in wealth and spirit. As a matter of fact, the important thing in life is regularity. Daily repetition of the activities of the day before. It's a fallacy to say "that all work and no play makes Jack a dull boy.". . .

Human beings are oddities in their thinking en masse—they are prone to follow false prophets to their own detriment, always seeking something for nothing—they rally to the slightest suggestion that something may be obtained for nothing, without effort, without ever weighing the possibility or probability that it is not within the province of mortal man to fulfill such alluring promises.

Men, of course, are forever making promises amongst themselves which they know to be impossible of fulfillment and have no intention of fulfilling at the time they are made—they make them primarily to attain some personal end or gain. . . .

There was a time in the history of this country when the people's concept of government was that the Government was a creature of the people. Today in the United States of America and in most parts of the world, the people have become the creatures of the governments they themselves have created by one false move or another. Individual freedom and the right to live one's life as one should is no longer the right of man on the North American continent or the world around, with but few exceptions.

The Marxian dialectic which regards man as a biologic creature serving the ends of the state has succeeded in setting up a tyranny over the mind and spirit of man in many parts of the world—the ultimate of this doctrine is the totalitarian state controlled either by one despot or by an elite oligarchy the world around.

Men for generations feared the privation of old age, so in their youth they worked and slaved and saved, so that they might not end their days in the poorhouse over the hill—they saved for the rainy day, for illness or adversity.

Today, when the worker diligently labors from a quarter to 80 percent of the fruits of his labor is taken from him, in order to provide for those who have not produced or saved for their old age or adversity.

For myself, fear has always been upon me and will always haunt me—fear of the unknown, dread of the known—and while I am capable of rationalizing the predicaments that others find themselves in, I have never been capable of rationalizing my own predicaments sufficiently to comfort or console myself.

In the translator's introduction to Kierkegaard's *The Concept of Dread* he said first "know thyself" (in that effort I have also failed W.W.S.), and he continued:

> Dread is a desire for what one dreads, a sympathetic antipathy. Dread is an alien power which lays hold of an individual and yet one cannot tear one's self away, nor has a will to do so; for one fears, but what one fears, one desires. Dread then makes the individual impotent, and the first sin always occurs in impotence—apparently, therefore, the man lacks accountability, but this lack is what ensnares him.

Kierkegaard was certainly much concerned with sin and the dread of sin, and in his gropings gave expression to many truisms as I see life and thought.

> That human nature must be such that it makes sin possible, is, psychologically speaking, perfectly true. If one were to think it, sin would become man's substance. It is easy for cunning common sense to escape the recognition of sin.
>
> Hereditary sin is so deep and dreadful a corruption of nature that it cannot be understood by the reason of any man, but must be recognized and believed by the revelation of the scripture.
>
> The account of the first sin in Genesis has, especially in our age, been regarded rather carelessly as a myth—sin came into the world by sin.
>
> Pelagianism lets every individual, unconcerned about the race, play his own little history in his private theatre.
>
> Dread is a sympathetic antipathy and not an antipathetic sympathy.
>
> Sinfulness is not sensuousness, but without sin there is no sexuality, and without sexuality no history.
>
> I would say that learning to know dread is an adventure which every man has to affront if he would not go to perdition either by not having known dread or by sinking under it. He, therefore, who has learned rightly to be in dread has learned the most important thing.
>
> If a man were a beast or an angel, he would not be able to be in dread. Since he is a synthesis he can be in dread, and the greater the dread, the greater the man. This is not affirmed in the sense in which man commonly understands dread as related to

something outside a man, but in the sense that man himself produces dread.

He who is educated by dread is educated by possibility, and only the man who is educated by possibility, is educated in accordance with his infinity.

The dread of poverty, the dread of unfavorable publicity, the dread of discomfort, the dread of disease, the dread of violence and physical suffering are compelling factors in the life of man—with many the dread of sin, as sin is understood, by those who dread it most, is often mitigated by the belief that there can be atonement.

The times or the age we live in moderate or increase our fears—without fear, man would grow fat and useless—and die.

My antidote for fear is sleep (it's my opiate) with my head under the pillow and the sheets piled up high—mayhap a childish hangover. . . .

I delay, postpone the issue. In my youth, I met the issues head on, but now I avoid them. I procrastinate maybe—and I wonder if that is not a serious fault. I frequently delay in order the better to marshal my defense, never my offense—but then, I seldom am on the offensive these days.

Eve meets any issue head on. . . .

I have a hard time accepting the world as it is today. Naught I do can change the present or the future the tides of destiny have set—the world I knew and heard about at the turn of the century is the world I could have favored most, but that is not to be again—there will be other times, but not those times, and so it has been ordered since the beginning of time and so it will ever be.

Aristotle accepted the world as it was—happiness was for Aristotle man's chief purpose and to have it a man must have a certain amount of worldly goods, a certain amount of good fortune—that is not Hedonism—Aristotle distinguished between pleasure and happiness.

Reason—but there are times when one can reason for others, but not for oneself—yet "The highest good is the life of reason."—Aristotle. . . .

"The happy man, the virtuous man, is the man who steers midway between the two shoals that threaten on either side to wreck human happiness. In every act, in every thought, in every emotion, a man may be overdoing his duty, or underdoing it, or doing it just right."—Aristotle.

You, my son, are inclined to overdo. . . .

With me, it has always been too much or too little—never in moderation. . . .

William James—need I tell you of him—well, I seem to fit into his "tough-minded" grouping, being Empiricist, sensationalistic, materialistic, pessimistic, irreligious (much of the time, altho very religious in early youth—I still have occasional lapses), Fatalistic, Pluralistic, sceptical. You lean to the "Tender-minded" gauging from the little I know of you. I suspect that you are Rationalistic—I know that you are intellectualistic, idealistic, whether you are religious or not I wouldn't know—I should say that you might be a free-willist—I have been a touch that way myself at times—monistic, maybe yes and then maybe no—time will tell. Dogmatical—a touch. . . .

Truth as I saw it and as you practiced it was what caused our separation—fundamentally—what colored Eloise's vision of truth was the difference between what the Pages of Ruxton and the Smiths of 30 Beekman had to offer materially. . . .

The futility of it all, the stark futility of human striving and aspiration—it appalls—the search for the true truth, so purposeless when one atomic bomb may destroy the universe. Today, we should live only for today, getting the most out of each and every minute. Tomorrow—for there may be no tomorrow.

The wastefulness—the uselessness—of all this effort of words to you—but it gives me momentary expression—occupies idle hands and helps the girl a bit who transcribes it all—otherwise it is wasted wordage.

It is not easy to see ourselves as we appear to others—our adulation of our own self-portrait is hard to dispel even when we eavesdrop and hear a much less pleasing, nay even unpleasant version of our deeds and thoughts—even an unbiased description of our physical appearance can come as a shock to our vanity. To evaluate oneself no higher than one's neighbor evaluates one is not so simple of accomplishment, but our own evaluation may be a truer one than another—especially of those seeking to be in our good graces, who only reflect the picture that we most like to see.

We, for our part, are always seeking what is not.

What ails me—my greatest comfort is sleep?

I worry and fret and stew about all manner of things—seldom outwardly, but everlastingly inwardly. So I sleep 8, 10, 12, 14 hours a day. And yet I well remember in my youth my sleep was often nil—an hour or two a day and sometimes not that. When troubled or beset, then to the bed I would go and sleep myself out of my dilemma.

I have no objective in life—I do not seem to be able to find a mark to shoot at—I weigh the pros and cons of all possibilities and finding the cons usually well in majority, I dismiss the object of my speculative interest. I see men venture into commercial, industrial life, yea, even political life, without the slightest knowledge of the pitfalls, the procedure involved, and no appreciation of their own limitations or availability for the task involved—like babes in the woods. Yet in their very naiveness, they succeed where others skilled and aware, fall by the wayside—so many gain by merely venturing. It sometimes makes you stop and ponder about the human race—it's certainly to the opportunist and not to the well prepared or trained education—bah! It's more often a greater hindrance than a help. . . .

Not only is sleeping one of the pleasant sensations of man, but eating is a pleasant indulgence—and crapping is the most enjoyable relaxation. Fucking has them all beat for there is nothing like a good straight screw—provided all the preliminary variations of perversity have been indulged in—the hors d'oeuvres so to speak.

As to food, I like to cook—soup is my favorite—waffles—beef—particularly steaks over a charcoal fire outdoors—mashed potatoes—sauté—scrambled eggs—vegetables—puddings—Fudge—griddle cakes—oatmeal—but soup, that's what I like best to do. . . .

And now you have a son as well as a daughter to guide thru the formative years of life—you will probably apply to your homelife, your wife and your children, a code of conduct contrary to that which you understood to have been mine.

I, for one, choose to believe, as I have often said before, that you are the better for having attained what you so far have attained in life, without reliance upon aid from your father. Had I chosen a different course than I have, and had I been sufficiently successful financially to maintain my family in the style to which it was thought by some they should have been maintained, I would have been prone to extend myself in providing lavish comforts and entertainment, particularly during the formative years—thereby offsetting harsh disciplinarian tactics, which I most certainly would have employed in the rearing of my sons, if their upbringing had been entrusted to me.

A great fault in my makeup was developed by the knowledge and assurance that I always felt while they lived that I could rely upon my parents in the way of material aid and assistance when confronted with adversity or in need, and on my wives and mistresses when my parents were no longer available for me to lean on.

I feel that you and your brother escaped spoiling to a degree in the household at Ruxton, altho pampered and raised in a most provincial atmosphere, with all the limitations that that pampering and provinciality imposed. Don't pamper your children—make them earn for themselves that which they desire most as they go thru life—do not raise them in a provincial atmosphere, whether it be scholastic, commercial, financial, political, economic or industrial. . . .

[Eloise, a few months after our marriage at Fort Benning, Georgia, went to New York to take up a scholarship she had won at the Art Students League. On one occasion she called my father and asked him to cash a ten-dollar check for a friend of hers. This request touched my father on a very sensitive nerve—his financial

situation and available credit. He asked Eloise who the hell she thought he was—Henry Morgenthau (then Secretary of the Treasury). She hung up the phone. Soon afterwards she gave up the scholarship and returned to Columbus, Georgia, where I was a mortar instructor at the Infantry School.]

On November 3rd, I wrote you as follows:

November 3, 1942

Lieutenant Charles Page Smith
36 Fox Avenue
Benning Park,
Columbus, Ga.

Dear Page:

Your wife's insolence Friday night was inexcusable—I told her I had talked with you and was about to give her your best, when she curtly stated that she was not interested—that she had had a wire from you.

I heard that Eloise and Richards had had quite a time of it while he was here—apparently she greatly enjoyed visiting the sophisticated haunts of New York's Cafe society with him—so didn't subject him to any of her petulance—she had always led us to believe that she didn't like those places.

Her failure to drop in or phone to say goodbye to Eve and myself would have been unpardonable from the most illiterate hillbilly—her cousin Ruth, who appears to have had about the same upbringing and background, seems aware of the simple amenities of life—so Eloise must know better.

On the way to the wedding, Eloise said she was going to ignore the Baltimore attacks on her and win her way into the Ruxton family—she stated that if anything happened to you, that she and any offsprings she might have by you would be entitled to your share of the so-called "Page fortune." I told her I didn't think it would run to very much, but of course it would be more than could ever be looked for from me.

Knowing there is little to be gained from us financially, may account in part for her rudeness—frankly, it was noticeable that as soon as she definitely decided to curtail her visit and no longer had any use for the little hospitality we might be able to extend to her, her strange attitude was accentuated.

Not being an art critic, I would not venture to pass judgment on any art work or to come to any conclusions from the criticisms of others. I was simply amazed at the wide difference between her report of the criticism of the critics and the statements made to me.

I trust that there is enough at stake in Baltimore for her to try and make a special effort to be polite to your family and your friends. . . .

My only regret in connection with my communications regarding Eloise is the fact that I permitted Eve to prevail upon me to delete from my original communication the things Eloise had said about me to Usui [a Japanese picture framer]. I have always felt I should have let you have that straight from the shoulder as well as telling you how she planned frankly and avowedly to get her share of whatever wealth she considered the Pages to possess, and that declaration as I may have mentioned before, she made en route from the hotel to the chapel, the day she married you—maybe it was all youthful enthusiasm a bit on the naive side. . . .

I have kept very carefully your communication dated January 3rd, 1942. It should have been 1943, because that was when you wrote it. You were not married in 1942. What always amused me about that communication was the fact that you never bore any resentment over the things your grandmother and your mother wrote about your then wife-to-be—they were pretty harsh. They were tough on Eloise and tough on her family and when I say tough I mean tough, because they were things which she had been born into and could not help, whereas, no matter how humble one's origin may be—there is no excuse for purposeless untruths.

You seem to feel that I should have shown greater patience and understanding of her conduct—I understood her conduct perhaps even better than you. I knew what she was interested in and what she was striving to attain—Baltimore held greater promise than New York—I have been confronted with the stupid lies of the female of the species many times in my life. In that respect I can think of only one gal, however, who was in a class with Eloise and that was Morris V.'s fifth wife, a little vitriolic redhead from California. She was 18 when she married Morris, who was 45 at the time. Russell Patterson couldn't trust her, but he fell in love with her—and for a time deserted his wife for her—he used her on the cover designs for *Ballyhoo* that made him famous. The truth wasn't in Lyle V. but men adored her and worshipped her, fought over her and squandered their time and money on her.

I gather that Eloise greatly improved under your mother's direction, but then only recently, in fact, this winter, I heard that all was not well and that she and your mother were not in complete harmony. I think that's unfortunate.

Lest you forget, the following is your letter of January 3rd, 1943:

> January 3, 1942
>
> Dear Father—
>
> I'm returning your Christmas present of the ten dollars and under separate cover the books you and Eve sent us for Christmas. I am sorry to have to do this. The fact is that after the things you wrote about my wife I would have very little dignity if I would still accept gifts from you.
>
> I've heard both sides of the unfortunate misunderstanding between you and Eloise and I feel that for a man of your maturity and worldly experience you showed a surprising lack of patience and understanding. However, this is beside the point. We both appreciate what you and Eve have done for us. Eloise was particularly upset that Eve should have received any impression that she was rude or unpleasant to her in any way because she has only the most pleasant memories in regard to her. We hold no rancor and no bitterness, but in view of the things you wrote me and your general attitude, I think it better for us to sever relations.
>
> Sincerely,
> /s/ Page

I do not know whether or not I ever sent you my letter of January 7th in reply to your letter regarding the 1942 Christmas gift—I seem to be in possession of the original, but just in case I didn't send it, I am inserting it here because it still clearly states my position and attitude in the entire matter:

January 7, 1943

1st. Lt. Charles Page Smith
36 Fox Avenue
Benning Park
Columbus, Ga.

Dear Page:

The Christmas money you returned—has been used to pay the Officers' Club bill, which you failed to take care of with the money that I sent you for that purpose.

It was interesting to get your letter confirming the severance of relations. Interesting because of what you had written me about the letters your mother, your brother and your grandmother had written to you and your then prospective bride—As I recall it, your mother was so ashamed of the union that she deliberately misled people as to the date of your wedding, so that she wouldn't be embarrassed by questions about your wife at Virginia's nuptials—that conduct you said you would never forgive—but in no time, to my surprise, you both were crawling back to Ruxton—kowtowing—"without dignity" and Eloise was boasting about it, and proudly displaying the gifts of jewelry that had been bestowed upon her from that quarter. Could it be, as Eloise pointed out on her wedding day, because the stakes for you both are high at Ruxton?—I had hoped you had more character than that.

It is difficult to comprehend how your wife could have failed to have been aware of her conduct up here, because it took such a decided change—toward Eve and myself—after she determined we could be of no further use—. I suspect she never behaved that way at Ruxton—I would have been tolerant, had I for one instant thought that she didn't know any better and wasn't aware of what she was saying or doing—There was nothing that Eve or I ever did that in any way warranted her impudence to us—.

Yes—our relations have been broken for some time, and will continue to be broken until your wife has apologized for her unspeakable behavior and has the common decency and courtesy to thank Eve for her hospitality. . . .

Perhaps my world-wide experience, with men and women, makes me in my maturity, discerning, critical and exacting.

I don't like deceitfulness and lying for any purpose, whether by you, your wife or your mother—Unfortunately, you have been placed in embarrassing positions because of the Ruxton attitude. In the long run, however, I think you will find it better to take a position, frankly and openly—as to what you want and intend to do—and stand by it. It was distressing to learn from you that you had prompted your wife to lie to me, and to lie to your mother.

In my old age—I am selective—emotionally, I do not approve of Premiers, Presidents, Diplomats, Politicians or little girls and boys who do not tell the truth, or who try to mislead people for their own selfish ends.

When I find someone lying about me to others, and then lying to me about others—I call a halt. . . .

Philosophically, I don't give a damn, for none of it makes any difference to me—As a matter of fact, only your egotism is involved—your pride and dignity at stake—Wasn't your dignity also at stake at Ruxton, after they had depreciated your wife to all and sundry?—or wasn't it?—

As for actuating reasons, they are sometimes diametrically opposed points, but as to facts, there are always two sides—the true and the false.

Every man should stand up for the woman of his choice, right or wrong—There is no doubt about that—altho there is nothing to prevent his trying to polish off a rough stone—particularly if it is a precious one and worth it.

I have had enough experience with husbands and wives to know that when either one or the other is told the truth about the other, the friendship of both is lost. Nevertheless, as your father, I could forsee that if Eloise continued unchecked, it would be a serious reflection on you, and I told her so—For a long time I sought to avoid the issue headon, because of the effect it might have upon her. I hoped it could be approached obliquely—but in the end, I was forced to be thus candid and frank with you for your own good. . . .

There should be no rancor nor bitterness between a father and a son, nor between a mother and a son, nor for that matter, between parents—living together or separated—Invariably, parents are primarily interested in the welfare and future of their children—true, their interest is usually a matter of personal egotism in wanting their images to always appear to the best advantage and to achieve the greatest possible success and honor in life.

As you have so aptly said, there is no reason for rancor or bitterness—there is not even a misunderstanding—all that is involved is the question of the behavior of a little girl who happens to be your wife, and my prerogative as an elder, to approve or disapprove, of unbecoming conduct—

I wrote you purely in the hope that you might gradually be able to bring about a little more respect for veracity and greater consideration for the acknowledged amenities on the part of the woman who bears your name.

Some prefer a world of fantasy—unreal, and thrive on lies. I happen to be a realist, believing the truth and trying to respect the rights of others who do likewise. It has always been my contention that while in Rome, one should do as the Romans do. I don't think it is a bit smart to be rude and crude in utter disregard for your fellowman. . . .

Love is blind, and that is as it should be, or there would be no mating season. I always thought I knew more than my father about women and things—but I lived to learn that he knew best—but that sage discovery was not made until he was under the sod in Trinity. . . .

If my dignity had bothered me—the way your dignity seems to bother you—I never would have gone along with your wedding plans, and cooperated the way I did—Now think that over. Minor things I can overlook, but obvious intentional rudeness, should be checked whether aimed at you, at Eve, at me, or anyone else.

Eve has always been devoted to you, and always will be, and that goes double for me. We liked your wife—we put up with a lot from her on account of you—but her latter day manners, her petulance and her unspeakable conduct were unpardonable.

It's your bed—you are the one to straighten it—clean it—or lay in it—and lying in it is usually the easiest.

And so! Me lad and lassie, adieu—May the world treat you well, right or wrong, and may you conquer it and yourselves.

Your devoted Father,
/s/ W. Ward Smith

When we decided to take the apartment at 31 Beekman Place, we put an ad in the paper, in order to sublet our 30 Beekman Place apartment furnished.

As usual, the *Times* brought results—there were many inquiries, due in part at that season of the year, to the desire on the part of commuters to take up residence in New York on account of the gasoline shortage. . . .

I made the deal for the apartment with Vivienne L. . . . She was living at the Hotel Royalton at the time, and I took her to the Algonquin bar, where we discussed the apartment and her guarantors—then the next time I took her to lunch at the Algonquin where we ran into Konrad Bercovici, and others connected with the publishing and writing game. . . .

There were many who wanted the apartment, but none who had the appeal of Vivienne L.—when I escorted her from the Algonquin back to the apartment to check it over, she gave in without any resistance—let me undress her—she played with my cock—loved to suck it—I figured that she was laying the town so I rubbed my cock with vaseline and put on a rubber—then I greased that. I hate the damn things—they always fit so tight and are so hard to get on—but she kept playing with my balls and my prick kept good and stiff—she was a pretty good fuck—she really loved it.

On one occasion when I came over to see her and her friend about something in the apartment—they received me in the nude. They were running around naked—that was too much for me—I went down on one while I fucked the other.

Whenever they came over to pay the rent, they would have little on under their outside dresses—I would pull up their skirts—open their waists—kiss the tits, play with their cunts while they would jerk me off or go down on me right in the doorway of the apartment.

Eddie Ballou used our Garden for a cocktail party of his own, and as luck would have it, I got into our tiny bathroom with two of his women guests. It wasn't my party, so I had a good load aboard—one girl was on the can—she pissed on my hand, while I finger-fucked the other one—then the girl on the toilet sucked me off while her friend played with my balls—just as I came, Eddie and a beau of one of the girls came pounding on the door—it was all over then—so we came out a bit distraught.

We had a little vegetable garden, as well as a flower garden, and a grill over which we cooked our steaks, when dining in the garden—we bought some garden furniture and had many very delightful parties out there on the banks of the East River, amidst the soot of the passing boats and the dust of the dirty city. . . .

I made some interesting studies in the back yard of the Hollywood models that I dressed in some of the old Parisienne costumes that Melba and I bought in Paris in 1929—then I made one with a girl in her bathing suit, holding samples of Tung Oil in various interesting positions in her hands, between her legs, etc.

One such picture made it appear as if the girl had a pencil between her legs. I could watch them undress and get into their costumes thru the mirrors or the bathroom window without their knowing I was watching. When I helped them tighten up or adjust their clothes I would feel them all over—I usually took the models' measurements first, and that gave me a chance to feel their thighs and tits—I would have a hard on—fix them a strong drink and then, when they undressed, go to work on them.

I paid them five bucks an hour, took their pictures in the back yard, and laid them in the livingroom. They were easy—one time I got two together—they were living together and loving one another. They were hard to approach, but when I got a few drinks into them it was simpler—then I encouraged them to love one another as they undressed—I got undressed too, and watched—and laying close to them on the sofa, jerked off as they went down on one another—they were hot babies and they loved it—no time for me, but how they could lap up one another's cunts and ass holes—to say nothing of the way they played with their tits.

I get a stiff prick as I write about it—memories about such things are that way. I suppose I will end this by jerking off or fucking the maid in the rear end.

One of the models that I favored that summer was a blonde—platinum blonde—she was quite lovely, but a bit hard.

The models would come to my office at 101 Park Ave. for inspection—that was largely filling out an application—then I would measure them—then I would eliminate—the ones I selected I would have come to 31 when I was sure Eve was out of the house—around eleven in the morning—the sun was just right then.

1947

Times are returning to normal, the stock market is declining, Republicans have been elected in a landslide across the nation—there are plenty of rooms in the Washington Hotels—the cabinet maker and repair man solicit your business—the District of Columbia is saturated with empty cabs—the dining car waiters on the railroad trains are courteous (and serve you quietly and decently—no more throwing things at you and rushing you out)—the parlor car porter polishes your shoes as you approach your destination and brushes the dandruff off your coat collar—he even cleans your hat—gentle folk are to be found riding in the Pullmans again once more properly clothed—Jews, in the Washington parlor cars are now few and far between, for their false god (FDR) no longer holds sway in the nation's capital.

Congress being out of session also improves the calibre of the riders. The niggers are still crowding the air-cooled, thank God, day coaches on the Baltimore-Washington route, almost 25% black—the trains are departing and arriving on their right tracks and once more generally are on time. And "Whitman's Sampler" chocolate candy is again openly displayed on the local druggist's counter. . . .

The Van Loon funeral set off a line of thought—made me reflect upon my own fruitless life—the narrowness and ruthless selfishness of my fellow man in his battle to survive.

I may never finish this or get caught up—so I will let my

thoughts wander here a bit lest when I come to where they should be put down I will no longer be here to do so.

I have scanned the rituals of the many sects—I know the dogma of my inherited faith—I well know the transitory nature of our daily life, and that the only certainty is death—that we have no control over our creation or extermination (except in a case of suicide, and I rather wonder whether that is as premeditated as we are prone to believe). . . .

People are forever planning and having their plans go asunder. Mine always do—just as death lurks stealthily around the corner—as Old Man Reaper shadows us from the cradle to the grave.

All there seems to be to life (and it is a maddening thought to some) is the material existence we know.

When life ceases to exist and passes out of the body, we then could make excellent fertilizer—but that would destroy the mystery of many sects.

That is really all we are good for after death—fertilizer. . . .

There are times when I seem to exist in cycles—perhaps I am inclined to over-sensitivity—nothing has ever come to me that I have ever sought, outside of women, no job I have ever wanted has been mine, nothing that could have benefited me materially has ever materialized—when I have been the instigator, in my own belief.

Whenever I have worked without an objective for the sheer love for what I was doing—and without compensation—things have come my way.

For example: I never sought the job of Secretary to the Governor—my real interest at the time was in the transportation facilities of the City, State and Nation, and occasionally I harbored a slight thought of being a Public Service or Transit Commissioner—when such thoughts occurred it was never the salary that occurred to me, it was the work that appealed.

But such notions were easily dismissed, for I was well aware that I never possessed the political qualifications (the Republican Party was not indebted to me).

The Secretaryship came out of a clear sky—the appointment to be Associate Chairman of the Small Loan Division of the Treasury Department came in the same way. More recently the small, petty honors—unremunerative—by the lively little local Republican Club were entirely unsolicited.

I was made head of the Actors' Fund, Endowment Fund Campaign thru no solicitations on my part—the "Hoover for President" activity was not of my own determination—W.S.S. was the doing of Karl Behr aided and abetted by Guy Emerson, as was the Mitchell parade.

The Preparedness Parade (World War I) was my father's idea—he thought there should be a Lumber Trade Division. Schuyler Meyer drew me into the 15th Assembly District fight—the banks on Long Island, were an idea of Father's—the Whit Organization, Joe Lilly's. . . . .

Life is full of contraries. FDR has a pleasing, yes, delightful personality and charm—acquired, of course. Developed over years—but economically, he is unsound and his advisers crackpots—he is a stubborn, dictatorial egoist, as lacking in administrative ability and sound business sense as he is overdeveloped with cultivated charm.

Our Governor—Dewey—is an upstart—a cute, sly, arrogant, ruthless, dictatorial, inflated egotist, a relentless slave driver obsessed with his own importance, and resigned in his own mind to the fact that he is a man of destiny. If elected President of the United States he would be as uncompromising and dictatorial with Congress and his Party as F.D.R. He is not a false-face like the President—he does not feign at charm in order to accomplish his purpose—he is direct in his ruthless dealings with his fellowman, whereas the President is always oblique and two-faced. Then too, Governor Dewey would bring, if elected, to the National Administration new blood with which to prime the rundown machinery—advisors and counsellors whose ability far exceeds anything the Democrats have ever had to offer in the National field.

Perhaps and in fact, I believe that for men to succeed in the highly competitive game of politics or in business or in finance or in commerce, or in industry, that they must be ruthless and heartless, and concerned only with their own destiny—dedicating themselves completely to their objectives and to hell with all and sundry along the path that they must tread to reach their destination.

I haven't been so gaited—perhaps that's why my existence has been so useless to myself and to my fellowman—why I have wasted and dissipated what I have, if I have anything.

If there has ever been anything in the balance that I have instigated myself or that I have wanted, the scales have always dropped against me.

And yet I cannot complain, because I have had much out of life, in a general sort of way—my senses have been appeased in many ways—perhaps my interests were and have always been too diversified. . . .

Americans are getting tired of being taxed to poverty in order to pour vast sums into the empty European pit, only to have the recipients of our bounty thumb their noses at us and seek by devious means to overthrow our form of Government, change our way of life, and reduce our high standard of living to the low levels to which they have been so long accustomed and from which most Americans' ancestors fled to escape the inequities of.

And so I come with these few observations on things current in 1947 to the end of the more or less colorless activities of 1943, as far as my personal existence was concerned. . . .

It used to be the movement of merchandise—the movement of precious metals—the movement of current invisibles—the movement of invested capital—the movement of temporary credit. Now it's the movement of the bowels that counts most.

AND THAT IS ALL FOR NOW

Afterword

The letter did not end; it stopped. It stopped, perhaps only coincidentally, with the reconciliation of Eloise and me to my father and Eve—at whose initiative I cannot now recall, certainly without those apologies my father had insisted must precede any healing of the breach. It was ratified, typically, by a great effusion of Christmas gifts for the children and handsome presents for ourselves.

There was visiting back and forth; father and Eve to our old tenement-building apartment in the Cambridge semislums. Eloise and I and the two children, Ellen and Carter, and then a little later, Anne, went to Sagaponac or Bridgehampton, once for the road races (which went past the front door) and once, as I recall, for Christmas, during the years I was in graduate school. Then later, after the Bridgehampton house had been sold for a large profit and my father and Eve had bought a farm in Stowe, Vermont, to Stowe and, in the last decade of his life, to Greenwich, New York, a small town near Saratoga.

My father's fortunes in this period were entirely dominated by Eve's professional life as a dress designer. In the middle fifties she left or was fired by Leonard and Levine. Her violent anti-semitism may have gotten too much for them to tolerate or she may simply have gotten tired of the nerve-wracking demands of the "rag business" and decided to extricate herself. In any event, she developed a line of knit twine handbags, placemats, and shoes which were farmed out for fabrication to the wives of, for the most part, French-Canadian farmers. My father undertook to sell the bags to fashionable women's stores and gift shops. He also ran a small dairying operation with a dozen or so cows and, typically, feuded with the natives, protesting the quality of workmanship done on the original improvements to the farmhouse he and Eve had bought and fixed up, much as they had restored the Sagaponac house, leaving bills unpaid and swearing vengeance on anyone who provoked his wrath. Vermont and upper New York State farmers are a tough and resourceful breed. On one occasion a disgruntled creditor got a lien placed on my father's Buick. It was locked in his garage pending payment of a bill for plumbing and for several months he and Eve commuted from Stowe to New York by train and bus.

He had a measure of revenge during a dry time for cows. When his and his neighbors' animals went dry, my father loaded his dry cows on a truck in the dark of night and carried them across the border to Canada where he got freshened cows that were giving milk. Thus surreptitiously he replaced dry cows with fresh ones and was delighted when word reached him that his fellow dairymen were thoroughly baffled by the milk tanker's report that Smith's cows were giving three hundred pounds of milk a day.

As he had earlier at Melvale, my father entered energetically into the not wholly unfamiliar role of farmer, albeit part-time. My impression was that the woven twine venture—Stowecraft it was called—was not an especially flourishing one. Certainly it did not permit my father and Eve to live in the style to which they had been accustomed when she was a topflight dress designer. After three or four years of knitted twine, Eve found another designing job in New York. They took an apartment in the city and bought the weekend and vacation house in Greenwich.

After I left graduate school and we moved to Santa Monica, where I took a position at the University of California at Los Angeles as an assistant professor of history, our contacts with my father and Eve became infrequent. My father called on the phone three or four times a year for long, rambling conversations, usually about politics, and when we moved to Santa Cruz with the opening of the new campus of the University of California in that community he and Eve visited us. There were presents at Christmas, though on a far more modest scale than formerly and on those rare occasions when we saw each other, there was much reminiscing and many references to the letter. He professed pride in my career and my modest accomplishments but he never really gave the impression of being interested in me as a particular person although he abounded in sentimental references to me *as his son*. The same was true with Eloise and his grandchildren. He tried to impress them with *him* but he showed little capacity to enter into their own rather interesting personalities. One felt that they, like my wife and I, had little reality for him. He could not engage any of us, son, daughter-in-law, grandchildren as people distinct from himself; we were all like extras in a play in which he (and to a lesser extent, Eve) were the stars. Or perhaps we were more like the scenery, the stage set itself, sounding boards, more or less inanimate auditors of his monologues.

Eve was delighted with him. In her eyes he was a person of infinite charm. She never tired of hearing the endless self-glorifying stories that so bored others—what he had said or written to Mrs. Roosevelt; how he had put La Guardia in his place, and told off that slob Hoover. She thought him a great wit, a brilliant intellect, and an enthralling conversationalist. She reveled in his power over headwaiters, in his imperious manners, and even in his violent and abusive temper. She thought him the handsomest man alive and never ceased to marvel how she—an ugly old maid—had managed to capture such a paragon.

My father, for his part, knew which side his bread was buttered on. He had been down too many times not to know up when he saw it. He attended faithfully to her needs. He squired her about with his great air of importance, demanding special courtesies and attentions for her, flagging down taxis while less imposing figures waited, getting the best tables, the best accommodations, the best service, and, not infrequently, paying for it all with a rubber check, because, despite the fact that Eve had what was, for the times, a very substantial salary, they always lived beyond it. The check-kiting, the false bank accounts, the pseudonyms, the subpoena servers did not cease with his marriage to Eve.

He shared the cooking (he had always had a penchant for cooking), got up every morning and prepared a simple breakfast for her and served it to her in bed, paid the bills and, for the most part, spent the money.

Although, as he himself observed, Eve had no interest in kinky sex, she resigned herself to his obsession so long as it was not flaunted in front of her or her friends. She and age eventually tamed him. The fires were banked, the ravenous sexual appetites diminished.

I remember being startled when, some six or seven years after his marriage to Eve he said to me, very casually, matter-of-factly, "I've gotten very fond of Evie." Indeed, he came, I would say, so far as he was capable of that uncertain emotion, to love her. Or perhaps he only became accustomed to her, which in itself is not to be taken lightly, men and women being what they are.

Eve I always liked. There was a directness about her that was appealing. I suspect that almost anyone who does a craftsmanlike or craftswomanlike job is in a measure redeemed by it, made more human or more real by it. Thus Eve always seemed more real to me than my father. She was tough and capable with an energy as vast as my father's, but one that was clearly focused. Her political ideas were simplistic. She accepted unquestioningly whatever my father said about politics and enthusiastically shared his anti-semitism, but she had a sense of humor and a body-wracking, hiccuping laugh that was infectious. She smoked incessantly and drank too much but she preserved my father from such grim fortunes as can only be imagined.

When he died quickly and easily of a heart attack in his seventy-fifth year, life was over for her. She did not wish to live. He remained for her the most wonderful, the most gifted, handsome man she had ever known. She began to drink incessantly. She visited us in Santa Cruz, two years after my father's death, still hopelessly bereaved, skimping along on some hidden savings and social security, but stubbornly refusing financial help. The night before she was to return to the house in Greenwich, which had become her permanent home, she broke her hip; the rumor was, dancing on a piano in a local bar. Her hip was set; she went from the hospital to a convalescent home where she could be near the doctor and get proper therapy and she turned the home upside down, smoking like a chimney, smuggling booze in, refusing to be quiet and tractable, steadfastly unwilling to behave like an old lady with a broken hip. One home virtually ousted her and in the one to which she was transferred I was constantly being appealed to to speak to my stepmother about her raucous and undisciplined ways.

Her drinking imperiled the mending of her hip. In fact she didn't care whether the hip ever mended or not or, indeed, whether she lived or not. Finally, still rebellious, she insisted on flying back to Greenwich. My daughter, Anne, accompanied her and got her settled. Kind neighbors attended her and a practical nurse cooked and kept house. Three months later she called a cousin of my father's in New York and told him that she had decided to blow her brains out (her brother and sister had both been suicides). While he was still remonstrating with her, she got a shotgun, went out on the porch, placed the gun against her head and pulled the trigger. She died some seven or eight hours later.

The principal riddle of my father's life was his obsession with sex. I always saw it as, in part, a consequence of his life in New York City. To me the city simply was (doubtless because of my association of my father with sex and with the life of the city) a sex-saturated environment. One was surrounded by women out of context, so to speak. They were not perceived, as one brushed past them in the streets, in crowded places, saw them on buses and above all, of course, on subways, as wives or mothers or people imbedded in some particular, defined social situation, but as mysterious, alluring sexual creatures, each seeming to promise a blissful assignation. That my father should have been so eloquent on the subject of what might be called "subway sex" seems significant to me, because of all the places one encountered women in New York, the subway was the most sexually suggestive if only because of the press of bodies stimulated by the motion of the train. It was one of those odd encounters of extraordinary if transient intimacy, in which the modern city abounds; eyeball-to-eyeball contact, body contact, olfactory contact that was at the same time outside of any normal context of social relationship. It was probably safe to say that people have never encountered each other in this fashion before in history. At the same time the experience of the subway was novel enough for my father's generation so that all these sensations, the potency of which was dulled for later generations of subway riders by custom and habit and by the deterioration of the stations themselves into noisome hellholes and the trains into foul vehicles of unpredictable velocity, were fresh and powerful. I believe that the fact that the subway was "underground" contributed to its sexuality; it was underground that dark and desperate acts had always been performed. The word itself suggested illicit affairs.

The city streets also, particularly of course in the Broadway area, reeked of sex, and it is clear that this atmosphere both excited and disgusted my father—one of the most vivid parts of the letter is his description of the area in the midforties off Broadway where the hotels St. Margaret and Coolidge were located; and what an irony that those seedy fleabags, those multistoried dens of iniquity, should have had those particular names!

In the mythology of small-town America, to which for perhaps unfathomable reasons I feel so close, the city has always been a symbol of sin, evil and wickedness. It was where the country boy went and lost his money and his virtue, returning shamefaced to the town, possessed by guilty secrets. Thus my father's sexuality was, for me, and I am sure for him as well, intimately connected with the city. I have always been aware, as a consequence, that I could not live in a city. It would produce and, in those brief times when I am in cities, has produced in me an unbearable sexual tension.

Conversely, when my father lived, however briefly or intermittently, in rural communities and small towns, his obsession moderated, grew less feverish and intense, more general—and for very good reason: the opportunities were infinitely less, and those women encountered belonged, for the most part, to some kind of social context that lowered the sexual temperature.

The problem also remains for me of my father's preoccupation with what were once called sexual perversions (and are today referred to as "kinky sex"), oral and anal sex, voyeurism, et cetera. The portions of the letter recounting these episodes were, frankly, most troubling to me both because I found them offensive and because they will offend many readers, among them people whose good opinion I value. I would have preferred to omit them on a variety of grounds. They could have been omitted without in any way diminishing the predominantly sexual character of the letter and of my father's life. We are told by many self-proclaimed experts on sexual matters that there are no such things as sexual perversions, that everything we enjoy doing we should feel free to do. The perversions are, as this argument goes, only in our minds. I did not retain such accounts in the letter because I accept this argument. Rather, I left them in because I felt that they had a conclusive psychological importance in the story of my father.

Some years ago Norman O. Brown praised "polymorphous perversity," the indulgence in every form of perversity, the tasting of all forbidden pleasures, descending into the depths in order to come out on the other side purged of the sexual anxieties and hang-ups accumulated over centuries of repression. My father ran that course and although I saw no signs that it freed him from anything, it seems to me it is part of the record, so to speak.

And what of the women who gave themselves to him with such abandon? What of them? What did they see in him? Certainly the aura of sexuality. And what else? The pure, simple, unadulterated, uninhibited power of sex, sex so much obscured, repressed, even maligned by the proper world. Did it need—did sex need—its pioneers, its explorers, its radical advocates? Was my father really an innovator, a precursor of the sexual revolution, a type which, appearing well in advance of its time, must suffer obloquy and chastisement by a society whose mores have been so flagrantly defied? Was he, like the Marquis de Sade, forced by the prudishness and hypocrisy of society to extremes of degeneracy? Or was he simply in the vanguard of the coming sensate culture, a forerunner of a general decline in moral standards?

I can only see him as a victim rather than a precursor. But yet, the story is clearly more complex than that. My father became pure act; from his violent disembodied rages to his reckless spending of money and semen, he tested the limits of man as a creature of self-gratification.

Sexual encounters were, for my father, I believe, an effort to overcome fear of death, to assert his own masculinity, which he confessed often to doubt, and, finally, I suppose to exercise a particular skill—an expertise—on which he prided himself.

I see my father as a victim, in part, of the transition from a prudential to a sensate culture (to put the matter in a rather fancy way), that is to say, nineteenth-century America had believed above all in control, in control of one's emotions, appetites, money, semen. Controlled, calculated, prudential behavior—what has been summed up as the Protestant Ethic of thrift, piety, and hard work—was the ideal and even, perhaps, the norm. George Washington was the hero of that consciousness because he was for his admirers a man of iron self-control. Tears or any excessive display of emotion were considered to be weak, effeminate qualities. The emotionalism of women was in sharp contrast to the "control" of men. My father grew up in the time when America generally, and the great metropolitan centers in particular, were on the verge of what has been called a sensate culture, a culture in which the immediate gratification of one's appetites and desires was replacing the old prudential behavior. The new ethic was the ethic of cheerful consumption rather than of saving, reserving, suppressing, storing away, retaining. To spend money, even money one didn't have and had to borrow, was to be a good American, to stimulate the economy, to keep cash circulating. Increasingly, money and semen were to be spent, not retained. There were already prophets of the new ethic that were eagerly read by those in the know—Freud himself, in a way; Havelock Ellis, Edmund Carpenter, the Englishman who advocated orgies and bisexual experience for sexual release; and, nearer home, Margaret Sanger, only part of whose message was birth control, the other being uninhibited sexuality and open marriage. My father read these authors and numerous others and became an enthusiastic advocate and practitioner of the new sexual freedom. He demonstrated, in his own life, what happens when control breaks down. He was, like a figure on the crest of a breaking wave, never really in control. One thus searches in vain for some clear point at which it was possible to say, "If only here . . . If he had only done this instead of that. . . ." He was like a skier skiing out of control, a surfer riding an impossible wave to an inevitable wipeout, a racing driver headed into a suicidal corner too fast. A curious combination of themes and forces converged in him—exploitive capitalism, the American success ethic, social ambition, the trend toward what the late C. Wright Mills called fictitious personalities, figures created by the media, the rise (or appearance) of national names and personalities, famous people, and the tireless promoting of them by newspapers, magazines, and radio. Promotion. Selling. Quick fortunes. Promotion, for instance, implied advancing something not particularly worthy on grounds other than the intrinsic merit of the thing itself. Besides promoting things an ambitious young man was expected to promote himself. In my father Horatio Alger joined forces with Casanova.

His violent rages provided another clue. I could not understand how these rages could be so transient, one moment furious shouting, the next smiling amiability. Rages that would have left me shaken for a day had they possessed me, passed from him as readily as the reflections of clouds on water. But the rages were like the sexual explosions. They never, or rarely, touched anything central *in him*. Perhaps that was why he so often doubted the reality of his own experience.

In a document as lengthy as my father's letter, what he has omitted may be as important as what is included (or, in some cases, more important). For instance, in the account of his brief period as Secretary to Governor Miller, the pages telling of the events that led to Miller's firing him are missing. There is only one specific reference to his feelings in that part of the letter. Much later, writing in a suicidal mood, my father recalls his temptation to kill himself when Miller told him that he must leave his administration and he speaks of the time as one when he reached the nadir of despair. I believe that, remarkably candid as the letter is, my father could not bear to allow his original account of that event to pass into my hands. That surely is a measure of the horror of the experience for him. There were some things that even he could not bear to tell, or, if he told them, could not bear to leave as part of the record of his life.

My father seldom speaks of *his* father in the letter and what he does say is in the nature of conventional filial piety. He describes him as handsome, honest, hardworking. It is clear enough that my father's mother—Honey—and aunts were much more important to him than his father or uncle, although Uncle Gov, with his yacht, seems to have made a strong impression. My guess would be that my grandfather held my father to a very strict standard, made a great deal of his weaknesses and was furious over his frequent lapses. I suspect that my grandmother and her sisters, on the other hand, spoiled him outrageously and that he came to feel a certain contempt for his mother as a consequence. Certainly, my father's letters to his mother, written after his father's death, are not pleasant reading. They are condescending and admonitory, asking for money in many instances and rebuking her for being selfish and complaining too much.

Then there are the frequent references in the letter to being a coward. In referring to his failure to enlist in the army at the beginning of World War I (and to his efforts to avoid being drafted), he speaks in an almost offhand way of his cowardice. He had flat feet and was thus ineligible on physical grounds. But he mentions that just the thought of begin shot at made him sweat with fear. His conviction that he was a coward seems to me to be related to his sense of the unreality of his own life. The philosopher, J. Glenn Gray, in his book about men at war, *The Warriors*, speaks of the cowards that he encountered in the army during World War II as men with little ability to relate to others. "The coward," he writes, "does not know the sense of a common effort and a common fate," [and] "has, unfortunately, not gained in its place any strong individuality or any full awareness of self. . . . The coward's fear of death stems in large part from his own incapacity to love anything but his own body with passion. . . . The inability to participate in others' lives stands in the way of his developing any inner resources to overcome the terror of death. . . . The coward, unrelated to his fellows, has an insufficient hold on life and is not in charge of himself or his fate."

I quote the passage at some length because it seems to me to provide an important clue to that sense of unreality that seems to have obsessed my father at many periods of his life.

If cowardice and the inability to love are, as Gray suggests, closely connected, they are often associated with the need to suffer and inflict pain. My father, I fear, enjoyed inflicting pain and suffering on others but he also needed to experience it himself. For instance, his virulent anti-semitism did not prevent him from having a number of affairs with Jewish women whom he professed to love passionately while at the same time disparaging them in the letter.

I believe that it was because he could not love that he continually degraded what is called too loosely "the act of love." Each violent and perverted sexual encounter was, in its own way, a plea for love. Although my father wrote constantly of loving, I could never find in meetings with him, in his treatment of others, or even in the letter itself, any evidence that he was truly capable of that emotion. Did he have some haunted, unarticulated sense that if, like the monster in a fairy tale, he could find someone to love him, he would become a splendid prince and was I, above all, the one from whom he hoped for release from that grim prison of unlovingness? Who, long before I was an actor in his life, refused him love? Or said or did something that made it impossible for him to love?

Another indication of my father's determination to punish himself and others can be found in his lifelong propensity to break off highly valued friendships on some startlingly trivial pretext. The case of Hendrik Van Loon is typical. His friendship with Van Loon was, among all his friendships, the one most treasured and featured. There are dozens of affectionate letters back and forth between the two men. My father bought literally hundreds of copies of his books to give to friends and relatives and Van Loon dutifully autographed all of them. My father applauded Van Loon as a genius, gave him in his "rich year" a handsome gold stopwatch from Cartier, and bombarded him with advice as to how to advance his career. Then because Van Loon did not instantly produce a Christmas card to be sent out from Melvale (my father wanted it done in three days) he wrote him a bitter, vitriolic letter declaring the friendship at an end.

While his relation with La Guardia was not a particularly close one, it was obviously one that my father prized. Again on some utterly inconsequential issue my father wrote him one of his "kiss-off" letters. He wrote many angry, vituperative letters, of course, to people that he did not know or knew only casually. He did know Hoover and he had been one of his earliest and most enthusiastic boosters; in time he became one of his bitterest detractors and wrote a long, denunciatory letter to him. Judge Robert McCurdy Marsh, who he had declared to be like a second father to him, who stood by him through a number of legal scrapes and embarrassments, and who managed his divorce from my mother, was written off by letter and physically assaulted. Poor Walter Piel, Harry Millar, Tommy Brodix, his drinking and whoring companions, all eventually got the kiss-off though in some instances there were eventual reconciliations. And me, the designated recipient of the fabled letter, his son and heir, because of some ridiculous contretemps with my wife, he wrote me an insulting letter, to which, by his own admission, I could only have properly reacted by anger and indignation, by a breach in our relatively recent and rather shaky relationship. So to punish and be punished was clearly a deep-seated need. It stemmed, I believe, from the same basic feeling of unreality that lay at the heart of so much of his behavior and, indeed, of the letter itself. The past was always more real to my father than the present. The past could be arranged and rearranged, recounted and reviewed, in a measure controlled, while the present had to be experienced, often in very excruciating ways, and the future, full of terrors and anxieties had, in some manner, to be neutralized. A classic way of neutralizing the future is, obviously, to be obsessed with the past. He tried to overcome the terror of the dream, of nullity, by striking out, by seeking to evoke the reassuring response, by what I can only understand to be strange cries of anguish, even in the midst of the most furious sexual debauches. Only in these moments when he was gripped by sexual ecstasies did he feel himself to be in touch with the fringes of reality. The physical violence, the verbal violence, the sexual violence, the suicidal moods, never really suicidal, always playing at suicide, too cowardly by his own account to really confront so final and desperate an act, all these come to one point: "Tell me that this is not a dream," or, conversely, "Waken me from this nightmare, and tell me it is a dream."

For me, the most appealing episode in my father's life was the Melvale venture. The mad energy with which he plunged into the undertaking, his impatience, his determination to reshape the whole environment in less than two weeks in order that he and Melba might celebrate Christmas in their new quarters was completely in character. He fantasized a country Christmas and, like a sorcerer, made it come true. He waved a magic wand and, presto, there was a farmhouse rebuilt even to the chimneys. One can be sure it set rural tongues clacking all over the county. No wonder he was called the Baron. Morever, he was no gentleman farmer; he got dirt under his fingernails, he planted cabbages, pitched hay, picked apples, plowed fields, took his produce to market, immersed himself in the arcane lore of rural life, made the farm a kind of universe from the center of which he, now Farmer Smith (as opposed to Politician Smith, Businessman Smith, and all the other half-formed and discarded Smiths), dispensed homely rural wisdom to anyone willing to listen. On one level he must have known it was only a charade, a play that would soon be over. But on another level he played the part with a furious gusto which I find irresistible. Was that really his problem? Was he, in fact, a kind of earth figure, a creature so elemental that only when he touched earth could he touch reality and, like Antaeus, gain fresh strength? Was he at heart a son of the soil whose powers were perverted by the alien atmosphere of a city that drew him back time and again like a magnet?

Certainly, his relationship to his city was a central fact of his life. He lived in the city, certainly in the thirties, by his wits and instincts, like an animal in the forest. He was aware enough of the ambiguity of his own feelings to see his constant travels as efforts to escape from the place where he was so essentially rooted, the place, most acutely, of his triumphs and defeats. I believe each of us has a destiny, dimly perceived though it may be, unrealized though it may be. It is a fate appropriate to our capacities—healing us and reconciling us to the world. The lucky ones discover it; the others pursue it. Perhaps it is just the current romanticism of "loving the earth" but I would like to think that my father's protean energies were meant to be rooted in the soil, in the common, consoling earth, and that, for a moment, he perceived this and entered into that realm with the instinct that he was coming home. Although he never again took up conventional farming, he never gave up a rural *pied-à-terre*.

One point that cannot perhaps be sufficiently emphasized was the ability that my father displayed in the various political and financial ventures that he undertook. Literally thousands of pages of the letter deal with these undertakings and one cannot, I believe, fail to be impressed by his remarkable organizational abilities. He was unsparing of himself and others in his efforts to achieve a particular goal: aid to the Jews, funds for the Actors' Memorial, War Stamps, Hoover's or Lowden's or Landon's presidential campaigns, Florida real estate, tung oil, the Queen Wilhemina Fund, the Mexican Tourist Bureau, the Anderson Air-Conditioner, the National Trailer Show, on and on. Certainly energy and intelligence, those usual guarantors of success, were not missing. But his extravagance, not simply in a specific financial sense, but in a total sense, his inability to contain or master his vision or his appetites brought everything eventually to nought.

One thing I wish to make as clear as I can. I have no illusion that in these efforts to account for my father's strange temperament I am in any real sense "explaining" him. I would be untrue to my own perception of human life and historical process if I left the impression that my father's life could, in any clear and final way, be explained in terms of some combination of psychological traits. I am not a psychoanalyst; I do not even believe in the efficacy of the science. I believe that it is far too often used as a form of reductionism—that is to say, the reduction of the infinite and ultimate mystery of human life and experience to a set of superficial formulas. Yet some degree of understanding (on the notion, perhaps, that to understand all is to forgive all) is necessary, or at least it is necessary to struggle to achieve it, and this, particularly, in the case of someone as closely connected as one's own father. Thus one moves from the specific acts and events to some general principle that will make clear a pattern, a connectedness, between the specific acts and events, so that they do not appear to be merely discrete, unconnected. Thus one gropes, inevitably, I suspect, for a theme, a principle, a perspective which will enable one to break free of the tyranny of the particular and gain a broader understanding. Having at least tentatively identified such themes one comes back to the particulars at least partially freed from them. I believe that the only substantial use of what might be called, loosely, psychological insights is that they increase and extend the range of our sensibilities; they make us aware of elements of character that we might otherwise scant or overlook entirely.

What I am trying to say is that if I were to rest on an amateur's (or even a professional's) psychological profile of my father I would have in the process evaded my real responsibility, which I understand to be reconciliation. Thus, whatever might be said about the particular persons and the historical forces—the milieu—that helped to shape his character, my father remains what he was very conscious of being—a sinner. And that is, in simple fact, what we all are, in the view at least of Christian orthodoxy. I am certainly very conscious that that is what I am. It is not, therefore, up to me to "forgive" my father—that is God's business. It is as a fellow sinner, on a somewhat less imaginative scale, that I can perhaps encounter him most sympathetically. Indeed, I suppose it is only so that I can escape a note of self-righteousness in regard to my father, a note which I am conscious of having had to struggle against throughout this undertaking, a note which I am sure affected, or infected, our relationships during his lifetime and of which he can hardly have failed to be aware.

To his dying day, my father remained obsessed by sex. In conversation he was as tiresomely repetitious about sex as about politics. But he did not need, after his marriage to Eve, to find verification or to seek reality exclusively in sex. Or, apparently, to search any longer for his son. And so the letter ended; from the record of a continuing journey, it became a legacy. One wonders if, in the twenty years between its abrupt ending and my father's death, he ever thought of destroying it. Such an impulse would, I suppose, have been suicidal. All then that would have remained of Ward Smith would have been the rapidly fading memory of a rather garrulous old man preoccupied with sex. There are plenty of those around.

The last thirty years of my father's life belonged, in a sense, to Eve. She was the reality principle in my father's life. His relationship with my mother was doomed from the beginning. Melba was a co-conspirator in his fantasy trip. Eve was the first person to attach him, at least to a modest degree, to the real world. He had reached out for her like a drowning man, reached out to this gawky, homely old maid and she had saved his life. She had loved him so much that she could not bear to live without him. So that unlikely match had turned out, after all, to be a classic romance. The sordid affairs and desperate expedients were finally absorbed in the last act of a drama of romantic love.

After my father's death when I returned to Greenwich for the funeral, I was relieved, as much for Eve's sake as my own, to find that I could weep for him. But I listened, with a kind of embarrassment, to her describing a man I did not know, the paragon, the "greatest."

I felt, aside from the perhaps too easy tears, the same detachment that I had always felt in regard to my father. I could not really mourn. I felt no sense of loss; indeed, none of the emotions a son might be expected to feel upon the death of his father. I did not even feel the fearful sense of my own mortality that seized me at my mother's deathbed three years later. Only a kind of nullity, an emptiness, a slightly apologetic sense of being unable to summon up emotions appropriate to the occasion.

My father's account of the night he searched me out at my division's encampment on the A.P. Hill Military Reservation in the piney woods of Virginia where I was on my way back from army maneuvers in North Carolina is, for me, the most poignant passage in the letter. Pearl Harbor had just been attacked. It was one of those strange moments in which world history and one's own personal history converge. I had met, on maneuvers, a young artist who I was determined should be my wife. In the light of that miraculous, staggering fact and the peace and certitude that the knowledge of it as ordained and irrevocable brought with it, I had little concern for anything else. The bombing of Pearl Harbor was of significance only as it might affect my prospective marriage. I do not even remember the encounter that was so important to my father.

Reading about our meeting in the letter, it seemed to me that the key to that document lay there on the page, so obvious that it was hard to see how I could have missed it. Perhaps I was so accustomed to the myth of the son's search for the father that I was insensitive to the equally powerful theme of the father's search for the son. The letter was the agent or instrument of my father's search, his effort to attach himself to an archetypal human role and thus introduce a principle of reality into his world of fantasy.

Small wonder I could not comprehend all this during my father's lifetime. He pursued me and I fled the emotional attachment that he at least thought might have saved him. The playing of the traditional roles of father and son which he sought so tirelessly I resisted with every instinct of self-preservation as long as he lived.

And then, after his death, his final stratagem came into play. He called once more to me beyond life in that vast, interminable, problematical letter, so repugnant and so compelling—a kind of plea or curse, a last petition for acceptance and understanding, for reconciliation.

So I am disposed to say: "Father, I read your letter and I have tried, after my fashion, to answer it. I accept your life, sadly misspent as it has always seemed to me to be. I have discovered a principle of reconciliation in Eve's love for you, her own Adam, fallen and redeemed. I am willing to be your son and acknowledge you at last as my father. I find I can weep again for you, better tears than those brief, bewildered ones I wept at your death. And weep, as well, for myself. I hope that is enough."